Hawkhurst

HAWKHURST

Christopher Green

CENTURY

LONDON MELBOURNE AUCKLAND JOHANNESBURG

To Annie, Joe and Nell

Acknowledgement
The author and publishers wish to acknowledge the
rôle played in the research for *Hawkhurst* by a
previous book: *Honest Thieves* by F. F. Nicholls (1973)

Copyright © 1987

First published in Great Britain in 1987 by
Century Hutchinson Ltd
Brookmount House, 62–65 Chandos Place
London WC2N 4NW

Century Hutchinson South Africa (Pty) Ltd
PO Box 337, Bergvlei, 2012 South Africa

Century Hutchinson Australia Pty Ltd
PO Box 496, 16–22 Church Street, Hawthorn
Victoria 3122, Australia

Century Hutchinson New Zealand Limited
PO Box 40–086, Glenfield, Auckland 10
New Zealand

ISBN 0 7126 1896 1

Phototypeset in Linotron Ehrhardt 10 on 11½pt by
Input Typesetting Ltd, London SW19 8DR
Printed in Great Britain by
Anchor Brendon, Tiptree, Essex

Chapter 1

Stumbling through brambles and dead bracken, the two youths ran as if the Devil had hold of their shirt-tails. Behind them, the hounds gave chase urged on by unseen masters. Black powder fireflies burned and a shot struck home. Every oath the older youth knew failed to ease its sting. He cursed the full-eyed moon for singling him out, and damned the crackling frost carpet that betrayed him to his enemies. He swore at his friend, who, slightly built and quicker on his feet, moved like a ghost twenty yards ahead of him. A low branch took his hat, raising an ugly weal across his forehead. He looked over his shoulder – there couldn't be that many game-keepers in Kent! He threw his fish net into the river but ran no faster. The gap, he knew, was closing so he bargained with God. To his relief, a hand of cirrus streamers masked the moon and darkness swallowed the hunters. Now, if only the earth would open beneath the dogs, he'd never cheat or steal again.

He did not see the man-trap. His foot had barely brushed the trigger when lightning flashed inside his skull. Muscle and bone yielded, and the roar of anguish that cracked the freezing air stopped the keepers in their tracks. Hair bristled on every neck as the stricken youth screamed like a dying animal.

'Help me!'

The cloud fist opened. The keepers came on. Blood glistened in the half-light as the trapped youth struggled to get up. He jerked his shattered leg. Again he cried out as all the nerves in his body turned to threads of liquid fire. Contorted muscles threatened to snap his spine like a dry twig and, in desperation, he battered at the ancient trap with his pistol butt. The first blow shot bolts of raw agony deep into his innards. The second put him into shock and his limbs twitched uncontrollably. He was close to blacking out when, as if in answer to an unspoken prayer, the spring that held those awful jaws shut snapped. Rusted teeth relinquished their grip and, though his foot dangled at a hideous angle, he was free. A towering sense of elation gave him new strength and he tried to run. However, one halting step and the world keeled over.

'Help me, George!' He hauled himself up onto all fours. 'My leg – it's broken . . .'

He reached out but his friend stood rooted to the spot. Had he reacted quickly, the younger lad might just have managed to drag his crippled accomplice to the river. Instead, transfixed by the charging dogs, he hesitated. As if by magic, the beasts were multiplying before his eyes. Soon, every tree and clump of frozen grass held its own snapping menace.

'Thomas . . .' he sobbed.

His brain commanded him to go back, but the lines of communication had gone haywire. His legs refused to obey. Then blind panic washed over friendship and loyalty. Suddenly, without taking any conscious decision, the boy turned tail and ran.

He did not hear the dog. With his friend's accusations ringing in his ears, he felt no pain as the animal ripped his leg from knee to ankle and bundled him into the thick winter waters of the River Teise. The cold was intense and drove the breath from his body. Fighting free of the undertow, he clawed his way back to the surface. A quick look confirmed that the dog had gone but, behind him, a dozen 'keepers lined the water's edge. One spotted him and a ragged volley drowned their angry voices. Pitch torches flared and the boy struck out for the opposite bank where, lost in the shadows, he heaved himself out of the sucking waters.

Crawling into the undergrowth, he tried to shut out his shame. But closed eyes and stopped ears were not enough. Coward! Traitor! Deserter! The injured youth's words impaled him as surely as any blade. His stomach turned over and he retched where he lay. Then, suddenly, the yelling ceased. And, like an onlooker at an execution, the

6

boy turned his gaze back towards the river. Back to where, less than a quarter of a mile away, his closest friend was fighting for his life.

'Damn your blood!' The youth screamed, lashing out with fist and skinning knife. 'Get away from me!'

Well practised in handling cornered animals, the game-keepers stood off and sent in the dogs. Frosted breath rose slowly into the still air as, ears laid flat, the pack circled its victim. Then, rushing forward, the boldest dog showed its teeth. The youth snarled back. Steel flashed in the torch-light. A hacking blow opened the beast's shoulder to the bone and the hoarfrost changed colour. His success, though, was short-lived. A second dog took him from the rear. A third seized his knife arm. A kill was imminent and the circle tightened. Jerking and thrashing, the crazed youth did not see the musket butt. It caught him behind the ear and for a merciful, all too brief moment, oblivion took away the pain. However, it returned with a vengeance as they dragged him back towards the highway. Instinctively, he fought them but, by now, his strength was gone. Chained and helpless, he threw back his head and, like the wild creature he was, howled to the moon. 'I'll have my revenge, George! I swear it! If I have to chase you to the gates of Hell itself!'

Hate and pain carried that dreadful promise across the river.

Deep in the dead bracken, the boy buried his head in his hands. He had gained his freedom, but doing so had cost him dear. That night, on the frozen banks of the Teise, a demon was spawned. The demon of all-consuming guilt. A demon that was to torment George Sturt for the rest of his days.

And half a lifetime on, Sturt watched the boy that was himself crawl from his bolt-hole and run – through frosted wood, branch and thorn raised against him. And run – to Goudhurst, over the Gore, into the village. And run – names through his head, Winchcombe, Glover, Shaddick, Wynter. And run – past lines of people, faces turned away. And run – in uniform, beating a drum. His drum. And run –

7

bells pealing. Bells? What bells? They don't belong! But still they peal, and peal again . . .

Image fading, Sturt turned from the mirror and identified the church bells that marked seven o'clock. He stood alone, thoughts shuffling into waking order, as Rye shook itself from sleep. Again he looked into the glass and saw – only George Sturt. He thought of Mary and the day dropped into place.

Although behind schedule, he ignored his gaping kitbag and listened to the rising street sounds. The sudden autumn cold snap lent a bustling urgency to the day's usual slow start. A flock of Romney sheep pattered to their doom. The death cart grated over ice-varnished setts harvesting the night's crop. Across the street, coarse female voices rose above the roar of cheated clients as the Crown and Rolls cleared its rooms. Sturt had heard the sounds a thousand times before, but this time they were somehow different. It was as if every man, woman and child, every bird and animal, was welcoming him back to their world.

Though he still couldn't believe it, he'd been given a second chance. A chance he did not deserve. But, he reasoned, would a drowning man reject a lifeline because others more worthy had already gone under? Perhaps. If he was a saint or a lunatic. George Sturt was neither.

He scanned the spartan billet. Wilsher's Lodging House was a rat-hole of a place, and much the same as any other forced to house the military. Fourpence a day bought precious little comfort for King George's loyal soldiers. But to Sturt, the damp-decayed walls, the resident wildlife, the sour-sweet perfume of overcrowded quarters were the pungent evocation of the only home he knew. And today he was turning his back on it. Just then, footsteps rattled in the passageway. The door swung open and Sturt dropped the lid on his lockerful of hopes and fears.

No attempt was made to disguise the overwhelming sense of satisfaction reflected in John Fairbrother's boyish features. He entered the room and, like an actor, paused, defying the audience to ignore his presence. A full hour late, he braced himself against the expected broadside. Sturt

8

knew the routine of old; John had been up to something and he was expected to coax it out of him. Time and again he'd risen to the bait only to fall victim to Fairbrother's infuriatingly childlike sense of humour. This time he was in no mood.

Turning his back, Sturt snatched the chevroned tunic of Regimental Colours Sergeant from a rusty nail hanger and laid it out as respectfully as he would a dead comrade. Fairbrother smiled. Sturt smoothed and folded his jacket, held fast by his friend's pale, gently mocking eyes. He snapped open his kitbag.

'The time it's taken, you could have packed for the entire regiment,' Fairbrother said.

'Some folk has an ordered way of doing things,' retorted Sturt. 'And some hasn't!' He glanced at Fairbrother's over-stuffed sack.

Fairbrother grinned. 'It doesn't matter. This time no officer's going to inspect it.'

Fussy as a housewife, Sturt rearranged his kit and placed the tunic on top of his spare shirt.

Fairbrother drew his cutlass. 'Out!' he urged – prodding a hole in Sturt's new civilian waistcoat.

Sturt stumbled backwards. 'John! For God's sake man . . .'

Fairbrother prodded him again.

'Grow up!' bellowed Sturt – and promptly tripped over his sword. A third lunge drew blood. Dignity pricked, Sturt unsheathed his hanger as Fairbrother hurled the carefully packed kitbag.

'Out!' he yelled.

Sturt caught his kit and dropped his blade. Fairbrother kicked it through the open door.

'Move yourself George Sturt . . .'

Furious, Sturt stood his ground. 'You'll go too far!'

Another crimson flower blossomed on his shirt front. And, jabbing like a punch-drunk street fighter, Fairbrother hounded him across the room.

'I said out!' He shoved Sturt into the corridor. 'It's time to take the world by the tail!'

At thirty-three years of age John Edwin Fairbrother was still the irritatingly boisterous youth adored by his mother and despaired of by his father. Born the first son of a prosperous Tonbridge cloth merchant, he had been expected to take his place in Society and the family business. Instead, the boy had devoted himself to the pursuit of pleasure. At seventeen he'd caught and fumblingly impregnated one of Kent's less virtuous daughters. Under increasing pressure to do the right thing – pay off the girl's family and go to work in his father's cloistered warehouses – John Edwin took drastic action.

One morning, having failed to drown his sorrows, the tortured youth was wrenched from gutter sleep by the remorseless onslaught of fife and drum. Convinced that death could offer no more exquisite agony, he faced a recruiting party of the Third Kent Foot. And, motivated more by the desire to stop the noise than evade his mounting problems, he stepped forward and pledged body and soul to the service of his King. Paraded around the town as an example to the nation's reluctant youth, young John had seriously considered murdering the drummer boy who seemed determined to emulsify his few remaining brain cells. Fifteen years later a bond of friendship held runaway village boy and renegade gentleman closer than the most acute observer might suspect.

Indeed, had such an observer first encountered them outside the Dog and Partridge he'd have been hard-pressed to believe they even liked each other. Fairbrother reached for the door and Sturt seized him by the scruff.

'First day out,' pleaded Fairbrother. 'We deserve a drink.'

'Business first.'

Fingers hovered above the latch. 'Ten minutes won't make any difference.'

A twist of the wrist and Sturt almost lifted his friend's toes off the ground. 'Horses!'

Fairbrother conceded, but voiced his protest as Sturt kicked him – a little harder than necessary – away from temptation.

*

Now stealing horses was a profitable if hazardous eighteenth-century occupation, and at the time in question Rye was suffering at the hands of a particularly successful gang of thieves. Even so, the precautions taken by Lot Dibdin seemed excessive to Sturt. Locked in the dealer's stable, yard gates barred and bolted, he faced an animal that, in his opinion, no self-respecting thief would look at. However, beggars could not be choosers.

Inspection complete, Sturt ran through his mental checklist. The mare was twelve years old if a day. She had bad feet and looked work-weary to say the least. Nevertheless there was something about her. She'd looked him in the eye, head up, ears pricked, as if she knew she was on display and meant to make the right impression. Sturt smiled. Pride. That was it, the old horse still had her pride! And then again there was the question of money . . .

Dibdin read his mind. 'A fine beast, master. And with the saddle thrown in, at a fair price.'

Fair or not it was all Sturt could afford. He had saved hard over the years, living a frugal, some would say puritanical, existence. But now, the three warm guineas clenched tight in his pocket were the sum total of his worldly wealth.

'Time was you could buy a decent pair for three guineas.'

'Then you must have been away a long time.' The dealer smiled. ''Course, you could always try the mule breaker.'

Outside a troop of dragoons passed by, drowning Sturt's reply. Dibdin waited. Sturt gazed gloomily at the mare. Pride or not, she wasn't what he'd intended.

Reluctantly he nodded – and just then Fairbrother appeared from the depths of the building with two magnificent saddle horses. 'I'd have thought the bay was to your taste,' he said.

Sturt stared blankly. 'What?'

'The bay! But if you prefer the chestnut . . .'

'What do you mean – the bay or the chestnut?'

'It's a difficult choice,' agreed Fairbrother. 'Perhaps Master Dibdin here could advise.'

Difficult choice . . . Dibdin advise . . . Sturt suddenly felt

11

himself suspended between two worlds; the one he inhabited, and the theatre of mayhem and illusion that existed in Fairbrother's twisted mind. A distant voice was nagging like a flea-bite. 'The gelding's surely got the legs, sir, but he don't have the same heart. If it were my money I'd be taking the mare every time.' For an instant Sturt considered that the two worlds might be one and the same. Madness must be contagious!

'Then it's the bay,' beamed Fairbrother.

Sturt started to speak but his friend rolled on. 'You're going home after fifteen years, and that demands a certain style. It's expected!'

Fairbrother paused and Sturt took his chance. 'You never know when to stop, do you? Always the buffoon! Always at someone else's expense! You know the farm cost me every penny – '

'They're paid for.'

Now he was going mad!

'Master Fairbrother,' explained Dibdin. 'He come down early this morning.'

It was a joke. Another of Fairbrother's infernal practical jokes! 'And this?' growled Sturt, glaring at the three-guinea thoroughbred.

'Borrowed from the knacker – at great risk to my professional reputation.' Dibdin laboured the point. 'If anyone saw that thing coming in here . . .'

Sturt couldn't have cared less. Head reeling, he turned on Fairbrother.

'A man of property needs a good horse, George. It's only fitting.'

'A neglected forty-acre farm does not make me lord of the manor. And I'll not get by on charity!'

'Charity be damned!' grinned Fairbrother. 'It's for you and Mary. My wedding present.'

Sturt stood silent, gripped by the strangest sensation. It belonged to the past and he ransacked his tidy memory. He drew forth a May Day – a long-dead May Day in Goudhurst. It was the only time Mary had ever cuckolded him. He'd caught her dancing with his closest friend and the hair-trigger rage of youth had set them at each other's throats. Well matched, the bloody, bare-knuckle contest was only halted when Mary threw herself at Sturt's feet. She begged him to stop fighting, promising in return never to dance with another man so long as she lived. He remembered how her generosity had tempered his anger, leaving him tongue-tied and flushed with embarrassment. Satisfied, he returned the incident to its rightful place.

Back in Dibdin's stable, he looked at Fairbrother and felt his cheeks burn. Anger waned, but it was a long time before he spoke. When he did it was to summon one of the dealer's much-abused apprentices. Sturt took a guinea from his pocket and sent the lad to pay off the knacker. It seemed he had acquired an extra horse.

As Sturt and Fairbrother were leaving Dibdin's yard, thirty miles to the south-west a solitary figure was crossing the bleak expanse of Seacox Heath. Wrapped in still-warm memories of the night, Thomas Kingsmill spurred his weary mount homeward and ignored the October snow flurry that bored in from the Channel. It had been a good night's work; more than five tons of tea, tobacco and geneva landed without the loss of a single tub or dollop.

In his mind a smuggler's lantern flashed. A familiar tightening gripped him beneath the breastbone. Fourteen years in the free trade, thirteen of them as undisputed leader of the Hawkhurst Gang, had not diminished the excitement generated by a blue light blinking at sea. Large wet snowflakes slapped against sodden greatcoat. The cold was seeping into his bones. And Chamber Cove tumbled from his memory, holding back the black despair that rises when exhilaration fades.

It had started quietly enough. The cutter had dropped anchor on time and, thanks to the skill of her oarsmen, the overloaded skiff ran in without wetting so much as a pair of boots. Eager hands copped hold of the umbilical tubline and Kingsmill waded into the surf.

As usual, he offered his hand to the bird-frail figure sitting hunched in the bows. And, as always, Richard Perrin

13

took it. Aided by his master, the gang's buyer urged his twisted body towards the dry land he held so dear. Over the years, this uncharacteristic gesture on Kingsmill's behalf had become a ritual performed at every landing. By now it was part of the accepted order of things because Perrin, a former carpenter prematurely crippled by rheumatism, held a unique position in the Hawkhurst hierarchy.

It had started some ten years ago when Perrin had been forced into the free trade in order to support a wife and young family. Fortunately, his physical disabilities were more than compensated for by a sharp intelligence and a natural head for business. This, combined with Kingsmill's ruthless genius for leadership, was the cornerstone of the gang's success. As buyer, Perrin insisted that he alone dealt with their financial backers, bought from the French, sold to the merchants and innkeepers of London and Bristol. He knew that if he should break a leg scrambling from an open boat, or suffer a momentary loss of balance and crack his skull on a sharp rock, Hawkhurst fortunes would sink into instant decline. Kingsmill knew it too. Therefore, the ritual at the water's edge was not so much a display of affection as a necessary safeguarding of valuable assets.

Sand spirals danced on the beach, stinging the eyes of men and horses. Soon, the landing settled into its regular pattern. And by the time Perrin had wrung the brine from his stockings and struggled into the saddle, he and Kingsmill were the only ones left on the shore. Above them, William Jackson led a string of straining pack animals up the narrow cliff track. At their backs, a rising tide swept tell-tale prints and droppings into the sea. And, beyond the breakers, throbbing arms pulled empty skiff back to mother cutter as she hoisted sail.

It was over, and so efficient was Kingsmill's private army that not one word had been spoken from beginning to end. He was fiercely proud of them. Through the years he had moulded a drunken, dissolute rabble of part-time owlers into a disciplined force that put the fear of God into every inhabitant of the southern counties.

Even dragoons of the regular army had little stomach for

service against smugglers. Chasing violent men who knew every channel and dyke on Romney Marsh, every track and gate on the densely wooded Weald, usually in the foulest weather, held no attraction for underpaid soldiers already sick of war with the French and Scots. An occasional tub of brandy dropped at a sergeant's billet, or left outside an officer's quarters, further insured against a dangerous upsurge of patriotism and duty.

And the riding officers of His Majesty's Custom and Excise Service posed even less of a threat. Thin on the ground, often senile, more often corrupt, and hated as much by the public as by the smugglers, these unfortunate preventive men were more than willing to 'turn their eyes to the wall as the gentlemen rode by'. Except that is, for Chief Riding Officer Brownrigg.

Concealed high on the headland, he looked down on the smugglers and saw rapid promotion. A uniformed figure emerged from the bracken some thirty or forty feet below his vantage point. Brownrigg wriggled like an excited child as, bobbing and crouching, Riding Officer Henry Jenner approached.

'Well?' demanded Brownrigg.

'They outnumbers us six to one,' said Jenner.

'Is it the Hawkhurst Gang?'

Jenner stared down the hillside. Kingsmill's force was now half-way between beach and skyline.

'Jenner?'

'Aye, sir.' The tone of the reply went unnoticed.

'Then deploy your men.'

Jenner glanced at the seven army rejects who had cost him so much effort. In his opinion every one was now a credit to the Service, and this over-ambitious half-wit was about to do for them all. He flushed angrily. 'They'll cut us to pieces!'

Brownrigg glowed with the reckless confidence of youth. 'They cannot know our strength. We hold the high ground. If they know what's good for them they'll surrender when challenged.'

15

'It's the Hawkhurst Gang down there,' said Jenner. 'Not some rag-arsed bunch of farm boys makin' an extra shillin'.'

But Brownrigg's ears were closed to reason. Thomas Kingsmill was to be his stepping-stone to success; the rank of Collector General beckoned as enticingly as a new mistress.

Hidden once more in the bracken, Jenner knew he had just made the biggest mistake of his life. Common sense demanded that he place Brownrigg under guard and take command himself. But, long conditioned to obey orders, he could not bring himself to do it. Now, as sweat beaded his forehead and his hanger slid noiselessly from its scabbard, he mouthed a silent prayer.

Then Brownrigg's voice bounced off the rocks – half an octave above its normal register. Sixty smugglers stopped as one and Jenner repeated his prayer. By the time Brownrigg had summoned enough spit to reissue his challenge Kingsmill's men were almost upon him. A musket ball splintered his right kneecap. He screamed and fell. Leaderless, Jenner's rejects took their cue. To a man, they dropped their long guns and ran – but by now there was nowhere to run to. Jenner rose almost wearily to his feet; too proud to turn tail, he stepped onto the track and fixed his sights on the nearest smuggler.

It was William Jackson, Kingsmill's ageing lieutenant, who stumbled on Brownrigg hiding in the ferns. Had he been given time, an appeal to Jackson's better nature would have made no difference whatever. A cutlass blade arced and the officer's lifeless body flapped like a headless chicken.

One shot and one hurried sword thrust had been the sum total of Excise resistance. From the moment Brownrigg drew breath to utter his challenge it had taken precisely three minutes to snuff out nine men's lives.

The wind turned to the north-east and the snow shower died away. Kingsmill re-ran the last bloody minutes but already images were fading. Had he finished off that impudent bastard with a musket or not? He couldn't remember and suddenly it didn't matter. Despair crept one pace closer.

It would be two weeks before the next run. Two weeks of boredom. A fortnight in which to brood. He had no family to enjoy (brother George didn't count). The novelty of wealth had long since palled. Women were a biological necessity. Nothing matched the charge of that winking blue lamp. Nothing that is, except for the Widow. Perhaps he would pay her a visit – then again, perhaps he wouldn't.

The mansion loomed on the horizon and unbidden his horse quickened its step. Kingsmill had chosen his house well. Perched on a hilltop two miles west of Hawkhurst, and equidistant between the highway and the Kent Ditch (that winding channel draining conveniently into Romney Marsh), its strategic position suited him, as did its location and austere architecture.

Surrounded by a high stone wall, the square-faced building harboured none of the trappings that money usually bought. Its furnishings were strictly functional, the only concession to comfort being fires that burned in every room throughout the winter. Kingsmill loathed the cold. It intensified the ever-present melancholy, and it made his bad leg hurt. The damned thing was giving him gyp now. He rubbed it and looked at the house. Wood smoke billowed from the chimneys. Becky Leggatt might be a sour-faced hag but she knew her master's ways. He spurred the stallion to a canter.

Two weeks . . .

Two weeks for the worm to gnaw at his insides – for the past to torment him.

'I'll not sell lace and linen!' Fairbrother's voice rattled along the narrow street.

'But you'd be a merchant,' said Sturt negotiating an obstacle course of beggars and traders, effluent and fallen masonry. 'Merchants are not shopkeepers.'

Fairbrother turned. 'Sometimes you sound more like the old man than he does.' He lost his balance on the greasy cobbles and slipped into the brimming open sewer.

Sturt grinned maliciously. 'It's the best offer you'll get.'

17

'No!' Fairbrother examined his boot. 'I'll re-enlist first!'
He walked on – there was nothing else for it but to dry out
at the Dog and Partridge.

It was Sturt who saw the cart. Slewing around the corner
of Church Lane, it bounced crazily along the quayside
leaving a trail of destruction in its wake. Had he shouted a
split second later, Fairbrother would have been caught
beneath the wheels. As it was, the wagon clipped his horse
and the startled gelding took off like a whippet – with
Fairbrother in tow. Man and beast splashed through the
stinking drain and swept aside the hawkers' stalls. Sturt,
struggling with his own animals, looked on as Fairbrother
was swallowed by a seething mass of irate bodies.

A cacophony of outraged voices, a jumble of flying
colours, a knot of indignant faces, then a sudden flash of
scarlet – and the world was once more on its axis. Bruised
and winded, Fairbrother stared up at the astounded boy
holding his bridle. Private Nathan Wykeham snatched a clay
pipe from his mouth and snapped to attention.

'Sergeant Fairbrother!'

Fairbrother levered himself upright. Wykeham's nose
wrinkled and, still rigidly to attention, he leaned back a foot.

'Smoking on duty, Private Wykeham?'

Smoke curled from the grass verge outside the elegant
town house that served as Regimental Headquarters for the
Third Kent Foot.

'Not me, Sergeant.' Tell-tale wisps escaped through the
gaps in his teeth.

'Ex-sergeant!'

'Yes, Sergeant!'

Fairbrother stepped forward and took his reins. Wykeham
teetered on the brink, testing the law of gravity to its limit.
Sturt, relieved that there was no serious damage, edged
discreetly upwind of his dripping friend.

Across the street, the driver of the cart elbowed through
the angry mob. Someone tripped him and he fell. If it hadn't
been for the excisemen he would never have got up. They
shoved back the crush and cleared a way to the Custom
House door. The driver dragged a sleeve across his

18

damaged snout and dropped the tailgate. The crowd fell silent. Beneath a blood-stained tarpaulin nine grotesquely stiffened corpses lay like broken toy soldiers. A riding officer threw back the sheet and a battered tricorn tumbled into the gutter.

'Looks like someone had a bad night.'

Wykeham inclined Sturt's way. 'Nine officers, so they say – seen off by the local smuggling celebrities.'

'Then they got what they deserved,' said Sturt. 'Hounding honest folk with their stupid laws – '

'There's nowt honest about the Hawkhurst Gang – right evil buggers they are.'

'You seem to know all about it,' said Fairbrother.

Wykeham tapped his nose. 'Keeps my ears open, don't I, Sergeant?'

The mob dispersed to salvage what they could from up-turned carts and stalls. Two officers lifted Brownrigg's body.

'Could be just the profession for an old soldier.'

Wykeham looked at Fairbrother but kept his distance. 'Smuggler?' he asked.

'Excise officer!'

'The career prospects look somewhat limited,' remarked Sturt drily.

'No more so than shopkeeping in Tonbridge.'

Sturt said nothing. Fairbrother turned to Wykeham and offered his hand. 'Take good care, Wykeham.'

The boy held his breath and nodded. 'You too, Sergeant.'

Fairbrother smiled. 'I take your point.' He led his horse off down the street – in the direction of the public bath house. Wykeham filled his lungs.

'A word of advice,' said Sturt.

'Sergeant?'

'The smoking of tobacco on duty . . .' Sturt picked up the smouldering dudeen. 'It stunts your growth – so they say!'

The snow clouds that had dusted Seacox Heath slid across the morning sun. Outside the Custom House, a mongrel dog licked crusted blood from Henry Jenner's favourite hat.

19

Chapter 2

Edward Winchcombe was convinced that he was dying. The awful pain in his guts had spread to his chest and legs. His mouth felt like a hot ashpit. And to cap it all, he was seeing things again. Rats it was this time – great green rats – scuttling over roof beams, climbing up and down the wheel irons stacked by his forge. He blinked them away but, deep down, he knew they'd be back to persecute him with more creeping horrors.

'Snakes,' he said. 'Bound to be snakes.'

He shuddered. It was three days now. Three days and nights without so much as a taste. Mary had ordered the innkeepers of Goudhurst to stop serving him on the say-so of that interfering leech. She'd then ransacked the house – his house – and emptied every flask and jug. Even the emergency supply he kept under the floorboards of her room had gone. Women. They were the bane of his life. Always had been. Always would be. And cursing him with two daughters was, to his way of thinking, God paying him back for a misspent youth. Leastways, that's what he always said. The truth of the matter was that he'd never so much as held a girl's hand until he was twenty-eight, and then it had been Elizabeth's – in Coppett's Wood.

'Women!' he grumbled, and the ginger tom needed no second warning. Perched on the tool rack, it dodged the wheel spoke (for the third day in succession) and opted for the safety of the house.

The house. Edward's walnut of a face lit up. That was it! Mary, who had inherited Elizabeth's thoroughness, had turned the house upside down. But she'd sent Jan to search his workshop. And Jan – God bless her – was more like her old dad!

He rolled up a sleeve and plunged into the festering heap of unidentifiable rubbish piled beneath the bench. A rat, the colour of spring cabbage, watched from the rafters as frantic fingers grasped cold stoneware. The rat, or was it Edward?, squeaked with delight – his youngest hadn't let him down!

Twopenny gin blasted his taste-buds and, eyes watering, he sank to the floor fighting for breath. He knew the stuff was undiluted poison but it was all he could afford. The memory of French cognac and finest Lowlands geneva taunted him. Thanks to Thomas Kingsmill and his bully boys the supply had long since dried up. Most folk just accepted it and said nothing – but not Edward. It irked him, and one day he was going to do something about it. One day . . .

A second swallow put everything to rights. His several terminal illnesses were miraculously cured. The falcon-fierce glare that terrorized every child in Goudhurst was replaced by a look of almost saintly benevolence. And the good humour and gentleness that he refused to expose to all but a select few suddenly flooded the lean-to workshop. Wheelwright Winchcombe was at peace with the world.

Unfortunately the peace was shattered before he had chance to enjoy it. Caught red-handed, Edward steeled himself for a tongue lashing, but Mary sailed past like a man-o'-war at battle stations. It was Jan who chided.

'Father! You promised . . .'

Wringing gin from his shirt front, Edward whined, 'It's damn-near mid-day!' He scowled at Mary as she tugged at the damp-swollen door to the house. 'A nip before a "long overdue" dinner never done no one no harm!'

Mary ignored him and slammed the door so hard behind her that a pair of roosting bats fell from the neglected thatch.

'What's put her in such a tear?'

'Reverend Brack,' said Jan. 'He says it's not decent.'

'What's not?'

'George staying here before the wedding.' Her soft blue eyes danced wickedly. 'Give her a right talking to, he did!'

Mary Winchcombe slammed a pot of grey stew onto the

21

hob-iron and pumped the embers. She was thirty-two years old, and the niche she occupied in the village scheme of things was labelled 'Handsome not pretty' and 'Proud as a bantam cock' – which was why she'd taken such fierce objection to Brack's unwarranted insinuation. Muttering to herself, she furiously pumped the bellows. The fire burned white hot. 'Of all the stiff-necked, pompous . . .'

'Nasty-minded?' Jan offered as she entered.

'Nasty-minded bigots! What does he take me for?'

'Seeing you waited so long for a man, happen he thinks you won't be able to keep your hands off of George!'

Mary stopped pumping. A tight, nervous giggle escaped Jan's lips and, to her immense relief, Mary laughed too. 'He might be right at that!'

Mary had borne her spinsterhood with dignity. Publicly respected and privately pitied, she was aware of her old maid status, and though the glimmer of hope had never been totally extinguished, even in her most despairing moments, it still stung. 'I wasn't short of an offer or two,' she said.

Jan chipped blackened bits of mutton from the bottom of the pot. 'The first I've heard of it.'

'Just shows you don't know everything then, don't it?'

Jan turned. 'You're making it up.'

Mary hacked at the loaf that her sister had baked that morning. Not blessed with culinary talents and conscious of Alan Wynter's love affair with his stomach, Jan had decided to get in some practice before her own impending marriage.

Unfortunately, practice does not always make perfect. To date, her enthusiastic labours had only resulted in an epidemic of chronic indigestion.

'Richard Pickett,' said Mary casually.

'He's got a wife and four children!'

'He didn't have ten years ago.' Mary gave up on the charred offering and wondered if Jan and Alan should go into the brick-making trade. 'It's burning,' she said.

Jan snatched the pot from the fire, blistering her fingers in the process, while Mary quickly cut a slice from the loaf she'd baked before dawn. Jan sat down and sucked her fingers. Richard Pickett was a revelation. 'Who else?' she asked.

Mary said nothing.

'Mary?' pursued Jan.

'It was years ago – I can't remember.'

'Who?'

After a momentary pause came the one name she would never have suspected.

'Thomas Kingsmill.'

A smile flickered at the corners of Mary's mouth. It wasn't often her sister was left short of an answer. She turned her attention to setting the table.

'Still . . .' said Jan, composure instantly regained. 'Richard Pickett – he must have been the best catch of your day.'

Mary laughed. 'I'm your sister, not your grandmother!'

In fact, the difference between them was twelve years; Mary was the first and Jan the last. There had been others, three boys and a girl, but none had survived their first year. Elizabeth died giving birth to Jan, and Mary had taken her place. Ever since, she had been the strong one, the driving force of the family – which was why this sudden outpouring of confidences was such a surprise. It was like discovering that your parents actually made love; slightly distasteful but wildly fascinating. Jan dug a little deeper. 'You couldn't have known George'd come back. Father says he went without a word to anyone.'

'Father lets the gin talk.'

Jan persisted. 'He might have been dead for all you knew. Then what?' Mary had resorted to her maternal role. 'You'd have waited, wouldn't you? You'd have waited for the rest of your life!'

Yes she would! Mary wanted to say it but couldn't – not even to Jan. It was as if admitting it would make her appear a silly, fawning woman – and that would offend her pride. Jan couldn't possibly understand. There was something about George that Mary herself found inexplicable. They'd grown up together, and in many ways they were closer than

23

family. And she couldn't remember not loving him. 'You're letting his dinner spoil!' she said sharply.

'You should have taken Thomas Kingsmill!'

Jan regretted saying it before the words had died away. Mary seemed to grow two feet taller.

'Listen Jan!' Her eyes blazed but failed to hide the hurt. 'He came back – back to me! That's all that matters, and I'll not have you stirring up mischief.'

'I'm sorry,' said Jan. 'It just doesn't seem fair . . .'

Mary sat next to her. 'I'm as sure of George as you are of Alan,' she said gently.

'Alan didn't disappear for sixteen years then pop up asking me to marry him!' Jan flushed. She'd done it again. Life would be so much easier without a tongue!

Mary put the pot on the table and handed her sister a ladle.

'Mind you,' Jan said by way of an apology, 'he took his time. And he'd still be dithering if it hadn't been for the May Fair.'

'What do you mean?' said Mary.

'Father got drunk. Remember? You had to put him to bed at Peter Glover's place. Alan brought me home. Alone.' She grinned hugely. 'Proposed the next day, didn't he?'

Old maid or not, the significance was not lost on Mary. 'What have you been up to?' she asked – dreading the answer.

'Neglecting your father's comforts!' boomed Edward. 'That's what!'

Mary was spared the details as, fortified by gin, the aged wheelright strode manfully across the kitchen. 'A man' – he banged a fist on the table – 'a man is entitled to his dinner!' He banged again for good measure, and sank into his chair.

Jan subjected him – and Mary – to her sweetest smile, then slid a plateful of barely recognizable stew under his nose.

That night, sleep was a long time coming to Mary. She lay in bed staring at the moon floating past the window, and allowed her usually well-ordered thoughts to run free.

24

There were so many unanswered questions. How would Jan and Edward cope without her? Could she ever fashion a home from the pigsty Enoch Trickett laughingly called a farm? What of children? The subject had never been broached and she was already past her prime. Head spinning, Mary closed her eyes and, unable to conjure one half-convincing answer, turned her attention to the present.

Saturday, 27 October 1747 was to be a turning point in her life. As from Sunday, 28th she would never pass another night alone. Admittedly she was to be denied the pleasure of sharing a bed with George for two weeks yet – her father had seen to that, insisting that his prospective son-in-law sleep with him and not in the spare room opposite Mary's. Nevertheless, they would be under the same roof. Her dream was a hair's breadth from reality.

The pictures careering through her mind slowed to a halt and focused on her man. Stern and unsmiling, no longer the buoyant youth of memory, Sturt stared back. Excitement bubbled inside Mary with a fierceness that surprised her. The Devil that was George Sturt possessed her very soul. She could feel him deep down. Smell the warmth of his body on the chill air. She reached out and the hawkish face dissolved. She whispered his name and night sounds crowded in.

Mary sat up and listened. Behind the wall to her left, poleaxed by gin, her father grunted like a rutting goat. To the right, Jan the perennial fidget tossed and turned. She tried to imagine Sturt at rest. Did he sleep on his back or his side? Did he snore? Were his feet, like hers, ice blocks winter and summer? Did he talk, or worse still walk, in his sleep? She'd heard stories of the terrible things some folk got up to whilst supposedly dead to the world! The prospects for their wedding night suddenly seemed less than idyllic. Mary laughed out loud. At that moment George was probably lying in some damp, bug-ridden lodging house pallet thinking exactly the same thing!

Still chuckling, she settled beneath the covers and, as the moon slipped from view, sleep stole silently into the room.

*

25

Ignorance can be a blessing. Had Mary known of Sturt's whereabouts just then it is unlikely that she would have slept so soundly or anticipated his homecoming with quite the same enthusiasm.

The evening had started in a perfectly innocent way; a leisurely dinner at the Spread Eagle, to be followed, so Sturt thought, by a quiet hour to collect his thoughts and an early night. John Fairbrother, though, had had other ideas.

As the grey splash of dawn lightened the window, Sturt turned in his sleep, tormented by the memory of Ma Collett's whore-house. He had gone along on the under-standing that he would view the evening's entertainment and nothing more. John could do as he pleased, he would limit himself to the pleasures of the grape. Presenting his well-travelled soldier's face he'd pretended that the display of naked flesh and over-rehearsed contortions merely bored him. He had seen things in India, tableaux of debauchery that defied the Western imagination. Even, he spouted rather too loudly, Nancy Collett would have learnt a thing or two. The brothel keeper's eyes had flashed, though her arsenic-bleached face gave nothing away. Long years at her trade had developed an insight into human nature that any decent citizen would have envied. And she'd seen it all before. Sturt had guilt stamped all over his face. It was as clear as day, he was cheating on someone and meant to vent his spleen on her. Never one to shirk a challenge, Nancy Collett had there and then resolved to bed him herself. She stepped forward and kissed him, as a tolerant mother would a petulant child, an inch below the peak of his hairline. To Sturt's cost, the gauntlet had been picked up.

Now, goaded by a particularly pungent image, he awoke to face her. Sleep gummed the sorceress's green eyes, her public face lay flaked on the pillow and the smell of stale sex turned his stomach. But he remained still, frightened of waking her before he'd gathered his alcohol-fuddled thoughts.

Guilt certainly outweighed the hangover. He knew that

26

his behaviour had been unforgivable. Nevertheless, he desperately sought some justification. Finding none he turned on John. Or was it the drink? Or Nancy's witchery? She rolled towards him. A hand touched his belly and the skin crawled in his groin. A purge! That was it! It had been a symbolic purging of the past. Somehow an act of gross indulgence seemed the most fitting way to flush fifteen barren years from his system. Logical or not, the explanation would do. He could face the future and Mary afresh.

In fact, the truth of the matter lay on a less elevated plane. Sturt was a creature governed by instinct and, once mellowed by brandy, a lamb before Nancy Collett's butcher's knife. To be brutally frank he'd got drunk and had a good time, but pride and an over-inflated sense of self-respect would not allow him to admit it.

He raised himself on his elbows and listened to her breathing. Sure that she really was asleep, he quickly pulled on his breeches and padded to the door. Nancy did not stir. Sturt hesitated; beneath the paint she was surprisingly handsome, almost beautiful. And good. So very good . . . He took his last half-sovereign from his jacket pocket and left it on the chair by the bed. The latch clicked shut and the rhythm of Nancy's breathing changed. She smiled. One jade orb opened and examined the coin before it disappeared beneath her pillow. She curled into a ball and was instantly asleep. Ma Collett's working day was finally over.

Silence was the order of the day as Sturt and Fairbrother led their horses out of Dibdin's stable. Iron-shod hooves struck sparks from granite setts and both men winced.

Fairbrother groped for the fogbound memories that made it all worthwhile but someone screamed inside his skull and frightened them away. He eased into the saddle. His liver was beating like a second heart. His stomach heaved and the tastes of the night bubbled up his gullet. Experience told him he'd feel better for being sick.

Sturt led the sorry column into the street as every bell-ringer in Rye simultaneously tried to outdo his rivals. Fairbrother whimpered. Sturt said nothing, but his face aged ten years as they clattered down the hill. A north-easter stung his eyes and swept the clinging sea mist into the Channel. He watched a solitary cormorant race the rising tide across the mudbanks of the Rother and plunge into the harbour. Crop full of mackerel, the great black bird surfaced alongside a sleeping Dutch lugger and paddled clear of the approaching *Greyhound*. Patrol over, the revenue cutter bumped the jetty. Yet again the log would read 'no contact'. Outside the Custom House, Rye's resident fishermen weighed the night's catch and haggled a price with Sabbath-breaking dealers. The sun climbed above the rooftops and their weather-tanned faces glowed. Sturt sucked in the sharp salt air – the day could only get better.

And it did. By eight o'clock heads had stopped pounding. By nine, stomachs were settled and the analeptic sun lifted their spirits and all the colours of a splendid Kent autumn.

Regrettably, not everyone travelling the highway that morning shared Sturt and Fairbrother's new-found sense of well-being. Sarah Dimer's day had started on a sour note and was showing no sign of improvement. The root of her troubles had slipped away like a thief in the night, taking their only horse and the rusting cutlass he'd bought from Ezekiah Jefford. Precisely what John was up to she did not know. Who he was with was all too obvious. The way the free trade dominated her husband's conversation was a constant source of sadness. There wasn't an evening went by without the Hawkhurst Gang's most recent, grossly exag-gerated exploit being told and retold. Thomas Kingsmill's shadow had hung over the Dimer's neat flint and brick cottage all summer. And Sarah knew that with John's luck, the gallows was likely to widow her before the year was out.

She was frightened; not because she loved him (liking him was asking too much these days) but because she was the product of a devoutly Christian upbringing. 'To do one's duty' was the highest of ideals. Her father had said so and hammered it into her ever since she could remember. At sixteen, desperate to escape such remorseless purity of spirit, Sarah had made her mistake. She had been drawn

28

into a world of excitement and illusion by a man ten years her senior. Unable to resist the driving ambition, the boundless promises, she had eagerly accepted his proposal of marriage. Thirteen years on, dreams replaced by harsh reality, she remained a prisoner of her father's moral principles. It was her duty to be concerned for her husband's safety, as it was her duty to cook his food. Or wash his clothes. Or allow him occasional access to her body.

Not that duty or any other socially approved-of thoughts were foremost in her mind right then. Stranded at the roadside, a cartload of turnips stuck fast in the ditch, Sarah could cheerfully have strangled John with her bare hands. After all, it was his fault. If he hadn't taken the mare she wouldn't have had to use General Wade, and by now their only current source of income would be safely in Rye waiting on the Monday market.

She made one last attempt to break the stalemate. Seizing the ancient donkey's halter, she tugged for all she was worth, but the beast swished a horsefly from its backside and refused to budge. Sarah was approaching the end of her tether.

'You've had fair warning and don't say you haven't!'

The dark threat elicited no response and the prospect of meat on the Dimer's table receded even further. Except perhaps for donkey steaks. It was a tempting thought that she dismissed with some reluctance.

'Be it on your own head then!'

She wrenched a thick hazel switch from the bank, but the General's ears suddenly pricked and her arm froze in mid-air. Sarah listened. Rising above the distant church bells was the distinctive drumming of horses at the canter.

She snatched a horse pistol from under the wagon seat, priming it as two mud-splashed riders led a sway-backed pack-horse into view. By the time Sturt and Fairbrother had reined their steaming mounts to a halt the firing piece had disappeared into the folds of her skirt. The two men assessed the situation. Sarah edged back against the cart.

'You could use some assistance, mistress,' said Fairbrother.

'Thank you, no,' she answered sharply. 'I can cope well enough.' The cart shifted and a choice turnip plopped into the curdled ditch-water.

Fairbrother dismounted. A brief examination revealed no damage to cart or cargo. Sarah's finger tightened on the trigger as he moved towards her.

'When I shout, lady, bite his ear.' He smiled. 'Hard as you can!'

There was an almost imperceptible pause before Sarah started to flounder. 'I don't understand you, sir. Bite . . .'

'His ear,' repeated Fairbrother. 'But not before I say.'

Again that reassuring smile. Sarah nodded and turned to Sturt. She'd felt his gaze from the moment they stopped and, well practised at deflecting unwanted masculine attention, she faced him with defences bristling. Usually a straight look did the trick, but this time it bounced right back at her. Nonplussed, Sarah failed to recognize that she was flattered. Cheeks flushing, she turned away.

'George?' said Fairbrother.

Sturt dismounted and they took a wheel each. Then, as veins popped and sinews cracked, the back axle slowly inched above the waterline. Fairbrother grunted in Sarah's direction and her jaws snapped shut – with spectacular results. Braying in agony, the donkey took off with Sturt and Fairbrother trailing like May Day streamers in the wind. Careless of convention, Sarah hitched up her skirts and sprinted after them, gaining ground as they fought to keep the cart on its axis. Fortunately, the General's old legs could not sustain the charge. Once he was safely at rest, Fairbrother unleashed his instant charm. Bowing low he offered his arm to Sarah.

'My pleasure, ma'am.'

Before she could refuse he'd lifted her onto the driver's seat and handed her the reins. The forgotten pistol slipped from her grasp and fell conspicuously to earth. Fairbrother stared at the delicate creature who might well have blown his brains out. Sturt picked up the firing piece and Sarah took it back without batting an eyelid.

'Not everyone as travels this road is a gentleman,' she said. 'I thank you kindly.'

A slap on its rump and the chastened donkey trotted on, and though the two men were visibly impressed Sarah felt foolish. She'd behaved like a helpless female. Biting an ear – it was so simple! Still muttering to herself, she approached a bend in the road and, without wanting to, shot a glance over her shoulder. Sturt was waiting for it, and again she turned away. Straight-laced Sarah Dimer was angry but didn't know why. She flicked at the General's mangled ear and hurried on to Rye.

As for Sturt and Fairbrother – they mounted up in silence. There was no need for words. The grin splitting Fairbrother's face said it all.

'God's Curse on English Justice!' Sturt's angry cry skimmed patchwork fields and bounced around the skeletal wood. Above his head, Will Scrimms's gibbet-hung corpse creaked like a ship at anchor. The tar-blacked face grinned at the living world below and a handful of rooks echoed Sturt's outrage as they took to the air.

'Just a thief or free trader,' said Fairbrother. 'Likely got all he deserved.'

'No one deserves that!' Sturt snapped. 'It leaves a man no dignity.'

'I doubt that dignity concerned him on the ladder,' remarked Fairbrother drily.

Before Sturt could answer, a sudden gust rattled Scrimms's irons and set him spinning like a child's top. Sturt spurred his horse to the junction with the Tonbridge road. Death itself was an indignity. He'd seen enough of it to know. But, deterrent or not, displaying a man's legally strangled remains in public was verging on barbaric.

He stopped by the mile post and Fairbrother joined him. Amoebic shadows raced across the equinoctial landscape. The year was dying but doing so gloriously. Somewhere a dog fox barked and a pheasant clattered to safety. Trees bending under the weight of the wind sighed like old men whose time had come. The only unnatural sound in the world was the musical clanking of Scrimms's chains.

The two friends sat tongue-tied and awkward. Keen to avoid each other's eyes, they watched the circling crows until Fairbrother could bear it no longer. 'Fifteen years.'

'Best part of.' The boldest bird returned to its perch and Sturt turned away. 'You'll not forget.'

Fairbrother's face remained impassive.

'The wedding!'

'Oh that.' The date had been branded on his memory since Sturt announced it almost a year ago. 'No, I'll not forget.'

One by one, in an ascending order of timidity, the rooks joined their leader on the gibbet and eavesdropped the stilted conversation.

'The next few weeks . . .' started Sturt.

'I'll take my ease within the chill bosom of my family,' said Fairbrother quickly. 'Hopefully, hound my sanctimonious sire to an early grave and squander his fortune loosening the corsets of Tonbridge!'

Those who did not know him would have considered that the flippant answer of an insensitive man; those who did would have recognized the misery it concealed. For once, the concern reflected in Sturt's eyes persuaded John to abandon the pretence.

'I'll consider my circumstances,' he said. 'Carefully.' Before Sturt could press him further he offered his hand. 'God-speed, George.'

Sturt grasped it firmly. 'God-speed, friend.'

Simultaneously, they reached out and embraced. That one fierce physical gesture said more about friendship than words ever could. Theirs had not merely grown out of familiarity; it had been forged in adversity, by the countless times each had trusted his life to the other. The bond between them was the one constant factor in both their lives and it would survive the disruption of marriage and an uncertain future.

A full minute passed before Fairbrother broke away and turned his horse towards Tonbridge. He did not look back and Sturt did not move. He merged into the distant trees and Sturt murmured softly, 'Take care.'

Over the horizon, thunder threatened. Scrimms swung to and fro seemingly urging Sturt to hurry home. However, 'walk on' was the command he gave to the mare. A new life lay disconcertingly close now, and he was in no mood to meet it at the gallop.

Chapter 3

A second roll of thunder heralded the downpour. Reflections in the village pond broke into a trot as Mary Winchcombe hurried her brood to church. Already late, they stopped on the Gore. Sheltering under the only oak in Goudhurst to escape the shipwright's axe, Mary glared at her sister.

'Nothing to do with me,' Jan protested. 'He was likely out poaching all night.'

And she was right. Alan Wynter had got home with barely time to change his clothes. Now, struggling to stay awake, cursing the stone in his Sunday best boot, he took the short cut through Peter Glover's yard and sprinted past the Bear and Billet. He was always late for church and Mary always roasted him, but today he had the perfect excuse. All he had to do was get in first, before she loosed one of her barbs.

Mary saw him as he skirted the pond.

'No bells are there?' Alan yelled quickly.

The challenge went unanswered. Bells were taken for granted and not one of them had noticed.

Alan beamed. 'Old Brack must be having a lie-in this morning.'

Edward cuffed him for his insolence and Mary's look sent them both scurrying up the hill.

Walking with Jan on his arm, Alan's eye remained fixed on the head of the family. Goading her was one of his greatest pleasures, and he knew just which nerve to finger. 'Word is you're going to tackle Thomas Kingsmill, Master Edward.' Jan elbowed his ribs.

'Then the word is wrong!' snapped Mary. 'And you should know better than to listen to gossip.'

'Who says it's gossip?' said Edward.

She rounded on her father. 'I do!'

'It's none of your business, girl!' retorted Edward. 'So don't get on your high horse with me!'

To everyone's surprise, Mary did not answer back. The rain intensified, transforming the rutted street into a water-course of miniature rills and cataracts. She quickened her pace. Bells or not, the rest of the village could get to church on time. Nevertheless, it was odd . . . For an instant an inexplicable foreboding gripped her, but Alan denied her the chance to rationalize it.

'Peter Glover says it's time someone made a stand.'

Edward rose to the bait. 'That's just what I been saying – '

'Say what you like, it's not going to be you!' This time, the tone of Mary's voice left no one in any doubt that the subject was closed. She sailed through the churchyard gates with Jan in her wake.

'They'll pay their dues,' Edward muttered confidentially. 'I'll see to it – next time they're in the village.'

Alan nodded the way he thought he ought to. 'Women!' he sighed. 'They've no idea.'

The game Alan had been playing turned sour the instant they set foot in the graveyard. Outside the main doors, Reverend Brack's congregation watched a human chain pass roped pairs of half-anker casks from church vestry to waiting cart. The Hawkhurst Gang were shifting contraband, and Edward wished that the ground would open up and swallow him.

'Mary has a point, Master Edward,' Alan said sheepishly. 'Best not do owt daft, eh?'

But his words were wasted on the old wheelwright. It wasn't as if he'd been blowing off in the Bear one night; he'd committed himself not two minutes ago. Courage boosted by the threat to his self-esteem, Edward forced a way through the crowd before anyone could stop him. Mary's stentorian objection fell on deaf ears as he strode towards the mounted figure by the porch.

'Thomas Kingsmill!' he called.

Kingsmill turned in the saddle. 'Master Winchcombe?'

'I'll have words with you!'

35

'And right heavy ones, I'll warrant, to put you in such a sweat.'

A hand tugged at Edward's sleeve.

'Master Edward? Don't do it . . .'

Pride was not one of Alan's vices; the source of his courage was an overriding sense of guilt. But Edward would not be dissuaded. Their ridiculous scuffling provided a welcome opportunity for the Hawkhurst tubmen to rest their aching arms. Edward pushed and Alan pushed back.

'And who's this charging about like a young bull?' enquired Kingsmill.

'My name's Wynter, Master Kingsmill. Alan Wynter.'

'Joseph Wynter's lad?'

'Aye, sir. Please, take no heed, he's lost hold of his senses – '

'The Devil I have!' Edward finally shook free. 'You hold your tongue, boy! We has business.'

A cutlass point jabbed him between the shoulder-blades.

'Go home, old man,' advised William Jackson. 'Else you'll fetch up with a sore head.' Another jab was imminent.

'Hold your hand and show some respect, William,' said Kingsmill with a smile. 'What business had you in mind?'

'Payment,' said Edward. 'For safe-keeping your cargoes year in and year out.' Kingsmill stayed silent, forcing him to elaborate. 'It were always the arrangement!'

'A long time since.'

'When Arthur Gray were running things – '

'Arthur Gray lost interest in the trade,' interrupted Jackson. 'What with falling down a well and all.'

What happened next was to become a subject of discussion and argument, not only in Goudhurst but throughout the southern counties for years to come. Exaggeration and embellishment aside, the facts of the matter seem to confirm that the whole bloody shambles was, as is usually the case, the result of a series of stupid mistakes.

Edward's ill-advised retort to Jackson started it off. Kingsmill's deputy lashed out and the old man fell senseless. As Jan and Mary rushed to his aid, Alan took up the fight. To the delight of the watching free traders, his ferocious

36

attack surprised Jackson, causing him to fall beneath the carthorse's hooves. Alan, remembering how he'd once seen a weasel finish off a buck hare, went for the throat. By now, the smugglers were drawn up in an expectant circle and bayed encouragement to their man.

Jackson responded wuth awesome efficiency. Thumbs gouging Alan's eyes, he threw the boy off balance and regained his feet. Jan screamed hysterically. Mary, unable to revive her father, appealed to their friends and neighbours. Frightened of involvement, the menfolk hesitated, until, that is, John Dimer crashed his sword pommel down on Alan's skull. The boy's knees buckled and Peter Glover, Goudhurst's giant blacksmith, suddenly rediscovered the grit that had once made him bare knuckle champion of Kent. The rest followed like sheep. But they were farm workers and saddlers, brickmakers and lath binders. They had never faced the Reculver shore patrol on Romney Marsh. Or routed the Rye dragoon squadron at Fairlight Cove.

Passion fuelled their first charge and the smugglers fell back. Glover tipped Kingsmill from the saddle. Jan dragged the cowardly Dimer from his perch on the wagon and flew at him fists and feet flailing. Unfortunately, the shock was too soon absorbed and the Gang countered. In the free for all that followed heads were split and bones were cracked, but miraculously not one fatal blow was delivered by either side. Until Kingsmill shot Mary Winchcombe.

Outraged at being unseated, he drew his horse pistol and aimed at the unarmed blacksmith. Fearing for Glover's life, Mary called Kingsmill's Christian name. He turned. And for the first time in seventeen years they looked each other in the eye.

That fraction of a second was all Glover needed. He struck Kingsmill a mighty double-fisted blow in the back and sent him reeling against a tombstone. The impact jarred his hand. The pistol discharged and the ball struck Mary in the stomach.

She sank to the ground without a sound. Villagers backed off. Smugglers closed ranks. Kingsmill stood over her as a crimson stain seeped through her muddied Sunday dress. A disjointed pattern of memories raced through his mind and his fingers slackened. The pistol fell to earth. Mary's breathing changed to a laboured rattle. A cry of anguish rent the clouded air.

'Don't touch her!'

The unaccustomed authority in Alan's voice stopped Jan in her tracks. Though still dazed, he knelt down and gently lifted Mary's head from the mud.

Kingsmill turned away and snapped at Richard Perrin, 'Is it all accounted for?'

The flustered buyer checked his tally; he detested violence and what he'd seen had turned his stomach. 'Yes.' he said. 'No! There's still the tea and tobacco.'

'Then we'll come back for it!'

No further orders were necessary. Perrin climbed aboard the cart and Dimer took a whip to the horses. The rest of the Gang followed, leaving Kingsmill alone in his native village.

He stared at Mary and felt nothing for her. Events had moved too fast as they had done once before. But the kind of pain and anger that had consumed him then, and for many years after, no longer touched him. Now, he was Kingsmill, leader of the Hawkhurst Gang. He needed no roots. He wanted no friends. He desired no one woman. All that he felt was an overwhelming compulsion to remind the world of who he was. He looked down at frightened faces and relished his power.

'Cross me again,' he roared, 'and I'll burn your village to the ground! I'll fill this graveyard to bursting!'

No one spoke. Above his head, a torrent of rainwater forced a long abandoned nest from a gargoyle's gaping mouth. A tiny, mummified corpse flopped onto the path and floated downhill. Kingsmill spurred his horse, leaving Goudhurst to weigh the cost of its impudence.

The last few miles seemed endless. Childhood memories rough and tumbled in the hop fields, laughed in the woods, whispered in every ditch. A derelict grain wagon lay rotting at the roadside, its rusting wheel irons standing like the ribs of an old skeleton. Sturt looked at them and two boys ran for their lives pursued by young Edward Winchcombe. The smaller boy toppled a pile of rim irons and the towering wheelwright sprawled head over heels. Shrieking with delight, his tormentors pushed and shoved their way down to the street, past the Bear and Billet and off across the Gore – hounded by a troop of French cavalry. The rain eased and, wooden sword in hand, an impish attacker lurked behind the hedge. Breathing suspended, his companion aimed a loaded sapling. The strike was timed to perfection. Yelling with all the lung power they could muster – cursing and blaspheming being essential components of any ambush – they slashed and blasted the enemy. Brains shot through, innards trailing, Sturt loosened his greatcoat collar and rode on.

A mile or so from Goudhurst, the road climbed high above the River Teise and wound through a plantation of hundred-year-old oaks. At a break in the trees, Sturt reined the nameless bay to a standstill and looked down on the best trout water in Kent. For centuries it had been a daylight haven for adventurous children, a night-time haunt of eager lovers. But now, many of the best trees had been felled, hauled off to the south coast shipyards to be sawn and split, nailed and jointed into the Channel battle fleet. No longer a vigorous green keeper of dreams and secrets, the wood wore the ravaged look of a war widow. A stab of regret homed on Sturt and he nudged his mount down the over-grown axeman's track. Down to the living water's edge. Down to his own brooding secret.

He dismounted where Isaac Dekker had so cunningly set his trap. The bay and the nag stood quietly, respectful as mourners at a funeral, while Sturt walked the yielding bank. Leaves the colour of rotten applies crackled underfoot. He looked across the water and a tearful youth blinked back. Somewhere a dog barked. He turned, squinting into the sun as it squeezed through a widening rent in the cloud ceiling.

Sounds familiar caused the hairs on the back of his neck

to bristle. At another time, in another place, he would have primed his musket, unsheathed his hanger, ready to engage approaching enemy troops. Now, though conscious of a quickening heartbeat, he merely watched as the Hawkhurst Gang rode south with their goods. Not a single rider wasted so much as a cursory glance on him until Kingsmill, riding at the rear, slowed as he always did at that particular spot. For an instant he looked down at the solitary figure standing by the water's edge. Sturt shielded his eyes from the glare, but the usual courtesy of 'Good day, sir' stuck in his throat. Half-buried memories stirred in both men's minds. Each reached out, groping for a piece of the past, a piece of the puzzle that had made them what they were.

All too soon the Gang and the moment were gone. Peace and natural ease returned to the wood though not to George Sturt. A dead friend dropped out of a tree. A forgotten enemy sprang from the bracken. An abandoned lover floated downstream clutching their dead child. Pain and pleasure ghosted through the trees like startled roes. Pain and Pleasure. Pain and . . .

A musket shot sent the rooks skyward, and Sturt's secret scurrying back to the void. Whether God or the Devil had chosen that moment to tear a rotten branch from the wood's oldest oak was open to conjecture, but what wasn't, was Sturt's desire to be about his business. He climbed into the saddle and spurred the mare – sharply – on towards Goudhurst.

A rumbling stomach reminded Sturt that he hadn't eaten since breakfast. Riding up the long lower hill, past Peter Glover's smithy, his mouth watered at the prospect of dinner. Mary was bound to have made a special effort, and he had every intention of doing justice to her more than adequate skills. Crossing the Gore he stopped. The village was unnaturally quiet. Houses were in darkness, streets deserted. Neither dog or homeless tom sifted the piles of domestic rubbish rotting in the alleys. And even the Gore lacked its regular complement of pigs and goats. The crawling feeling in Sturt's gut had nothing to do with hunger pangs. An old soldier's instinct could not be packed away with his unwanted uniform. He'd known times like this before – in France where entire villages had been abandoned by panic-stricken inhabitants fearful of the advancing English. But this was Goudhurst. His home. No blood-crazed invader threatened here.

Muffled voices floated down the street and the tension in his body eased. He'd forgotten that it was Sunday, and, by the sound of it, Reverend Brack was hurling thunderbolts from the pulpit. For a moment Sturt wondered if, with the passage of time, the ghosts of his service past would cease to trouble him. Recognizing wishful thinking for what it was, he nudged the bay on; past the browning stain outside Widow Shaddick's timber and daub cottage, up the winding hill, on top of which squatted Goudhurst church, like some massive greystone frog.

Inside, the nave was packed to bursting point. Virtually every man, woman and child in Goudhurst sat, frightened and subdued, listening to the row going on beneath Brack's elevated pulpit. Like a terrier snapping at a chained bear, Alan Wynter squared up to Peter Glover. He'd never done it before, not whilst remaining within ear-cuffing distance anyway, but at that moment he was angrier than he'd ever been in his short life.

The blacksmith's recommendation to abandon the village forever, moving the entire population to some unspecified safe location inland, had roused him to a fury and, come what may, he was going to say his piece. Shouting Glover and his growing band of supporters down, Alan urged them to fight back. Glover countered. They had done so that afternoon – and been punished for their recklessness ten times over. Undeterred, Alan appealed to their sense of pride – and justice. Honourable men could no longer face the wall as the gentlemen rode by, he argued. And attack was the best means of defence – a recruiting officer had told him so only last month whilst filling his head with tales of battlefield glory in a vain attempt to entice him to take the King's shilling. They must organize, form a militia, then

41

Kingsmill and his murderous crew would not dare trouble them again.

Ignoring Glover's perfectly reasonable enquiry as to who was to arm and train this village army – bearing in mind the military's well-known aversion to doing anything that might provoke the free traders – Alan blundered on, gathering momentum as he sensed the argument slipping from his grasp.

His family, like everyone else's, had lived in Goudhurst for three hundred years or more. He would not be pushed out. Running from a gang of drunken bullies with his tail between his legs was something he could not live with. Something no decent, God-fearing man with half an ounce of courage and self-respect could live with. Because, if he did, one day he would have to explain why to his children; to those who, too young to know better, believed in him; those who, sitting with him now, confused by the dreadful events of the day, trusted him to do what was right.

For a moment the weight of village opinion hung in the balance. All eyes were on Glover as he turned to Alan. Sturt entered unnoticed as the blacksmith started to speak. Gently, and without malice or mockery, Glover applauded the boy's noble stance. In principle, he agreed with everything he had said. He shared the same feelings, the same sense of outrage and shame, but his instinct for survival told him that Alan was wrong. Resistance would only result in too many widows, and, when it all boiled down, a proud corpse was of no practical use to a fatherless family. Conscious that the balance was tipping, Alan played his one remaining card. His voice rose by fully half an octave as he blurted out the words: 'Glover's way,' he said, 'is the coward's way!'

Again the silence. The anticipation. But the older man resisted the clumsy goad and turned to face friends and family. A vote was the only answer, he said quietly, a free and open vote to see how many cowards were with him. At the back, Sturt could scarcely believe his ears. He felt like an intruder on some private grief, but didn't know what or whose it was.

All at once, stones and mortar seemed to quake as the church erupted in an explosion of near-hysterical voices. Opinion and counter ricocheted from the ancient roof timbers. Francis Felkin and Tom Austin, normally the meekest of men, stood toe to toe, flailing the air with clenched fists as each tried to outshout the other. And as for the guiding hand, the calming influence of Reverend Enoch Brack . . . He was leaning over the lip of his carved oak eyrie, a look of supreme resignation etched deep into the lines of his ferrety countenance. Within minutes, it was obvious that the vote was going to be a formality. Youthful passion lay defeated. Mature discretion had carried the day. Goudhurst was to be abandoned.

Itching to discover the root of such a fantastic state of affairs, Sturt stepped out of the shadows. Alan saw him at once and called his name. Every head turned as if operated by the same invisible string. Insults and arguments dribbled away as the ex-soldier strode down the aisle. By the time he was half-way to the altar, the only sound in the world was the harsh ring of iron boot nails on granite flags. He stopped no more than a yard from Alan and Glover.

'Evensong has changed some,' he said and looked straight at Brack. The priest turned away, refusing to meet his gaze.

'A special meeting, George,' explained Glover. 'Everyone in the village . . .'

A quick glance around the nave was all Sturt needed. 'Who stands for the Winchcombes?' he asked. Peter Glover's eyes shifted to his boots and Sturt looked at Alan.

'I – I think we should talk outside,' said the boy, struggling to keep voice and emotions under control.

Again Sturt looked at Glover. The blacksmith nodded, 'Best go with the lad.'

Sturt turned on his heel and, as he passed each pew, looked at the person sitting next to the aisle. Without exception, they either picked imaginary specks from their clothing, or blew their nose on a rag wipe, or simply avoided his eyes. Countless possibilities tumbled through his mind – but one rose to the fore and refused to be dismissed. Mary. It had to be something to do with Mary. Alan banged the heavy

43

oak door shut behind them. Peter Glover waited for the echo to die then spoke calmly. 'On a show of hands. Those for going . . .' A forest of arms reached for the roof. 'And those against.'

Not a single hand was raised.

Passing through the yew-dotted graveyard, Alan wanted to tell Sturt but somehow the awful words refused to come. ''Appen Master Edward should do the talking,' he said, and nervously fingered the ugly swelling behind his ear. Sturt did not press him; he merely squeezed his shoulder and opened the gate. Leaving his horses tethered outside the Bear, they turned left into Back Lane and approached the Winchcombes' house. Rats clattered in the darkness as man and boy walked in silence. Stepping over the brimming open sewer, they entered the house. In the kitchen, Alan took a smoking tallow candle from the table and led the way upstairs. He opened Mary's bedroom door. The soft glow of an oil lamp spilled into the narrow passage and he stood aside.

What happened to Sturt as he entered that tiny, low ceilinged room was outside his experience, and almost beyond endurance. He'd seen death many times; sometimes quick, sometimes slow, it was never easy and inevitably messy. He'd seen it often enough to know that Mary was dying. But stretched beneath a single sheet, face colourless as water, barely breathing, she looked as peaceful as a sleeping child. The world seemed to stop. He did not see Edward hunched in the chair, his roughly laced facial wounds leaking onto his only linen shirt. Nor did he see Jan, red-rimmed and almost as ashen as her sister, tearing linen strips with Ma Shaddick. All he saw was Mary. His Mary. Dying. And taking what remained of his life with her.

Somewhere deep inside, a terrible scream ripped through his innards, paralysing all feeling, leaving him helpless, teetering on the brink of the abyss. No one moved, No one spoke as he stood in the doorway consumed by the terrors within. Eventually, someone whispered her name. Sturt realized that it was him and the spell was broken. Kneeling at the bedside, he was about to speak it again when Jan's weary voice intruded.

'The Hawkhurst Gang was here, George – collecting a run cargo . . .'

Sturt looked at her and she shut up.

'There was an argument,' said Alan, 'a stupid argument what got out of hand. Mary was shot.'

The bald statement hung in the air like a gibbeted thief, but the lad offered no further explanation. Sturt turned to Edward. Tears diluted the dark streaks trickling down the old man's face as he answered the unspoken question.

'It was Kingsmill,' he said. 'Your friend Thomas Kingsmill!'

Again the scream within; only this time it was followed by a musket shot. A voice, an angry juvenile voice leapt from the distant past and filled the living present.

'I'll have my revenge on you!' it roared. 'I swear it. If I have to chase you to the gates of Hell itself!'

Sturt leaned over the bed and kissed Mary gently on the lips.

'You'll have your chance of revenge, Thomas,' he murmured.

'I promise you!'

Chapter 4

Early on the fourth morning after Mary's death, Sturt stood at her graveside. Bare-headed, wrapped in his high-collared greatcoat, he rose out of the mist like the Reaper himself, a fact not unnoticed by Enoch Brack as he scuttled down the hill clutching his personal bundle and the church plate. Somewhere, a stormcock sang to the wind that ripped through the leafless elms. Sturt sank a little deeper into his coat.

There were no tears, no outward sign of sorrow to betray the agony. He merely stood, staring at the mound of rich Kent earth, beneath which his mortal remains would one day lie beside hers. Not a God-fearing man, he believed that death was the end of everything. Over the years, he'd seen many comrades die in action; some marched to meet their Maker joyously; others, rejecting their faith as the darkness crowded in, expired in stark terror. Ever since his first skirmish and through countless later battles, he had searched for the sense of it all, for some hint that beyond the carnage lay a celestial plan based upon a system of natural justice. But, in nearly twenty years' soldiering, he'd failed to catch so much as a glimpse of any such scheme. Therefore, to his way of thinking, there was no God, no Paradise to come, and what hope there was existed solely in the way a man conducted himself during his short span.

Nevertheless, standing there cold and alone, he prayed. He asked – no, begged – for a little more time on Earth. Time to find Kingsmill. Time to exorcize the guilt and slake the thirst for vengeance that now consumed him. Time to kill or be killed. Just then, the sun punched a jagged hole in the clinging grey blanket and warmed his back. Sturt took it as a sign that someone or something, somewhere, had heard him.

He offered silent thanks, then, looking at the precise spot

46

where he imagined her face to be, said clearly and with hoarfrost in his voice, 'Each owes the other now, Mary. It's time to settle.' A door banged shut and Alan Wynter called his name. Mary's face faded and Sturt turned and walked towards the church.

Dorothy Shaddick was sixty-one years old. Widowed by a rotten appendix some forty years earlier, she was midwife, leech and village arbiter rolled into one. A natural respect for her years, allied to a combination of near-legendary common sense and a talent for plain speaking, had made Ma Shaddick one of Goudhurst's most influential citizens. Though to look at her that morning, lost in the crush, apparently nodding off in the same seat she'd occupied since some indeterminate point in the previous century, it was hard to credit that she was anything more than a dried-up old hag sliding, without protest, into the grave. But it was Dorothy who had forced the second vote.

Mary's death had affected Dorothy deeply, more so than any of the many tragedies that littered her past. It had been her pleasure to drag Lizzie Winchcombe's first-born into the world. She'd patched up young Mary after innumerable childhood knocks and scrapes, done her best to remove Kingsmill's ball – then sobbed as she'd stuffed and blocked, dressed and wrapped, her too-young body for the benefit of churchyard worms. Personal outrage, injustice, disgust, she'd experienced before, but never had she been gripped by such a feeling of utter waste.

The first meeting had taken place while she'd been striving to staunch a massive internal haemorrhage. Deprived of that platform, she'd lobbied and cajoled, blustered and threatened, until the opposition had wilted. Her timing, as always, was deadly. Four days had been just long enough for tempers to cool, panic to subside. And supported – to devastating effect – by the brooding presence of Edward, Dorothy had touched on every raw nerve she could find. The long shadow of shame hung over the population of Goudhurst and she'd exploited it to the hilt. Knowing full well the consequences of doing so, she'd had no qualms, no stab of conscience, about forcing them to reconsider. Now, task completed, tired and nagged by her rheumatics, Ma Shaddick melted into the background as Sturt again faced Peter Glover.

'Well, tell him!' urged Alan.

Never a good loser, the blacksmith glared at him. 'You tell him!' he snapped, then sat down.

The lad drew breath, but at that moment two hundred or more people were looking at him and his tongue turned to chalk.

'We're staying put!' Jan's words rang out from the second row.

'To face 'em . . .' explained her father unnecessarily.

She squeezed his hand and Alan found some spit. 'That is – if you'll lead us.'

If! Sturt wanted to embrace the boy and shout for joy. Instead, he merely fingered the carotid pulse, throbbing at twice the normal rate beneath his ear, and nodded. Terrified of exposing his feelings in public, he turned away and, like a predatory wolf cleaving a flock of sheep, strode down the aisle. He knew what they were thinking. The sergeant had just been promoted general; now it was up to him. But with no arms or strategy, and troops such as these, he needed time to think. He reached for the doorknob.

Alan's shout stopped him like a slap in the face. 'George . . .' Speaking for all, the lad asked the question that Sturt was dreading. 'What do we do?'

John Dimer was up to his old tricks. Rye had always been his favourite thieving ground (he put it down to the sea air – and the fact that its teeming warren of hilly streets and alleys offered a better than even chance of escape). Standing at the corner of Bell Yard where it opened onto the harbour, he watched as, nosegay clamped to pox-scarred nostrils, the Hon. Josiah Shovel negotiated the filth and street traders with equal distaste. Dimer's method was simple and to the point; find a spot where a blocked drain had flooded, stick out a boot as the intended victim passed by, then lift watch and purse under the pretext of helping said gentleman, or lady – he harboured no prejudice – out of the effluent. Even at a time when close proximity to all things organic was the norm rather than the exception, the effect of such a ducking on one of breeding guaranteed Dimer time to lose himself in the crowd. It had worked unfailingly for years and, though he was now a respected member of the smuggling profession, he felt obliged to keep his hand in.

This time, distracted at the crucial moment by the fracas on the quay, he mistimed the strike. Out shot the leg. Down came Shovel's fashionable heel – firmly onto Dimer's instep. Dimer squealed and buckled, thereby chinning himself on the pommel of the gent's blade. Cuffed about the ear for good measure, the would-be pickpocket may well have retired to the Dog and Partridge had not the afore-mentioned fracas drawn him like a moth to a flame.

Limping past the moored revenue cutter, *Greyhound*, Dimer craned his short neck but could see nothing. Fish-wives and soot boys abandoned slab and street, joining him as he burrowed into the rapidly swelling crowd. The source of the disturbance seemed to be outside the Custom House itself. Peering past the party of riding officers struggling to hold the mob at bay, he could see three pack-horses and a bay mare tethered to the rail. Beyond them, a pair of tide waiters, grateful for the extra money, carried oilskin-wrapped packages into the building. Snatches of a dozen conversations buzzed about his ears.

'Run goods,' explained a muscular cord-wainer.

'Hawkhurst goods,' confirmed the know-all pot boy from the Green Man.

The mob surged forward and, before he could dispute such a preposterous supposition, an old bunter dropped her hand into Dimer's crotch.

'Part of a stored cargo, your honour.' Her face seemed to turn inside out as, fingers working like mating spiders, she flashed her diseased gums in his direction. 'Turned in by some loon from Goudhurst, see.'

Skin crawling, Dimer shook himself free as the mob surged again. He didn't believe it – couldn't believe it! No one, not even a lunatic, would dare. Elbows flailing, he pushed to the front, eager to ask them as would know for sure – but a musket butt sank into his bread-basket, discouraging all thought of further enquiry.

'You has to have an appointment. Mr Collier won't see no one without one.' The officious clerk looked up from his blot-stained ledger. 'It's his way see.'

'He'll see me,' said Sturt.

The scrivener smiled oilily. 'I'm sorry, sir . . .'

A 27-pound dollop dropped onto his desk.

'Tea,' explained Sturt patiently. 'Best Indian. Come all the way from France.'

Inky fingers touched the oilskin as if it was alive.

'There's seven hundred pounds of it – lodging in your strong-room this very minute.'

Gaping like a gaffed fish, the quill driver stared hard at him.

'You can tell the Surveyor General my name is Sturt. George Sturt.'

His Majesty's Surveyor General of Customs, one Cloudesley Collier, was a sensitive soul. Born and bred within the tranquil confines of a Staffordshire farm, he'd found the constant bustle of a busy Channel port such a distraction that, within a week of his appointment, he had been forced to abandon his grand office overlooking the fish quay and move into the riding officers' duty room at the back of the building. John Dimer knew as much because it was his responsibility to deliver the Surveyor General's weekly ration of contraband – and dropping it in the narrow alley off Shoe Lane, rather than at the front door, made life easier for all concerned.

Squatting beneath the window, ear glued to the weatherboard wall, he strained to catch the gist of the agitated exchange within. Collier was furious with his uninvited visitor – and rightly so. Not only were his perks in jeopardy but, when Kingsmill got wind of the day's events, his very existence would be called into question.

Regardless of the image he liked to present to the world

at large, Dimer's own position within the Hawkhurst hier-archy was tenuous to say the least. Recruited into the company on George Kingsmill's personal say-so, he was despised by Jackson and disliked by the rest – with the all important exception of Thomas Kingsmill. He seemed to recognize some obscure hidden talent in Dimer, and even entrusted him with the odd task that would normally have gone to one higher up the pecking order. So, never slow to exploit an opportunity to improve his status, Dimer threw caution to the wind and sneaked a look through the window.

He did not recognize the gaunt, straight-backed figure taking a tongue-lashing from young Collier, but sensed a military bearing. He tried to ease the window open, but the Surveyor General, who also hated draughts, had securely bolted it. Muttering curses to himself, Dimer squatted beneath the sill where he caught tantalizing snippets until, without warning, Collier's visitor turned nasty.

Insatiably curious, Dimer risked another look and saw the man lean across the desk, and administer a verbal assault of such ferocity that the exciseman was left floundering. And though he could not hear the actual conversation, Dimer had no trouble in guessing its content. He dropped out of sight as, denied further opportunity to speak by the stranger's abrupt exit, Collier tapped a keg of smuggled geneva and downed a large measure. Equilibrium partially restored, he donned Kevenhuller and tunic. Breathing deeply, he waited for his cheeks to cool then left the room. Dimer, by that time, was half-way back to the quayside where, faced by Rye's resident squadron of dragoons, the mob had dispersed to spread the news.

On the jetty, a few split heads were raised as Sturt pushed past the soldiers. Boiling angry, he threw himself into the saddle and led his string up Old Turnstile towards the castle.

Collier stepped out onto the veranda and watched him go. At the corner, Dimer returned, hid his face and pretended to remove a stone from his boot. The clerk slid into his master's shadow.

'He wanted me to arrest the Hawkhurst Gang,' said Collier. 'All of them!'

The inky sycophant shook his sparsely thatched head in disbelief. 'Poor scab must be damaged about the cranium.'

The Surveyor General looked at him. 'I advised him to try the Army.'

Dimer suppressed a snort of amusement and scuttled away as fast as his stumpy legs would carry him. Cloudesley Collier didn't know it, but that statement had just saved his skin.

Forking horse manure from the dung cart, Sarah Dimer silently cursed her husband – wherever he was. Their scrap of land just off the Roman road east of Iden Green was not the best in Kent and, like a good marriage, required constant care and attention. She cursed him again – this time out loud. He'd been promising to feed her potato patch for weeks, but whenever the subject was broached John seemed to remember pressing business elsewhere. Now, with the onset of winter draining the autumn colours from the Weald, Sarah had been left with no option.

She turned a forkful of heavy earth and a blood blister the size of a farthing tore away from the palm of her hand. As she sucked it clean, the ring of iron plates on Roman setts startled the mistle-thrush following in her wake. Clattering with alarm, the timid creature dropped a leather-jacket and sought refuge in the yew copse behind the house. Wary of all who travelled the highway in daylight or darkness, Sarah reached for her ever-present horse pistol. Caught in the open, flight was out of the question, so she stood her ground and watched the solitary rider and his pack animals rise above the brow of the hill. Barely a chain's length from the road, she recognized Sturt at once. The same feelings that had disconcerted her at their previous meeting stirred again. Feelings that had remained dormant for so long that she failed to recognize them.

For an instant, a smile threatened. 'Good day to you, sir,' she called.

Her greeting had no more effect on the muffled figure

than the first spots of cold rain sweeping in from the sea. No snub was intended. Sarah Dimer simply did not exist in Sturt's world just then. The problem of how to safeguard the lives of two hundred innocent people put at risk by his ill-considered action consumed him as he rode slowly on towards Goudhurst. The heavens opened and Sarah ran for shelter.

Inside the stable, she kicked an empty milk pail at General Wade's stall. One more forgotten feeling had slipped out of the memory chest – but this one she did recognize. It was feminine pride – severely ruffled to boot! Sarah sat in the doorway and watched the rain. Deep inside, dangerous forces were gathering strength, and the prospect of them breaking loose frightened the very life out of her.

At the same time, it sent a delightful shiver of excitement coursing through her veins.

'What the Devil did you expect?' asked Peter Glover.

'Those in authority to do their duty,' said Sturt.

Alan straddled Sturt's legs and pulled off his sodden boots. Life flowed painfully back to frozen toes as he flexed them in front of the flames. He did not look at Glover pacing the Winchcombes' kitchen like an expectant father; that look of despair had been ingrained in his heavy features since the second meeting and Sturt was sick of the sight of it.

'As I said – you've been away a long time, George.'

The blacksmith looked out of the window. Candles flickered in those across the way. Somewhere, a dog barked, and Tom Austin's lads chanted a scurrilous rhyme ridiculing England's German royal family as they prepared for bed. For a moment, all seemed well in the world. A charred log fell from the grate and sparks flared on Sturt's stockings, leaving tiny black spots where the wool had burnt.

Glover turned and again paced the beaten earth floor. 'Kingsmill employs more excisemen and soldiers round here than King George.' he said. 'No one's going to risk his neck chasing after his own paymaster, now is he?'

At the table, Jan sat next to her father. Eyes fixed on

Sturt, she eagerly awaited some brilliant retort, some subtle change of strategy that would deflate the tiresome black-smith. Instead, Sturt leaned back in the chair and closed his eyes; every joint ached, and his backside felt as if it had been flayed.

'I'm sorry,' he said quietly. 'I should have listened.'

Jan's disappointed gaze shifted to Alan who shrugged his shoulders and toed the smouldering log out of harm's way.

Glover sat down. 'So what do we do now?'

'Sort it out!' said Edward purposefully.

'Just what in God's name does that mean?'

No one seemed to know.

Glover got up again. 'There's dozens of them, maybe hundreds – all armed! What have we got?' He didn't wait for an answer. 'A broken-down collection of farm boys and old men shaking scythes and pitchforks!'

Sturt shifted in the chair, the heat was making him drowsy.

Outraged by Glover's spineless whining, Jan turned on him herself. 'What if it had been your wife or sister?'

'I appreciates your feelings, Jan,' he said patronizingly. 'Really I do. But this is man's business – '

'We all voted!' snapped Alan. 'Everyone agreed.'

'Not everyone, boy!'

A cockroach clattered across the rush mat. Alan stamped on it.

Glover said, 'If we'd given back the cargo – like I said, and made it plain as how this was the last time, happen they'd have left us in peace!'

Sturt's eyes opened. 'A gesture of defiance would only dent his pride,' he said. 'And Thomas has a long memory.'

The blacksmith towered above him but, big as he was, fear had got such a grip that he appeared frail and vulnerable.

'I know how it is for you, George. Believe me, there ain't no one I'd rather see strung from a gibbet . . .'

Sturt leaned forward and adopted a calm, matter-of-fact tone, as if describing one of the less palatable facts of life to a confused child.

'He'd wait, Peter. Then come back when you least expected him.'

Unfortunately, Glover completely misinterpreted his attempt at rational explanation.

'You're the most devious man I ever knew George Sturt! We've got to fight them now, haven't we? You've left us no choice!'

To be fair to Sturt, he had appealed to the Excise and Army in good faith but, on the road from Iden Green, the advantage of their position had finally dawned on him. Frightened, Peter Glover might be – stupid, he was not!

'It's a perfect opportunity,' Sturt said. 'They'll be coming to collect a cargo. A routine operation. The last thing they'll be expecting is more trouble.'

Jan flashed the briefest of smiles at Alan. George hadn't failed them after all – Glover's silence was testimony to that.

'It doesn't make sense,' said Richard Perrin. 'Who is he?'

'Who he is don't matter!' snapped Jackson. 'We'd better pick up the rest before he puts us in the workhouse – and put them Goudhurst scabs in their place while we're about it!'

'No.'

'Buying is your business, Richard. Keep your snout out of what don't concern you.'

Perrin looked at Kingsmill. 'Thomas . . .'

The gang leader turned to Dimer who was standing inside the door.

'All right Dimer.'

'Yes . . . Thank you, Master Thomas.' He opened the door and Becky Leggatt hurried down the candlelit passage, back to her kitchen. 'I only done what I thought best – all things considered . . .' Dimer dipped from the waist, as if avoiding a blow. Jackson got up from the settle and the informer quickly took his leave.

Closing the door, Kingsmill's lieutenant lifted the ale pot from the hearth iron and mixed another jug of hot. 'If we don't rap their knuckles fast, every farmer's lad in Kent will be yapping to the Excise or stealing from us himself.'

Perrin nodded. 'Probably.' He gazed at the charts, Channel Islands and mainland maps, neatly laid out on the table. A year's work seemed to be slipping away from him.

'Burn the village!' continued Jackson, getting into his stride. 'Stake the stranger and a few of their menfolk out between the tide lines – '

'I agree we should take some action,' said Perrin. 'But it's got to wait.'

'They'll take it as a sign of weakness!'

The buyer unrolled a detailed map of the south coast. 'I think they know you better, William.'

Jackson took that as a compliment. The mix of gin and ale took the lining off his gullet. He grimaced – the ale was barely lukewarm.

Perrin carefully weighted the corners of his vellum map. 'If you please, Thomas.' Puzzled by his leader's uncommon lack of interest, he waited until Kingsmill joined them at the table. 'This run has taken me the best part of a year to set up.' He pointed to the routes traced in black ink. 'Every detail – choice of landing sites, safe houses, alternative roads home. All worked out and agreed with the Chichester Gang. But if we delay – even by a day or so – to take reprisals against Goudhurst, they'll back off sure as God twisted my hands.'

'Let them.'

Jackson's lack of imagination was a constant source of irritation to Perrin. 'We cannot handle this cargo without them,' he explained wearily.

'We always managed before.'

'We've never tried to land so much at one time before!'

A head louse fell out of Jackson's wig and into the English Channel. He fished it out and broke it in two.

'You were against a joint venture from the start, weren't you?' asked Perrin.

Jackson shrugged. 'I don't trust Shepherd Fairall no more than he trusts me.'

'But he trusts me, William – and I've given him my word.'

56

Jackson got up and drew a glowing poker from the grate. He jabbed it into the ale pot and watched the clouded liquor boil. He'd had his say, the decision would come from another quarter.

That Perrin was a brilliant buyer and organizer was indisputable, but even more important was the fact that he was trusted the length and breadth of the southern counties. Not only those directly involved in the free trade, but their gentlemen financiers, the soldiers from whom he bought information, the customs officials he bribed, knew him as a man of honour – a man of his word. Which is why the leader of the Hawkhurst Gang thought carefully before speaking.

'We'll delay the landing,' said Kingsmill.

'We can't!' In a rare display of temper, Perrin banged both swollen hands on the table top.

'I warned them.'

The buyer shook his head. 'You're making a mistake, Thomas . . .'

Kingsmill rose to his feet. 'Go to Chichester. Convince Fairall we're not wanting to cheat him. Tell him . . . Tell him we need to sell the Goudhurst cargo to raise our share of the capital.'

Perrin struggled out of his chair. 'He won't believe me!' Sweat beaded his brow. In twelve years, he'd never dared shout like that. He braced himself, but Kingsmill turned away and dropped into his favourite highback.

'Then tell him something else – just convince him.'

Sharp-edged features lit by the flames, he took on the appearance of a large predatory bird about to strike. 'I've had a bellyful of Goudhurst,' he said quietly.

It was almost midnight when Sturt led his saddled mare out of the Winchcombes' stable. A door clicked shut on its wooden latch and Alan Wynter hurried from the house. Sturt gave him the reins and boosted him aboard. The rain had stopped and, chased by a freshening south-easter, the thinning nimbus bank raced on to less troubled parts of the country. With luck, the waning moon would light the highway and help the lad to make good time. Alan shortened the stirrup leathers and Sturt slid a horse pistol into the saddle holster.

'Just in case,' he said.

'I wouldn't know what to do with it.'

'Take it anyway.'

Ready to go, Alan did not move. 'We're in a right mess, aren't we, George?'

'Yes.'

The knot in Alan's gut tightened. 'I'd best get on then.'

With Goudhurst long since tucked up for the night, the alley was pitch black. Sturt took hold of the bridle and walked them out onto the street.

'Take care of my mare.'

Alan nodded.

'Keep your eyes open . . .' Sturt slapped the horse's rump and she took off like a thoroughbred. 'And don't stop for anything!'

Unused to riding such a quality animal, Alan frantically lengthened his rein and gave the mare her head. As he cantered up the hill, the clouds released the moon. Caught in the pale light, Goudhurst's church dominated the skyline like some massive ecclesiastical fortress. With the square stone tower thrusting to the heavens, Sturt wondered if the God he didn't believe in was trying to tell him something.

'Alan . . .'

Horse and rider slipped over the brow of the hill. Jan's face registered disappointment and concern.

'Was it important?' Sturt enquired.

'No,' she lied. 'Not really.'

He cupped her face in his powerful hands. Hard and calloused as they were, Jan was overwhelmed by the kindliness he so rarely showed.

'He'll be back tomorrow afternoon.' Sturt smiled. 'You can tell him then.'

She gripped his wrists in case he should let go. 'I don't know what I'd do if anything happened to him, George.'

'Nothing is going to happen to him.'

'He ain't never been more'n eight mile from Goudhurst

in his life.' Tears welled and she willed them not to break. 'I miss him when he's not here. I get lonely.'

Sturt drew her to his chest.

'I asked our Mary if she was ever lonely.'

Jan looked up at him. The smile had gone. The familiar mask again obscured the softer side of Sturt's nature.

'She said no one could be lonely with so much to look forward to.'

He released her. 'You can help me close the stable,' he said, then walked away.

Jan watched from the doorway as he trimmed the wick of the smoking oil lamp.

'Was Mary the reason you ran away?'

He picked up the mare's feed bucket. 'Who said I ran away?'

'Father.'

Sturt closed the stall gate and left the bucket by the grain sacks stacked against the back wall.

'Was she?' asked Jan.

'No.'

Persistence was a Winchcombe characteristic and, like her elder sister, Jan had more than her fair share. She sat on the hay piled almost to the apex and waited.

Sturt turned. 'I said no.'

'She always thought it was her fault. She reckoned you got panicky 'bout getting wed afore your time.'

He crossed to her. 'She was barely fourteen!'

Jan grinned. 'But she had plans!'

He flopped down beside her and shook his head. 'It seems to run in the family.'

'I told Alan we were betrothed on his tenth birthday,' said Jan with a laugh.

A long-eared bat ghosted into the stable, squeaked indignantly at the intruders and flew back out. Up in Enoch Trickett's top meadow, a dog fox scolded the moon for making its life so difficult. Caught in the lamp's soft glow, Jan bore an unnerving resemblance to Mary. Back straight as a ramrod. Grey/blue eyes that looked into a body. Bold eyes that probed and questioned, searching for the man within.

'Why did you?'

'It doesn't matter any more.'

Sturt wanted to look away, but those eyes wouldn't permit it.

'She waited all those years for you. No other man got near her.'

The words had escaped before he could catch them. 'I waited too – in my own way.'

Silent as a priest in the confessional, Jan peeled another layer.

'It just took me a long time to realize what I was waiting for,' he explained.

'She knew you'd come back. I'm glad you did.' The eyes relaxed their grip. 'At first, I thought you had a brass nerve – but I'm glad you did.'

'For Mary.'

'For both of you.'

Sturt got up and fiddled with the tack hanging from a row of blacksmith's nails hammered into a low beam. For no good reason, he took a halter from the last nail on the left and hung it on the second from the right.

'I could have been here a day sooner.'

As if it was too heavy for the shoulders supporting it, Sturt rested his head against the beam. For once, his body lost its parade ground stiffness and he seemed to shrink an inch or two. Jan was bursting to ask the obvious question but sensed it would be a mistake to do so.

'I needed time to take it all in,' said Sturt softly. 'One day and she'd still be alive.'

'Or you'd be dead too.' Jan dropped her eyes She was trying so hard to be grown up. 'Life's not very fair,' she murmured. 'Is it?'

Sturt turned to her. Squatting on his heels, he gently squeezed her hand. A tear splashed onto his coat sleeve.

'Keep tight hold of that man of yours, Jan Winchcombe. Don't give him half a chance to get panicky and run.'

Her hair brushed his face as she shook her head. 'I won't – don't you worry.'

She looked at him and he thumbed the wetness from her cheek. 'George . . .' Again she pressed against the lean muscles of his chest. His arms clasped her so tight, he took her breath away. She smelt of the woods and fields. His lips brushed the top of her head. She tasted like Mary. For a long moment they clung like lovers; then her breathing changed and he could feel her heart beating faster.

'Killing Thomas Kingsmill . . .' she said. 'It won't bring her back, George.'

'No.' Again he inhaled the smells of her warm body. 'But it might let me sleep easier.'

Chapter 5

Sturt had given up on basic drill and tactics before breakfast. Shooting practice never got started due to a singular lack of reliable weapons. So that left close combat instruction. Though the prospect of the Hawkhurst Gang getting amongst Goudhurst's newly formed militia was the stuff of nightmares, Sturt had stuck doggedly to his task all morning. Parry and counter, thrust and block; the words had sunk in but never quite synchronized with the actions.

Now, stretched out in Ben Edge's field below the church, Sturt took a well-earned breather. Perhaps, he mused, their best chance would be to show themselves and hope the enemy died laughing. He watched a buzzard soar above the elms beyond the graveyard, and took a long pull on a jug of ale. Peter Glover joined him. Twenty yards away, thirty-four exhausted militiamen sat against the drystone wall and compared bumps and bruises.

'No good, is it, George?'

Sturt was not in the mood for one of Glover's doom-laden prophesies.

'Hand to hand, they'll chew us up and spit us out.' He dabbed at the weeping wound above his right eyebrow. 'What did I do wrong?'

'You tried to cut when you should have parried.' Sturt offered Glover the jug. 'A few real weapons would make all the difference, Peter.'

'I got my missus and Jan organizing the women,' said the smith. 'Begging and borrowing from all the outlying farms – on the quiet, mind.'

The look of surprise on Sturt's face caused Glover to smile. 'If I'm destined for the worms,' he said. 'I surely mean to take a few with me.'

He returned the jug. Across the field, John Cuplinn and Philip Blandy had fallen asleep, while Esau Besswick leaned over the wall and deposited his breakfast in a fresh-dug grave.

'When do you think they'll come?'

'On past record ... perhaps a week.'

'Time to forge a few decent blades?'

Glover nodded. 'And cast a gross or two of musket balls.'

The distant beat of galloping horses drew not only their attention but George Kingsmill's too. Sent to spy by his brother, he'd slipped past the aged sentry dozing outside the churchyard gate and, for the past hour, had enjoyed the entertainment. Now, uncomfortably close to the highway, young Kingsmill threw himself to the ground as three lathered horses and two riders swept by. Beyond the wall, Sturt got up and cocked his musket.

Wood pigeons and rooks scattered as the horsemen slowed to a canter and entered the field. Sturt threw his musket to Glover and ran towards them. Caked in mud, grinning all over his sweat-stained face, John Fairbrother parted company with his steaming mount.

'George!' he cried.

The two men embraced.

'It's good to see you,' Sturt said.

Like stags in combat, they remained locked together.

'You saved my life,' Fairbrother said. 'Tonbridge was fair strangling me.' He looked at Sturt. 'I'm so sorry about Mary, George.'

Since her death, Sturt had just about managed to contain his feelings, but that simple statement from one so close caught him unawares. He wanted to say so much to John but Edge's paddock was not the place. Now was not the time. 'Come and meet the Goudhurst Militia,' he said.

Only old Edward found the energy to rise as Fairbrother inspected the troops. 'Sweet Jesus ...' he murmured. 'Alan?'

Bone weary, the lad slid from his saddle and led the blowing pack-horse forward. Fairbrother untied the canvas cover across its back and pulled it clear. 'Fortunately' – he addressed himself to Sturt – 'I didn't come empty-handed.'

Hunched behind the Winchcombes' family plot, George

Kingsmill was no longer amused. Reinforcement in the shape of a second strange face was neither here nor there, but twenty new muskets and enough powder and shot to wage a small war was an altogether different kettle. The proceedings had taken a distinctly serious turn. His boot left a clear imprint on Mary's grave as he took to his heels.

'Bit of a shambles . . .'

Sturt and Fairbrother looked at him.

'Today's training session,' explained Edward. 'Not quite what you're used to.'

'I've seen worse recruits,' said Fairbrother. Then he thought again and turned to Sturt. 'I must have seen worse recruits.'

'At least they're still here,' said Sturt.

'And they'll not let you down now,' Edward said firmly.

Sturt took his tobacco pouch from his jacket pocket and packed a clay pipe. Fairbrother poured Edward a fourth measure of cognac. The heavy atmosphere that had dominated supper was easing with every swallow. Nevertheless, the old man was hard work. Fairbrother guessed correctly that, deep down, he was a shy man who felt awkward with strangers – even friendly ones.

'The gossip in Tonbridge says you're not the only ones to have suffered. This Kingsmill seems to have half of southern England in his pocket.'

Edward drained his glass. 'He's got a real talent for the free trade.'

Fairbrother handed him the flask.

'There ain't a tub of geneva or a pound of tea between here and the Dorset boundary moves without his say-so,' said Edward. 'Refuse him a beast of burden or talk out of turn and he'll stamp all over you.'

'You seem to know a good deal about him.'

'He was brung up here. Him and his no-good brother.'

Sturt tamped his weed and poked a taper into the front parlour grate.

'George knows him better than anyone, mind. They was thick as thieves as lads.'

The dry Virginia leaf crackled as Sturt sucked the smoke into his lungs. Ignoring John's quizzical look, he sat back in Edward's rocking chair.

'I haven't seen him in seventeen years.' The air clouded blue as he exhaled. 'It's a long time. People change.'

Edward swallowed his brandy and cast his mind back more than twenty years. He remembered how George had been a high-spirited pain in the neck then. Always hanging around his yard with Kingsmill. Plaguing the very daylights out of him with infuriating practical jokes. However, where Kingsmill's tricks and schemes were spiteful or designed to hurt, George's bore the stamp of an altogether more likeable personality. Even while driving Edward and his neighbours to distraction, there was a complete absence of malice. And close as they were, that was the crucial difference between the two boys. Kingsmill was a morose, mean-spirited individual, while George always showed generosity in his dealings with the world – always exhibited a genuine affection for his fellow man.

Looking at him now, though, brooding by the fire, it was hard to believe that he was the same person. And it wasn't just because of Mary's death. The wheelwright had sensed it a year ago when, sent home on sick leave, George had surprised the entire village by proposing marriage to Mary. Edward sighed. Yes, people did change – and more often than not for the worse. He put down his empty glass and got up. 'I'm off to my bed,' he said, eyeing Fairbrother's flask. 'Can't stand the late nights no more.'

Fairbrother pushed the legally purchased spirit across the table. 'Take it,' he said. 'Help you sleep.'

'I thank you kindly, Master John.'

Mind and body slowed by the alcohol, Edward carefully negotiated the furniture and paused at the door. He looked at Sturt, drawing on his pipe, staring at the coals, and a lump rose in his throat.

'If I hadn't got greedy and kicked up a fuss, Mary would still be alive.' He cleared his throat. 'She'd be sitting here now and we'd be planning a wedding, not a war.'

He waited but Sturt gave nothing. Not a word of comfort.

65

Not even a look. The old man took a lighted candle from the dresser and climbed the stairs. Drunk or not, sleep would not come easy to Edward Winchcombe.

Fairbrother joined Sturt at the fire.

'You were too hard on him, George. He's miserable enough.'

'Yes.'

An icy draught blasted through the badly fitting window and Fairbrother raked the embers. Sparks cascaded up the chimney. 'In all the years – you never mentioned this Kingsmill. Not once.'

It was an invitation to talk, to get off his chest all the things he wanted to say earlier in the day. But, somehow, the moment had passed. 'No,' said Sturt.

Fairbrother sat on the black iron fender. 'You've done it again, haven't you?'

'What?'

'Dropped us in the dungheap. This time, up to our necks!'

Sturt tapped out his pipe. 'Thank you for coming, John.'

Chapter 6

Mending was Sarah Dimer's way of coping with a crisis. Patching and sewing, darning or shoe repairs, she'd turn her hand to anything that might help her weather the storm triggered by her husband's nocturnal wanderings. Recently, she'd patched two pairs of breeches, stitched a tear in her everyday grey dress, sewed up four pair of holed yarn stockings, replaced the buckles on her Sunday shoes and renailed the heels of his underemployed work boots.

Dimer pulled on his long coat and picked up his hanger. 'I'm off then.'

Sarah unpicked a perfectly good patch.

'Sarah . . .'

'I heard you.'

He put on his hat and caught his reflection in the darkened window. 'I do it for you, you know.'

It was her silences more than the rows that made him feel such a failure. In all of their thirteen years together, she'd never once called him such, but she had the uncanny knack of making her feelings felt without a word being spoken. He crouched beside her chair, resting the cutlass across his knee.

'Thomas Kingsmill trusts me, Sarah. It's taken damnnear six months, but soon I'll be in on every landing. In two or three years, I'll give you everything you want – money, big house, servants – '

'God help you, John, sometimes you're so stupid!'

She tore the neatly stitched patch off his only nightshirt.

'You blame me because there ain't no children, don't you?' he said.

'Of course not – '

'You always have!' The cutlass clattered to the floor as he rose. 'I've failed at everything else, so it must be my fault – isn't that it? You expect me to fail, Sarah!'

'You expect yourself to fail.' She put down her needles. 'I don't know whose fault it is. It doesn't matter any more. What I want –'

He turned away from her.

'All I want – is a little peace of mind. A husband home at nights. Not chasing over the Marsh with the Hawkhurst Gang. Or laying dead in some ditch . . .'

Sensing her anguish, the always pregnant tabby dropped from the mantelshelf and jumped onto her knee.

'I don't want houses nor anything else bought with dishonest money, John.'

'Well I do! I want it all! I want folk looking up to me for a change. I'm sick of them laughing and whispering behind my back!' His fingernails dug into her shoulders. 'When I'm up there – like Kingsmill – fetching my own cargoes from France, they'll respect me. And if they don't, they'd bloody well better watch out!'

She dropped her eyes and he shook her.

'Don't you see? It'll make up for everything, Sarah!'

'It's what you think of yourself that counts.'

'The Shaddick family motto!'

'My father lived his life believing it.'

'They strung him up for holding run goods!'

'Left without him knowing so! The Law hung him for not informing against them as put it there – the Chichester Gang.'

'Then more fool him!' He released her and picked up his cutlass.

'John – I don't want the dragoons dragging you out one night. I couldn't bear it.'

He buckled the sword belt around his waist. 'Things is different here.' The tip of the scabbard scraped across the floor. 'No one's dragging me nowhere. Kingsmill's got the dragoons and the Excise scared witless. It's all right . . .'

The cat hooked its claws into her apron and purred.

'Honest – it's all right. Look.' He reached into his coat pocket and pressed five coins into her hand.

'Five shillings. Just for driving a cart!'

Sarah's fingers instinctively closed about the warm metal pieces; five shillings was a lot of turnips . . .

'More to come,' he said and hitched up his hanger. Sarah touched the hilt; there was dried blood ingrained into the hand guard filigree.

'Bit of a scramble with them Goudhurst folk. It's all right – I wasn't hurt – '

'Who was?'

'No one.'

She picked up her sewing. Again, silent disapproval – undermining him, making him feel like dirt.

'No one as matters anyhow!'

One of the coins split his lip, the rest struck the front door and rolled across the floor. Sarah sprang to her feet and the cat ran for cover.

'Take your blood money!'

Dimer did just that.

'Save it for a coffin. At least you'll hang for good reason!'

The door banged shut and Sarah stood trembling with rage. She'd loved her father dearly but, at times, she hated him for her inheritance. She wished she could reject his moral values, discard his principles. She knew it was wrong to live by a code that condemned innocent men to the gallows, that forced others to live out their days in avoidable misery. If only she had the courage to do what she knew was right for her. If only she could believe in a fair-minded God. If only she believed in miracles. If only . . .

Dimer spent the night at the Black Dog in Hawkhurst where he'd intended to drink himself to oblivion. However, events were gathering momentum and his mind was soon occupied by matters other than domestic problems. Young Kingsmill's report had really stirred things up and, as a result, they were both shivering in Coppett's Wood soon after dawn.

The object of their attention was Stephen Diprose, Glover's apprentice. They'd followed him from the village perimeter and now watched as he cut wood for the forge. The faint sounds of combat carried from Edge's field and

George Kingsmill gave the nod. 'I'll grab him,' he said softly, 'you hit him.'

Dimer nodded.

Cramped muscles screamed, seized joints cracked, as they rose from the dew-wet bracken.

'I haven't got a gun.'

Young Kingsmill gave him his own.

Relishing the balance of a fine piece, Dimer gripped the pistol by the butt and stalked his quarry.

Ma Diprose's only son laid into a dead beech with a vengeance. In his opinion, he should have been training; others less able – older – should have been detailed to cut wood while he did his bit to defend hearth and home. Chips flew as the blade bit into the trunk. He freed it and swung the axe over his shoulder – thereby putting Dimer's nose further out of joint than his own. Caught right between the eyes with the blunt end of the steel head, he didn't scream, he just gurgled like a contented baby and sank to his knees. Absolutely astonished, the boy spun on his heel – only to be poleaxed by a perfect right cross from Kingsmill.

Blood and mucus flowed from various holes in Dimer's face. The extent of his injuries suddenly dawned and he started to wail.

'Sshh!' urged Kingsmill. 'For Christ's sake – shut it!'

'My nose . . . He's busted my bloody nose!'

Terrified of discovery, George grabbed him by the scruff and hauled him to his feet. Poking and probing, he carefully inspected the damage. There was no doubting that the nose was a right mess. The smallest of pulls and gristle grated against something. Dimer squealed like a punctured pig. It was definitely busted.

'No,' said George knowledgeably, 'it's a scratch – barely touched you.'

He let go and Dimer folded.

'Come on, John – they'll have heard you bleating past Romney!'

A quick search revealed Dimer's pistol beneath a blackthorn.

'Grab a leg,' Kingsmill urged him.

Half-blinded by the elephantine swelling, Dimer did as he was told, and Diprose's face ploughed a furrow through the undergrowth.

'Scratch be buggered,' Dimer moaned. 'It's busted – bloody busted!'

Caught squarely on the point of the jaw, young Stephen had no recollection of being trussed across the saddle, nor of the bone-jarring cross-country ride to Hawkhurst. Deeply unconscious, it took a vinegar-soaked rag to jar his senses. Head bursting, he opened his eyes but could scarcely distinguish light and shade. More vinegar. A stinging pain across the side of his face, then the other side; someone was hitting him . . .

He threw up an arm, trying to deflect the blows but it was wrenched painfully up his back. He tried to rise but could not. Held fast, he gave in and the hitting stopped. Wits unscrambling, he blinked the world back into focus. Faces, there seemed to be hundreds, surrounded him. And voices, harsh and excited, baying like a crowd at a cock-fight.

Slowly, the sharp predatory features of a face he knew so well materialized before his eyes.

'Good day, Stephen,' said Thomas Kingsmill softly.

Apart from an odd whimper from Dimer, the only sound in the main room at the Black Dog was the crackle of burning logs. Thirty men stood in a circle around Stephen Diprose. Though close to wetting himself, the boy stood proud and defiant. Determined not to show weakness, or betray his friends, he held Kingsmill's steady gaze. Jackson stood at his shoulder. Perrin sat alone, as far from the sport as possible.

'I want their names, Stephen. And I want to know why they're poking their noses into my business.'

Diprose tensed his legs, a futile gesture to stop them trembling.

'Names.' So softly did Kingsmill speak that he might have been reassuring a frightened child.

'Go to the Devil!'

The Gang's leader sighed, as if to say that what he was

71

doing was a regrettable necessity. He stepped back and the circle widened.

Little Harry Sheerman and Jonas Cobby held the boy's arms while Jackson stripped him of boots and breeches.

'You're wasting your time,' he yelled, 'I'll tell you nothing!'

His underwear shredded.

'Get off of me!' He lashed out with his bare foot and caught Sheerman low in the gut. The smugglers released him. Naked from the waist down, the boy pulled at his shirt-tails, trying to keep himself decent.

Kingsmill picked up a riding whip and the room again fell silent. He dangled it under Diprose's nose. The lad turned away.

'Look at it, Stephen.'

The peculiarly knobbled leather touched his chin.

'It's loaded with lead shot. William is a craftsman with it. He can open you quicker and cleaner than a surgeon. I've seen him work down a man's back one rib at a time, then turn him over and fillet him like a codfish.'

Diprose could not take his eyes off the tiny lead balls painstakingly stitched into the lash.

'A name. Give me a name.'

'As I said . . .'

Before the boy could utter the insult, Kingsmill had handed the whip to his lieutenant and moved out of the way. Jacketless, waistcoat loosened, Jackson smiled at the boy who instinctively retreated. Sheerman stretched out a foot and he fell heavily to the floor. Jackson raised his arm. Diprose curled into a ball, desperately trying to protect himself.

The lash caught him across his exposed genitals, and the animal roar that escaped his lips sent Perrin hurrying from the room. The boy's body snapped rigid as a broomstick and Jackson struck again; this time across the belly, slicing deep into soft flesh.

'Sturt!' the boy screamed. 'It's George Sturt! Now for pity's sake – stop it! Please stop it!'

Jackson lowered the whip, the name meant nothing.

George Kingsmill pushed his way to the front and looked at his brother.

'He's changed, Thomas. I swear you wouldn't have known him yourself.'

The leader of the Hawkhurst Gang said nothing, his face betrayed nothing. Jackson and Cobby lifted the boy from the floor. Every muscle in his body was locked in a spasm of agony, his shirt-tails were stained crimson, blood and urine flowed down the inside of his thighs. And he was crying.

Kingsmill stepped forward and looked deep into his eyes – then took the whip from Jackson.

It had been a long, frustrating day in the field, and Jan's cooking had done nothing to lift their spirits.

'It was lunacy to even consider squaring up to them,' Sturt said. 'We'll have to try something else.'

'Like kidnapping a regiment of dragoons.' The acrid taste of incinerated mutton surged up Fairbrother's gullet.

'Skirmishing,' suggested Sturt. 'Catch them on the highway – hit and run.'

'I doubt they can run, never mind hit!' John belched discreetly, pardoning himself.

'And you call yourselves soldiers?' Jan wrapped Alan's mercifully simple supper in a clean cloth. 'The answer is obvious,' she declared.

'It is?'

'We hide.'

No response. She knotted the cloth slowly, savouring her moment.

'On the rooftops, in the bell tower, anywhere we can. As you said, George, they won't be expecting more trouble – so everything seems quiet and we let them ride right into the village.'

Jan smiled.

'Won't know what hit them, will they?'

Half out of the back door, she could not resist a parting shot. 'I suppose your officers did the brainwork.'

73

It was a good half-minute before Fairbrother broke the embarrassed silence. 'The answer is obvious,' he mimicked.

The commotion outside the front door wiped the thin smile from Sturt's face. He rose as, breathing hard, Peter Glover followed Edward in. The old man was carrying Diprose's bloodied axe. 'Found it up Trickett's Wood,' he wheezed. 'Ain't no sign of him.'

Because of Diprose's disappearance, Sturt ordered a round the clock watch on all approaches to the village. Alan relieved Ben Edge at ten, but his idea of guard duty and Jan's did not quite coincide. Teeth chattering, hands and feet frozen numb, he lay pinned like a butterfly to a board. His stomach rumbled for the bread and cold beef two feet out of reach. She shifted her weight and he breathed again.

'I'm supposed to be doin' guard duty,' he complained.

The point of her tongue danced along the row of good teeth still occupying his upper jaw.

'And I'm supposed to be feeding your stomach, not your carnal appetite.'

If the truth were out, he'd have settled for his supper, but once her mind was set Jan usually had her way.

Again her tongue, probing and teasing. A hand was working at the buttons of his breeches and, despite the chill, all was not dormant down there. Realizing that his only hope of avoiding starvation was to concede to her demands, he hoisted her skirt. Wrestling with half an acre of winter petticoats, the reek of vinegar stung his nostrils.

Jan's eyes burned star bright. 'Don't want any careless accidents, do we?'

Icy fingers took her breath away as they touched her warmest spot.

'Alan – they're freezing!'

'Then you warm 'em for me.'

With one quick movement, he shifted his body and threw her onto a carpet of sapless ferns. Breeches at half-mast, member erect, Alan knelt between her raised knees like a fertility god of the Old Religion. A rotten branch dug into her right buttock, there'd be a bruise tomorrow. She wriggled clear of it and drew him down. Keen to avoid further contact with his fingers, she took hold of him and raised her hips. Alan's mouth locked onto hers and his belly rumbled. The sweet smells of her body aroused him further. The tang of vinegar reassured him. She rocked like a cradle and her warmth swallowed him up.

That initial joining excited Alan as much as it had done after the May Fair when for fear of shaming himself, he'd lain so still Jan thought he'd died of a seizure. He lay still now, they both did, but for an altogether better reason. Locked together like some mythical eight-limbed creature, Jan Winchcombe and Alan Wynter silently declared their love to the grass and the trees, to the earth and the sky, and to God himself – simultaneously praying that He might forgive them for enjoying that most prized of forbidden pleasures!

A low drumming broke the moment. Jan twisted free of his kiss and listened. Horses, three perhaps four, coming fast from the east. Alan rolled off her and onto his supper. Breeches around his calves, he stumbled about the under-growth until he found his musket. Cocking it, he stood at the roadside waiting to issue the challenge that Sturt had taught him. A hefty shove sent him flying. Dead bracken cracked as Jan bundled him to safety.

Three horses stopped exactly where he'd stood; one broke wind and dropped its steaming load. No one spoke. Something fell to the ground and the riders were gone. Jan released the stale air from her lungs and Alan rose cautiously to his feet. He wasn't frightened; adrenalin was surging around his system and pure exhilaration had kept him hard. Unaware of his own absurdity, he hitched up his pants and listened.

Beech and oak groaned under the weight of the wind. He walked back to the highway and a stag beetle splintered beneath his bootless heel. So sharp were his senses just then that he could feel the heat of the horse dung.

The softest of moans brushed his ears and floated away.

'Hello . . .' Alan pointed his long gun at nothing in particular. 'Who is it?'

75

Nothing moved. The creatures of the night waited for the tragedy to run its course.

'I said who's there?'

A bloody hand reached up and closed about his knee. Reflex action lifted both feet from the ground and jerked his finger on the trigger. Gun smoking, heart pounding, Alan looked down at a vaguely human shape curled up in the long grass.

Half a mile to the east, Jackson and Harry Sheerman heard the shot and spurred their mounts on towards Iden Green. Stephen Diprose was back with his people.

And he was dying. There was no pain; the bolts of agony that had ripped through his nervous system, the fire that had consumed every inch of his flayed body, making him writhe and shriek on the floor, had ceased when Kingsmill exposed his bowels. The shock of that one blow should have killed him, but something happened inside his brain and he seemed to part company with his physical self. After that, he'd stopped screaming, stopped trying to protect himself, and lain like a submissive dog until Kingsmill's rage had burnt itself out.

Stretched out on the Winchcombes' kitchen table, he watched the thick needle rise and fall as Dorothy Shaddick closed another gaping wound. He listened to his mother crying in the parlour, and Edward trying to comfort her. He sensed Alan's presence but could not see him. He heard Jan tearing bed linen to bind him, and felt Sturt's warm breath on his face. He opened his mouth and dark blood spilled out. The words were his, but he could not relate the clear thoughts, the cold facts that he wished to communicate, to the sub-human noises emanating from that mutilated thing on the table.

Sturt bent a little closer.

'I told him about you, George – you and Mary.'

Arms and legs started to tremble. Bodily defences were breaking down. The pain was coming back.

'I didn't mean to – but he went berserk – '

'It's all right, Stephen, it doesn't matter.'

76

'I couldn't do anything, say anything, to stop him! He went on and on . . .'

He covered his right eye with a hand; tears leaked from the congealed mass that used to be the left.

'He wants his cargo – and he wants you, George. Most of all he wants you!'

Dorothy mopped his abdomen and her own stomach turned over.

Diprose twisted, then arched. Waves of agony, each stronger than the previous one, again surged through him.

'That's why he didn't kill me clean – so's I could carry his message . . .' The words stuck like rocks in his throat, but he had to speak – had to warn them. 'He says he's goin' to burn the village and everyone in it . . .'

His whole body was shaking now. Dorothy dabbed at his groin and he moaned.

'When?' asked Sturt.

Jan wiped his mouth and held his clenched fist. 'For the love of God, George – leave him be!'

Sturt tasted blood and sweat as his lips touched the boy's ear.

'When Stephen?'

Red and white lightning was flashing inside Diprose's skull.

'The day after tomorrow!'

Lacerated guts burst, and he screamed and thrashed. A flailing arm caught Jan across the breast, knocking her to the floor.

'George!' cried Dorothy. 'Master Fairbrother!'

The two men dropped their weight across legs and chest. Alan vomited over his blood-soaked jerkin and blundered out of the room.

Slowly, the boy's strength ebbed. The screams subsided and a dry rattle escaped his lips. Stephen Diprose, blacksmith's apprentice, aged seventeen years and four months, was dead.

Sturt rested one limp hand on top of the other, and closed the eye staring at the ceiling. Fairbrother helped Jan to her feet and eased her into a chair. Never had one man's

77

death affected him so deeply. Breathing hard, he turned on Sturt.

'What the hell is it between you two?'

Sturt winced at the memory. The snap of the man-trap echoed all the way to the banks of the Teise.

'Help me!' Kingsmill cried. 'It's broken – get me out of this!'

Keepers ghosted through the trees, dogs were closing fast, but all he saw was the running figure of George Sturt.

At the gap in the oak plantation, where the axeman's track ran down to the water's edge, the leader of the Hawkhurst Gang stood and watched his innocence die. So clear were the images, so keen the memory, that it might have been yesterday. He rubbed his shin where the bone had mended and saw the splash as Sturt hit the water. Hounds and hunters dissolved into the blackness. He stood alone, held in the cruel jaws, yelling and cursing. Then he too faded. One figure remained on the opposite bank. One cowardly, sobbing figure. George Sturt. More than his friend, closer than family. The other half of the whole.

A dry twig snapped behind him and he turned, hanger raised to strike.

'It's all right, Thomas,' his brother said quickly. 'It's me, George.'

The cutlass remained poised above his head as he stepped out of the shadows.

'Are you all right?'

For what seemed an eternity, George Kingsmill's life hung in the balance.

'Thomas . . .'

Then his brother sheathed the blade and mounted his horse. Without a word or backward glance, he turned the beast for home and viciously spurred its flanks.

George leaned against a fat oak and waited for the banging in his chest to stop.

'George Sturt . . .' he muttered. 'I wish to God you'd never come back.'

He looked at the river and fond memories stirred. Lizzie Shadwell had deflowered him down there.

A knock at the door broke Kingsmill's train of thought.

'Master Thomas?'

'I told you to leave me be!'

In the passageway, Bekky Leggatt looked at the Magistrate.

'Be it on your own head, your honour.'

She opened the door and retreated.

For ten years, Rye's Senior Magistrate had been a major investor in Hawkhurst ventures. Indeed, had he not been cursed with a weakness for the gaming houses of London, he would undoubtedly have amassed a fortune to rival Kingsmill's own. As it was, he lived from run to run: borrowing to finance a cargo, which in turn paid off his most pressing debts and staked another night at the tables – where he would inevitably lose; then borrow again; another run; another ruinous evening ... So turned the circle of his existence. A less intelligent man, a less talented schemer, would have long since fallen from the tightrope and ended his days dancing the hempen jig. But Robert Lamb possessed not only the instinct to survive, but harboured a huge appetite for the game itself. Money aside, he revelled in the irony of maintaining a privileged position in society, thanks solely to his dealings outside the Law he so ably represented.

Which was why, chilled to the marrow, he was standing in Kingsmill's gloomy parlour when he should have been taking his pleasure at Nancy Collett's whore-house.

'Good evening, Thomas.'

'What the Devil do you want?'

Lamb moved his bulk towards the hearth. 'I've been instructing Richard in the finer points of rolling dice ...' Perrin limped cautiously into the room, but kept his distance. 'I thought you might be in the mood.'

Kingsmill dropped back into his chair. 'Good night, Robert.'

Anyone else would have taken the hint; Lamb planted

himself in front of the fire. The easy smile was no longer in evidence. The smell of scorching velvet filled the room.

'I'm informed you're thinking of delaying the landing.'

The briefest of looks cut Perrin to the bone.

'I'm not thinking of it.'

Lamb shifted as his stockings started to discolour. 'If this venture were to fail, it could prove somewhat embarrassing to me. Unnecessary unpleasantness with creditors – that sort of thing.'

'Then you should stick to playing with Richard.'

'I'm talking about being ruined, man!'

He sat down and the backs of his larded thighs blistered. He got up again. 'I'm mortgaged to the gills, Thomas.'

Mind elsewhere, Kingsmill stared at the flames.

Powder from the Magistrate's over-elaborate peruke dusted his head and shoulders. 'I'll go to Chichester myself – to ease Fairall's mind,' he said. 'Tomorrow. But only if Richard is on his way to Roscoff.'

'I'll decide when Richard sails.'

Lamb stepped back. His shadow crept up the wall and across the low, beamed ceiling. He adopted the tone he reserved for sentencing felons in court.

'If you let me down, I'll see every gentleman backer and dealer from Bristol to London town drops you like a leper. I'll see you hounded out of existence. And I'll see Shepherd Fairall take your place.'

The threat was not an idle one. The smuggling gangs needed not only their investors' money, but the political protection afforded by involving so many of the upper class in the free trade.

Kingsmill's face betrayed nothing, but the point had been taken.

The Magistrate perched his cocked hat six inches above the crown of his head and took his leave. Perrin hurried after him. He'd gambled on Lamb's high opinion keeping him safe; it seemed to have worked and he had no desire to test his luck further.

'I'll take the morning tide, Thomas,' he said.

He was halfway to the front door when Kingsmill stopped him with a shout.

Iron strap hinges groaned. The door slowly swung open and Perrin entered. To his relief, his master was still in the chair.

'Not until I tell you,' Kingsmill said quietly.

By specifying a day for the destruction of Goudhurst and its inhabitants, Kingsmill had made a rare mistake. His intention had been to make public his contempt for the opposition and give them time to sweat. And initially, it worked. News of Diprose's death sent a wave of panic sweeping through the village, and only with Peter Glover's wholehearted support did Sturt manage to check it. He argued that a direct confrontation was playing into their hands. Given a day to dig trenches, fortify sniper positions, set their trap, Goudhurst's Militia would have the advantage of facing the enemy on their own ground and terms.

Preparations started long before dawn. Children stripped lead from the church roof and humped it to Glover's forge where it was melted and moulded into shot. Some women twisted paper cartridges. Others dug trenches around the Gore where Sturt and Fairbrother applied a final polish to the Militia's improved marksmanship.

Soon after sundown, the two ex-soldiers watched 143 women and children gather on the road outside the church. They'd seen refugees before, but always foreigners. Never their own. And as that sad caravan bade an emotional farewell to its menfolk, the magnitude of what they were demanding from the people of Goudhurst weighed heavily on John Fairbrother. For the men in the village, tomorrow was going to be a long day. For those waiting at Sturt's farm, it would seem like an extended lifetime.

The mood inside the Black Dog was less sombre. A sporting day was anticipated, and the smugglers' traditional preparation was to spend the night before soaking their brains in gin and ale. Sixty men had been called and they'd been arriving in ones and twos all evening. By the time Dimer

81

entered, the inn was bursting at the seams. Smug as a Cheshire cat, he found George Kingsmill in the back room with Lizzie Shadwell. Oblivious to the fact that he was intruding – thanks to the half-bottle of brandy he'd drunk on the ride from Iden Green – Dimer joined them.

'George – Mistress Lizzie . . .' he beamed.

The lack of response went unnoticed, and he produced an oilskin-wrapped package from his coat.

'Got somethin' to show you – summat special!' A gleaming horse pistol wafted back and forth under Kingsmill's pointed nose. 'Brand new!' said Dimer proudly.

George weighed the balance while Lizzie chewed his ear. 'A truly fearsome weapon, John.'

Dimer took it back. 'And cost a fearsome lot of money too!'

'What are you going to do with it? Shoot the tongue out of that nagging wife of yours?'

Lizzie bit a grubby lobe.

'I'm going to shoot . . .'

The barb interrupted Dimer's brandy-fuddled train. Suddenly he was hurt – deeply offended. The pistol clattered onto the rough tabletop as he rose unsteadily to his feet. 'I'll have you know, my Sarah is all a man could desire in a wife. And I loves her dear!' He picked up his new toy and put it to his temple. 'I swear I'd sooner shoot myself than harm a hair on her head!'

George nursed his ear and stifled a chuckle. 'Who are you going to shoot, then?'

Dimer sat down and fiddled with the irritating bandage around his nose.

'Tomorrow . . .' he confided. 'Maybe I'll wing me a villager or two. Then again . . .' He leaned across the table, face split by a grin like an open wound. 'I just might shoot the balls off of that old sod Jackson – given half a chance!'

Lizzie giggled. A great booming laugh shook George's wiry frame. Tomorrow promised sport of the very highest order!

Two miles to the west, a solitary light burned inside Kingsmill's fortress home. Unable to sleep, he had paced the sprawling house for hours, finally settling in the kitchen to hone his blade. He needed no company. Alcohol would have merely dulled the senses – and he wanted all five at their sharpest when he faced George Sturt. He was going to kill him. And he wanted to see and hear his death, smell it and taste it, touch the actual moment of extinction. He sliced a finger testing the edge of his steel. For him, the dawn could not come soon enough.

Sarah Dimer looked out of her bedroom window. It was two in the morning and still more riders were Hawkhurst bound. This time there were three, and she thought she recognized Elijah Peck's grey gelding trailing behind. She watched them climb the hill beyond her two small fields and merge into the birch coppice. The clatter of iron shod hooves faded. The dogs in the yard fell silent. The moon was up and it burned like ice in the winter sun, casting hard-edged shadows as far as she could see. Be it a run ashore or transfer from safe house to London, it was a bad night for Hawkhurst business. John, of course, had said nothing, but she knew. She always did. There was a chill in the air that owed nothing to the weather. Instinct told her that violence, even murder, would be done before she saw her husband again. If she saw him again. Sarah Dimer returned to her bed – and images of death went with her.

'You were right, it's the perfect command post.'

Fairbrother looked down on the village from the top of the church tower. At a glance, Goudhurst appeared to be at peace with the world. Closer inspection, however, revealed gunports cut in window shutters, barricades in the alleys, deep trenches violating the even green of the Gore.

Sturt filled his pipe and leaned on the parapet. 'We used to sneak up here as boys,' he said. 'A handful of stones at his stained glass would have Reverend Brack out in a flash and we'd be up the ladder like lightning.' He struck a spark in his tinder box. 'It was our fortress against the world.'

Fairbrother looked at him. 'You never mentioned him, George.'

'We grew up together – closer than brothers.'

Tinder crackled and Sturt sucked a flame deep into the bowl.

'We'd sit up here and daydream the future,' he said. 'Who'd be the best soldier. Who'd make the biggest fortune. Who'd marry Mary Winchcombe. That caused more fights . . .'

He watched a hunting barn owl quarter the graveyard and drop on a careless vole behind the Wynters' family plot. Tobacco smoke rose vertically in the still, cold air. 'Mary couldn't bear him near her.'

'Was she the reason?'

'No.'

Sturt turned and looked south. Towards the sea. Towards Hawkhurst. 'I deserted him, John. The one time he really needed me.'

Words stuck in his throat. Drawing on his pipe, Sturt was uncomfortably aware of the strict moral code that governed his life. He had been barely seventeen when the keepers had surprised them, yet even now he made no allowance for youth or inexperience. Guilt had not diminished with the passage of time. Running away, he knew, had been intrinsically wrong. And, as nothing could change what had happened, he saw no point in talking about it. However, that same sense of right and wrong told Sturt that John was entitled to an explanation.

'As a result,' he said, 'he got three years in Horsham Gaol and I kept running until I enlisted. I never told a soul. I was too ashamed.'

'Why didn't he turn you in?'

'That's not his way. Thomas likes to settle his own scores.' Sturt shivered and closed the flap of his greatcoat. 'I sometimes wish it had been me who got caught.'

'Three years prison in return for a clear conscience?'

Sturt turned. Mary's death had deepened the lines in his face. Caught in the moon's stark light, he looked older than his thirty-four years. 'It would have been a bargain,' he said.

Below them, the owl hooked powerful talons into the remains of its victim and flapped noiselessly over the church roof as a faint hammering floated up the hill. Beyond the Bear, an oil lamp flickered in the street.

'Peter,' said Fairbrother. 'Boarding up.' He looked at Sturt. 'You know we'll likely lose tomorrow?'

'Yes.'

'But it doesn't matter so long as you both settle your score.'

They were cruel words. Words that made Sturt sound as bad as Kingsmill. He wanted to deny it. Wanted to ram the accusation back down John's throat, but in all honesty he couldn't. 'Peter could use a hand,' he said.

Lifting the trap, Sturt looked down at Jan Winchcombe wobbling on the ladder. She had refused to be evacuated with the rest, and had spent the evening assembling ammunition pouches. Two dropped at Sturt's feet. 'A present,' she said, 'for Thomas Kingsmill.'

Chapter 7

The grey light of dawn spread across the eastern sky and chased the night to the horizon. In Edge's Wood, a storm-cock opened its throat and called the day to order. John Fairbrother closed his eyes, absorbing the warmth of the sun as it climbed above the Weald. He stretched his arms wide and filled his lungs with cold clean air. Sunrise was a celebration of life itself – and there was nothing quite like the threat of extinction to make a man appreciate it.

Sturt rammed a split ball down the barrel of his spare musket and looked down onto the village. Between the graveyard and the Gore, forty armed men were in position but it would have taken an exceptional pair of eyes to spot one of them. He leaned his long gun against the castellated parapet. Goudhurst was as ready as it would ever be.

At first, he thought it was distant thunder, but a glance at the cloudless sky told him otherwise. They were coming. And, as expected, by the Biddenden road. Sturt shaded his eyes and looked into the sun. His pulse quickened as he listened. The rumbling, the soft clink of harness, the bois-terous yelp of drunken voices grew louder. The buildings – the very stones and timbers of Goudhurst seemed to brace themselves as the Hawkhurst Gang wound slowly up East Hill.

The trap-door flew open and Jan followed her father up the ladder. Below, Alan and Peter Glover loaded their muskets.

'Alan?' called Fairbrother.

Face strained and anxious, the boy looked up.

'Do you want me to do it?'

He shook his head.

'Are you sure?'

He nodded. 'I owe them for Mary too.'

Jan watched him trot after Glover. She meant to speak, but couldn't think of anything to say.

An arm snaked around her shoulder, making her start. 'Don't fret,' said Edward. 'Peter will see him right.'

Sturt did not see Fairbrother descend the ladder, nor was he aware of Jan or Edward. His concentration was focused on the road. On the point where he would catch first sight. He picked up his musket and a terrible fore-boding gripped him. He knew it was Kingsmill he'd seen at the river, but he'd been nothing more than a silhouette against the sky. After seventeen years, what if he did not recognize him?

The crown of a three-cornered hat rose out of the ground like an excavating mole. Edward tugged at his sleeve and he dropped below the parapet. Doubts subsided as Kings-mill led his private army into view and stopped by the churchyard gate. Sturt raised his musket, but trees and other riders obscured the target – it would have to be Jan's way.

Half-way between church and Gore, two figures stood in the middle of the road. Neither was Sturt. So, anxious lest he be cheated again, Kingsmill scanned windows and rooftops. Nothing stirred. He nodded to Jackson, who nudged his horse forward a pace.

'We want the cargo!' Jackson yelled. 'And George Sturt! Give them over now and no one else need suffer. I promise!'

Alan and Glover stood their ground.

'If you don't, we'll take 'em anyway – and kill you all!'

The blacksmith's ball fell a yard short. Alan's grooved the horse's shoulder, causing it to rear and unseat its rider. By the time Kingsmill gave the order, Glover and the lad were in full flight.

A great roar of anticipation preceded the smugglers' shambling rush down the hill. Behind them, Sturt and Kingsmill watched as the hares ran for their lives. Reaching the Gore unscathed, they jumped a rampart of beaten earth and fell into the ditch behind. John Fairbrother slapped Alan's shoulder, then stood up in full view of the enemy and raised an arm. Lead flew harmlessly overhead as the mounted smugglers bore down on him. Surging past the blacksmith's forge, a sudden metallic snap interrupted their progress. Leg bones shattered, Harry Sheerman's old mare nose-dived and thrashed in the mud – first victim of Peter Glover's cleverly concealed man-traps.

Fairbrother dropped his arm. 'Now!' he yelled.

The Goudhurst Militia showed themselves – over the churchyard wall, on the rooftops, at the windows and alleys, dug in on the Gore. Before Kingsmill could speak or move, another crippled beast went down and Sturt commanded them to fire.

The volley killed three horses and Sam Hone. Kingsmill instinctively sought cover, as confusion sent his men scurrying in all directions at once. The day had lost its sporting edge. Caught in the lethal confines of the street, some turned back up the hill, while others dismounted and recklessly hurled themselves at the marksmen on the Gore.

Unable to see Kingsmill, Sturt fired at the nearest man. His ball took the gang leader's brother squarely in the nose and fragmented inside his brain. Almost before he hit the ground, John Dimer was out of the saddle and running. 'George?' he cried. 'George!'

At the church, Jan took Sturt's gun. She handed him the spare while her father sat on the floor reloading like a professional. 'Kingsmill . . .' she shouted. 'There!'

Sturt saw him run from the stable behind the Bear.

'He's dead!' Dimer's shrill voice carried. 'They killed George dead!'

Kingsmill dropped to his knees and stared into his brother's sightless eyes. High above, Sturt took aim.

'Him in the tower . . .' Dimer wailed. 'I seen him!'

Kingsmill turned and, momentarily distracted, Sturt fired a split second too soon. With blood leaking from a graze in the neck, Kingsmill scrambled to his feet and melted into the blanket of smoke belching from Felkin's carpentry shop. Half-concealed by the choking shroud, Dimer – in a moment of ill-considered heroism – dragged George's body past hostile guns and over the brow. Safely out of range, he sicked up, rolled onto his back and listened to the sounds of men dying not fifty paces distant.

With the smugglers in retreat, order and discipline collapsed. Flushed with success, the Militia ignored Fairbrother's orders and took to the streets. The smoke thickened as the flames spread to Glover's forge. Sturt blundered about the village desperately searching for Kingsmill, who, in turn, ran from building to building looking for him. But such was the chaos, so dense the smoke, that they passed within twenty yards and never caught so much as a glimpse of each other.

Casualties on both sides mounted. Screened by the fug, escape was suddenly a realistic possibility and the Gang fought a ferocious rearguard while the villagers, seduced by the prospect of totally annihilating the enemy, exposed themselves to unnecessary and deadly risks.

Kingsmill and Jackson rallied their men opposite the church. But, with a clear road home to hand and the villagers closing fast, the temptation to run won. Peter Glover led the charge that swept Goudhurst clean. Conceding that the day was lost, the leaders of the Hawkhurst Gang suffered the indignity of having to turn tail and run. Slowest off the mark was Jackson, and Glover bore down on him, gaining with every stride. Sturt, following close at heel, realized the danger and shouted a warning. Too late. Slow on his feet Jackson may have been, but his sword arm was the equal of any. In one movement, he turned and struck. The cutlass blade caught Glover above the right eyebrow and cleaved him to the lower jaw. He was dead before he hit the ground. To a man, the Militia hesitated. The Gang closed ranks and covered Jackson's dash to safety. A last shot from Kingsmill lodged in Tom Austin's liver and Fairbrother grabbed Sturt by the arm.

'Stop them, George! They'll be cut to pieces!'

The battle had lasted less than thirty minutes and Sturt finished it with a shout. Eight smugglers and three villagers lay dead; Austin would not see the dawn and Ashley Scotcher would lose a leg. Whether the widows of Goudhurst and their children would agree or not, the victory would prove to be worth the price. The Hawkhurst Gang were human after all. And though the effects on Thomas Kingsmill's hitherto invulnerable reputation would only show in the months to come, the damage had been done. At that moment, he stood by his brother's corpse – defeated – and looked up the hill.

Sturt walked forward; his face a mirror image of Kingsmill's. One thought ran through both minds, but it was Kingsmill who gave voice to it. Fingering his bloody neck, he drew breath and bellowed.

'It's only just started, George! I swear to God – it's only just started!'

Chapter 8

It had been the coldest night of the year so far, and the derelict watch-tower had provided scant comfort for those perched on its topmost platform. Eyes barely visible between brim and muffler, George Sturt shifted his aching backside for the umpteenth time and again scanned the Romney Levels. The coming dawn washed the eastern sky, adding shape and colour, revealing latticed sewers that swallowed the unwary, sheep tracks that served as highways for the Hawkhurst Gang. Rotting timbers groaned under the weight of the wind and Sturt levered himself upright – slowly lest stiffened muscle or sinew should tear. He shuddered and stretched. The sun touched but did not warm. They would not come now. A grunt intruded and he turned. Hoarfrost dusted lash and stubble, ageing Fairbrother twenty years. He moaned again and rolled over, unusually troubled by his dreams.

Sturt shook him. 'Time to go John.'

The words fell like soggy snowflakes and Fairbrother knew there was no cause for alarm. He sat up, blinking the hostile world into perspective. Given the chance, he would gladly have returned to his nightmare. 'Five nights and not a damned thing . . .'

Sturt pulled him upright and cramp seized a leg. 'Holy Jesus!' Fairbrother stamped his foot and the tower swayed alarmingly. 'If Kingsmill doesn't kill us, this godforsaken place will!'

Sturt rolled his blanket.

'We're wasting our time, George. They could shift a boat-load of brandy right under our noses and we'd sit here in blissful ignorance!'

'You've got a better idea?'

Fairbrother had been trying to think of one for the past week. He gathered his things and eased himself onto the

91

ancient ladder. A hand on his shoulder stopped him. Sturt was staring at a hunched figure some fifty yards distant.

Burdened with the best part of a hundredweight of contraband, Jos Burney approached a deep ditch and conjured a heavy plank from the marsh grass. Bridging the gully, he wobbled across, then pulled the board after him.

'Why only one?' whispered Fairbrother.

'I don't know, but it's better than none.' Sturt cocked his pistol.

The tubman hurried westward, towards Hawkhurst, and though they were down the ladder in seconds, there was neither sight nor sound of him. Cursing quietly, Sturt found the crossing board and his tracks. They led to another yawning sewer. Lacking any other means of crossing, the two men prepared to jump.

A short run, a last minute adjustment, and they were airborne. Hanging over the widest point for what seemed like an age, they could do nothing when two pairs of hands reached up and seized their ankles. Sky and ground changed places and the earth swallowed them up.

The trap had been expertly sprung.

By any yardstick, Sturt and Fairbrother should have died where they fell. But the most carefully laid plans can fail at the moment of execution. Over-eager to despatch Fairbrother, Harry Sheerman lost his footing in the clinging silt and knocked himself senseless with his own sword pommel. As he hit the water, Burney jumped from the brink and impaled himself on Sturt's raised blade. Which left Jonas Cobby and young Matt Sarmon. Pack animals deprived of leadership and the safety of numbers, neither was a match for their intended victims. Sturt drowned the boy in the mud. Fairbrother retrieved his useless pistol and bludgeoned Cobby into submission, pausing only when he cried out for mercy. Sturt's mood was less charitable. His cutlass had caught Burney in the groin and passed through gut and liver. In one clean action, he drew it out and turned on Cobby.

'Please . . .' was all the terrified free trader could manage.

But Sturt was in a killing frenzy. He lifted Cobby's chin and the point of the blade pricked his windpipe.

'Don't . . .' he cried. 'I'll do anything you want!'

The pinhead of pressure eased the merest fraction, and Jonas Cobby sensed a chance to live.

'Anything at all – sir!'

Fairbrother hammered at the iron-strapped pass door. Inside, an irritable officer drew back the bolts and turned a key in the lock.

Sturt looked at Sheerman. 'Remember,' he said. 'As it stands, attempted rape will get you seven years in the colonies. But one word about Kingsmill and you'll dance the jig.'

Bound and gagged with his own muffler, the smuggler could only grunt his protest.

Sturt cut Cobby loose. 'You sit tight and keep your mouth shut.'

Head gaoler Alfred Dash opened up. Fairbrother entered and the door banged shut.

Down the street, Ben Huggins stopped shovelling free manure from the open drain and edged his handcart a little closer, hoping to drift into earshot. Sturt and Cobby said nothing. They just sat beneath the high greystone wall and waited on Fairbrother. The curious farmer stared at the corpses draped across their saddles like freshly butchered meat. Blood leaked from Burney's wounds. A crimson thread trickled down his leg, dripped into a wheel rut and ran downhill, thickening as it cooled in the freezing air. Greaseless hinges squealed as the prison gates swung open. Cobby glanced at Sheerman, who strained at his bonds, all the while hurling unintelligible abuse at his former comrade.

A scruffy officer led Sarmon's and Burney's horses into the enclosed yard.

Dash blinked at Sheerman. 'Why the silencer?'

'He's got a venomous mouth,' said Fairbrother. 'I suggest you scour it with vinegar when you scrub him down.'

The gaoler's good eye drifted, lingered agonizingly long on Cobby, then swivelled in Sturt's direction. Without another word, he took Sheerman's rein and returned to the world he knew best. A world of pain and misery where Alfred Dash dispensed favour or punishment as the mood took him.

Fairbrother mounted up. 'Your mother is supposed to file charges by Monday.'

'My mother?' queried Sturt.

'Sounded better – worse – than my sister.'

Steel tips pricked chestnut flanks and Fairbrother cantered down to the quay as Rye shook itself from sleep.

'Come Monday and you don't show,' Cobby whined, 'they'll let him loose!'

'By then,' said Sturt. 'It won't matter.'

Ben Huggins watched them go, then returned to his dredging. He was sure that he had witnessed an event of significance – though precisely what it was, defeated him.

Sturt, not trusting Cobby, took his family hostage. With no choice, and a battered silver timepiece in his pocket, the wretched free trader turned his back on wife and children and rode hard for Poole.

Fairbrother had remained uncharacteristically quiet throughout. But, driving the Cobbys to Goudhurst, he'd done his best to calm the frightened children, telling grossly exaggerated stories of his exploits against the French and heathen Scot. For almost an hour, Mollie Cobby had sat beside him, not listening, clutching the youngest, gaze fixed on George Sturt. She knew of him; there was hardly a soul in Kent who did not know of the death of Mary Winch-combe and the confrontation in Goudhurst. Suddenly, through no fault of her own, her family was under threat from all sides. She'd learnt to live with the shadow of the gibbet, and even Thomas Kingsmill. But Sturt was some-thing new. Something beyond her experience. A human being so consumed by the quest for revenge that he was willing to abandon all recognized standards of behaviour, whatever moral code he had lived by, in order to snuff out the life of one other man. And not knowing what to do to protect her brood, she'd prayed – to the God that regularly

94

failed her. Prayed, with great conviction, for the safe return of her stupid, weak-willed man.

At the Winchcombes', Jan had done her best to reassure her, providing food, settling the children into Mary's room while Sturt and Fairbrother cleaned up. Her father's permission or opinion about what amounted to kidnapping had not been sought. Sturt had simply issued an order: the Cobbys were to remain in the village until he said otherwise. His manner had not encouraged dissent but, as with Fairbrother, sullen silence accurately reflected Edward's – and Jan's – feeling on the matter.

Keen to be on the road, Sturt chivvied Fairbrother as he led his horse out of the stable. In the yard, Jan barred his way. She offered a bulging cloth bag. 'Breakfast!' she snapped. 'Not that you deserve it!'

Taking the bread and cold meat, Sturt mounted up.

'George . . .'

The tone was unmistakable. If he'd closed his eyes, it could have been Mary calling.

'Don't go.'

'I have to.'

Jan stepped forward. 'Please – no more killing. Our Mary wouldn't want it.'

'It isn't just for Mary.'

Fairbrother could barely contain his surprise.

'Someone's got to stop him, haven't they?' Sturt turned to Fairbrother but avoided his eyes. 'John . . .'

Fairbrother climbed into the saddle.

'George . . .'

Again that tone.

'You won't forget the wedding?'

'No.'

'Promise. Both of you.'

Sturt did not answer.

'We'll be there,' said Fairbrother. 'I promise.'

She smiled at him then lifted on her toes, inviting Sturt to bend forward. He did so and she kissed his cheek. 'Take great care, George.'

He wanted to speak but dared not, lest the floodgates should open. His fingers brushed her hair and he was gone.

'What about me?' A look of mock indignation spread across Fairbrother's scrubbed face.

Jan ran to him and hugged him so tight that he almost fell off his horse. 'I expect you to take care of the both of you.'

Before he could answer, Sturt called and Jan slapped the gelding's rump. Leaving the yard, Fairbrother saw Mollie Cobby at an upstairs window and felt dirty. Riding past the smithy, he caught sight of Peter Glover's widow and his anger returned.

Struggling to control the jumble of emotions racing through her mind, Jan entered the kitchen. Her father sat brooding by the fire. 'Holdin' women and little 'uns hostage . . .' he moaned. 'Frightening them witless. It ain't decent!'

'Then you should have said as much to George, shouldn't you?'

The retort stung like a slap in the face. Upstairs, a child started to cry.

Set back from a minor crossroads two miles east of Poole, the farm was hidden from travellers on the highway by the elm coppice planted by Caleb Jessop's great-grandfather. Forewarned by the mongrel dog tethered to the byre, Jessop and his sons waited in the yard as William Jackson led forty weary riders down the track through the trees. Behind them, Kingsmill stood at the cross. There was no sun; horse and rider steamed beneath a pewter sky. He fingered the grubby linen strip tied around his neck. The wound inflicted by Sturt's ball had festered and was giving him hell. He rubbed wind-blasted eyes and looked back the way they'd come, scanning and re-scanning the empty winter landscape. Jackson approached. Kingsmill's eyes fixed on the point where the road slid over the brow of Sopley Hill.

'They'll not come now, Thomas – not in broad daylight.'

'They should have caught up by Southampton Water.'

'Trackin' the levels at night ain't easy – '

'Romney is our ground! I ought to have seen to it myself.'

'Then we'd have lost Shepherd Fairall for sure.'

The nor' wester gusted strongly, startling Kingsmill's mount. He struck it viciously across the neck, twice, three times, before the beast settled.

'You're frettin' over nowt,' said Jackson with scant conviction. 'Harry Sheerman knows what he's doin'. Come this time tomorrow, he'll have him in Ringwood, you'll see.'

Kingsmill wasn't listening. A rider had crested the brow and he was straining to identify him. Frozen to the marrow, John Dimer lurched towards them, whimpering every time his raw backside struck the worn-out saddle he'd bought from Ezekiah Jefford.

Disappointed, Kingsmill turned to his lieutenant. 'I don't trust Fairall,' he said. 'And Dimer's a nose for ferreting. Send him into Poole – see if our new ally has done his business.'

Jackson nodded. He didn't trust Fairall either, and would have suggested taking such precautions himself – had he only possessed the wit to think of it.

Kingsmill turned his horse and took the road to Cadnam. Jackson waited for Dimer, whose exhausted nag chose that moment to stumble into a deep pot. Dimer squealed out loud as needles of agony shot through his rump. Eyes watering, he parted cracked lips, subjecting Jackson to the oiliest of grins. He guided 'Fury' onto Jessop's track, desperate to be free of his mobile torture chamber.

'Not yet . . .' said Jackson softly.

Dimer hoped he'd misheard.

Jackson showed his own blackened teeth. 'A job for you first.'

Kingsmill tethered his horse behind the stable and, keeping to the shadows, entered the stone-flagged yard. No smoke rose from the tall chimneys, not even a stable boy was about his chores. The White Hart was sleeping late. Up on his toes, he approached the porched entrance. Steel rang on black iron as his scabbard struck an empty feed bucket. The watch geese murmured and he stood still, holding his breath until they settled. The smallest of movements caught his

97

eye. A drape at a first-floor window had fluttered. Was it the wind? Or a hidden observer? Instinctively, a hand sought the pistol stuck in his belt then, remembering the reason he was there, he relaxed and tried the latch.

Inch by inch, the well oiled door opened until the gap was sufficient for a man to enter. Square-toed jacks in hand, he eased into the darkened bedroom and carefully put them down. At the far end, close to the fireplace, stood a curtained four-poster. He hesitated. A cinder fell from the grate and pulsed in the hearth. Kingsmill skated across the scrubbed board floor, legs stiff in case his tendons should crack and betray him.

Two days' growth snagged the weave as his cheek brushed the embroidered screen. He reached for the overlap and drew the curtains slightly apart. As he did so, the barrel of a horse pistol slid through the opening and lodged against his Adam's apple. Thomas Kingsmill, leader of the Hawkhurst Gang, most powerful individual in the southern counties, had been uncharacteristically careless – and knew it.

'Now open it,' a voice said softly.

He drew the curtain back and faced his captor. Like an undiscovered classical statue, Hannah Payne knelt in the middle of her bed wearing nothing but a smile of triumph. Kingsmill raised his hands but she shook her head. The pistol barrel, and her eyes, dropped below his waist. Kingsmill removed his sword belt and started to unbutton his breeches.

By nature a creature of the night, the Widow slept on, warm under the blankets, breathing easily, mind and body at peace with the world. Not so Kingsmill. Naked beneath his still damp surtout, he stood at the open window looking east. The day had improved but he was unaware of the sun warming his fingers on the sill. His mind was working overtime. Countless images troubled him, and at the centre of every one was George Sturt. Escaping him. Tormenting him. Haunting his every moment. Rational analysis would have quietened his fears. After all, Sheerman was a talented assassin, who had never yet failed him. Perhaps that was it. Killing was relatively easy – a sniper's bullet, a blade under the ribs down some dark alley. But he'd ordered them to take Sturt alive, and that was an altogether different matter.

The piercing note of a post-horn intruded as the Southampton mail coach approached. It was almost noon and he should have been gone long since. His clothes were on the floor; the pistol on a chair close to the bed. He moved it out of reach and took off his coat. Foot raised, he was about to step into his breeches when the Widow rolled over and snatched them from him.

'Damn you, Thomas! You'd treat your whores with more consideration!'

'Now, Hannah . . .' he blustered, acutely conscious of his own absurdity. 'Don't start – give them back!'

She waved them tantalizingly out of reach. 'At least you'd leave them a shilling or two before crawling away!'

'I said give them back!' He lunged. And missed – cracking his bad shin on the bed leg for good measure.

Before he could try again, one quick movement had sent his best leather riding breeches out of the window. Billowing on the breeze, they floated down to the brimming horse trough. For a split second they lay spread-eagled on the meniscus then sank to the depths. Fist raised, Kingsmill turned on her but, before he could strike, she threw back the bed covers – and smiled!

Though thirty-seven years old, Hannah Payne's body was the envy of her serving girls, and the subject of more male fantasies than any actress on the London stage. Kingsmill's hand remained frozen aloft. She opened her knees and pulled him down. Kissing him, she drew his anger like a wasp sting; then bit the tip of his tongue – hard.

'I'll not be used, Thomas.'

Tasting blood, he dabbed at the injured organ with the back of his hand. 'You were sleeping. I should be half-way to Poole . . .'

A hand slid down his belly. 'Got something better there, have you?'

'Not better – younger.'

Her fingers closed about his privates.

'It's business!'

'Liar!' She squeezed and his eyes popped like a child's on Christmas morning.

'It's the truth, Hannah! I swear to God – '

'Your business is with Shepherd Fairall – tonight.'

She released him. He lifted onto his elbows, taken aback by the extent of her knowledge.

'My business is to know what goes on,' she said. 'Otherwise, scabs like you and Fairall might take advantage of a poor widow.'

Kingsmill had known her for eight years or more, and couldn't remember anyone taking advantage – not and having lived to boast of it anyway. He knelt up and inspected the damage.

'What happened in Goudhurst?'

He didn't answer.

'Thomas . . .'

'They killed my brother, George.'

She sat up and the smells of her body enveloped him. 'Is it settled?'

'Not yet.'

Her hands closed about his neck.

'I have to go – '

'Was it George Sturt?'

'The Devil take your questions!' He tried to pull away but she was deceptively strong in the arms.

'Who is he?'

Their noses were almost touching.

'Tell me.' The edge had gone from her voice; the tone was soft, almost gentle.

Kingsmill relaxed his muscles. 'A piece of the past,' he said. 'And he's none of your business, Hannah. Nor Fairall's. Nor your talkative friend, the Magistrate's.' His eyes held her. 'Understand?'

She pulled herself up and straddled his knees. Her tongue danced in his mouth. She shifted her weight and swallowed him up.

*
100

A shrill blast, a yell from the postillion, and the mail coach was on its way. They waited as it turned onto the highway, then Sturt urged the lathered mare on. Fairbrother gazed longingly at the White Hart.

'George . . .' he called.

Sturt stopped again. He was eager to reach Poole, but the horses were undoubtedly done in. 'Twenty minutes,' he said. 'No more.'

Hannah Payne stood at the window buttoning her bodice as they entered the yard. Fairbrother felt her eyes and, though aching from head to toe, instantly sprang to life. Bowing with an elegant flourish, he subjected her to his most irresistible smile. She ran a cold, professional eye over the mud-spattered strangers – they might just as well have been meat on her kitchen slab.

Sturt dropped to the ground. 'You're losing your touch.'

The Widow's son, Samuel, took his rein and he entered the inn.

'Forty minutes, boy,' said Fairbrother. 'See they're watered and fed good oats – no husks!'

Samuel led the animals away as Kingsmill appeared from behind the brew house. Wet leather clung to his crotch. He swung into the saddle and glared at the Widow. Spurs gouged matted flanks and the geese scattered. Hannah Payne chuckled quietly to herself. The power she wielded over him gave her immense satisfaction.

'Time to go.'

Fairbrother stood in the hearth, roasting the backs of his legs whilst packing a dudeen with herb tobacco. 'There's no rush, George. Cobby won't show before dark.' He dipped a lighted taper into the bowl and sucked on the clay stem. 'And God knows what we'll do when he does.'

The point was not lost on Sturt but, peeling a flake of dried mud from his Dettingen, he chose to ignore it. He jammed the hat onto his crown and finished his drink, unaware of young Samuel squeezing through the crowd by the door.

Strangers at the White Hart were always cause for

concern, and the lad had just searched their saddlebags. Having found nothing to link them to the Excise Service, he reported to his mother, then retired to his favourite perch on the stairs with a mug of hot.

A compulsive observer of the human condition, Sam Payne carried an old head on twelve-year-old shoulders. Sturt and Fairbrother intrigued him. They weren't gentry, though one exhibited pretensions of style, and they couldn't possibly be farmers or merchants. Everything about them screamed army: their bearing, the quiet authority of those used to giving orders a hundred times a day. So what were they doing at the White Hart with a run in the offing? Gin and hot ale blistered his lip. He watched his mother home in and clear the table nearest the fire – she had her suspicions too.

Rebuffed once, Fairbrother made no further effort to charm the lady, restricting conversation to the weather, state of the public highway and the ever-rising price of ale. Sturt remained oblivious to her presence. Deep in thought, he considered the alternatives unfolding, now that they had a spy in the enemy camp.

'George . . .'

He'd left his tankard balanced on the high iron fender, and scraped his chair backwards so that the Widow might reach it. She leaned across him and he caught the unmistakable scent of sex. She held his look, though not for the reason he thought.

She watched them leave from the kitchen window. In the front parlour, a noisy argument was developing amongst a platoon of foot soldiers en route for Chichester. Who was going to pay for the next round? Ranks closed and nominated Corporal Shard. Badgered by the chanting of his Christian name, George Shard eventually gave in and called for the serving girl.

With drunken cheers ringing in her ears, Hannah Payne dismissed her suspicions and turned the joints of beef over the fire. It was too much of a coincidence. After all, George was probably the most popular name in Hanoverian England.

Chapter 9

It had taken Dimer most of the day to complete his task. Now, with darkness drawing in, he hobbled back down the jetty, increased the pace as he passed the Custom House and headed for Fleet's Coffee House. Tethered to a hitching ring in the wall, his much-abused nag dozed on its feet whilst, under the window, a legless blind man picked out a simple tune on a tin whistle. At his side, dressed in tattered red jacket and trousers, squatted an Indian bonnet monkey. It shook its begging bowl at the passers-by, chattering and panting whenever a coin was donated. About to mount, Dimer paused. His hand dropped into the monkey's bowl and coins jingled. The cripple thanked him. The primate, however, screamed with rage. They'd just been robbed of a day's takings.

Slumped in the saddle, Fairbrother looked up as they passed the Custom quay. Though Dimer had gone, the monkey still raged and the noise caught his attention. He noticed that the cripple too sported the remnants of a crimson uniform. Closer inspection revealed it to be that of a private in the Third Kent Foot – their old regiment. Fairbrother whistled at the monkey and tossed a bright shilling. The tiny creature caught it and turned a somersault.

'God bless you for your kindness, your honour!' cried the cripple.

Behind them, a door banged. An officer left the Custom House and crossed the street to where the *Swift*, a privateer Revenue cutter, lay alongside the jetty. Sturt dismounted outside the coffee house.

'We can't do it alone, George.'

Sturt looked at the Custom House. Inside, a clerk was lighting candle lanterns. 'No,' he said.

'Be reasonable,' Fairbrother argued. 'They would make all the difference.'

Sturt tied his rein to the ring. 'We'd best find lodgings.'

Fairbrother slid from the saddle. 'He can't have bought every revenue officer in England! There must be a few honest men left.'

The cripple stopped playing, turning his head to catch the conversation.

'If there are, we don't need them,' said Sturt.

Fairbrother knew the mood; knew that arguing was a waste of breath.

But Sturt continued, as if trying to convince himself. 'They'd likely foul it up – Kingsmill might slip away.'

Sightless eyes widened at the mention of his name.

'Or someone other than yourself might shoot him!' It was an unworthy jibe but Fairbrother was tired and angry. Before he could apologize, Sturt had turned his back.

'We do it my way,' he said, stepping onto the walkway outside Fleet's establishment.

'There'll be dozens of them – you'll be lucky to get one clear shot!'

'One is all I need.' Sturt opened the door.

Concern for his friend's deteriorating state of mind showed in Fairbrother's face. In all the years they'd known each other, all the times they'd faced the possibility of extinction together, he'd never once questioned Sturt's judgement, never doubted his instinct. But Mary's death had wormed into his soul. Judgement had become clouded, instinct distorted.

'I'm sorry, George . . .' he murmured, and walked towards the Custom House.

'John!'

Fairbrother's pace quickened.

'John!'

Heads turned. Chilled knuckles stung as he rapped on the stout oak door.

'Damn you!' Sturt ran after him, barging a laden fish porter, dodging amongst gin traders and sailors' whores.

Hairy fingers tugged at the cripple's coat. The blind man

took Fairbrother's shilling and tucked it into his coat cuff. 'Kingsmill . . .' he wheezed. The stumps of his legs drummed on the pitch pine boards. 'Thomas Kingsmill!'

'Well?'

'Fairall done his bit and more, Master Thomas.' Relishing his moment of glory, Dimer slowly unbuttoned his greatcoat.

'Dimer . . .' said Kingsmill threateningly.

The Hawkhurst Gang's newest recruit inclined towards his master and beamed. 'There ain't a single soldier left between Poole and Chichester.'

'I don't believe it!' Jackson snorted. 'How?'

'Check he'd done it, you said. If you wants to know the ins and outs – ask him yourself!'

Jackson jumped to his feet and Dimer backpedalled – there were times he wished he'd been born mute.

'He had two of his own men informed against.'

Kingsmill spoke quietly, but the effect of that simple statement was devastating. Dimer and Jackson gaped like fish out of water. To inform against your own was the most heinous crime a free trader could commit: retribution was traditionally swift, invariably painful, and always fatal.

'Discreetly of course. Then he put the word about that there was to be a gallows rescue in Chichester.'

'And is there?'

The look answered Dimer's question. Confused and more than a little frightened, he sat down, trying to make sense of it all. Fairall had committed the cardinal sin, and Kingsmill seemed to be condoning it. If that was the case – what security was there for any of them?

'But Master Thomas . . .' he bleated.

Kingsmill leaned back in Jessop's favourite chair. Candle-light danced across his face, emphasizing the dark smudges beneath his eyes, giving already gaunt features a decidedly cadaverous appearance. He was impressed by Fairall's ruth-less single-mindedness but knew it would be bad form to admit it. His eyes closed and he was instantly asleep.

Only the tock of a long case clock broke the silence in James Milner's office. The Commissioner of Customs had listened carefully to Fairbrother's story and, though wildly excited by the prospect of taking on the Hawkhurst Gang, thought it prudent to maintain the dignity of his office and weigh the situation in silence – for a minute or two at least. Observing the fire in the young man's eyes, Fairbrother rested his hands on the polished oak desk and waited.

Henry Kemp stood at his master's shoulder. His opinion had not been sought so he too waited, secure in the knowledge that whatever course of action Milner decided upon would be the wrong one. Indeed, rectifying the new Commissioner's gaffs had become a way of life for Kemp – and there were times over the past few months he wished he'd never abandoned his previous trade. A soft rumble interrupted his train of thought. Sturt was drumming his knuckles on the curved frame of a bay window. Determined to take no part in the proceedings, he looked out at the *Swift* and watched her crew plaiting hemp, chipping paint, patching storm-damaged canvas.

Fairbrother cleared his throat. 'George . . .'

He stopped drumming and, like a petulant child, sought another diversion. Unfortunately, he chose the map of the district pinned to the wall. A hand-coloured masterpiece, it was Milner's pride and joy, purchased at extortionate cost to give the office that veneer of professionalism he thought necessary to impress visiting superiors. Sturt carefully traced the coastline with a grubby finger and a dark smudge surfaced off St Alban's Head.

'An extraordinary story!' Milner's voice hovered close to the top of its register. 'Wouldn't you agree, Kemp?'

'More like fanciful, if you're askin' me.'

Sturt glanced at Fairbrother. 'I told you!'

To Milner's relief, he went back to the window and recommenced the drumming. The Commissioner shook his head – sharply – like a labrador with an earful of water. 'You disappoint me, Kemp.'

'I does my best, sir.'

Milner rose and paced the floor, carefully avoiding the

expensive rug given by his mother. 'A half-wit could invent a more convincing story.'

'Yes, sir.'

'Which is why I am inclined to believe it.'

Fleeting as it was, Kemp caught the look of satisfaction on Fairbrother's face. The silky tongued stranger had manipulated and manoeuvred with great skill. Personal flattery, combined with the carrot of rapid promotion and public acclaim, had worked its spell on the gullible young exciseman. Nevertheless, Kemp was determined not to let Fairbrother have things all his own way; leading Poole's Commissioner by the nose was his prerogative.

'Beggin' pardon,' he said, 'but we don't know nowt about these gentlemen.'

'Instinct, Kemp?' Milner breathed perfumed air into his face.

'Yes, sir.'

'A nose for the truth . . .'

Kemp repeated the oft-quoted phrase. 'Is an exciseman's greatest asset.'

The Commissioner beamed. 'Precisely so!' He turned to Fairbrother and offered his hand. 'We are at your disposal, sir.'

'All seven of us,' Kemp muttered mischievously.

The sense of satisfaction dissolved instantly. 'Seven is your full complement?'

'Strange as it may seem' – Kemp took a generous pinch of cheap snuff and sneezed – 'recruiting is a mite difficult around here.'

'I'm sure Kingsmill will lose sleep – '

'Shut up George!'

Milner returned to his desk and spoke with what authority he could muster. 'As His Majesty's Commissioner of Customs, I am empowered to enlist the assistance of any military unit in the district.'

'They're all in Chichester.' Kemp was back at his shoulder. ' 'Cos of the 'angings – sir.'

'The Poole troop is in Chichester, Kemp. The Dorchester and Weymouth squadrons are not!'

'How many men?' Suddenly interested, Sturt moved to the desk. 'Altogether.'

'Fifty, perhaps sixty.'

The clock struck six. The echo of the final stroke died and Chief Riding Officer Kemp collected his hat. 'I'll send Dekker, then.' He looked at Sturt and Fairbrother. 'But it still smells queer to me.'

There was no salute, not even the smallest gesture of respect before he walked away.

'Wait!' Milner rose. 'Gentleman' – Kemp snorted his nostrils clear and hawked into his hand – 'I suggest you arrange lodgings for the night. Ma Sharkey's should suffice. She changes the sheets weekly and supper is an event.'

'We're obliged to you,' said Fairbrother.

Again, the ostentatious shake of the head. 'I am merely doing my duty. The onus lies with you, sir. Or to be precise, with your man Cobby.'

'Unfortunately!'

'He'll show!' snapped Sturt. 'You just get your horse soldiers here by first light.'

Kemp showed them out and closed the door. Milner fingered the filigree hilt of his dress sword. 'Your informant?'

'Sir?'

'Who was it?'

'No, sir!'

Again, the sickly scent of rose water mouthwash affronted Kemp's nostrils. 'Strictly between ourselves, man.'

'It ain't done . . .' But backed up against the wall, Kemp had nowhere to go. 'Hannah Payne. Her as runs the White Hart at Cadnam.'

'And the source of the rescue attempt rumour?'

Kemp didn't need to answer, his expression spoke for him. Milner backed off.

'I'd best haul Dekker out of the gin shop.'

The door closed almost noiselessly.

Left alone, Milner poured a liberal measure of run cognac and smiled to himself. The balance had undoubtedly tipped

108

a fraction his way. And he intended to enjoy his moment to the full.

Outside, sleet was driving down the street, slapping against weatherboard buildings, forming great puddles in the ruts and pots. On the way to Ma Sharkey's, Sturt put his hand in his purse and a shilling dropped into the cripple's bowl.

By ten that evening snow was falling steadily. In the New Forest, puddles had iced over. And, though the trees took the sting out of the wind, the lone horseman waiting in the shadows clamped chattering teeth shut and dusted snow epaulets from the shoulders of his threadbare wrap rascal. Not three hundred yards away, folk were wallowing in the warmth and comfort of the Red Lion. He could hear them, swilling ale and geneva, enjoying the pleasures of a good inn on a bad night. A fat plume of smoke rose from each chimney. Firelight danced behind bottle-thick windows, casting a rosy glow onto the frozen carpet outside. The rider sniffed and cleared his raw throat, certain that he was coming down with a fever. As if to confirm it he sneezed, startling his half-perished mount. Soft words calmed the beast; then he pulled slouched round hat about his ears, frost-stiffened muffler over his nose and stuck one numbed hand into his crotch. If they didn't come soon he would surely freeze to death.

Slumped in a high-backed chair close to the front parlour fire, Shepherd Fairall was aware of a faint tremor in his right leg. He wasn't cold and he wasn't ill. It was simply the waiting. He hated it; hated waiting for anyone or anything; always had, always would. It was something to do with losing control, having to rely on others in a profession where one mistake led to the ladder. The trembling and acid belly were merely the physical manifestations of his inner torment. He belched and tasted bile. They were more than two hours late. Most of his men were so gilded that, should trouble ensue, they would be worse than useless. He belched again and peevishly pinched the ear of his deerhound spread in the hearth. The animal responded with a token growl and moved its massive head out of reach. Two hours . . . He'd failed to stop his imagination working on the various possibilities. Reason and clear thinking had deserted him. Treachery and destruction seemed to threaten from every quarter. He rose and went to the window.

The darkened houses of Ringwood were losing their identity beneath the deepening blanket. He peered at the wood and a thousand hostile faces stared back. He listened and a muffled rumble betrayed the presence of an invisible army. His breath misted the glass. He wiped it clean and saw only trees. His mind was playing tricks. Or was it? The rumble persisted, the hound had heard it too. Dragging itself from the fire, the great beast jumped up at the window and, tail beating the heavy air, started to bay. Smoaker Mills got up, urging those who were able to do likewise. Fairall hurried back to his chair. Robert Lamb looked on with undisguised amusement as the Chichester Gang bobbed like corks in a heavy swell. His admiration for Kingsmill increased with every new venture!

Pistol primed, Mills was half out of the door when his master stopped him. 'Smoaker . . .' Lamb's face had provided the key. Realizing that the game had to be played to the finish, Fairall shook his head. 'Sit down,' he said quietly.

Cobby abandoned the safety of the trees and waited in the middle of the road. All around him, snowstorm and blackness merged, transforming the New Forest into the stuff of nightmares. Slowly, ghost-like figures materialized two by two. He recognized Kingsmill leading the column and his guts turned to jelly. The gang leader did not stop until he was within touching distance. Jackson held back, halting the rest with a gesture.

'Where is he?'

Cobby had rehearsed his story over and over, but could not summon the spit to speak. A hand clamped around his windpipe.

'I said where is he?'

110

Something seemed to give behind Cobby's eyeballs. The world started to disintegrate as he fought to fill starved lungs. 'Dead!' he rasped.

Kingsmill physically reeled, as if he'd been struck by a musket ball. If he hadn't been holding onto Cobby he would have fallen from the saddle. He squeezed even harder. 'You're lying!'

'I'm not . . .' Cobby squirmed and thrashed, desperate to tear free. 'Thomas – I swear it! He's dead!'

Suddenly the awful pressure was gone. His lungs ballooned. Blood seeped from ruptured vessels, spraying from nose and mouth as he coughed.

Sitting motionless, Kingsmill now held him with his eyes. The initial shock had passed: instinct and intellect were regaining control. 'Then where's the body?' he asked.

The pain in Cobby's throat was acute; dark clots and mucus bored holes in the snow as he cleared his damaged airway.

'Where?' Again, that cruel fist reached out.

'Hidden! At the Burmarsh Tower . . . I was hurt – couldn't do owt else.'

Kingsmill searched for the slightest hint of a lie. Conjuring images of Mollie and the children, Cobby held his gaze.

'What happened?'

'I don't know . . .' Mollie was fading and he talked faster. 'Honest I don't! I got pole-axed. When I come round it were like a knacker's yard – they was all done in . . .'

Kingsmill neither moved nor spoke, but Cobby knew he was losing ground.

'Except Sturt,' he said quickly. 'His head were split, but he was still breathing. I knew how bad you wanted him, so I dragged him to the tower – '

'What did he say?'

The question threw Cobby, he had not anticipated it. 'Nothing . . .'

'He must have said something!'

'No!' Honed steel pricked bruised larynx. His voice fell

111

to a whisper. 'I watched him die, Thomas.' Very carefully, he reached inside his coat. 'This was in his pocket.'

Kingsmill pulled off a glove with his teeth and took the battered timepiece. Inside, the lid was engraved with a name. George Edward Sturt. A long moment passed, during which no one dared draw breath for fear of breaking it.

The watch case snapped shut. The cutlass point sank deep into the nearest trunk. Like a bereaved father, Kingsmill started to moan. A deep, haunting note, it sent a shiver through those within earshot. Then, rising in pitch and power, finally erupted into a full-throated snarl of animal rage.

Jackson spurred his mount forward. 'Thomas.' He shook his shoulder. 'Thomas!'

Kingsmill stopped screaming and flopped onto his horse's neck. 'It's over now. Finished. And we've other business to hand.'

Jackson reached for the watch. Kingsmill drew his hand away and sat bolt upright. Cheated of the vengeance that gave his life meaning, he felt nothing. All he could see was a youthful face. Sturt's face – smiling at him. He closed his eyes but that grinning mask stayed with him. George Sturt was dead and it still was not over. He would continue to plague him; haunt every moment, waking and sleeping, until that infinitesimal beat in time when Thomas Kingsmill also ceased to exist.

The door burst open. The dog leapt forward. Had Fairall not kept a tight grip on its choker, Kingsmill would have killed it. Dimer pushed his way through the crush of snow-wet riders and hovered at the door. Mills dragged the hound out of harm's way. Jackson watched for signs of hostility, while Robert Lamb sat tight in his corner, aware that he was witness to history in the making. The amalgamation of Hawkhurst and Chichester Gangs had long been a dream. He had discussed it often with Perrin. With a territory stretching from the Thames to the Exe, from the Channel to the Severn, such a union presented mouth-watering possibilities for profit. Assuming the resolution of one outstanding problem. The rival gang leaders faced one another. Fairall's guts rumbled. Kingsmill noticed the shake in his leg and beamed expansively, exuding trust and friendship. 'Shepherd . . .' he said warmly.

Outside in the courtyard, Cobby was violently sick.

Chapter 10

The darkened courtroom resembled a vision from Hell. Judge, officials and jurors hid behind inquisitor hoods. Above the bench, broken Scales of Justice spun in the motionless air, flanked by a naked lunatic and a grinning death's-head.

In the dock, Sturt stood alone, held prisoner by a shaft of brilliant light emanating from no definable source. There had not been a trial. The charge was obvious. The evidence common knowledge. All that was required was a verdict. And sentence.

The gallery hushed as the diminutive foreman rose and approached the dock. Mary Winchcombe removed her hood. She smiled, kissed him full on the mouth and pronounced him guilty. The walls shook as the mob stamped and pounded. The rest of the jurors filed past the accused. One by one, John Fairbrother, Alan Wynter, Jan, Edward Winchcombe, Peter Glover, Sarah Dimer, removed their hoods, kissed him and confirmed the verdict.

Across the room, Thomas Kingsmill stood and donned black cap. Old army comrades piled kindling about Sturt's feet. Friends and half-forgotten acquaintances thrust blazing torches into the pyre. And Sturt screamed, fighting against the rough hands that held him.

'Come now. Rouse yourself, master . . .'

Sturt seized Esdor Fleet's wrist and his nightmare shrank from the daylight.

'What time is it?'

'A quarter afore seven!' snapped Fleet. 'And I've a right to be chargin' you bed and board!'

Neck and back twinged as Sturt levered himself upright. 'Has anyone been asking?'

'No they ain't!' A sleeve dragged across a slimy snout. 'Not as I'm surprised mind. Some "gentlemen" would sell

114

their souls to the Devil to duck out of payin' their way in this world!'

The death's-head smirked and vanished.

Sturt tossed him a coin and Fleet bit into the soft metal. 'I'll be fetchin' your breakfast,' he said, and shuffled back to the grease pit he called a kitchen.

Sturt got up. Fairbrother was still asleep in the hearth. They'd waited all night for Cobby; John had passed out around two while he had resisted for a further hour or so. The question now was what to do next. He rejected aimlessly searching the countryside for Kingsmill's base. Perhaps they'd got the wrong coffee house! Grabbing his coat, Sturt realized that Fairbrother was watching him. 'He could be anywhere,' Sturt said. 'There must be two dozen coffee houses and taverns.'

'But he selected this one,' Fairbrother replied. 'And he said to wait.'

But for how long? In twenty-four hours the cargo would be ashore and Kingsmill gone. Patience had never been Sturt's strong point. They had to do something, anything, while there was still time. He went to the window and looked out.

The snow had turned to a steady downpour and, caught in the dawn light, Poole Harbour looked like a sheet of hammered lead. The distinctive clatter of horses at the gallop broke the silence. Their problems were about to increase.

Soaked to the bone, Riding Officer Dekker led the Dorchester and Weymouth dragoons down the street and along the jetty. Before the officer in command had dismounted, Milner was out of the Custom House. A curt exchange and he ran across the street, barging the blind cripple as he scrambled onto the walkway.

Fairbrother opened the door, depriving him of a grand entrance.

'There's forty dragoons out there!'

Sturt pulled on his coat.

'I took your word . . .' Milner blustered. 'In good faith!'

And Sturt had given it in good faith, though there seemed

115

little point in saying so. He squeezed past the exciseman and walked down to the deserted quay.

Deeply embarrassed, the Collector felt like the boy who cried wolf. His professional credibility was in tatters and he didn't know whether to stay or go. While he dithered, Fleet brought in two plates of bread and cheese.

'Master Sturt?' he enquired.

'Will be back,' said Fairbrother. 'But you can leave them both.'

Like all decent citizens, Fleet despised the Excise Service and, had he not been of a cowardly disposition, would have refused to serve Milner. He settled for banging the plates down onto the table – then beat a hasty retreat.

Fairbrother pushed a chair in Milner's direction. 'Things always look better on a full stomach, James – particularly at this ungodly hour.'

A reassuring smile decided the issue. After all, John Fairbrother was a man of vast experience – to ignore his advice would be churlish in the extreme.

Further down the coast, a grey mist clung to the horizon, obscuring the curve where sea and sky met. The rain had stopped, the last of the snow had been washed into the Channel and, high on Duriston Head, Henry Kemp lay on his oilskin cape, tossing bits of bread to the gulls. It was his favourite time of day. A time of peace. A brief respite from Agnes's whiplash tongue. To his delight, a juvenile black-backed snatched a morsel of crust from his out-stretched hand and rose effortlessly on the updraught.

Like most earth-bound bipeds, Kemp envied the birds their freedom, their simple, uncluttered existence. Where he differed from his fellows was in the pleasure he derived from merely watching them. During his years at sea, he'd spent many hours admiring gannets diving in the wake, countless days observing the same fulmars following the ship. Alone on watch or up the mast, he'd talk to them; asking time and again – why? what was the purpose? In his more fanciful moments, the tiny creatures simply valued his company. Feeling bleak and homesick, they were heralds, there to carry news of his untimely demise.

A handful of crumbs fell over the cliff edge like leftovers from the night's blizzard, but the gulls let them go. Twisting and turning overhead, they screeched a warning.

'Still at her worst first thing, eh, 'Enry?'

Kemp sat up and smiled. 'You know, Gilbert, they say it's a scientifical fact that folk mellow as they get older.'

'So I've heard.'

'My Agnes defies the Sciences.'

Gilbert Pett nodded sagely and stopped his wagon. 'Her and my Martha together.'

Kemp offered his flask. The elderly farmer took a long pull while the exciseman leaned over and peered into the back of the cart. He was not surprised to find it empty, but felt obliged to go through the motions. 'All this dashing about could see off a man of your years – like as not.'

Unsynchronized eyeballs swivelled in their sockets. Pett swallowed the last mouthful of ale.

'You ain't bin doin' a bit of nightwork for Shepherd Fairall, by any chance?'

The farmer backhanded his foamy mouth. 'Have you?'

'I packed it up while I was winnin' ' said Kemp. 'Never heard as you did.'

The old man grinned. 'I needed a rim fixing and stopped over in Wareham. I was expected home last night, but you know how it is . . .'

'You'll be in hot water.'

Pett pictured the reception and sighed. 'Martha will have my balls.'

'Could be worse.'

The logic of Kemp's argument defeated him.

'Can't be considered essential equipment at your time of life, now can they?'

Pett chuckled and returned the flask. 'Struggle on, 'Enry . . .'

He flicked his whip but, before he'd gone ten yards, a rear iron worked loose and slapped into the ooze. Pett stared at the rimless wheel in disbelief.

'The one you had done?' enquired Kemp, trying hard to keep a straight face.

'English craftsmen!' wailed Pett. 'Mark my words, they'll be the death of us all!'

Kemp retrieved the iron and threw it into the cart. 'Just drive easy,' he said. 'Stay out of the ruts and it should see you safe home.'

Grumbling and cursing, the farmer lurched down the dipslope. Kemp mounted up. Turning for Poole, he took a last look at the sea.

The mist had lifted and there, caught like a hare in the open, was a ship hull-down on the horizon.

For fully half a minute, the exciseman studied her mast pattern. Main course and mizzen, cut and rake, finally dropped into place. As of right then, he owed masters Sturt and Fairbrother a sincere apology.

'Here,' Kemp said. 'About twelve mile off-shore.'

Sturt looked up from the map. 'And you identified it?'

'No two ships have the same mast pattern or fly the same kites,' Milner explained. 'And Kemp sailed on *Three Brothers* for more than five years.' Giving his words time to sink in, the Collector carefully removed the map and laid it on his desk.

'How can you be so sure she's carrying for Kingsmill?' asked Fairbrother.

'She displaces three hundred ton or more,' said Kemp. 'Ain't another ship workin' these waters big enough to shift your outsize cargo.'

'Might she not be about her legitimate business?'

Kemp smiled. '*Three Brothers* never run a legal load since the day she first floated.' He turned the map. 'From her position, she's come from Roscoff or Guernsey. And with this nor'-nor'-wester blowin' she was 'avin' to beat to windward to 'old 'er course. Now, if she was 'eadin east, say for Romney Marsh, she'd 'ave bin flyin' up the Channel with a soldier's wind.'

Three blank faces indicated that an explanation was in order.

118

'The wind on 'er beam.' He paused. 'Everythin' points to a landin' in the west.' A calloused index finger swept East Dorset. 'Somewhere around 'ere.'

'Where there's a dozen possible landing sites!'

'That's right. But beggin' pardon, Master Sturt, with wind and tide as they are, we can ignore all bar two.' He pointed out the tiny indentations in the coastline. ' 'Orse Rock Bay. And all of eight mile away, Chamber Cove.'

'Which would you choose?' asked Sturt, memorizing the positions of both.

Kemp shrugged. 'In this weather – neither. If it eases, one's as good as the other.'

The wooden wheeled clock struck a half after ten. Milner sat down, uncomfortably aware of the responsibility resting on his young shoulders. The desire to deliver Thomas Kingsmill in chains had not waned, but the memory of his public humiliation still made him flush. 'My feeling is to take the cargo while we can.'

'No!' exclaimed Sturt.

'A heavily laden lugger is no match for the *Swift*, sir. With Eachard's dragoons aboard, we can deal Kingsmill a savage blow.'

Sturt towered over him. Barely in control, he spoke slowly. 'Take that ship and we lose the Hawkhurst Gang,' he said. 'You'll never get a better chance to make your name.'

Milner got up and moved to the window. With the length of the room between them, he felt confident enough to speak his piece. 'Your informer has lost his nerve, Sturt – he's betrayed you!' To discourage interruption he turned away. Eyes fixed on the *Swift*'s seven pounders, he continued. 'Trusting him was undoubtedly a mistake. We were both at fault, but the choice now is straightforward.' He turned back. 'Take the freighter or end up with nothing.'

Sensing that Sturt was about to boil over, Fairbrother took evasive action. 'And you, Kemp,' he said quickly, 'what do you think?'

'I agrees with Master Sturt, sir.'

Again, Milner's cheeks coloured.

119

'It's my guess they'll abandon the run tonight, heave to and wait for a break in the weather.'

'Which will be when precisely.'

The irritation in his master's voice was not lost on Kemp. ''Ard to say, sir. Not afore tomorrow, maybe even the day after. Either way, *Three Brothers* ain't goin' nowhere right now. We could afford to give this Cobby feller a bit more rope. That is, if you've a mind to.'

Under pressure Milner tended to chew his mouth, and a large blood blister was forming inside his cheek. He poked it with the tip of his tongue as he crossed to the desk. Picking up the map, he rehung it on the wall. 'Have Captain Johnstone prepare to sail.'

'Damn you to Hell, man!' snarled Sturt.

Jaws clamped shut and the blister burst. Bloodied teeth showed as the collector addressed Kemp. 'But tell him to wait for the late tide.'

Kemp was already on his way. 'Aye, sir!'

The door banged shut and Milner turned to Sturt. Dabbing at his mouth with a fine silk kerchief, he spoke quietly and with great purpose. 'Your man has until the quarter after midnight – and not a second more.'

That night, heavy black clouds kept the temperature above freezing and thunder rattled around the western sky, warning of the deluge to come.

Outside Rye Gaol, a bored guard amused himself by stoning the vermin in the alleys and drains with bits of fallen masonry. A shrill squeal confirmed a third direct hit. Satisfied with his tally, he leaned back against the massive gate and shook the stiffness out of his throwing arm. Behind him, a key turned in the lock causing him to snap to attention.

Alfred Dash opened the pass door. Leaving it ajar, he offered his man a jug of heated ale. 'To drive the chill from your bones, Simon,' he said.

The guard took it and inhaled the vapours. 'You're a real gent, Alfred.'

Those few words were the last he spoke. Greedily swallowing the scalding liquor, he failed to notice a second figure in the doorway. Chains clinked softly as Harry Sheerman raised his arms. Too late, the sentry heard him and took the cudgel full in the face instead of behind the ear. He fell without so much as a grunt.

Dash dropped to his knees. 'Curse your blood!' he hissed. 'You've done for him!'

Unconcerned, the free trader held out his manacled hands. Rye's Senior Gaoler shook his head. Sheerman produced a leather money bag from his boot and Dash pocketed five gold guineas. Using his muffler to deaden the noise, he struck off the irons with two expert blows of a hammer.

'There's a saddle horse in the flux dresser's alley.' He turned his back, closed his eyes and braced himself. 'Do it quick – and not too hard, mind.'

Sheerman rubbed his raw wrists then lashed out with all his strength. Bone splintered, and a fragment pierced Dash's brain. Face down in the mud, his eyes rolled up into what was left of his skull and he twitched like a wrung chicken.

Wasting no time, Sheerman turned him over and retrieved his money. A quick look to check that there were no witnesses to his butchery and he took to his heels. Watched by dozens of tiny red eyes, he led his mount out of the shadows and down to the harbour.

Outside the gaol, Alfred Dash died without fuss. For a moment, the smell of blood hung on the air and a rat scuttled over the cobbles. It started to rain as needle-pointed teeth tore cloth and human flesh. Within seconds, Sheerman's victims had vanished beneath a mass of writhing black bodies. By the time they were found, even their families would have been hard-pressed to recognize them.

Fifteen minutes before midnight, Sheerman was fast approaching the village of Herstmonceux. In Poole, Sturt and Fairbrother were kicking their heels at Fleet's Coffee House. Henry Kemp joined them. The mood was sombre. Sturt had retreated even further into himself; so, for the want of something better to do, the ex-smuggler took out a pack of cards and dealt two hands. Grateful for the distraction, Fairbrother placed a shilling in the pot.

He had warmed to Kemp, and while they played, told him of the grudge between Sturt and Kingsmill. The shorter, though suitably embellished, version of his own life story followed, and by the time Esdor Fleet approached the clock was striking the quarter.

'Master Sturt . . .'

A snort was the only indication that his words had registered.

'Someone to see you.'

Sturt shot to his feet – Cobby hadn't failed him after all! But where was he? Sturt anxiously scanned the crowded room. The elation that had surged so strongly dribbled away as a stunted figure emerged from the forest of legs.

'Sturt?'

A hand reached up and lightly touched his own. 'Yes,' he said, stepping back.

'George Sturt. From the village of Goudhurst in Kent?'

'I said yes . . .'

The bonnet monkey took exception to his tone and chattered angrily.

'What of it?'

Credentials verified, the rain-damp cripple inclined in Sturt's direction. 'I got a message for you,' he breathed.

Alongside the jetty, the *Swift* bobbed high in the water snapping tight fore and aft painters. The tide was on the turn, and under the anxious eye of Captain Johnstone, the dragoon officer ushered his troops aboard. Within minutes the cutter would be creaming across the wide expanse of Poole harbour and Kingsmill would be out of reach.

'Try and stop them, Henry.' Sturt turned to Fairbrother. 'Get Milner down there – drag him out by the ears if you have to.'

Both men were running before Sturt had entered the narrow passageway between Fleet's place and the shipwright's premises. Instinctively, a hand dropped to his pistol butt.

'Cobby?' he called softly.

Angry voices drifted up from the quay as he moved into the shadows.

'Over here.'

The free trader appeared from behind a pile of empty fish baskets stacked in the smelliest recess of the alley. Wet through and frightened, he stopped six or seven feet short. Sturt covered the distance in one and grabbed him by the scruff.

'Where were you?'

'Kingsmill don't trust no one! I couldn't get away – '

Sturt's grip tightened, but something moved behind the baskets. A kick sent them flying and he dragged John Dimer into the open. Foxed legless, oblivious to his predicament, he threw an arm around Sturt's shoulder and smiled.

'It's all right,' Cobby said quickly. 'He don't know if it's day or night.'

'Who is he?'

'John Dimer.'

The name half-registered, the face meant nothing.

'We was sent to fix a busted cart.'

Juniper vomit erupted from mouth and nostril. Sturt dropped his captive like a hot cinder.

'Got a thirst for two,' said Cobby, watching his companion flounder in his own mess. 'Cost me damn near two shillin's to get him in that state.'

'When?'

The smuggler edged out of reach. 'Tomorrow night. Call out is one o'clock.'

'Where?'

Dimer groaned and retched again.

'My family?'

'Safe,' said Sturt. 'Where?'

'You'll not go back on your word – '

The heel of Sturt's hand caught him squarely in the chest and he bounced off the clapboard wall.

'Where?'

'East Dorset . . .' Cobby wheezed, racked by the pain in his bruised sternum. 'Horse Rock Bay.'

Sturt was almost back in the street when he stopped. 'Pick him up,' he said. 'And get yourselves back.'

'Back!' Cobby grasped his arm. 'I've done my share! You promised . . .'

'If you go missing, they'll know.'

'How do I explain that?' He pointed to Dimer. 'Kingsmill will kill me!'

'You convinced him once – do it again.'

'I can't . . .' The crack in his voice was a manifestation of overwhelming despair.

Sturt tore free. 'A prison hulk is a death trap. Hundreds die before they ever reach the colonies.'

The saddest of sounds escaped Cobby's lips, only to be carried away on the night wind. The past two days had been the worst of his life. Time and again his world had threatened to split apart at the seams but, sustained by the illusion that having betrayed his friends Sturt would release him and his family, he had managed to hold himself together – just. Now the bubble had burst. Death and destruction crowded in and he seemed to shrink a little.

Sturt reached out. This time, the touch was reassuring, the tone deceptively easy. 'Do it and I'll see you slip away on the beach. No one need ever know. I give you my word.'

The last vestige of resistance was gone. Tired and despirited, Cobby righted his stinking companion and guided him out of the alley.

A month ago, Sturt would have been incapable of inflicting such misery, even on the likes of Cobby. For an instant, he despised himself but the commotion on the jetty prevented further analysis of his declining sensibility. Arms twisted up his back by a pair of burly troopers, Kemp was being frogmarched down the gangway. He fell on his face and Sturt ran, spurred on by the knowledge that the balance had again shifted in his favour.

Kemp picked himself up as Sturt barged past the soldiers. He sprinted up the gangway and faced the dragoon

124

commander. 'I know where it's to be, Major.' Try as he might, he could not contain his excitement. 'Hold off until tomorrow and the Hawkhurst Gang are yours for the taking.'

To any soldier with an ounce of initiative it was an irresistible opportunity, but independent thought had never been Jonathan Eachard's strong point. What modest progression he had made in the Service had been due to his blinkered devotion to duty, his unquestioning willingness to obey orders, however trivial or distasteful.

'I presume, sir, that I am addressing George Sturt?' The look was one normally reserved for beggars and urchins.

'You are.'

'I take my orders from the Collector, Sturt, not you.' The words seemed to fall off the end of his nose. 'And my orders are to sail.' He turned his back. 'Carry on, sir.'

The *Swift*'s captain was on his way when Sturt pressed his pistol to the officer's temple. Eighteen years in the army had brought him into contact with more Major Eachards than he cared to remember. Bitter experience told him that rational argument would be a waste of breath.

'Order your men to stack their muskets.' He glanced at the captain. 'You too.'

The pursuit of profit was Ashley Johnstone's driving force; heroic gestures he happily left to others. A nod to the bos'n and the crew threw their weapons into the hold. Eachard radiated disgust, but something was happening on the jetty and his attention drifted. Too late, Sturt remembered the troopers. A look of triumph swept Eachard's humourless features as his men prepared to shoot. Annoyed with himself for making such a basic mistake, Sturt turned sideways to the marksmen thereby reducing the target area. Nevertheless, he braced himself for a shot that was never fired. Eyes closed, Kemp launched himself at the soldiers and, as luck would have it, propelled them into the freezing water.

In a fit of pique, Sturt clipped Eachard's ear with his pistol, causing it to colour and swell. 'Do it!' he snapped.

All of a sudden the confrontation was over. Soldiers and

sailors filed ashore and mustered on the jetty. The cutter shifted, squashing rope fenders between hull and chiselled granite. The tide was ebbing fast; she'd be going nowhere for at least twelve hours.

Sturt prodded Eachard down the gangway as Milner and Fairbrother came running. Behind them, a pair of Mother Ashton's least tainted charges left the Custom House, grateful for an early night.

A clap of thunder drowned the steady beating of the rain. Powder from his sodden foretop streaked the front of Milner's coat starchy white. Fairbrother hung back as the angry Collector bearded Sturt.

'You'd better be damned sure!'

Fifty pairs of eyes swivelled in Sturt's direction.

'Tomorrow night,' he said, shoving the pistol back into his belt. 'Horse Rock Bay.'

He did not wait for Milner's response. The tension had slackened and fatigue finally breached his defences. He was bone tired and it was time to sleep.

Chapter 11

At first light it was still raining, but the temperature had risen to an acceptable six above freezing. Sturt rose soon after ten and shook Fairbrother fifteen minutes later. By eleven, Milner, Kemp and Eachard had formulated a plan of action. By half-past, Sturt and Fairbrother had given their approval and time was starting to drag. By mid-afternoon, every possible contingency had been exhausted, and the remaining daylight hours were passed in silent contemplation of the bloody business to come.

In Ringwood, Kingsmill slept even later than Sturt, not breaking his fast until midday. The afternoon he spent resting, conserving energy, wallowing in self-pity. News of Sturt's death had brought no peace. He'd been cheated again. Frustration and a sense of helpless outrage tormented him. Memories beyond that night at the river sprang to life. Thick and fast, stinging images tumbled through his mind, overlapping, dissolving one into another. Moments of youthful innocence, of security, friendship and trust. Brief years of happiness destroyed when that same special friendship was betrayed before the advancing keepers.

Dusk brought the Chichester Gang, and the realization that moving their share of the cargo back to Hawkhurst would have to wait for an improvement in the weather. Killing time on Fairall's ground did not appeal, and three hours later Kingsmill felt far from easy as Robert Lamb helped him into his greatcoat.

'Two days should see the highways passable, less if the Lord blesses us with a southerly blow.'

Kingsmill did not share the Magistrate's optimism. 'It was never part of the plan, Robert.' Buttoned up, he wrapped a coarse wool muffler about his face.

'Neither was the second coming of the Flood,' said Lamb, handing him his hat and opening the door. 'The carts would bog down before you were past Southampton Water – we'd lose every bag and cask.'

'It leaves too much in Fairall's hands.'

'The farm is safe, Thomas.'

Kingsmill paused. 'You can't be sure of that, he's the Shepherd's man.'

Lamb glanced at ninety armed riders waiting in the torchlit yard and lowered his voice. 'Fairall thinks that he's his man . . .' Dettingen cocked hat bumped plain as he moved closer to Kingsmill. 'With debtors' prison staring me in the face, I can't afford any unnecessary risks.'

An overpowering smell of bad fish intruded. The Magistrate buried his nose in a bag of dried herbs. Kingsmill took his reins from Dimer and climbed into the saddle.

'And if it's any consolation,' Lamb mumbled, 'the good Shepherd has no desire to extend the association either.'

Kingsmill looked straight at his rival. 'It isn't!'

Blazing pitch sent plumes of oily smoke curling into the night sky. Long shadows danced up the walls, slid over the rooftops like cats on the hunt. No one moved. No one spoke. All felt the tension. Kingsmill paused at the head of the column. Anticipation, always worse than the event, gripped every man. Indulgent thoughts of home nurtured the doubts, provoked a dozen silent appeals for courage to the Almighty.

So strongly did that momentary spell hold them that nobody noticed the rider until he entered the yard. It was Jackson waiting by the lead cart who saw him first and called out. The tone rather than the warning itself shook Kingsmill from his introspection. He turned as his men broke ranks, clearing a path for the exhausted intruder. Clots of phosphorescent white mud clung to his coat and steam rose from the gelding's matted flanks, giving the impression that man and beast were about to catch fire. So threatening was his presence that even Kingsmill's heart missed a beat.

Jonas Cobby's jammed in his throat.

He'd recognized the rider and was desperately forcing his way through the crush when Dimer's shrill voice echoed around the yard.

'God preserve us all!' he wailed. 'It's the ghost of Harry Sheerman!'

Man or spectre, the name meant nothing to Fairall. 'Who's Harry Sheerman?' he asked.

'Shut up, Shepherd!' breathed Lamb, standing on tiptoe to get a better look.

'It's a trap, Thomas . . .' Sheerman pulled on the reins and his mount stopped for the first time since leaving Rye. 'Cobby's turned you in to save his own hide.'

Kingsmill did not move. The pulse in his neck quickened as adrenalin surged through his veins. Even so, begging the question that mattered, his voice remained calm, betraying nothing. 'And Sturt?'

Sheerman nodded. 'Alive. And waiting on you to show your face.'

Relief struck with the force of a hammer blow. Kingsmill gripped his horse's mane. A sigh of deepest pleasure escaped his lips and carried on the wind. Self-control regained, he stood in his stirrups and scanned the multitude of faces staring at him.

'I seen him, master' – Dimer waved an arm in the general direction of Southampton – 'Slidin' out the back – makin' for the woods . . .'

A furlong from safety, Cobby twisted in the saddle and discharged his pistol. More by luck than judgement, the ball ripped into living tissue and a horse went down, taking three or four others with it. Sixty yards of pitted highway was now the difference between sweet life and extinction. Once amongst the trees, Cobby knew it would take an army to root him out. He gave the grey her head but, sliding and stumbling in the mud, she could not get into her stride. A yawning pot, a jolting peck, and his horsemanship was tested to the limit. Fear kept him on her back, gave him the strength to lift her from her knees as Jackson and Smoaker Mills broke free of the mêlée and resumed the chase. Both men fired. Instinctively Cobby ducked but the balls dropped short.

He laughed out loud. 'Too late!' he cried. 'Too late!' Nothing but Divine intervention would stop him now.

The rider emerging from the trees cut short his premature celebration. At first he thought he'd been outflanked, but the face – unmistakably female – said otherwise. Then it struck him. Mollie! His spirits rose – it was the only logical explanation. She must have slipped away from Goudhurst and come looking for her man. Come to guide him safe home ... But there was a flaw in his reasoning. The set of the jaw was strong where Mollie's was weak; the mouth sensuously wide, not thin and well-organized. Suddenly, the world spun off its axis and the earth rose up to meet him.

Hannah Payne had timed her move to perfection. Waiting until the very last moment, she'd turned her mount broadside on and barged the grey clean off the highway. Clutching his ricked knee, Cobby dragged himself to his feet and leaned against a tall beech. His dash for freedom was over. The grey mare thrashed in the mud, legs hopelessly tangled in her reins. Half-crippled, unable to run or hide, Jonas Cobby unsheathed his hanger. Pain and terror filled his eyes with tears but he refused to let them run. He was angry; deeply ashamed of informing against his friends, of inflicting such misery on the family he loved, so determined to die with what dignity he could muster. He also knew that token resistance would provoke instant retribution, and hopefully a clean finish.

Jackson seemed to confirm as much as he bore down, cutlass raised. The Widow stood back, leaving him room to work. One slashing blow and Cobby's blade shattered. The second would have cleaved his skull but Kingsmill held it with a shout.

Denied even the small mercy of a quick death, Cobby's resistance crumbled. He slid to the ground and wept. Great shuddering sobs racked his frame as Jackson and Mills dragged him back towards the inn.

Kingsmill waited in the yard; expression rigid, eyes glittering like those of a predatory animal. Cobby fell at his feet and curled up, a grotesque caricature of some foetal creature rudely ripped from the womb. Unnoticed, the Widow dismounted and stood close by. Behind her, the mob was baying for blood.

Kingsmill squatted on his heels and spoke disarmingly softly. 'Jonas . . .'

Cobby looked up. His tear-streaked face contorted as obscene images sprang from the bowels of his once innocent imagination. The protracted agonies of unspeakable disease, the eye bursting stricture of a hemp cravat, the universal terror of not knowing what lay beyond the grave – at that moment, the leader of the Hawkhurst Gang embodied them all. And more. In one respect, he was worse than death itself. The Reaper was at least impartial when gathering his sad harvest. Thomas Kingsmill was chillingly selective, taking sadistic, almost sexual, pleasure in destroying those who dared to oppose him.

Courage and dignity gone, Cobby pissed in his breeches. 'Please . . .' he said, voice barely audible above the din.

Kingsmill shuffled a little closer. 'Will he be there – at the bay?'

Like a chastened child, Cobby dropped his eyes. 'Yes.'

'And soldiers?'

'Yes.' His supper was rising in his gullet so Cobby swallowed hard, then made a last desperate attempt to save himself. 'I swear to God I'd have said nothing' – Kingsmill stood up and turned away – 'but he's got my family, Thomas – waiting on transportation!'

Jackson lashed out with his boot. 'I say stretch the scroat's neck and be done with him!'

'No!' snapped Kingsmill. 'He goes with us.' Ignoring Cobby's screaming protestation, he suddenly started to chuckle; gently at first, then progressively louder until his whole body was seized by a fit of humourless laughter.

Fairall shoved Jackson aside and grabbed Kingsmill's sleeve. 'For Christ's sake,' he said, 'that bastard almost had us in the gallows cart!'

Kingsmill tore loose. Blows were imminent when Robert

131

Lamb squeezed between them. 'Now, Thomas,' he said nervously, 'take hold of yourself . . .'

Kingsmill cupped the Magistrate's bloated face in his hands. 'Robert, it's perfect!' He beamed. 'He'll be there waiting – expecting us on the beach.' Again, he laughed. 'His trap will be sprung all right – but not quite as he planned it!'

'The Devil it will!' said Fairall.

Lamb bobbed out of harm's way as Kingsmill gripped his rival by the collar and slammed him against the stable door. 'You'll do as I say!' he snarled.

Younger and stronger, Fairall twisted free. 'I'll not put my neck in a noose so's you can settle an old grudge!'

Both reached for their blades.

'Richard is right, Thomas.' Hannah Payne stepped out of the crowd. 'Sturt is your private business. Right now the cargo comes first.'

For a moment, neither man moved. Then, in one smooth action, Kingsmill drew and raised his hanger. 'Damn you to Hell!' he roared.

'I wouldn't advise it.' Something in Fairall's tone made him pause. Slowly, Kingsmill turned and looked around the yard. A dozen muskets were aimed at his head. Forty more ensured that Jackson and the rest could do nothing but bear silent witness to an execution – should his desire for vengeance override his instinct for survival.

Chapter 12

Sturt saw the cormorant as it turned the eastern headland. It put down on the rocks beyond the surf and, stretching its wings, began to preen. Something was wrong. Soldiers and civilians all felt it, but each wanted someone else to say so. Perched on the exposed promontory since a half after twelve, it had been a miserable two hours. Offshore, huge waves were crashing onto the natural limestone breakwater. Directly below, the tide was ebbing and sand spirals etched crazy patterns on the empty beach.

'Nowt on the road,' Kemp said softly. 'No sign of a ship neither.' He sat down and Milner shot bolt upright. Pummelling a cramped leg, the Collector looked at Eachard.

The officer shook his head and stood up. 'The least we can do is take a look,' he said. Fairbrother turned to Sturt, who narrowed his eyes against the wind and said nothing.

Ten minutes later, he made his way down the winding track. On the beach, dragoons and excisemen scurried back and forth, grateful for the chance to stretch their limbs.

'Nothing!' snapped Eachard.

'Chamber Cove,' said Milner.

Kemp nodded. 'Be runnin' it ashore this minute.' He looked at Sturt, who turned on his heel and started up the headland.

Milner clattered after him. 'It's chasing shadows! They'll be long gone . . .'

Sturt kept climbing. 'We've bugger all else to do!'

'George?'

He stopped.

Fairbrother was at the water's edge, staring out to sea with a young trooper. 'Over here!' he yelled.

'Gash from some passing merchantman,' said the soldier.

'I don't think so.' Fairbrother pulled off his boots and waded into the sea. Ten yards out, he recognized it as a

133

half-anker cask; at twenty yards, he realized that it was fixed, tethered to something under the water. A seventh wave lapped above his crotch and took his breath away. Paddling with his hands, he was almost there when he stubbed a toe and cried out.

'John?' Sturt called from the beach. 'What is it?'

As if by prior arrangement, the last of the cloud cover raced towards the horizon. Pain forgotten, Fairbrother stood motionless, peering into the murky water, waiting for the sand to settle. What he'd kicked was a short wooden post. Tied to it was a bootless foot.

Fairbrother shifted his gaze. 'Sweet Jesus . . .' he murmured.

Pale lit by a waning moon, Jonas Cobby's sightless eyes stared up at him. Securely staked out, gagged with his own stock, he had heard them high on the headland, torn his wrists to shreds trying to attract their attention. Then, as the incoming tide washed over him, he'd died – silently screaming, railing against the injustice of it all.

And Chamber Cove it was. Evidence of the Gang's presence was scattered about the beach; boot and hoofprints, a carelessly discarded short hemp, a pile of still warm horse dung. Unfortunately, the bridleway leading down to the cove had been churned to a quagmire. Tracking was out of the question. Sturt knew it and had not even bothered to look. Inwardly he was raging. A unique opportunity had been squandered – and how Kingsmill had found out remained a mystery. The thought occured to Sturt that perhaps he had demanded too much of the luckless Cobby. He pushed it aside. Cobby was a fool – he could not be held responsible . . .

Dawn was fast approaching when Henry Kemp struck flint on steel. Burning pitch roared in the wind. He crouched at the roadside and examined the grassy verges where they had turned the carts. From the ruts, he estimated at least a dozen, all fully laden. Admiration for the audacity and skill of his former comrades was unreserved until his attention was taken by one imprint in particular. Kemp stuck his torch in the moist earth and fingered the groove. There was something missing . . . An oak splinter drew blood and the answer dropped into place. Sucking the wound clean, he leapt to his feet. They were fallible after all!

Sturt was silhouetted against the eastern sky. The impression was of unnatural size, as if he and his shadow had grown together. Hunched in the saddle, he not only seemed to be shouldering the cares of the world but, like a judge or hangman, carried the smell of death with him.

Kemp hesitated. The implications of his discovery were stark and uncompromising. If he was right, Jonas Cobby would not be the night's only casualty.

It was Martha Pett who opened the door. Hearing the horses, fearing the worst, Gilbert had slipped into the yard and made a run for it. Breathless, he paused behind the byre. There were soldiers everywhere. His only chance was to reach the wood and seek sanctuary with his sister in Dartmouth. Inching past the sty, he startled a sleeping sow and blundered into the vegetable plot with two troopers in pursuit.

Outside the house, Martha appealed to Major Eachard. 'Please, sir,' she said, 'don't hurt him – he ain't got the wherewithal to damage no one!'

And that was the truth: for all his niggling faults, Gilbert Pett was neither malicious nor dangerous. Somewhere beyond the late crop of potatoes, a shot was fired and a man cried out.

Kemp turned his back as Martha flew at him.

'Judas!' she sobbed. 'I hope you burn in the fires of Hell!'

A riding officer dragged her off and bundled her back into the house.

Kemp crossed the yard and stared miserably at Pett's cart. He kicked the rimless rear wheel. Proved right, he felt no pleasure. The Petts he'd known for twenty-odd years, and though not exactly close, they were more than acquaintances. A distant shriek made him wince. The old man was paying a high price for driving Hawkhurst goods.

John Fairbrother called from the barn. A quick look

135

inside confirmed that, in one respect, the ex-smuggler had been mistaken. Pett was not just a driver for Kingsmill – his barn was packed to the rafters with run goods. Every tub and dollop, all the wads and lace from the *Three Brothers* were neatly stacked amongst the hay and stored apples.

A sense of euphoria reverberated around the ancient building. Dragoons whooped and cheered, riding officers laughed and jigged. Milner breathed a sigh of relief. He would go down in history as the first exciseman to take a cargo from Thomas Kingsmill. Promotion was assured.

The celebrations left Kemp cold. Looking from face to face, he saw only greed. Each man was already spending his share of the booty, amd he felt tainted by what he'd done. A hand touched him lightly on the shoulder.

'Go home, Henry.' Fairbrother nodded in Milner's direction. 'He doesn't need you now.'

Outside, the light of day hurt his eyes and Kemp shielded them with an arm.

Across the yard, Sturt stood alone with his thoughts. He'd stopped believing in God a long time ago. Over the years, what had carried him through his bleakest moments was a deep-rooted sense of natural justice. An occasional spark of human compassion; a sometimes obscure, but always present, balance between good and evil kept a semblance of order during that passage of time between birth and death; provided a yardstick with which a man might measure his true worth. As of that precise moment, George Sturt no longer believed in anything. Like Jonas Cobby, he had realized too late that there was no justice in a world dominated by Thomas Kingsmill and his kind.

He mounted up as a dying old man was carried back to the house in which he had been born.

Hannah Payne stepped over the comatose figure of Smoaker Mills and made her way downstairs. Earlier tensions had evaporated. Goodwill and geneva flowed freely as the Hawkhurst and Chichester Gangs celebrated their triumph in style. To the tortured strains of a three-stringed fiddle, Jackson blundered about the floor with the Red Lion's prettiest serving girl. Richard Perrin sat quietly in a corner, absorbing Lamb's account of the battle of Goudhurst. Standing at the fire, Shepherd Fairall watched the Widow. Her presence had surprised and disturbed him. He'd done business at the White Hart for years, never realizing her connection with Kingsmill. Her explanation for being in Ringwood, keeping an eye on a personal investment in the cargo, had failed to convince. Running through his mind were countless morsels of information let slip during their more intimate moments. Names in particular: of investors, informers, tenants and owners of safe houses – all of whom could be of use to an ambitious rival. Easing through the crowd, she brushed his arm and was gone without a second glance. Refusing Jackson's drunken invitation to jig, she peered into the gloomy back parlour, nose twitching at the stench of fish.

'You'll find him outside Mistress Payne . . .' John Dimer shuffled into the light and took off his hat. 'Sitting all by himself, he is.'

He was about to show her where when she blatantly looked him up and down. Blushing like a boiled crab, Dimer melted back into the shadows.

There was something about his fawning manner that set her teeth on edge.

Though the sun burned bright, the day was in sombre mood. A thinning ground mist chilled the air, leeched sparse winter colour from the wooded landscape. No birds sang as Hannah Payne crossed the cobbles. Beyond the stable, Kingsmill sat still and bent, a grey shape beneath a twisted, shadowless yew. He did not hear her. He saw nothing but the smooth metal object in the palm of his hand. The Widow stopped and watched from a safe distance.

A tiny muscle flickered above his right eye, the only indication of the turmoil within. Every fibre of his being screamed Injustice. He'd been cheated again. Fairall, Circumstance, the World – all had conspired to rob him of the chance to settle with Sturt. Despair erupted in a futile, violent gesture. Springing upright, he hurled Sturt's silver-cased timepiece against the brew-house wall. Lashing out

137

with both feet, he scattered the fragments about the yard; then, frenzy subsiding, dropped heavily to his knees.

Hannah Payne turned and walked back to the inn. Soft words and comforting gestures had no place in Kingsmill's world just then. And she knew better than to risk her health for no good reason.

Chapter 13

Dawn broke dry and clear. Three days without rain and the highways were again passable to coach and cart. Kingsmill was anxious to be on his way home and despatched a rider to warn Gilbert Pett of their imminent departure.

Two hours later, that messenger traversed the skyline at a dangerous canter and dropped down to the narrow track that led back to Ringwood. His mount stumbled into a deep rut, almost unseating him. He slowed to a trot. After all, there was no rush. The damage was done and the news he was carrying would be about as welcome as a papist in Canterbury. His mind ran in circles. He believed Martha Pett, yet he didn't believe what had happened. It couldn't have been Cobby, so how had they known? Perhaps there was another informer . . . He shook his head and hawked into the carpet of browning chestnut leaves. Thinking was down to others, his brain couldn't cope with any more. And anyway, there were matters of more immediate, personal concern. He was merely the bearer of bad news but, considering his master's current state of mind, that guaranteed him no protection at all.

A stinging blow with the whip caused his mare to kick and rear. As he entered the Forest, Harry Sheerman called down every curse and blasphemy he knew and wished them on the meddlesome bastards who'd stolen their cargo.

Behind him, a greatcoated horseman slithered recklessly down the hillside anxious lest he lose sight of his quarry.

Getting a man back into bed had never required such an effort. After Sheerman had gone, her ingenuity had been taxed almost to its limit. But . . . She smiled, smug as a Cheshire cat, and slid further down the bed. Lying next to a sleeping lover, exercising the senses, was one of life's great pleasures. She listened to his breathing, easy and

139

relaxed, so different from normal. Curled up on his side, only the back of head and neck were visible. She burrowed into the thick black hair and traced his vertebrae with the tip of her tongue. He tasted salt sharp and made her mouth water. He shifted. She shifted onto her back and inhaled the sweetest of smells. Fingertips danced over those cool delights resting soft and mobile on his thigh. He sighed and she felt her muscles tighten.

'Thomas?'

The snort was hardly in keeping with the mood.

'I've told the Shepherd to load my tubs with yours.'

It took a moment but her words finally penetrated. Kingsmill rolled over and looked at her.

'I'll ride as far as Cadnam with you.'

He shook his head. 'With William and Richard, not me.' He wriggled up the bed, avoiding the soggy patch between them. 'Sturt is still in Poole.'

'Has he been seen?'

'No. But he's there or thereabouts.'

The Widow lifted onto her elbows and the counterpane fell away, revealing her breasts. Kingsmill's head dropped. His mouth searched for a nipple but she seized him by the ears. 'How do you know?'

He shook free. 'Take my word, he'll be looking for me.'

Turning to face him, she sat back on her heels. A slap discouraged quick fingers. 'If you stay here, Fairall will kill you.'

He shook his head. 'He'll help me.'

'Into the grave, he will.'

'It's in his interest.'

She inclined towards him. 'How?'

'The run was a success...' He reached out and she twisted away. 'But, until our business is done, Sturt remains a threat.'

'To you. He has no quarrel with the Shepherd.'

'The Shepherd is greedy. His share of the cargo won't satisfy him for long. He'll want more – and that will give him a personal interest in my well-being.'

140

He made a grab. This time, she was a fraction too slow and he pinned her down.

Unable to move, she glared up at him. 'The cargo wasn't all he wanted!'

He laughed, mocking her clumsy attempt to distract him, then clamped his mouth to hers. Anticipating resistance, he wedged a leg between her knees but they opened and she drew him to her. Fingernails raked his lean back, etched strawberry furrows from waist to thigh as he entered. The Widow hooked her heels around his calves and gripped him.

'Or got,' she breathed.

True or false the thought had registered, the image had been conjured. Kingsmill shrank inside her, and she squeezed him out like a grape pip.

'Mornin', Sergeant.'

'Private Bootie . . .'

Fairbrother's hand froze on the Custom House doorknob. 'How on earth did you know?'

A broken-toothed grin split the cripple's face. 'A blind man soon gets to recognize a friendly footfall. But I ain't no private no more.' He fingered the triple chevron on his sleeve.

'Of course.' Fairbrother moved towards him, taking care not to step on the monkey. 'And if I may say so, the rank does foster a certain elegance.'

'Keeps the chill off me chest, if that's what you mean.'

'Philistine!' Fairbrother opened the door.

'Sergeant?'

He stopped.

Bootie held up a golden guinea. 'Found it in a pocket – stitched to the linin'. Reckon you must have forgot about it.'

Fairbrother looked into the dead eyes. In his time, he too had faced death and maiming more often than he cared to remember. Yet somehow he'd survived intact. Raised in a devoutly Christian home, he believed in God – up to a point. Luck was what it boiled down to and, to date, his had always been good.

'It belongs with the tunic,' he said. 'Put it back now, before some urchin steals it.'

The clerk's office was empty when Fairbrother entered but a candle lantern burned inside the dingy strong-room, and cast two long shadows through the open door.

'I counted them myself, Peckover,' one said angrily. 'Last night!'

The other hunched its shoulders, as a man might against a cold wind. 'Then you was likely tired,' it whined. 'Easy to make mistakes when you is fatigued, sir.'

The shadows moved away and Fairbrother looked in. The room was piled from floor to ceiling with Kingsmill's contraband. A narrow gangway separated dry goods from spirits, and he watched Milner's clerk back into a pile of tubs.

The Collector towered over him. 'There were one hundred and twenty-six tubs of cognac!'

Archibald Peckover struggled to keep his feet. 'With respect, sir, one hundred and twenty-two – '

The stack collapsed beneath his weight and the aged quill-pusher rolled down the gangway on four-gallon wheels, taking the legs from under his master for good measure.

'Good morning, James.' Fairbrother's intervention saved Peckover a beating.

'John . . .' Milner retrieved wig and dignity. 'I was about to call on you.'

'Dekker.' Fairbrother said. 'I've just seen him at Fleet's Coffee House.'

Milner dusted the seat of his velvet breeches and opened the door to his office. Fairbrother looked at Peckover, who was all ears in the corner.

'One hundred and twenty-six,' said Milner. 'I suggest you count them again.'

The clerk waited a full minute before moving. Satisfied that they were not coming back, he carefully unbolted the

142

side door and handed four tubs of brandy to the youth waiting in the alley.

'They're at the Red Lion in Ringwood – Kingsmill, Fairall, perhaps forty others.' The Collector sat behind his desk and beamed. 'We have them by the throat, John!'

'Dekker saw Kingsmill – in person?'

'At an upstairs window with some jaded whore.'

The pulse in Fairbrother's neck beat faster. 'We'll wait for the London escort.'

'The Devil we will!'

'Eachard's troops would not last five minutes in a direct confrontation.'

Milner toyed with his sand-shaker. He didn't have the experience to argue the point, and knew it. 'And I thought George was the cautious one,' he said.

'He is.'

'Yet he's gone off to Goudhurst knowing full well that Kingsmill is close to hand.'

Fairbrother went to the window and perched on the ledge.

'I lied to him.' He held the exciseman's gaze. 'I told him that one of your riding officers observed them last night, beyond Havant, riding east.'

'And he took your word – without verifying the facts with me?'

'In twelve years, he's never once had cause to doubt my word.'

Bootie's monkey jumped up at the window, fogging bottle-thick pane with yellow breath.

'Mary Winchcombe's sister is getting wed. It's important to the family that George is there. And . . .'

The primate flattened its face against his fingers.

'He feels he owes them for her death. Even so, I had to twist an arm up his back.'

'I feel sorry for him.'

'He wouldn't thank you for it.'

'The man lives for nothing but killing Thomas Kingsmill.'

Milner rose and, though still early in the day, poured two

glasses of Madeira. 'Correct me if I am wrong, John, but I suspect that he was a fine soldier.'

The cloying sweet liquor slid down Fairbrother's gullet.

'Hard on his men and harder on himself. By reputation, he was an over-zealous disciplinarian, but in forty-one engagements his section sustained fewer casualties than any other in the regiment. Exceptional best describes his qualities.'

'With discipline the key to his success.'

'Probably. I've never really thought about it.'

'And now he's lost control.'

Fairbrother drained his glass. The young Collector was beginning to irritate. Even so, he resisted the temptation to put him in his place – perhaps because he knew he was right.

'Exceptional, he might have been, but his actions now are not rational. He wants Kingsmill regardless of cost, to himself or others.'

'And should he, by some miracle, succeed, you stand to gain more than anyone.'

'I make no secret of it,' Milner said quietly. 'Chasing the dregs of Hampshire from one miserable bay to another is not how I intend to eke out my days. Nevertheless, it gives me no pleasure to see a man like Sturt tear the living flesh from his bones simply to slake a thirst for revenge – justified as it may be.'

Fairbrother refilled his glass. 'I beg your pardon, James.'

'He's your friend; were he mine, I'd defend him with equal vigour.'

The Harrison long-case struck ten. Outside, Riding Officer Dekker passed by, en route for a bed and someone else's wife. An awful thought occurred to Fairbrother.

'Kemp,' said the Collector, anticipating his question. 'I sent him to keep watch the minute Dekker reported back.'

Fairbrother returned to his seat at the window; the lad was learning fast.

'A few basic precautions would not go amiss,' he said.

'Such as?'

144

'Extra patrols between here and the New Forest. A guard outside, doubled at night, just in case.'

'What are you expecting – a frontal assault?'

'They did it in Goudhurst.'

'And got their knuckles well rapped!'

Milner joined him and looked out at his jetty, his cutter, his harbour. No doubt about it, he liked being the King's Collector, albeit temporarily. A flash of well-pressed scarlet caught his eye as the bonnet monkey led Bootie into the weak winter sun now warming the Custom House veranda.

'Your old regiment?'

Fairbrother nodded. 'He served nine years – before my time.'

'What happened to him?'

'He didn't say. I didn't presume to ask.'

For a moment, neither man spoke. A familiar tightening in the pit of the stomach was nagging Fairbrother, dampening his natural high spirits. Worry and doubt reflected in his expression.

'Do you think it's contagious?' asked Milner.

He didn't understand.

'George's obsession,' explained the collector. 'His jaundiced evaluation of the human race.'

'Only as far as Thomas Kingsmill is concerned.' Fairbrother put his glass on the desk and crossed the room. 'The Army develops a suspicious mind, James. If you are lucky, it's what keeps you alive.'

Milner opened the door for him.

'Call it an old soldier's professional jitters, or what you will. I just have a nasty feeling.'

Becky Glover's cheeses teetered precariously on top of the ham hocks boiled to perfection by Sal Diprose. They, in turn, threatened to overbalance the still steaming joints of beef that Lizzie Edge had been roasting since dawn. Bending beneath them all was Edward Winchcombe. Inwardly cursing wasted biceps, he twitched like a hanging day rope walker whilst struggling to counter the natural law of gravity. Had he been able to move the task would have been easier. However, one violent movement and he knew that the beast would be out of the alley and halfway to Rye before he could blink.

'Tread softly, boy, don't frighten him.' Bristled chin wedged Becky's cheeses tight against his chest. 'Easy now. Easy . . .'

Alan Wynter squeezed past the old man and slid into the narrow passageway where he loomed menacingly over the troublesome creature. Pin-bright eyes stared up at him. One pale ear flapped forward, giving the impression that it needed mending. Like bare-knuckle fighters, man and quadruped weighed each other's weaknesses. For one, it was a matter of life and death; for the other, a niggling irritation on an already bad day.

The softest of grunts presaged a dash for freedom. Alan stopped breathing. It would be one grab with no second chance. Nerves tight as a drumskin, he prepared to strike.

'Don't go bruisin' 'im,' nagged Edward.

He glanced at his prospective father-in-law, bending ever lower under the weight of his burden.

'Cop 'old! Cop 'old!'

Concentration in tatters, Alan mistimed his lunge.

Squealing fit to burst, the piglet shot through his legs and was off down the hill while he was still snatching at thin air.

'You bungling donkey!' yelled Edward. 'You'll run all the fat off of 'im!'

'Then you should try coppin' 'old yourself – 'stead of standing there blowing off and doing nothing! As usual!'

Words almost failed the old man, but not quite.

'Get after 'im!'

Alan avoided the clumsy kick.

'And show some respect, you ain't family yet!' The echo of his voice died away and the old man fell silent.

A combination of thinning mist and soft morning light played cruel tricks on failing eyes. Peter Glover, Tom Austin, even George Kingsmill and his dead cronies, seemed to appear and disappear as Alan sprinted crazily down the hill. A lump rose in Edward's throat. The hairs on the back of his neck stood up and he turned, as if to acknowledge a shouted greeting from a friend.

Squinting into the sun, he looked up at the church. Was it or was it not Mary standing at the gate, smiling, waving at him? His arm rose involuntarily, and a cheese fell to the ground. She laughed. He was about to call her name when Alan's triumphant shout broke the spell. Clutching a hind trotter, the lad fell headlong and disappeared into the confines of Packer's alley.

'God preserve that porker,' muttered Edward as he tottered after them.

Concern deepened the closer he got, prompted by a third unidentifiable, definitely female, voice rising above the din.

Turning the corner, Edward stopped in his tracks. 'God preserve us all!' he breathed.

Alan, still holding the porker's leg, lay spreadeagled on top of a furious young woman who, not unnaturally, was doing her utmost to dislodge him. And with the pig wriggling like a demented eel, he was hard-pressed to protect himself from his victim's violent assault.

'Get your hands off me! You – you ham-fisted oaf!' she roared.

Edward quickly piled cheese and meat onto Ben Packer's doorstep.

'Beg pardon, mistress . . .' wailed Alan.

The pig twisted and shook itself.

The slap echoed like a pistol shot. 'Don't do that!'

'No offence meant . . .' Alan protected one ear from her two-fisted attack and tried to roll away. Unfortunately, every move he made, no matter how small, seemed to make things worse. A raised knee caused him further anguish, and loosened his grip on the trotter to boot.

In the nick of time, Edward seized the pig and proceeded to examine it, inch by inch, for damage.

Alan scrambled clear and, sure that he was out of range of flailing fists and feet, coddled his throbbing privates.

Dignity in shreds, the woman sat bolt upright and Edward finally recognized her.

'Sarah!' he cried. 'Sarah Shaddick!'

Wide green eyes flashed in his direction. 'Sarah Shaddick as was, Master Edward! Sarah Dimer now.'

Thrusting the pig at Alan, he helped her to regain her feet.

'I can't believe me eyes . . .' he said, beating the dust from her rump. 'You've filled out right handsome, Sarah!'

'You haven't changed at all!'

He sighed. 'Ten year slows a man down, if nowt else.'

She slapped his wrist. 'The ravages of time don't seem to have affected your hands much!'

She bent and gathered up the remnants of an impoverished bunch of wild flowers that she had been carrying before the collision.

'And it's twelve years, not ten.'

The broadest of smiles spread across Edward's face. 'It's a rare treat to see you again.'

Alan shuffled uncomfortably as she kissed the old man lightly on the cheek. He held the pig tighter and it bit him on the chin.

Straightening a crushed stem, Sarah said, 'They were all I could find. I picked them for Aunt Dorothy.'

'The whole village turned out for her. She was lucky Sarah, it were over right quick.'

'I didn't even know she was ailing.'

'Neither did we all, 'til the very last.'

Sarah lifted a faded dress from the mud while Edward retrieved a tattered collection of dog-eared papers and ancient parchments tied loosely together with hemp string.

'Her medicines book,' he said.

Sarah nodded. 'She left it to me, along with her best Sunday dress. And there was I, sure she'd given me up forever.'

'She missed your visits.'

Again those clear green orbs.

'She told me so,' he said.

'I missed them too.'

He squeezed her hand. 'What was it between you two? She never said.'

'Aunt Dorothy disapproved of my choice of husband. We

148

had a terrible fight before the wedding and she threw John out of her house.'

Edward waited for her to finish the story. 'And that was all?'

'Yes.'

The old man shook his head. 'I swear I'll never under-stand folk if I live to be a hundred!'

Alan coughed as loudly as he dared, silently beseeching Edward to clear his way and allow him to go.

'Get that porker home,' said the wheelwright, taking pity. 'And see he don't get loose again.'

'Yes, Master Edward. I'm sorry, Mistress . . .'

'Dimer.'

'Mistress Dimer. I didn't mean you no incon-venience . . .' Passing too close for comfort, he bobbed like a courting grebe then beat a limping retreat.

'And don't forget to come back for these here cheeses and things!' Edward grinned and offered his arm to Sarah. 'I'll walk with you.'

She took it and they walked slowly up the hill, attracting the occasional glance and comment from those villagers surprised to see her back in Goudhurst.

'You remember Joseph and Fanny Wynter?'

Sarah nodded. 'The house opposite Aunt Dorothy's. They died in a fire when I was little.'

'That's their lad Alan.' He opened the churchyard gate. 'A bit slow-witted, but he's God-fearing and honest enough.'

'For what?'

'He's marrying my Jan tomorrow.'

'Poor Jan!'

'He'll do.' Edward smiled. 'But don't you tell 'im I said so.'

They entered the graveyard and took a tortuous route between weather-worn tombstones.

'Sarah – you'll come to the wedding?'

'I don't think so.'

'Why ever not? Send for this no-good husband of yours, I'd like to cast an eye over him.'

149

Mischievous Edward might have been, malicious he was not. However, misinterpreting his suggestion, Sarah immediately went on the defensive.

'No!' she said, a little too sharply. 'That wouldn't be possible.' She relaxed slightly and explained. 'His work takes him off and about a lot.'

'Will he be waiting at home?'

'There's no one waiting at home.'

'Then you've no excuse! Stay over, we'd be right pleased.'

They had arrived at Dorothy Shaddick's freshly-filled grave. In the churchyard's quietest corner, adjacent to the four hundred year old yew, her last resting place was probably the most peaceful spot in Goudhurst.

A large earthworm glistened in the weak sunlight and burrowed easily into the loose soil, starting the inevitable process of decay. Soon, in the overall scale of things, Dorothy Shaddick would be no more than a memory to family and friends, and a small but vital component of the good Kent earth.

Sarah watched the tip of the worm's tail slip beneath the surface.

'I couldn't,' she said. 'I don't belong any more.'

'But you know everyone, girl . . .'

'They'll have forgotten me.'

'Nonsense!'

'Everyone but Mary and Jan then.'

The pause was infinitesimal.

'Mary's dead, Sarah.'

The weight of those terrible words, delivered in a flat, unemotional tone, made her physically stagger. The question screamed to be asked, but words evaded her.

'I thought you must have heard. Just about everyone in Kent seems to know.'

Sarah shook her head and leaned against a tall stone.

'I fancied you didn't want to talk about it, you and she being so friendly, like.'

His eyes settled on a fine new headstone close by. Sarah studied the roughly chiselled inscription which read 'MARY WINCHCOMBE. 1715–1747.' There was no hint of the

150

tragedy behind the fact, no public statement to fire the imagination of future generations resting tired legs on a hot Sunday afternoon. But somehow, that simple granite stone with its diagonal quartzite stripe seemed to embody the sadness of the world.

Sarah knelt down and fingered the letters. She did not move for some time. Childhood memories did not flood back. All she felt was pain; for Mary, for Edward and Jan, and for herself. Then, as the initial shock receded, nightmarish thoughts and images forced their way into her consciousness. She looked at Edward.

'How?' she asked.

'There were some trouble in the village, three week back – '

'The Hawkhurst Gang?'

Suddenly, the old man's control was going and the best he could manage was a brief nod of the head.

Sarah's tears were already flowing as she turned back. 'I didn't know,' she whispered. 'God forgive me, Mary – I didn't know!'

Laying her aunt's flowers on her friend's grave, Sarah Dimer sobbed her heart out. Deeply touched by her distress, Edward laid a hand gently on her shoulder, thought of Mary and George, then wept with her.

John Dimer was now cold, bored, and busting to know what was going on in there. He'd been sent to keep watch for passing Excise patrols, but that had been two hours since and no one had brought him so much as a jug of hot or bite of bread and dripping.

Squatting on numbed heels beneath the chestnut tree in the yard, he tossed gravel at the watch geese, taking particular delight in provoking the gander. Patience finally exhausted, the great bird lowered its head, thrashed the air with its wings and sent him packing.

His cries for help were ignored inside the inn, where the Hawkhurst and Chichester smugglers had split into their respective groups. The air was blue with tobacco smoke. No one spoke. And with the leadership conspicuously

151

absent, the atmosphere prickled with tension, threatening to boil over at any second. Someone coughed and forty heads turned. At the door, Sheerman sat with Jackson; while Mills stood by the fire with his close mates Dunne and Tapner. Each watched the others and strained to hear what was going on in the back parlour. For the most part, the muffled voices remained unintelligible though occasionally they rose excitedly and a few words or sentences could be gleaned.

At that moment, they reached an angry climax then fell completely silent.

After a brief interval, the door opened. Tight-lipped, Robert Lamb strode across the room and left by the front door.

No one moved. Sheerman looked at Jackson and raised an eyebrow. Kingsmill's lieutenant got up and entered the parlour where his master sat at the table with Fairall and Perrin.

'Well?' enquired Jackson cautiously.

All eyes turned to Kingsmill.

'We take it back,' he said.

Fairall stood up as the Widow appeared in the doorway. 'Lamb snaps his fingers and you jump to please!'

There was no response from Kingsmill so he continued. 'He takes his share of the profits all right and bleats when things foul up. The one thing he doesn't do is risk his own neck!' Pushing past the Widow, Fairall was on his way when a word from Kingsmill stopped him.

'If you haven't got the stomach,' he said, 'we'll do it without you and take your share as a bonus.'

'How?' demanded Fairall. 'They've got every last tub and dollop under lock and key in Poole Custom House. And when they move it, I'll wager there's more dragoons riding escort than you can shake a stick at!'

A charred log disintegrated in the hearth as he fisted the door, and sent a column of sparks rising to the blackened ceiling.

'When you've a half-way workable plan,' he said, 'let me know and I'll come running.'

This time he did go and the Widow crossed to the fire. 'Perhaps Sturt will give it back . . .' she said, 'as a favour to an old friend.'

Skilled as she was at teasing Kingsmill, there were times when she went too far. Perrin recognized this as one of them and stepped in before his master could rise to the goad.

'There may be a way, Thomas . . .'

Kingsmill eased back into his chair.

'It's risky,' continued the buyer, 'but they'll never expect it – and it just might catch them napping.'

Chapter 14

Edward had taken his time walking back to the house. With so many contradictory emotions in play, he was feeling his years and needed a moment to reflect. Scraping his boots on the step, he was half-listening to the industrious hum within when the door opened and Alan stepped out.

'Where are you slopin' off to?'

'The Bear.'

'That's what you think.'

'That's what I know!' said Alan, pulling on his jerkin. 'It's like a madhouse in there.'

As if to prove his point, a chorus of female voices rose another octave and sent him running for cover.

Edward was livid but lacked the energy to give chase.

'Come back here, you idle young scab!' he blustered impotently.

'No! I've had enough!' said Alan as he disappeared from view. 'I wish I'd joined the Army like George!'

Edward pushed open the door.

The kitchen presented a tableau of organized female chaos. Half a dozen village matrons were preparing and marshalling enough food and drink to provision a small army when Edward slipped into the room. Peering through steam and flour dust, he looked in vain for Jan and almost fell victim to a high-speed tray of honey tarts precariously balanced at the end of a large sticky woman he did not recognize. Dodging out of the way, he bobbed between mixing bowls and heaving bosoms until he found sanctuary on the stairs.

'I wish he'd joined the Army an' all!' he yelled to no one in particular.

Jan stood at the window gazing over the Weald. The countryside was buttoning down its topcoat for the winter

154

and it was the quiet time of year for the farming communities around Goudhurst. Apart from a handful of ewes, pregnant with next season's lambs, grazing in the high pastures, and cutters at work amongst the elms of Blackbush Wood, the landscape was at rest. Peaceful. A picture of rural normality, this was the world in which Jan had always felt happy and safe. A world with no place for the events of past months. Pehaps it was the wedding, perhaps it was just one of those days, but her natural ebullience was lying as dormant as the earth. Her father knew so at once and left his tetchy disposition out on the landing.

'I can have the horse and cart ready in ten minutes,' he said.

Jan started. 'I didn't hear you.'

'You could be off to Great-uncle Herbert's in Hastings before anyone missed you.'

'Don't!'

'Lots of folk change their mind at the last, you know. I'm sure the boy would understand.'

'If I considered it, even for a second, you'd kill me!'

Edward grinned. 'Try me and see.'

'Oh, father . . .'

Jan ran to him and buried her head in his chest. He held her tight and her hair caught in his beard.

'Tomorrow should have been our Mary's day,' said Jan, 'not mine.' She swallowed hard. 'I miss her!'

'I miss her too.'

'I miss her moaning and nagging at me. I miss her organizing and bossing us about. Day in and day out. I feel sick every time I think of her . . .'

'Yes,' said Edward. 'So do I.'

He swept the strands of hair from her face, then sat her on the bed. Taking her hand, he paused for a moment then started to speak in a soft, calm voice.

'When the smallpox took your mother, it seemed like the end of the world to me. We'd had just six year together, then . . . Nothing. There was you and Mary of course, but that made it so much harder. You see, every time I looked at either of you, all I saw was Elizabeth.'

155

One by one, a handful of rooks settled in the large copper outside the window and eavesdropped the conversation. Edward saw them and lowered his voice.

'I had this gun.'

He paused again. Deeply ashamed of the secret that he had kept for so long, he shifted his gaze away from his daughter.

'Your grandad's pistol, it was. And one day I sat down and decided to damn myself to Hell by doin' us all in.'

The baldness of the statement took Jan completely by surprise, but she said nothing.

Her father continued. 'But all I had were this rustin' old gun. So I sold our milk cow to Enoch Trickett, borrowed his nag and used the money to buy a brace of horse pistols down in Rye. You see, I couldn't face having to reload twice over.'

He leaned back against the wall and found the courage to look at her.

'That night, up in your bedroom with three loaded guns, I waited for you both to go to sleep. Mary was her usual organized self and went out like a snuffed candle. But you . . .'

He stroked her head.

'If it weren't wind at one end, it were wind at the other! I must have sat there two hour or more with you blowin' an' gruntin' fit to pop.'

Jan's cheeks flushed scarlet. It was true. Mary had always complained when they were children. And nowadays it was Alan. 'Go on,' she said, deeply embarrassed.

'I didn't even hear Dorothy Shaddick. She'd brung me a bit of supper, same as always, and come upstairs to find me with you over my shoulder and three primed horse pistols on the table.'

He shook his head.

'God knows what ran through her mind, but she put down my supper, picked up them pieces, and went without so much as a word.'

Taking a pipe from his pocket, Edward packed it with cheap tobacco.

156

'I didn't know what to do. The belly gripes got worse and you started screaming. Mary woke up. Nothing I did seemed to make no difference. By four in the morning I didn't know if I was coming or going . . .'

He paused.

'What I did know was that I was frightened to death that I was going to lose you too.'

He smiled.

'I didn't. Mary and me sat up all night and, somewhere around dawn, you managed the most almighty fart and dropped off there and then!'

He lit his pipe and drawing deep, felt the pungent smoke tear at the delicate tissue of nose and throat.

'We was so grateful we fell asleep where we sat. After that I reckoned I could cope with anything. Bringing you two up decent. Thomas Kingsmill and the Hawkhurst Gang. Anything.'

Jan lifted his hand to her cheek. 'Until Mary.'

'Including Mary!'

He took his hand away.

'I'm lucky, Jan. I've still got you. And after tomorrow it'll be you and the dimwit. Then after that . . . who knows?'

Jan smiled and wondered how much her father really knew.

'It hurts when them we love gets took,' he said. 'And we can't never forget them. But life goes on. The world don't split itself in two . . .'

He put his pipe on the mantelshelf and cradled her face in his calloused hands.

'We has to go on. So you make the most of tomorrow, eh? And we'll all get by.'

The story had exposed another of Edward's many facets, and Jan thought none the less of him for revealing his moment of weakness. In fact, spirits restored, she sat with her head resting on his shoulder, content in the warmth and security that he offered. Her inner strength, inherited she knew from both parents, was again flowing.

Tomorrow she and Alan would become one, and with her father to guide them, they need fear no one. Though

157

the Kingsmills of this world might maim and kill, they could never destroy the love that bound the likes of Winchcombe and Wynter together.

Chapter 15

A subtle change had occurred during the long ride east and it was giving Sturt considerable cause for concern. He was being troubled by what he could only assume to be an attack of guilt. Harsh words had been exchanged that morning and, with hindsight, he knew that he had been wrong. John's argument had roughly encompassed the points raised later by Milner – though he would never have dreamt of admitting it to the precocious young Collector. Sturt, for his part, had steadfastly refused to give an inch. He had left for Goudhurst in a huff, only half-convinced by the report that Kingsmill had been seen leaving the district. Twice he'd turned back, wasting a good hour, but as his temper had cooled a glimmer of light had started to flicker in the black vault of his mind. Like a persistent itch it had plagued him, forced him to acknowledge its existence then, after three hours in the saddle, left him no alternative other than to be honest with himself.

He had taken advantage of his friend. John had left home and family in Tonbridge without a second thought and put his very existence at risk simply because he had asked him. In return, he'd been taken for granted, shot at, used and abused without so much as a cursory thank you.

Sturt conceded that he had good reason to be feeling guilty. Kingsmill may well have become his obsession; he had no right to expect the same from others.

As for the Winchcombes – he not only liked them but cared deeply about what happened to them. In many ways Jan and Alan represented what might have been with Mary. He'd lost sight of that and had John to thank for ramming it down his throat.

His desire to destroy Kingsmill burned no less brightly. The man was not merely a cancer devouring him from the

159

inside, but an affront to human decency, a blight that must be wiped from the face of the earth for the good of all.

For the good of all.

That was the shift in thinking that Sturt now recognized as a hand reaching into his grave. But, the question whether or not he had the courage to stretch up and clasp it, dare to consider that life might yet have something to offer other than the hunt, the kill, a lonely old age, and a solitary death, would remain unanswered. For the time being at least, thanks to the oddest of sights now laid before his disbelieving eyes.

A pair of beautifully crafted riding boots were protruding from a deep ditch and pointing, square heels uppermost, to the sky. At the verge, a riderless bag of bones was cropping greenery around a half-empty flask of geneva with the precision of a barber-surgeon.

A low, gurgling moan indicated that the owner of the boots was somewhere in the immediate vicinity. Sturt dismounted and approached the ditch.

In it, doubled up, wedged fast with his chin jammed up against his knees scarcely an inch above the surface of the water, was what appeared to be the frayed remains of an aged human being – though Sturt would not have sworn to it in open court.

It blinked bloodhound eyes and grunted acknowledgement of his presence.

In return Sturt did the decent thing. He seized it by the scruff and hauled it wheezing and snorting out of the stagnant culvert. Restored to terra firma, what was now to all intent and purpose an old man, massaged cramped muscles and arthritic joints while Sturt stepped back in a futile attempt to avoid the organic aroma breezing his way.

'My heartfelt thanks, sir. I had resigned myself to a watery grave,' said the smelly creature, wringing a gill of brackish liquid from his coat-tail. 'Daniel Chater, boot and shoe-maker of Fordingbridge – at your service.'

An ostentatious low bow proved his undoing and the shoemaker was back in the ditch before Sturt could move.

Again, he dragged him out.

'To whom . . .' spluttered Chater, removing a brilliant green water snail from his left ear. 'To whom do I have the pleasure of addressing myself?'

'George Sturt – freeman of the village of Goudhurst.'

'Master Sturt, I am indebted a second time.'

Attempting another bow, Chater wobbled on the brink.

Sturt caught him by the collar and held him at arm's length.

'The pleasure is all mine, Master Chater,' he lied.

The shoemaker leaned towards him, exhaling enough neat alcohol to pole-axe an ox. 'If you would be so kind as to assist me into the saddle . . .' Yellow lips parted, revealing the blackened stumps of two large molars standing proud of a diseased lower jaw.

'Don't move a muscle!' said Sturt, wiping a tear from his eye. 'Try and stay out of the ditch.'

Chater nodded conspiratorially. 'My word, sir – as one gentleman to another.'

Glad to extend the air space between them, Sturt approached the derelict nag with caution. Unobserved, Chater retrieved his flask as his rescuer caught the loose reins.

'Damned rented animal tossed me in the cut!' The flint that he booted was the size and shape of a duck egg, and it struck the horse squarely on the muzzle.

Sturt's arms barely maintained contact with their sockets as the agnonized gelding reared and kicked. For a good minute it was touch and go whether he would calm the animal or have his brains dashed out by its hooves. With the outcome resolved in his favour, Sturt grasped the shoemaker firmly by the throat.

'I said not to move a muscle!'

'Take my advice, sir . . .'

Again dragon's breath. Sturt's head snapped back as if he had been punched on the chin.

'Never rent a saddle horse,' Chater continued. 'In my experience all such beasts are of a malevolent disposition and possess a devilish sense of humour.'

161

As Sturt shook him, the old man's flask worked its way through the hole in his pocket and fell at his feet.

'I would have thought that the geneva was the root cause of your predicament, Master Chater.' He picked it up and returned it. 'I doubt this poor creature can carry, let alone throw you.'

The rubber-legged ancient shot him a look as black as the ditch-water, then attempted to slot his foot into a stirrup iron. Sturt did it for him and boosted him aboard. Horse and rider pointed west.

'Fordingbridge is the other way.'

'I am obliged, sir, for the geographical information.' The words dripped off the end of Chater's purple-veined snout. 'But I happen to have business in Poole.'

'Then I suggest you toss your flask into the ditch. I wager you'll not make half a mile otherwise.'

The shoemaker sighed.

'Master Sturt. The nature of my business in Poole is twofold. One – to procure a consignment of the finest imported leather, for the making of footwear for the gentry. Two – and more important – to gain brief respite from the whiplash tongue of the nagging hag I had the misfortune to marry some forty-one years since.' He allowed Sturt time to absorb this information then continued, 'And you, sir, sound more like her than she does!'

With that parting broadside, Daniel Josiah Chater doffed slouched round hat, dug spiteful heels into wasted flanks and resumed his regal progress. Suitably chastened, Sturt chuckled to himself as the old scroat sailed into more trouble. Approaching the bend, he narrowly avoided contact with an eastbound rider. Cursing and scolding, he clung to its mane while his nervy mount lurched from one side of the highway to the other.

Sturt stepped back as Magistrate Lamb passed at the gallop, then roared with laughter as the gin-sodden shoe-maker disappeared from view.

Chater had faded from the forefront of his mind by Peters-field. A near-full moon had risen as he'd left Crowborough

162

and he'd taken supper at the Green Man in Lamberhurst, speaking to no one, troubled by the jumble of thoughts and emotions spinning around inside him.

Revived by a full belly, the last four miles passed quickly. Yellow lights flickered welcomingly as he approached the village. On the Gore, a barn owl was quartering on noiseless wings and pale woodsmoke spiralled into the still air above the Bear and Billet. Somewhere a dog barked and a neighbour cursed it for waking the children.

Sturt stopped by the duck pond. He was home and, to his surprise, pleased to be so. Or he was until the distinctive click of a musket being cocked made his skin crawl.

'Just stand where you are, Mister.'

Sturt did as he was told without argument.

'Who are you and what's your business?'

He recognized the voice and breathed easier. 'My business is none of yours.' Keeping his head down, he deliberately mumbled the words.

A sharp jab in the back made him grunt.

'You'll tell me, else I'll blow your top off!'

'Then you'd better shoot.'

The hands holding the musket trembled. 'Are you sure you wouldn't rather tell me?'

Sturt smiled to himself and nodded.

'Be it on your own head then – ' Wheeling his horse on the spot, Sturt kicked the musket out of Alan's hand and dealt him a hefty blow to the shoulder. Sprawled in the dew-wet grass, the lad sat up and faced his assailant.

'George! I could have killed you!'

'I doubt it. The way your hands were shaking, chances are you'd have shot yourself in the foot.'

He reached down and hauled Alan to his feet.

'Though I'm glad to see the Militia on its toes, shouldn't you have found a relief tonight?'

'It was my turn on the roster,' said Alan, 'And I'd only be in the Bear makin' myself poorly. At least I can put my thoughts in order out here.' He picked up his musket. 'What happened with Kingsmill?'

163

The question was perfectly justified, but Sturt could not bring himself to answer it. 'Where's Edward?' he asked.

'At home,' replied Alan. 'Making Jan's life a misery, I'll warrant.'

A quick look to check that they were alone and he lowered his voice.

'If I'd known getting wed were such a doin's,' he said, 'I swear I'd have took a mistress.'

Sturt gave him a long look. 'I'll talk to you later,' he said, then walked his horse up the hill.

Passing Dorothy Shaddick's cottage, he failed to notice Sarah Dimer lighting a candle lantern at the window. Draping a shawl of Romney wool about her shoulders, she stepped outside as he entered the Winchcombes' stable. She'd recognized him at once and her pulse had quickened. Breath clouding the night air, she shivered and went back inside.

Bolting the door, Sarah sat by the fire, puzzled by the effect he'd had on her. Confused and a little angry, she scolded herself for succumbing to Edward's persuasive tongue.

On the Gore, Alan let his imagination loose on what had happened between Sturt and Kingsmill. Behind him, the hunting owl dropped like a stone and ripped the life from a careless fieldmouse burrowing into Sam Boys's potato clamp.

Edward was not making Jan's life a misery. He was sitting quietly at his fireside, nursing a pot of ale, wrestling with mixed feelings while Becky Glover altered Mary's wedding dress to fit Jan. Adjusting the hem, she lifted it an inch above the ankle.

'You put that back, Becky,' said Edward sharply. 'I'll not have my daughter looking like a trollop in church!'

'Father!'

The gleam in his eye contradicted his tone of voice. Jan stuck out her tongue and raised the dress to her knee. A knock at the door brought it down like a curtain.

'If that's Alan,' she said, 'tell him the wedding is off if he so much as casts a shadow in here.'

She hid behind Becky's comfortable bulk and urged her father to open up. Moaning and groaning, he levered himself out of the railback and lifted the latch.

Sturt entered, loaded with packages.

'George!'

Jan ran to him and threw her arms around his neck. He kissed her on the forehead, then ran an eye over her dress. Knowing that it had belonged to Mary, he said, 'Reckon I might take you off young Wynter's hands myself tomorrow.'

'George . . .'

He put down his parcels and she hugged him again. Edward closed the door and went back to his chair.

Jan looked at Sturt. 'Where's John?' Anxiety put the slightest crack into her voice.

'In Poole.'

'He's hurt?'

'No.'

'Dead?'

'No!' He smiled reassuringly. 'One of us had to stay, that's all.'

Becky glanced at Edward but Jan beat them both to it.

'What happened?' she asked.

'The bastard gave me the slip – made a complete fool of me!' was what Sturt wanted to say. Instead, he picked up the largest package.

'From John,' he said. Then, offering the rest, 'And these are from me. They're not to be opened before tomorrow.'

Jan accepted them. 'Thank you. Thank you both . . .'

Though no longer frightened of him, she still found Sturt slightly intimidating. Itching to question him further, she hesitated – just long enough for Becky to chip in.

'Upstairs Jan and out of that dress, or I'll be sewing gone midnight.'

'Ten minutes won't make any difference – '

'Do as you're bid,' said Edward. 'George ain't goin' nowhere. You can talk his head off over supper.'

165

Half-way up the stairs, Jan stopped. 'I'm so glad you're both safe.'

'Then see you thank God for it,' said Becky, hustling her up to her room.

Irritated, Sturt dropped into a chair. Widowed by the Hawkhurst Gang, Becky Glover still reached out to God. Alone in her bleakest moments, she probably justified such appalling waste by believing that some vague deity had good reason to spill her husband's brains in the street; that there was a mystical guiding hand destroying her family, depriving her children of a father's love, for their own good. Doubtless, some church-instigated, half-cocked theory concerning salvation of the immortal soul through suffering on earth. Sturt couldn't accept that. As a child, the priests had drummed into him that Christ had suffered for man's sins. If that was so, it seemed to him that the human race, or the majority of it – the meek, the honest – spent their span being punished for their virtues.

It didn't make sense. The fact that otherwise clear-thinking people, whom he liked and respected, could do themselves the injustice of swallowing such nonsense plunged him into despair. The carrot of Christian comfort, reassurance, an easy answer to the unanswerable questions that had tormented man since the dawn of time, carried no weight with George Sturt. Mary had challenged his thinking on countless occasions but never succeeded in moving him. He did not fear death, only the manner in which it was achieved. Existence began with a moment of earthly passion and, for most, ended with a painful, undignified exit. There was no greater scheme of which man was a part. Life ended in death. He was sure of it, and the arrogance of his opinion never occurred to him.

A swallow of Edward's fine strong ale rejuvenated his palate if not his disposition.

'We took the cargo,' he said.

'Kingsmill?'

Sturt took another mouthful and shook his head.

'Are you all right?' asked Edward, offering the obligatory dudeen.

166

'I'll survive. What have you done with Cobby's family?'

A taper flared in the grate, threw a harsh light onto the wheelwright's tired face as he sucked on the clay stem. 'Becky's got a second cousin Gloucester way. I had Jack Tunley take 'em.'

Sturt reached for the taper. 'Cobby's dead.'

That stark announcement stung like a slap in the face. Anger surged and for a moment Edward remained silent, struggling to contain it. 'Then you'll have to see them right!' he said.

'It was Thomas,' Sturt explained, 'not me.'

Two mischievous small boys sprang from the past. Caught stealing wheel irons for stick and hoop, they kicked and yelled as he bundled them out of the yard. It was Thomas, not me, cried one. No! It was George, not me, bleated the other. So to be fair the young wheelwright cuffed them both and sent them packing with an earful. Edward looked at Sturt, studied that severe, tortured profile, and felt very old.

'Did you do as I asked?' queried Sturt.

The question jolted Edward back to the present. 'I've had a man watching Hawkhurst since the day you left.'

'And?'

'Nothing. It's as quiet as the grave.'

'You're sure? You've had someone there all the time?'

Edward nodded. 'Day and night.'

Sturt cursed himself for ignoring his instinct. Had he believed in God, he would have begged for a simple, comforting explanation for Kingsmill's absence. As it was, the hand of uncertainty gripped his innards and gave them a twist. There was something in the wind and he was powerless to stop it. Edward tactfully withdrew to fetch more ale and he sat brooding by the fire, a miserable victim of his own pragmatic nature.

A heavy overnight frost ushered in a bitingly cold dawn. Had it not been for the extra warmth provided by the bonnet monkey sleeping inside his tunic, Bootie might well have frozen to death in his alley. Eager to get his blood circu-

lating, he was propped against the Custom House wall by
0800 hours, methodically sucking the life back into wooden
fingers while the primate consumed the remains of a frugal
breakfast.

A known footfall preceded the welcome sensation of
aromatic steam on chilled facial flesh.

'Do you more good than porter this morning, General.'

Bootie took the mug of scalding tea from the guard. 'God
bless you, Master Greenslade, you're a proper gent.' He
flattened himself against the wall to avoid the wind driving
in off the harbour and enjoyed the heat on his hands.

On the jetty, Fairbrother turned up his collar to protect
his ears. Passing the hoar-dusted *Swift*, he skated over icy
setts, eager for the day's update on the Hawkhurst Gang.

At his desk since seven, James Milner signed the letter to
his London superior and sealed it with an official mark.
'Peckover!' he called.

Reluctant acknowledgement filtered through from the
clerk's room. 'In here!'

Leaning against the doorframe, his peculiar posture gave
the impression that the quill-pusher's only set of underwear
was too tight.

'It's a hundred and twenty-two, Master Milner,' he
whined. 'On my life, I done counted them four times over
now.'

'I want this despatched to London.'

Relieved, the clerk shuffled across the room and took the
letter. 'Yes, sir. You can leave it to Archibald Peckover.'

'And you should know that I intend to supervise the
transfer of the Hawkhurst cargo personally. Kemp will take
command in my absence.'

'Yes, sir. I hopes you has a very pleasant journey...'
Bobbing like a cork float on a spring tide, he moved his
insectiform body to the door with surprising speed.

'Peckover...'

He flinched. The tone bore an uncanny resemblance to
that used by his wife when she had a bone to pick.

'Four tubs of cognac,' the Collector said purposefully. 'By the time I return.'

Peckover seemed to wilt. He had tried every trick he could think of to retain possession of what he considered to be an underpaid employee's legitimate share of the booty, but his master's persistence was beginning to wear him down.

'Sir,' he complained, 'you're doing your most willing servant a monstrous injustice . . .'

His words carried no conviction, even to his own ears, and it was only Fairbrother's timely entrance that spared him further embarrassment. In his haste to escape, he cracked one knee on the arms chest, the other on the door edge, and collapsed into his chair nursing both.

On any other day, Fairbrother would have seen the funny side. As it was, he shut the door and approached the Collector.

'Good morning, John.'

'Has Dekker reported in yet?'

'Give the man a chance! Kemp will barely have had time to relieve him.'

Fairbrother sat down. 'Then I'll wait.'

Outside, the cripple blundered through a stiff-fingered rendering of 'The King' and Milner recalled his clerk. Breeches rolled above the knees for damage inspection, Peckover limped in. 'Sir?'

'Breakfast,' said Milner, 'as soon as you have found a rider.'

'Yes, sir.'

The door closed behind him and the Collector turned to his visitor. 'They have not moved one inch beyond Ringwood.' His voice oozed reassurance. 'They're under constant surveillance and the dragoons will be here first thing tomorrow.'

'Kingsmill is up to something,' said Fairbrother. 'I know it. Why else would he still be waiting around?'

Milner shrugged. 'I have no idea, but he can plot and scheme until his brain bursts. There is nothing he can do.'

He got up and warmed the backs of his legs at the fire. 'I have written to the Surveyor General this morning – '

'Only right and proper . . .'

' – advising him of your contribution.'

Outside, the cripple stopped playing and a faint buzz of excitement rose above the clamour of the day.

'It could be to your advantage.' continued Milner.

Fairbrother did not share the Collector's enthusiasm, but neither did he wish to appear churlish. 'Thank you, James,' he said. 'Most kind of you.'

A hearty slap on the shoulder lifted his backside out of the chair. 'There is a new profession staring you in the face, my friend!'

'There is?'

'Excise officer!'

Fairbrother's dry laughter momentarily drowned the noise in the street.

'You and George,' continued Milner, 'you're both eminently qualified – potential collectors even. And I am prepared to offer my personal endorsement!'

Fairbrother softened. The thought was generous. He shook him by the hand. 'Again, thank you. But the Excise Service is a little too close to the Army for my taste. I've had more than enough of people telling me what to do.'

A tapping at the window intruded on Milner's disappointment.

'Beg pardon, sir.' Buffeted by a rapidly swelling crowd, Peckover struggled to hold his ground. 'I think you'd best step outside a minute.'

As Milner and Fairbrother forced a way through the crush, Kemp and Greenslade eased Dekker from the saddle as carefully as they could. Out of harm's way in the alley, Bootie heard the mob surge forward eager for the sight of blood. A shot over their heads sent the ghouls backpedalling.

Peckover, acutely conscious of public hostility towards the Service, slipped back inside and closed the door.

A quick glance acquainted Milner with the seriousness of Dekker's condition. He turned to Peckover's face at the

170

window and yelled, 'Get the army surgeon as fast as you can!'

Peckover left by the side entrance, mouthing thanks to the Almighty for removing him from the firing line, while abuse and horse dung flew as Milner and Greenslade carried their comrade inside.

'I found him half a mile from Ringwood,' said Kemp. 'They'd dumped him at the side of the highway.'

'Did you check the inn?' asked Fairbrother.

The question was expected. Nevertheless, Kemp took his time before answering. 'I did what I could for him . . .'

Fairbrother's eyes were burning holes.

'Yes I checked the inn!' Kemp said. 'They've gone – every last one of them.'

Milner and Greenslade had lifted Dekker onto the desk and were removing what was left of his clothing when Fairbrother entered.

The riding officer had taken a severe beating. A boot heel had burst an eyebrow, a cutlass blow had left an ear dangling from his skull. Nose and teeth were shattered. A lead-loaded whip had ripped clothes and flesh from his upper torso. The bizarre angle of his left leg indicated that it was broken below the knee, and his hands were unlikely to be of further use to him.

Fairbrother was reminded of what they'd done to Stephen Diprose, and the same sense of outrage that had coursed through him then returned with a vengeance. He turned away. Kingsmill had done a thorough job, his sadistic mark was there for all to see. But something was wrong. Quite what it was eluded him . . . He turned back and leaned forward to catch the words dribbling from Dekker's mouth.

'My own fault . . .' whispered the officer. 'Got too close. Careless.'

'Dekker?' Fairbrother spoke clearly and a fraction slower than normal. 'Have you any idea where they went?'

That sorry head turned almost imperceptibly towards him. 'They left me for dead . . .' He grinned a death's-head grin, spilling fragments of teeth and gum onto the walnut veneer. 'They thought I was finished – but I were foxing . . .' His words rattled ominously in his throat. 'I heard every word!'

Fairbrother lifted him into a sitting position. On the field of battle, he'd seen men drown in their own blood whilst waiting for a surgeon. 'What did you hear? Where are they?'

'Gone . . .' Dekker coughed warm clots into Fairbrother's hand and his breathing eased. 'I told Kingsmill we knew what he was up to – hangin' about, hopin' to jump the escort – '

Without thinking, he shifted his damaged leg and pain scrambled the intricate controls that keep the body's myriad components functioning as one recognizable entity. Nerves and muscles went haywire. Twisting and jerking, he messed his pants while Greenslade held him down. He screamed like a fox in a gin-trap, then his nervous system lapsed into a state of shock. The agony dulled and he flopped back onto the table.

Milner placed a thick ledger beneath his head. Fairbrother wiped his hands. Once more that awful smile split Dekker's face. 'They couldn't get out fast enough,' he crowed. 'They've all gone 'ome!'

Fairbrother stepped back and scanned the bloody, near-naked body. Burst eyebrow, slashed ear, lacerated ribs and crushed fingers, broken leg . . . Each was an excruciating injury, deliberately inflicted to cause maximum distress but not, as in Diprose's case, to threaten life.

Now it made sense to him. There was method in Kingsmill's cruel madness!

'Outside, gentlemen, if you please.'

Fairbrother turned. The surgeon was already stripping off his tunic and laying out his instruments.

'Do you require assistance, sir – in case he should resist you?'

The sawbones took two broad leather belts from his kit and declined Fairbrother's offer.

'Will he live?' asked Milner, helping to strap his man down.

'He's been abused most savagely. But with luck and my best efforts . . .'

Having confirmed Fairbrother's theory, Surgeon Officer Oakes spit on his small forceps, wiped them on a sleeve and started digging shot out of Dekker's chest.

Next door, Milner leaned against Peckover's rickety table. Glad that he hadn't taken breakfast, he filled his lungs with unpolluted air. 'Unfortunate . . .'

'For Dekker? Or you?' asked Fairbrother.

Milner looked at him. 'It was a God-given opportunity, John, and we've let it slip.'

'Perhaps.'

Fairbrother crossed to the door and Kemp opened it. Excitement over, the mob had dispersed and Bootie was back under the window. He turned at the threshold.

'Thomas Kingsmill never left anyone alive by accident, James.'

Fairbrother buttoned his coat and stepped outside. Deep in thought, he crossed the street and walked slowly back to his lodgings. Passing the Patriot Arms, he was unaware of the figure loitering in the stable yard.

John Dimer watched until he vanished amongst the working fishwives on the jetty. Satisfied that his job was done, Dimer fetched his horse and headed for the highway.

173

Chapter 16

It was four the following afternoon and the November light was fading. Above the village, a weak sun touched the western wall of the church tower, lifting the colour of the stones in an otherwise achromatic landscape.

Beyond the squat yew, Sturt stood alone at Mary's graveside. Dressed in Sunday best, he was unaware of the onset of night, brooding as he was on an earlier turn of events.

Initially, the day had unfolded in the prescribed manner. Soon after dawn, panic gusted through the Winchcombe household like a February gale. By eight o'clock it was bedlam as minor problems assumed the proportions of major disasters. Buttons maliciously detached themselves from cuff and bodice, hooks refused to couple with their loops, a shoe went missing, and Lizzie Jefford dropped the game pie she'd left cooling on the kitchen sill. By eleven, Edward had sampled every jug and cask, and was at peace with the world. By half-past, Jan was stepping into her sister's dress. At twelve, flanked by George and her father, Jan Winchcombe strode joyfully up Goudhurst Hill and into wedlock.

In the churchyard, a pipistrelle swept past Sturt's ear and disappeared into Tunley's beech coppice in search of insects. Sturt disliked bats and the tiny creature had startled him, broken his train of thought as the wedding group approached the packed church. Leaning against a neglected tomb, he tucked cold hands into the warm pockets of his armpits and tried to pick up the thread.

In his mind's eye, he saw himself open the heavy oak door. Saw again two hundred heads turning as one. Remembered how, a split second later, he'd picked out the face that had thrown him into confusion. A face he'd seen for the first time a few miles from Rye. A face that had stayed with him ever since. He remembered every feature. That dark mane tumbling freely to her shoulders. Those green eyes holding his gaze. The straight nose with that odd bump at the bridge. That wide, generous mouth . . . He pictured every crease and blemish as if she was standing before him now. He reached out. His fingers touched Mary's headstone, but his thoughts remained inside the church where the ceremony seemed to go on forever. Sturt stood and sat, sang and muttered meaningless words as required. He thought of Mary but took every opportunity to glance over his shoulder, searching for that face in the crowd. Once he caught a glimpse of her and his pulse rate quickened. Edward elbowed him in the ribs and he turned away.

Outside, he'd kissed Jan, shaken Alan by the hand, and failed to find her as the congregation drifted homeward. Left alone, he drifted to Mary's grave, in search of what he did not know. Comfort? Reassurance? Forgiveness even? More hungry bats vacated the belfry as he tried to analyse his feelings. He knew who she was. The image of her sitting on her donkey cart, horse pistol in hand, was fixed in his memory. Before he could stop it, a half-smile had escaped his lips. Perhaps it was because he admired her spirit, appreciated her courage, recognized an exceptional woman for what she was.

The smile faded and he walked away from the grave. The truth was screaming for recognition and he did not want to acknowledge it in front of Mary. Feelings that had lain dormant since her death had been aroused at her sister's wedding, surged at the sight of that nameless woman who looked the world in the eye and defied it to look back. Guilt was troubling Sturt. He had betrayed Mary in thought if not in deed, and his puritanical nature allowed for no such lapse. Not that Mary's memory was enshrined on some high pedestal. He was no paragon of virtue. Looking back over the army years, he had behaved consistently badly with women and never given it a second thought.

This time however, it was different; not only because Mary was dead, but because somehow his own moral code had been breached. Had he cared to push the thought to its limit he may well have concluded that his feelings were perfectly natural. Nothing more than the second most powerful human instinct making its presence felt. Instead, he chose to get angry. So, banging shut the churchyard gate, he stormed down the hill. He'd spent half his life racked with guilt over the way he'd betrayed Kingsmill. Now there was more of it, coming at him from every side. And he didn't like it. He didn't like it at all.

Two hundred yards away, Sarah Dimer sat in front of her aunt's chipped looking glass. She often studied her face; not for narcissistic reasons but because she was fascinated by the way it reflected the most intimate details of her life. The history of her relationship with John was there for all to see. The disillusion in her eyes and the shadows beneath. The fine down-turned lines at the corners of her mouth. The two vertical furrows etched deep into her brow, cata- logued each event of a ten-year descending spiral.

What held her attention at that moment however was not what she knew, but something she had forgotten existed. She stared hard and long into the mirror. It wasn't imagin- ation, nor the light from the flickering candle. There was a spark; admittedly a small one but, nevertheless, a spark once more flashing in Sarah Dimer's eyes, firing her base instincts in the most shameless way imaginable.

A broad open smile swept the wear and tear from her face. Fear and exhilaration had set the adrenalin flowing, breathed life into the most private corners of mind and body. For as long as she could remember, men had been drawn to her like moths to a flame but, stern and unyielding as he appeared, Sturt was the first to appeal to her in years.

'But why?' Perrin protested. 'I'll only slow you down.'

Forty armed riders, each leading an unladen pack animal, waited outside the White Hart at Cadnam.

'It's a bold scheme, Richard.' Kingsmill mounted up as John Dimer approached with the buyer's horse. 'It would be a pity to miss seeing it put to the test.' He took his place at the head of the column where Shepherd Fairall joined him.

176

Dimer offered Perrin a greatcoat. 'I took the liberty of fetching it from your room, Master Perrin,' he said. 'It being such a chill night an' all.'

Wishing he'd kept his mouth shut, Perrin took it. Because of his palsy, riding caused him severe discomfort, and he knew that if things went wrong and they had to run he would be the first man caught. Refusing help, he struggled into the saddle and went to the back of the line. Experience had long since taught him when to protest and when to keep his mouth shut.

'Ready, Thomas,' Jackson called from the stable lean-to where he had loaded Sam Payne's pony with long-handled axes and crowbars.

Widow and son appeared at the inn doorway.

Kingsmill said, 'I'll give you Sturt's ears.'

'I'll settle for my share of the cargo,' she replied.

Fairall spurred his mount. 'Time to go!' he snapped, then led the Sussex contingent out onto the highway.

The Hawkhurst Gang waited. Jackson urged his master to give the word, lest they lose face in front of the opposition.

Deliberately taking his time, Kingsmill pulled on riding gloves, adjusted a stirrup length. The Widow watched him. With the scheming done, the waiting over, all that remained was the execution. And that was his forte. The thought struck her that had he taken to the Army instead of the free trade, he would have long since become a national hero. Her eyes did not stray until he had vanished into the night.

'Cut plenty of firewood, Samuel,' she said softly. 'We're in for a long night.'

On the road, they soon caught up with the Chichester Gang. No objections were voiced as the east countrymen barged through their ranks, riding hard for Poole. His allocated task and personal share of the cargo occupied the thoughts of every man but one. Blinded by obsession, Kingsmill could not see beyond laying hands on George Sturt.

Sturt waited until nine o'clock before leaving the house. Two hours nursing the brandy bottle had eased his anxious state of mind and dulled the guilt, honed the illicit sense of

177

anticipation. Now, possessed of an uncharacteristic lightness of spirit, he tucked the oilskin wallet inside his coat, buttoned it, and strode down the hill.

Hanging high above the Weald, a full moon soft washed the silent village, lighting his way as he took the short cut through Fletcher's alley. Crossing the Flimwell highway, the thought occurred that even Kingsmill would think twice before taking to the road on such a night. Feeling easier, he increased his pace, drawn on by the sound of a quicksilver jig dancing on the breeze.

The Gore was lit by two huge bonfires burning at either end of the duckpond. Between them, under the beady gaze of Becky Glover, sucking pig and fattened lamb turned grotesque circles over beds of white-hot charcoal. At Becky's heels, boss-eyed children up past their bedtime, hovered like hungry kestrels, waiting their chance to steal a taste. Undersized boots and clogs curled in the heat as they shuffled closer to the prize. Momentarily distracted by a diversionary strike at her sweetmeats, Becky rapped blistered fingers with a basting ladle and scattered her tormentors amongst their dancing parents.

Warming his backside at the flames, Sturt helped himself to mulled ale and stole a baked potato from a grubby boy's stick. He scanned the makeshift dance floor and smiled at the newlyweds, bobbing and turning in the crush. Close by, a mane of black hair leapt in the torchlight. His gaze locked onto Sarah Dimer jigging like a demon with old Edward. The blood surged in Sturt's veins, striking heart and brain with the force of a breaking wave.

The music came to an abrupt end. The wheelwright called for more. Glistening with sweat, he dismissed Jonathan Deal's clumsy attempt to cut in and led Sarah back into the fray. The village band struck up a spirited reel and Sturt lost sight of them.

'We thought you'd deserted us.'

Someone walked over his grave and he shivered. The voice belonged to Jan but the inflexion was Mary's. For a moment, he stared at her, blank-eyed and wordless.

'Slipped off back to Poole,' explained Alan.

'No . . .' said Sturt. 'Poole is in the capable hands of John Fairbrother. Until tomorrow, that is. Tonight is a celebration, so not one word about Thomas Kingsmill or run goods. Understand?'

Simultaneously raising their right hands, the Wynters pledged to remain silent on the subject. Then Jan giggled and Sturt slapped her rump. Turning to Alan, he said, 'Now, before your wife and I put these so-called dancers to shame . . .'

The oilskin wallet was warm to the touch as Alan took it.

'It won't bite you, boy!'

He opened it and glanced at the wad of legal-looking parchments.

'What is it?' asked Jan.

'His farm – '

'Your farm,' Sturt corrected him. 'As from today.'

Alan fumbled for words. 'George – you can't . . .' was the best he could manage.

'I want you to have it.'

'You're not going to come back, are you?' Suddenly, Jan's buoyancy had gone and she looked at him with wounded eyes. 'Ever?'

'I didn't say that.'

'Then why?'

'As I said, I want you to have it.'

Jan took the wallet from Alan. 'It's very generous, George – but no.'

Sturt's hands remained in his pockets. 'Enoch Trickett let the place go. It's almost derelict. If someone doesn't move in soon it will fall to bits.'

Jan shook her head.

'It's my wedding present.'

'You've given us enough already.' Her eyes drifted to the exotic silks and Indian elephants carved out of ivory that held pride of place among the mundane domestic gifts.

'Those are from John as well.' Sturt touched her cheek. 'Take it.'

'One condition,' said her husband.

179

'Alan!' Jan rounded on him like a veteran.

'Name it,' Sturt said quickly.

The boy seemed to grow. Then, speaking in a carefully measured fashion explained. 'When you've sorted your business with Kingsmill – come home. You and me. We'll work the farm together for a year then see where we stand.'

Even Jan was impressed. Such cleverness was usually beyond Alan.

Sturt did not hesitate. 'Agreed,' he said, shaking him by the hand.

'Alan!' Three heads turned together as Sarah Dimer approached with Edward. 'Get your father-in-law a drink. I think he's done himself a mischief!'

'Nonsense!' croaked the apoplectic wheelwright. 'Just gettin' me second breath . . .' His knees buckled and Sturt helped him to a stool. Head immersed in a pot of ale, he felt the life returning to his legs.

'You ought to know better at your age!' scolded his daughter.

Edward grinned at her. 'I do know better, but what's that to do with anythin'?' Belching loudly, he drained his mug and demanded a refill from Alan.

Meanwhile, Sturt and Sarah stood silently staring at one another. Neither face gave anything away. The space between them crackled like the air before a thunderstorm. Jan thumped her father in the ribs, almost knocking him from his perch.

'Eh?' he gasped. 'Oh!' Standing up, he performed the formal introduction. 'George, you remember Dorothy Shaddick?'

'I remember.'

'This is her niece, Sarah.'

'Master Sturt and I are already acquainted.' Sarah's words were directed at Edward, but she was looking straight into Sturt's eyes.

'I trust you'll have no need of your horse pistol tonight, Mistress Shaddick.' Sturt thought he detected a hint of colour in her cheeks.

180

Sarah closed her fist and John's wedding ring disappeared from view. 'Sarah,' she smiled, 'my name is Sarah.'

Jan gave the oilskin wallet to Alan, then, stepping between Sarah and Sturt, took his arm. 'About that dance,' she said, and led him onto the floor.

'Our Mary told me once and I couldn't believe it.'

'Told you what?' Sturt asked.

'That you used to be known around Goudhurst for your fancy footwork.'

'What makes you think she was referring to my dancing skills?'

Jan laughed and Sturt spun her around the floor. The musicians upped the pace and Edward moved Becky out of harm's way as they sailed past. Though pleased to see Sturt enjoying himself, the wheelwright was determined not to be outdone. He drew his old friend's widow as close as common decency allowed and demonstrated a few steps of his own.

Surprisingly light on his toes, Sturt responded in like manner and danced the old man to a standstill.

Over at the pond, Alan and Sarah solemnly declared an end to hostilities. Then, slightly drunk, he carved long, thin strips of pork from the spit and fed them to her with his fingers. The act itself was perfectly innocent, but the image was intimate, even sensual.

Sturt watched them, chattering and laughing, until Nat Dekin lurched across his field of vision. With one effortless movement, he spun Jan the way a child would a top, caught her around the waist and felt her head come to rest on his breast. Inhaling her female fragrance, he brushed his face against the curtain of fair hair. They were in the midst of a hundred sweating bodies, moving in the firelight like one great shapeless creature of the night. Intoxicated more by atmosphere and imagination than alcohol, Sturt felt a stirring in his crotch. He inched away from Jan before she felt it too.

'Did you mean it?'

He looked at her.

'About coming home.'

181

'I agreed, didn't I?'

'All too easily.'

He smiled. 'I'll try it.'

Jan was not convinced.

'I can't think of a better alternative,' he admitted.

Dekin and his partner left the floor and Sarah reappeared. Sturt edged Jan to her left so that he might get a better view.

'She's a married woman!' Jan scolded.

A momentary pause and he answered, 'So are you.'

Before she could elaborate the difference, her feet lost contact with the ground as Sturt again whirled her around the Gore.

By the ebbing fire, Sarah licked pork juice from her chin, and watched every step and turn he made.

Soon after midnight, Edward's stamina finally gave out and he joined Jan and Alan at the fire. Poking the embers, he salvaged a charred potato and added it to the remains of his supper. The momentum had slackened. The music was less frantic, and the cooked carcasses had been reduced to a pile of picked bones. Most people now sat around talking and drinking. Some, stone drunk, just sat. A few with exhausted children reluctantly drifted home, leaving three or four couples on their feet. One by one, they too gave up until only Sturt and Sarah remained.

They did not speak, they did not touch. They merely looked. But had their naked bodies been locked together in a spasm of all-consuming passion, their minds could scarcely have been closer. A murmur of interest rippled through the village audience and Jan snorted disapproval.

'From what she hinted at,' said Edward, 'it ain't bin that much of a marriage.'

'It's still a marriage!'

Alan mopped his plate with a bread doorstep. 'Can't see why you're getting so het up,' he said. 'They're dancing' – he crammed the soggy wedge into his mouth – 'just dancing.'

And for another timeless thirty minutes, Sturt and Sarah

continued to do just that, oblivious of the critical eyes upon them.

Resplendent in dress uniform and full-bottomed peruke, James Milner studied his reflection in the darkened window. Adjusting the hang of his sword, he bowed to himself.

'Surveyor General,' he muttered.

Not satisfied he repeated the action, this time eliminating the agricultural footwork.

'Surveyor General, sir.'

He thought of the reception awaiting him in London. Ambition triggered endless possibilities. He stooped again, adding an elegant flourish of the arm.

'Mr First Minister,' he breathed.

Then, after final rehearsal, he bowed so low that he chinned himself on his extended knee.

'Your Majesty!'

Memorizing crook of back and angle of elbow, he held the absurd position and practised – smiling!

Pulling the most extraordinary faces, his repertoire ran from a passable impersonation of a fishwife in labour to a gross caricature of respectful submission. Overstretched tendons forced him to rise. Resetting his Kevinhuller, he glanced at the window where to his consternation, the face in the glass was framed by a well-dusted campaign wig and Dettingen.

John Fairbrother smiled, causing the Collector severe embarrassment.

Outside, the guard sneezed and hammered on the door. Milner entered the clerk's room and threw the bolts. Annoyed at having been dragged from his sick-bed in order to mount guard, Officer Greenslade made a point of coughing his cold germs into Fairbrother's face as he entered.

'Thought you might appreciate the company.'

Milner locked up as his uninvited visitor cast an eye over his uniform.

'But if you are otherwise engaged?'

The Collector turned on his heel and went back to his

office. The musket hanging from Fairbrother's shoulder, the sword and pistol in his belt, had not gone unnoticed. He was checking up, casting doubt on Milner's professional competence. Silently cursing his clumsiness, Fairbrother took a bottle from his pocket and prepared to pour alcoholic balm on injured pride.

Not two miles away, Dimer dropped from the saddle and faced his master. 'Two guards and no soldiers,' he said.

'But?' said Kingsmill.

'The cutter is still alongside.'

Richard Perrin emerged from the shadows. Behind him, only the soft clink of harness betrayed the free traders waiting in the wood. 'Privateer or Excise?' asked the buyer.

Dimer shrugged. 'I dunno. But she's got five four pounders pointing straight at the Custom House door.'

Shepherd Fairall approached, followed by Smoaker Mills. 'Perhaps we could steal the cannons,' he suggested sarcastically, 'as well as the cargo.'

Kingsmill just about managed to ignore the jibe. He mounted up, consoled by the knowledge that Fairall's long overdue come-uppance was fast approaching.

It was almost midnight and the tide had reached its peak. From a dockside alleyway, a short distance beyond the Custom House, Harry Sheerman kept watch on the *Swift*. Whether by accident or design, her guns were indeed trained on the Excise Headquarters and posed a serious threat should they try to break in as planned. While he pondered the odds against surviving a broadside of grapeshot, boot nails clacked on greystone and a familiar twisted figure limped by flanked by two juvenile whores. Money exchanged hands on the jetty. The man melted into the darkness and the whores teetered up the *Swift*'s gangway. A brief conversation, a further transaction, and they went below with the nightwatch.

Problem solved, Sheerman turned to Fairall and grinned. Priming his pistol, he was about to go when a hand on his shoulder stopped him.

'There's no rush, Harry,' said Kingsmill. 'We'll wait a while.'

Sheerman saw no reason to delay, but nevertheless did as he was told. Pocketing the firing piece, he caught the discordant strains of a scurrilous song wafting on the wind.

The excisemen heard it too, and they hurled abuse at Daniel Chater as he lurched along the quayside. Gloriously drunk, the ancient shoemaker continued to sing his heart out until an over-sized cobblestone upended him outside the Custom House. Grateful for any diversion, the officers hauled him to his feet.

'God bless you, gentlemen! You're an upstanding credit to your service!'

He breathed neat gin into Greenslade's face, making the exciseman's eyes sting.

'Get off home, old man,' he advised. 'Sleep out tonight and tomorrow you'll wake up dead.'

His young subordinate laughed mirthlessly at the feeble joke. Chater retrieved his cap and threw an arm around the senior officer's shoulder.

'Sir!' he shouted confidentially, 'death would be a welcome release. The Devil himself could devise no cruelty more refined than sharing a bed with Dorcas Chater!'

And with that definitive summary of forty-one years of sexual and emotional deprivation, he went about his business.

Unfortunately, that meant relieving the pressure on a straining bladder. He chose to do it in a nearby alley where, deep in the shadows, he concentrated hard on not falling over and not peeing on his boots. Sighing with pleasure as the pain receded, Chater was suddenly aware that he was not alone. He glanced over his shoulder. Kingsmill was standing right behind him. Alarmed, the old man was starting to yell but Sheerman clamped a hand over his mouth.

Death was imminent when Dimer called out, 'Daniel?'

Jackson hesitated and Dimer appealed to Kingsmill.

'Make him stop, Master Thomas! The old sot is distant family – second cousin to my mother or summat like.'

185

Chater nodded furiously.

'And,' Dimer added, 'he holds contraband regular, he does. In his boot store.'

Nine times out of ten Kingsmill would have been unmoved by such a plea, but for no good reason he chose to be generous. Perhaps it was the pleasure he derived in exercising absolute power that gave Chater his life.

'Take him to the horses,' he said.

Jackson sheathed his blade and clipped Chater behind the ear with a pistol barrel. The shoemaker's world went dark and Sheerman hoisted him onto Dimer's shoulder.

When Chater did not reappear, Riding Officer Greenslade assumed that he had collapsed in a stupor and promptly forgot all about him. Though he didn't know it, the exciseman had just condemned Chater to an unenviable place in the history of the free trade.

Fairbrother's bottle had served its purpose. By one o'clock, Milner was stretched out on the chaise with his good humour restored.

'A King's Collector,' he said, loosening his waistcoat, 'is to all intent and purpose, his own man. Admittedly, there is always someone to answer to, but that applies to any position of authority. In practice, one is left to exercise one's own initiative.'

Fairbrother moved from the window to the fire. Tense and preoccupied, he had been pacing the room, half-listening to the young man's continuing attempt to enlist his services.

'Meaning you're not just a soldier under a different hat,' he said.

'An Excise officer can take pride in his work, John. Unlike the military, we are not despised by the mob.'

'From what I have seen, you're not exactly welcomed, either.'

Milner sat up and poured the last few drops of brandy into his glass. He was getting nowhere so tried a change of tactics. Coming clean, he appealed to Fairbrother's sense of duty.

186

'In truth,' he said, 'the Service is desperate for men of your experience and ability. And until it gets them, the likes of Thomas Kingsmill will continue to run riot.'

The point was well made but Fairbrother was weary. In recent weeks his inner strength had waned, and with it his hitherto unassailably optimistic opinion of the human race.

'With respect James, the root of the problem lies not with the quality of your officers.' He had thought deeply about the free trade's place in the scheme of things and, for once, had reached an accurate conclusion. 'Society needs the Kingsmills and Fairalls,' he explained. 'They satisfy a demand.'

'But at what price?' Coming so quickly, the retort sounded trite and naïve.

'Indeed. But I am afraid that murder and mayhem are perfectly acceptable today, James – so long as no one who matters gets hurt. Nevertheless' – he selected a pipe from Milner's rack and helped himself to herb tobacco – 'had you asked me two weeks ago, I might have been tempted.'

'And now?'

Fairbrother drew the sweet smoke deep into his lungs.

'My father's cloth empire is looking increasingly attractive.'

Richard Perrin sat on an upturned fish basket and watched the jolly boat glide noiselessly towards *Swift*. In the past hour the water level had dropped some three feet, leaving the cutter's gun pointing at the jetty wall. Kingsmill, he conceded, had waited for good reason. Rope fenders squashed between timber and stone as her painters pulled tight.

Feigning climax, a female voice rose above those of the crew and cracked the silence hanging over the harbour. Outside the Custom House, Greenslade smiled, envying the sailors their luck.

And Perrin shifted on his perch. He'd spent his money well, reducing Smoaker Mills's task to a formality. He lost sight of the skiff as it disappeared behind the cutter's seal-sleek hull. Seconds later, Mills pulled over the seaward gunwale and led his bootless assassins down into the fo'c's'le. A brief pause, a solitary scream quickly stifled, and the palsied buyer glanced nervously at the Custom House, where the guards were arguing over who was now doing what to whom.

Perrin trembled. It had started. Men and women had just died and there was no turning back. He gave the nod and two sinister figures materialized on the quay. A splash of geneva, a few adjustments to headgear and clothing, and they were transformed into amiable inebriates. Striking up a tuneless rendition of Chater's bawdy ditty, they tacked towards the Custom House.

Drink was offered and accepted. Greenslade's man swigged a flask and presented his throat to Harry Sheerman. One smooth stroke opened it from ear to voicebox, and he died a quick, silent death.

Dimer was not so skilful and missed Greenslade's jugular by half an inch. With his vocal chords severed, the exciseman gaped like a gaffed fish and turned on his murderer. Fingernails stripped the flesh from Dimer's face. He stabbed and stabbed again. But the exciseman was as strong as an ox and refused to go down. Sheerman finally bundled him to the ground and lay on top of him until he was still.

In a fit of pique, Dimer slung the flask into the alley where it struck a bundle of rags beneath a derelict fish cart. Something grunted so softly that Dimer did not hear it.

'Keys!' hissed Sheerman as he signalled to Kingsmill.

Forty men ran towards them while Dimer went through Greenslade's pockets. 'He ain't got 'em . . .' he breathed.

Sheerman fared no better and Kingsmill ordered them to smash the door. Fairall struck the first blow, shattering the lock with an axe. The third split the frame. Jackson kicked it down, and Peckover's room was suddenly full of armed bodies clamouring to get into the strong-room.

Milner fired from the doorway, taking Tom Cox in the back of the neck. Jackson stepped over him and struck the Collector with his hanger. The blow almost decapitated him and he was dead before he hit the floor.

188

At his heels, Fairbrother had no chance to defend himself before the blunt end of an axe hit him squarely in the face. He fell like a butchered heifer. Fairall kicked him for good measure then shoved those nearest into the strong-room.

'Every dollop of tea,' he yelled, 'and as many tubs as you can carry!'

An elbow in the back sent him reeling. Kingsmill barged past and burst into Milner's office. He scanned the empty room, unaware that Bootie was listening outside the window. Astonishment registered in the cripple's face when Kingsmill screamed at Jackson, ordering him to leave the cargo and find Sturt.

Within seconds, order was restored. Fast hands moved tea and spirits from strong-room to street, where human beasts of burden staggered to the horses then ran back for more. In the doorway to Milner's office, Fairbrother tried to rise as his senses returned. Strong hands seized him by the collar and slammed him against the wall.

'Where is he?'

A blurred figure punched him in the mouth, again scattering his senses.

'I said, where is Sturt?'

The man was no more than inches away, roaring into his face. Fighting the encroaching darkness, Fairbrother blinked Thomas Kingsmill into focus. He felt no fear. The pain of his injuries exploded like sunbursts, but somewhere else, on a different plane, in another time. All he could see and hear, feel and smell, was Kingsmill. He tasted his breath as the hands tightened around his throat.

'Where's Sturt?'

Suddenly Fairbrother was laughing. His worst nightmares had combined, invaded the real world, and he was laughing! He heard himself say, 'Well out of your reach,' then a searing, screaming pain seemed to split him in two and he remembered nothing more.

The cutlass blade rose and fell, twice and again. Like a woodsman cutting kindling, Kingsmill hacked at Fairbrother's helpless body until his rage blew itself out.

*

189

Streamers of cirrus cloud slid in from the west, casting ghostly patterns across the face of the moon. A pitch torch spluttered and went out. The wedding party was in its dying moments and in ones and twos the few remaining villagers were on their way home.

It had been a special night for Edward, one of the best of his life. Now, sitting alone, sucking on his pipe, he listened to the weary band playing for Alan and Jan. Rising and turning, linking and breaking, they danced in a world of their own. Alan drew her to him, and as they swayed together, kissed her long and tenderly. Edward watched them and resolved to stop calling him the boy.

His eyes drifted to the fire where Sturt and Sarah sat close to the pulsing coals. A lump rose in the old man's throat and he pushed Mary back into the deeper recesses of his mind. Back to that special place reserved for her and Elizabeth. Sarah he liked, cared for almost as a daughter. Sturt he respected. But whereas Alan and Jan, with their youth and optimism, gave him some hope for the future, those two silent figures shimmering in the ember haze represented the pain of the past. Sarah because of the happy memories she stirred, Sturt because he carried the smell of death with him, and unless he could exorcize his obsession with Kingsmill, he would destroy himself and all those close to him.

Edward suddenly felt angry. Sarah deserved better and he would tell her so. He started towards them but something stopped him. The Sarah he had watched grow up with Mary had been a fragile creature; this Sarah exuded strength and resilience. Perhaps with God's help she might be the one to shift Sturt's focus, drain the pus that was rotting his soul . . . The wheelwright turned back. Wishing them well, he headed for home and the strong hot toddy that would bring deep, dreamless sleep.

Sturt, meanwhile, took Sarah's hand and she opened it, revealing her husband's ring.

'I've been married for twelve years, George.'

She looked into his eyes, searching for the man within.

'I was barely sixteen. To look at he was nothing at all

190

and he hadn't two farthings to rub together. But he was a whirlwind of ideas and ambition. When he talked, the dreams sprang to life.'

The smile only lasted for a second, but it was the saddest he'd ever seen.

'He made it seem as if the whole world belonged to no one but us.'

Sarah raked the ashes with her heel and a half-burnt fragment of beechwood burst into flames.

'I stopped loving him a long time ago.'

Her tone was flat and matter of fact. Only the tremor at the corner of her mouth hinted at the horrors behind the mask. She looked away.

'Sarah.' Sturt cupped her face in his hands.

'He's gone and got himself mixed up in the free trade – '

'It doesn't matter.'

'With Thomas Kingsmill!'

The shock effect of those three words caused physical pain. Sturt drew back as if he'd been shot or run through.

'He was here, George . . ' She paused. 'When Mary was killed.'

'Your married name – ' he demanded. 'What is it?'

Her answer evoked the sour smell of vomit and Sturt remembered an alleyway in Poole, saw Cobby, and that obscene thing rolling in its own mess. The name rattled like a musket ball around his skull. Dimer. John Dimer!

He turned away from her as Alan wheeled Jan in time to the music. In his imagination, Sturt saw himself dancing with Mary at their own wedding. Arms clasped around each other's waists, they spun faster and faster. Laughing. Until a shot rang out and the image disintegrated.

A sound from pre-history stopped the dancing newly-weds, silenced the band. Sturt was up on his feet, an awful violent presence that briefly threatened Sarah's very existence. Then he was gone and she sat staring into the coals.

Pain and confusion were on the rampage. Something she had not dared dream about had been offered then snatched away, within the space of a few hours. She was being punished; by whom and for what she did not know. But she was serving her time in purgatory right now. Sarah Dimer cursed her honesty. Why hadn't she lied to him? Why?

Chater's eyes were falling from their sockets as Kingsmill dragged him to his feet. Steel glinted in the moonlight, and, anticipating the inevitable, the shoemaker squeezed them shut and prayed for a quick end.

But Kingsmill hesitated, as if caught between two planes of existence. Face set in a rictus of hatred, spattered with Fairbrother's blood, he stood in front of forty witnesses looking like a vision from Hades. Though anxious to be gone, no one dared speak until Dimer stepped forward with his horse. He offered the reins and a shiver of apprehension ran through him. Quite why he had taken such a risk was never clear to Dimer but there was no doubt that the old man owed him his life.

Abandoning the cross of private anguish, Kingsmill returned to the world of contraband and corruption, murder and confrontation. He cut Chater loose and mounted up.

'Breathe one word of this to anyone,' he said 'and you'll wish I had cut your throat.'

Dimer pulled the shoemaker to one side as Kingsmill spurred his mount. Eighty horses followed. Left alone, Dimer removed Chater's gag.

'He meant it, Daniel.'

Unable to speak, the shoemaker nodded. Dimer climbed into the saddle and took a dollop of tea from his pack mule.

'That should sweeten your discomfort some.'

Chater caught it and watched him go. Suddenly his stomach turned over and he sicked up his supper. As the spasm subsided, a soft scuffling sound startled him, triggering instant panic. There was something moving on the quay, outside the Custom House. Chater had no desire to know who or what it was. He hid Dimer's tea under his coat and ran as fast as his legs would carry him. Keeping to the shadows, he thought of Dorcas. For the first time in forty years, he couldn't wait to get home.

Across the street, the bonnet monkey chattered a warning

192

but Bootie bumped into Greenslade's corpse. Reaching out, the blind cripple touched the exciseman's lacerated neck then licked his fingers. The jetty was silent except for the friendly sounds of the sea. Bootie shuffled to the doorway and listened. All he could hear was the pounding of his own heart and the monkey panting.

'Master Fairbrother . . .' he called softly. 'Are you there, sir?'

Casting a long shadow, he knuckled inside where Milner and Fairbrother lay motionless on the floor. Cocking his head like a hunted animal, Bootie sniffed the air.

'Sergeant Fairbrother?' he called – more in hope than expectation.

Chapter 17

There was no one at home when Sarah got back, so, taking advantage of the peace and quiet, she ran the events of the past few days through her mind. For once, guilt and duty, the measures of her daily existence, were pushed aside and her own wants and needs rose to the fore. Where her husband was she did not know, and neither did she care. A turning point had been reached. The future, in the shape of George Sturt, was staring her in the face. Those few minutes sitting by a dying fire in the early hours had convinced her. She knew it and was sure that, deep down, he did too. The havoc created by her refusal to deceive had clouded the issue momentarily. Now she saw things in a clearer light. Their lives had touched. The magic had been invoked and could not be denied. Sooner or later, their paths would cross again and she would not let him go so easily a second time. As she was always telling herself, time was short. Old age could not be taken for granted.

And so, with the sleet clinging to her shoulders, Sarah Dimer set about the morning chores with a lightness of spirit that unnerved the yard dogs – more used to the sharp edge of her tongue than an affectionate scratch behind the ears. Emptying night soil, she turned her attention to the hungry scratchers bickering at her heels. Reflecting her state of mind, a handful of seed corn supplemented the usual kitchen scraps.

Then, for no particular reason, her arm froze in mid-throw. No sound or movement had triggered the alarm, merely a feeling. She turned on her heel and wet flakes slapped against her cheek.

Beyond the potato strip, a rider was trampling her turnip crop as he led a heavily burdened pack animal towards the house. Sarah shivered. The last few grains fell from her fingers to be claimed by the black rooster.

By the time she had run inside and primed her pistol, the rider was entering the yard. Fumbling with the latch, Sarah stepped out of the house as he peeled a greasy muffler from the lower part of his face. Her pulse rate doubled. The rodent eyes, large fleshy nose, deceptively feminine mouth were all-too horribly familiar. Turning the gun on him was a reflex action. But before she could shoot, he jerked the lead rein causing her husband's horse to rear. A low, sobbing moan hung on the wind then died somewhere beyond the pigsty. With one easy movement, William Jackson cut the hemp holding Dimer across the saddle and he flopped face down into the mud.

'John!' cried Sarah.

She ran to him and rolled him onto his back. One split eye swivelled in her direction. The other was a purple egg shut tight against the cruelties of the world. Trying to speak, he could not shape the words and a pitiful sob bubbled through the mess that had been his mouth. He reached out, searching for her face. Sarah drew back sharply and sprang to her feet.

Again, she aimed at Jackson. This time he spurred his horse and she took the full force of a boot in the ribs. She crashed against the stone water trough and the pistol was jolted from her grasp. Skidding across the cobbles, it struck a cart wheel and discharged harmlessly into the air.

Half-stunned, Sarah could only stare while the pain ripped through her body. The desire to kill Jackson was overwhelming, but her legs would not work, so she just sat there feeling stupid, until disgust and outrage finally forced enough air into her lungs to produce one long cry of anguish.

Dimer moaned softly. His favourite terrier had slunk out of the barn and was licking blood from his mouth.

'Get away!' rasped Sarah.

She threw a handful of mud and the dog ran for cover.

Jackson watched impassively as, crawling on all fours, she lifted John's head from the stones and urged him to get up.

'Sarah Dimer?' The tone was calm and controlled.

She twisted towards him.

195

'Ask him if it was worth it for a dollop of tea.' Then, releasing Dimer's mount, Jackson turned his own and walked on, back towards the highway.

The significance of his words was beyond Sarah. Sleet turned to rain. Strength returning, she ignored her own injuries and dragged John bodily into the kitchen where she dressed his wounds as best she could. By noon she had finished and, with half a pint of gin dulling the pain, he drifted off to sleep on the settle.

In their bedroom, she carefully strapped her ribs and eased into bed. Shock was setting in. She needed sleep, but her own pain, pulsing beneath her breast like a second heart, was too fierce. She summoned Sturt's face. The throbbing seemed to ease. Then John called her name and all the old feelings of guilt returned.

'No!' she whispered through clenched teeth. 'No!'

Work-scarred hands beat tiny clouds of dust from the straw palliasse. She had made her choice. There could be no turning back.

Sturt swept past the cripple, who was sitting on the bottom step, and ran up the winding staircase to the second floor. Long and narrow, the dragoon sick-bay looked like a gun deck, stank like a bilge. At the far end of the room, someone was sitting by the only occupied bed.

Sturt hesitated. All at once, he felt ill-equipped to deal with the situation facing him. Thoughts of John had dominated the long ride west but, surprisingly, the past had taken second place to the future. Memories of fifteen years shared experience meant nothing. All that mattered was that his friend would live; would recover sufficiently well to gather up the threads of his disjointed existence and find the peace of mind that had eluded him for so long. Though slight, that shift in Sturt's perspective was profound. It was as if a shaft of sunlight had penetrated the armour that encased his cold obsession to destroy Kingsmill. It excited and frightened him. Excited, because an unexpected splash of colour was permeating the bleak landscape of his inner world.

Frightened, in case his resolve to settle the score should be diluted by reason and common sense.

Approaching Southampton Water, it had occurred to him that Sarah Dimer had a lot to answer for. She was creeping into the very fibre of his being – despite his best efforts to exclude her.

'George.'

The voice was familiar, and Henry Kemp rose to his feet as Sturt approached.

'Henry.'

Sturt's eyes were drawn to the waxen face framed by the off-white grubbiness of soiled bed linen.

'What are his chances?'

Kemp had been dreading the question and could only shake his head.

'What does the surgeon say?'

'You know what they're like, George – don't give much away at the best of times . . .'

Sturt's eyes bored into him.

'No one expected him to last this long.'

Those few words relieved Kemp of a heavy burden and, like a Papist absolved in the confessional, he suddenly could not stop talking.

'They've sent a new Collector – with more dragoons than I've ever seen,' he said. 'Front-line troops, at that. Come down from Scotland – not the dregs we're used to round here . . .'

Sturt was hardly listening. John's breathing was so shallow that it could not be detected by eye alone. He had to touch a cheek to feel the warmth of life and know that somewhere, in a world beyond reach, John was fighting a desperate battle for survival.

'His name is Shearer,' continued Kemp, 'and he's got orders to go after Kingsmill – hunt him for as long as it takes.'

'No.'

So emphatic was the reply that Kemp picked up his coat and turned to go.

'It's the best chance you'll get,' he said. Then, as an

197

afterthought, added, 'Think on it, George. I reckon you owe him that much.'

Sturt waited until the exciseman had gone from that gloomy chamber of suffering and despair. Then, heart in mouth, he took hold of the sheet and slowly drew it back. The strength momentarily drained from his legs. Hardened as he was to death and battlefield carnage, he was unprepared for the extent of Fairbrother's injuries.

His immediate reaction was to rend and destroy anything that came to hand. Seizing the water jug by the bed, he was about to hurl it against the wall when he suddenly felt absurd. So he put the jug back and sat down.

Sarah sprang to mind – angering him again. This time, for betraying John by allowing an outsider to intrude on their private grief. However, what he failed to realize was that Sarah and John were the two people who mattered most to him. And it was perfectly natural to seek comfort from one whilst grieving for the other. Nevertheless, he banished Sarah to the subconscious and, taking hold of a lifeless hand, George Sturt wept for his friend.

Clean salt air flushed the stink of the sick-bay out of his nostrils as he stepped into the street. Thoughts elsewhere, Sturt did not hear Bootie calling his name and walked on until the bonnet monkey, chattering like an angry wren, gave his coat-tail a sharp tug. He stopped and, turning back, saw Bootie knuckling through the icy puddles.

'What is it?' he snapped irritably.

'It was you they were after, Master Sturt,' replied the cripple. 'The feller what done for Master Fairbrother asked after you by name.'

Sturt squatted on his heels and the blind man felt his breath in his face.

'I'd got my 'ead down in the alley, sir – '

'Was it Kingsmill?'

Bootie hesitated. He knew the answer that Sturt wanted to hear, and nothing would have given him greater pleasure than to provide it. But his better judgement told him to resist the temptation to please and stick to the facts.

'I couldn't swear for sure. But there's some bugger what could.'

A tremor that had nothing to do with the freezing weather ran through Sturt, causing his hand to shake as it touched the cripple's shoulder.

'Tell me,' he breathed.

'I heard him, Master Sturt,' said Bootie, equally excited. 'God strike me dead if I didn't! In the street – the minute they'd gone. Whoever it was must've seen every last one of the murderin' scroats.'

For a moment, Sturt remained motionless. Then, without a word of thanks, he was up on his feet and melting into the seething tapestry of merchants and tradesmen, urchins and pedlars, going about their business on Poole waterfront.

Bootie propped himself against the gin shop wall and the monkey settled on his lap. Scratching the creature's head with one hand whilst searching for a coin with the other, he said softly, 'The King says Master John'll walk out of that rat hold on 'is own two legs.'

The coin turned in the air and the monkey watched it drop into the mud. Fingertips as deft as a lacemaker's found it and danced across the upturned face.

Bootie sighed. 'We'll make it the best of three,' he said. 'Always more reliable is the best of three.'

Three times polished steel flashed in the smoky lamplight, and three times a roar of approval rattled around the rafters of Jude Shadwell's barn. Blood spots flew and flecked the faces of those members of the Hawkhurst Gang leaning expectantly over the pit. Kingsmill's russet champion launched another sustained attack, demonstrating why it was undefeated in more than forty contests. Yet Robert Lamb remained optimistic. His money was riding on Jackson's challenger. And when it finally struck back, opening a wicked gash across the champion's breast, his spirits rose. He looked at Shadwell, who was still taking bets, and beamed knowingly. Unable to make himself heard above the din, the landlord of the Black Dog responded with a confident shake of the head and shortened the odds on

199

Kingsmill's bird. The contest approached its climax. Kingsmill faced Jackson across the bloody arena and each urged his bird to greater effort, unaware of Harry Sheerman shouldering his way through the crush.

A haze of horse sweat hung on the thick air as the free trader loosened his sodden greatcoat. Squeezing in alongside Kingsmill, he leaned his saddle-weary backside against the parapet and glanced into the pit where Jackson's best was proving no match for the champion. Needle-sharp spurs struck home time and again until, its throat in shreds, the challenger went down flapping in its death agony.

Sheerman stepped back.

'Well, you were right,' he said. 'He was in Goudhurst.'

Kingsmill's gaze remained fixed on the dying cockerel. The moment of death, the passing from one state to another, had fascinated him since he was a child.

'And now?'

'Taken hisself off to Poole.'

The pulse in Kingsmill's neck quickened as the death shudder ceased.

'I can raise fifty men within the hour, Thomas. We'll be there by daybreak.'

'No.' Kingsmill turned away as the victor crowed in triumph.

'But I thought – '

'Patience, Harry.' The hint of a smile lifted the corners of Kingsmill's mouth. 'Give him time to bury his friend. We'll cross paths soon enough.'

Reaching into the pit, he lifted his bird and carefully removed its spurs. A cursory examination revealed that the champion's wounds were not serious. So, caressing the creature as gently as a mother would her child, he walked away, leaving Robert Lamb to count the cost of another ill-judged wager.

Sheerman shook his head. There were times when the workings of his master's mind defeated him.

The lodging house was cold, its walls streaming with damp.

200

The room had been without a fire for three days causing a film of ice to form on the cheap window glass.

Fairbrother's possessions were scattered all around: spare shirt across a chair back, shaving gear on the rickety washstand, dirty stockings tossed carelessly onto the floor close to his kitbag. The clothes he had been wearing during the raid on the Custom House had been returned and lay folded on the bed, creating a bizarre impression of normality.

Something rustled behind a rotting skirting. Sturt did not hear it. Wrapped in his greatcoat, he sat in an ancient carver, resting his feet on the cold hob. His gaze remained unblinking as he stared at John's brown-stained coat. Only his hands, clenched so tight that the knuckles shone like polished stones, gave any indication of what was happening behind the eyes. Pain and outrage consumed him. But he was mentally and physically exhausted. Right now, rational thought was beyond him. So he sat there allowing memories and emotions to flare, merge one into another, until daylight had finally gone. Then, with his mind swept clean by the purgative effect of such gross indulgence, his sense of purpose stirred again. He shivered, became aware of the chill numbing his flesh, creeping into his bones, and stood up. Pacing the floor, he considered his options, made his decision, and left.

The door banged shut and the room was again in the possession of its unseen inhabitants. Outside, the street sounds had lost their daytime urgency and taken on the more relaxed tone of evening. Inside, the cockroach squeezed through a gap between skirting and floorboard. For a moment, it remained motionless, tasting the air with its antennae. Then, having detected the sour sweet odour rising from Fairbrother's jacket, it crawled slowly but purposefully towards the bed.

Archibald Peckover peered around the door and slid into the Collector's office. Kemp and Michael Shearer had not heard him knock and ignored the nervous cough that was meant to attract their attention.

The new Collector sat at his desk studying his predecessor's much-prized map of the south coast. Kemp stood at his shoulder, and between them they marked every possible landing site within the boundaries of what was generally assumed to be Kingsmill's territory. The caterpillar of crosses tracing the beautifully drawn coastline seemed endless, confirming Kemp's opinion that, even with Shearer's dragoon reinforcements, the possibility of a patrol stumbling upon the Hawkhurst Gang during a landing was so remote as to be unworthy of serious consideration.

Peckover coughed again, a little louder.

'What is it?' snapped Shearer, without looking up.

'Excuse me, your honour.'

He paused, waiting for his new master's attention to shift his way. Instead, Kemp shot him a malevolent glance and the obnoxious clerk winced, as if kicked by an invisible boot.

'A gentleman to see you, Master Shearer.' he whined.

This time, the Collector did look up. 'I said, no interruptions, Peckover!'

'And I remembered, so I did. But it's, Mister George – '

A shoulder caught the quill-pusher in the back, cutting him off in mid-sentence. A look of surprise swept Kemp's face as the visitor entered.

'Sturt,' said Sturt, finishing off Peckover's introduction. Then, crossing to the desk, he offered his hand to Shearer. 'George Sturt. And you and I have business, sir – concerning Thomas Kingsmill.'

'The Shepherd will not be pleased to discover you back on his quarter,' said Lamb. He wiped the smoke-stained window pane with his sleeve and watched Richard Perrin ride out of the tavern yard, bound once more for the contraband warehouses of Fecamp.

'Kent is crawling with dragoons and militiamen, Robert,' said Kingsmill, who was sitting with Jackson and Sheerman. 'You said so yourself.'

Lamb turned from the window. 'I doubt if Fairall will consider that a good enough reason,' he said.

'Then again – what Fairall don't know won't hurt him, will it?' said Jackson with a sly grin to Sheerman.

Lamb ignored it and joined them. He helped himself to a cognac. Untouched by the convivial atmosphere spilling over from the cockfight, he felt tense and anxious. Normally he trusted Kingsmill's judgement implicitly. His record over the past ten years spoke for itself. But this time, the cold logic that was the cornerstone of his success appeared to be lacking. Since the raid, the authorities had been up in arms – literally. Therefore, landing a cargo on Fairall's doorstep, with all the additional problems of transport and distribution, would undoubtedly increase rather than reduce the risk. Surely, it made better sense to cease operations until the dragoons were required elsewhere? Until the temperature of official outrage returned to its usual ineffectual level?

'You're a hard man to please, Robert.'

The tone was slightly mocking and interrupted Lamb's train of thought.

'It's a straightforward run,' continued Kingsmill. 'You'll show a quick and healthy profit.'

The Magistrate said nothing, but searched Kingsmill's eyes for a solution to the puzzle. To his surprise, the gaze that could dissolve the strongest man's innards slid away. The missing piece fell into place.

'Perhaps so,' he said. 'But – ' He paused.

'Yes?' said Kingsmill.

Lamb glanced at Sheerman, then turned back to Kingsmill. His face remained expressionless as he asked, 'Where's George Sturt, Thomas?'

Sitting in Shearer's office was the answer to the Magistrate's perceptive question, listening patiently while the Collector outlined his plan to storm Hawkhurst and drag Kingsmill out in chains.

Sturt remained silent as Kemp tactfully pointed out that his lawyers would have Kingsmill out of gaol before they could turn the key – even if it was possible to get him in there in the first place, which, of course, it wasn't. Taking the Gang at the coast, Shearer's only other suggestion, Kemp also dismissed on the grounds that, without an informer, they would need half the King's Army to watch every beach and cove between Poole and Romney. A gloomy silence fell, presenting Sturt with the opportunity to voice his own eminently more practical plan of action.

As a result, Shearer's dragoons were on the road by first light the following morning. Armed only with the information that there had been an eye-witness to the mayhem at the Custom House, patrols descended upon every village and hamlet within thirty miles, where they nailed up proclamations offering an unprecedented reward of two hundred guineas for information leading to the conviction of anyone involved in the raid. But such was the reputation of the East Countrymen, as the Hawkhurst Gang was known west of Portsmouth, that not even the carrot of financial security for life could loosen a single tongue. Sullen silence was the reaction everywhere and the pile of depressing reports on Shearer's desk grew higher by the day.

Sturt, reluctant to sit around waiting for a miracle to happen, took to the road with Kemp and his fellow riding officers. For days they searched out and questioned the tenants of every isolated farm within sight or sound of the eastbound highway, only to run up against the same wall of silence. Initial enthusiasm dribbled away. By the end of the second week Shearer was again considering a suicidal assault on Kingsmill's headquarters.

Therefore, it was fortunate that Henry Kemp decided to stop off at the Headless Woman in Fordingbridge as, late that evening, he dragged his weary body homeward. It had been a bitch of a day. Soon after dawn he had questioned a family of tinkers outside Cranbourne and been savaged by their dogs for his pains. Although his torn leg was still nagging, his spirits rose as he entered the squat, reed-thatched inn.

It was packed – always a good sign. The landlord was friendly and the mulled ale much to his liking. So, squeezing through the tap-room crush, Kemp claimed an unoccupied stool next to the misted window and glanced across at the bent figure of Daniel Chater as he addressed a rapt audience of regulars.

The old shoemaker was in full flow. Revelling in his own importance, he embroidered every detail of his encounter with the Hawkhurst Gang. The mention of Thomas Kingsmill's name, dropped with studied nonchalance, had Kemp spluttering into his beer. Heads turned and, anxious to avoid drawing attention to himself, the exciseman dabbed at his ale-stained waistcoat with a well-used nose rag whilst straining to catch what Chater was saying. Just then, one of the shoemaker's less gullible neighbours cast doubt on his story. He stiffened then, firing a look at the doubter that would have felled an ox, picked up his folded coat and solemnly unwrapped John Dimer's gift. A dozen backsides lifted from their seats as he slammed the oilskin package onto the table with a flourish.

Heart banging, Kemp drained his pot, resisting the temptation to do anything rash.

Now, with his audience hanging on every word, Chater re-enacted the scene outside the Custom House. He personally despatched both guards and was breaking down the door with Kingsmill himself when the shrill tones of his long-suffering wife cut him off in full flow. Before the gin-fuddled shoemaker could move, Dorcas Chater had beetled across the room and seized him by the ear. Up on his toes with his neck twisted like a hanged man, Chater surrendered the last vestige of dignity and pleaded for mercy. Dorcas remained unmoved. Aware that, this time, her husband's notoriously slack mouth could be the death of him, she ordered instant silence. Then, to the raucous delight of all those watching, she dragged him unceremoniously towards the door.

Pausing only to harangue the landlord for allowing her husband to make such a fool of himself, Dorcas slackened her grip and Chater wriggled free. Showing a surprising turn of speed for a man of his years, the shoemaker dodged around Kemp, retrieved his precious dollop of tea and bolted for the back door with Dorcas snapping at his heels. The door slammed shut. A well-timed blow connected and a howl of agony skidded along the wet street.

Laughter rattled around the Headless Woman's ancient

205

roof timbers and Kemp joined in. He called for another jug of ale and moved closer to the fire. Perhaps it hadn't been such a bad day after all.

'I found it hidden in a ditch, your honour. On my life, it's the truth!'

Chater was so frightened that he was in danger of wetting himself. Kemp and an excise patrol had dragged him from his bed in the middle of the night. And now, still in his nightshirt and breeches, he stood before Sturt and Shearer. The Collector picked up the incriminating dollop of tea and turned to his senior riding officer.

'Kemp,' he said coldly.

Kemp stepped forward and, deliberately taking his time so that Chater might have a moment to think on what was to come, removed top-coat and vest. Muscle control deserted Chater as the exciseman took an oak belaying pin from his master.

'For the love of Christ,' he wailed, 'I'm an old man!'

Shearer and Sturt went to the door.

'Call me when he changes his mind,' said the Collector.

'Yes, sir.' Kemp took a practice swing.

'Master Sturt!' Chater's voice was hovering close to the top of its register.

Sturt paused.

'You know me, sir! Tell them I'm just a shoemaker. I had nothing to do with it. I swear . . .'

'I'm sorry, Daniel.' The tone was convincingly sympathetic. 'It's out of my hands.'

Kemp seized Chater by the scruff and raised his club.

Shearer opened the door.

Chater shrieked, 'Wait!' then he collapsed onto the floor and curled into a pathetic bony ball. 'Please . . .'

Sturt nodded and Shearer pushed the door to. Taking a beat to hide his disgust behind a mask of assumed concern, Sturt lifted the old man to his feet and sat him down in the Collector's chair.

'You don't understand,' Chater sobbed. 'I can't – I daren't!'

Shearer's fist struck the desktop and bounced the lid from his inkwell. 'Then I'll hang you! And gibbet you on your own doorstep!'

'Compared to Thomas Kingsmill's idea of justice,' retorted the shoemaker, 'the gallows would be a blessed relief!'

The truth of that grim statement was not lost on Sturt or the exciseman. From somewhere, Chater dredged up the remnants of his courage and Sturt realized that they were in danger of losing him.

'No, sir,' said the shoemaker, quieter now, more controlled. 'Beat me to death if you will, I'll not give evidence in court.'

'You don't have to.'

The old man was sure he was hearing things.

'One word,' continued Sturt, 'and you can walk out of here. Forget it ever happened.'

He took the tea from Shearer and slid it across the desk. Like a rabbit hypnotized by a dancing stoat, Chater could not take his eyes off the oilskin Judas.

Sturt loomed over him.

'Who gave it to you?' he asked.

Chapter 18

The soiled dressing was stuck to his head. Dimer grimaced as Sarah peeled it off.

'Go easy,' he complained.

'Be still then.'

She parted his matted hair and examined the half-healed wound.

'How is it?'

'You'll live.'

'No thanks to that madman Jackson!'

Sarah rolled a clean strip of linen.

'What did he mean about the tea?' she asked.

Dimer gave her a sullen look.

'John?'

'I gave a dollop to Daniel Chater.'

'Part of the Custom House cargo?'

'That's none of your business!'

She swabbed congealed blood from his scalp with vinegar. It stung like the Devil, making his eyes smart.

'I'll see things right with Kingsmill,' he said, squirming on his seat. 'Soon as I'm back on my feet. It was a stupid mistake – that's all.'

'Like killing Mary Winchcombe.'

'Who?'

Dimer let out a cry of pain as she slapped a muslin pad onto his head. Moving closer, she held it in place with one hand and wound the bandage around his head with the other. The closeness of her body took his mind off his injuries and he reached for a breast. Sarah moved behind him.

'You can help me back upstairs after supper,' he said with a smirk.

'I don't think so.'

'I'll be all right – just give me a hand on the stairs.'

'No.'

He twisted towards her. 'Tomorrow then.'

Again, that childlike tone that so exasperated her.

'I no longer want you in my bed, John.'

The expression on his bruised face was that of a six-year-old deprived of his Sunday treat.

'I mean it.' She spoke firmly, trying not to let her irritation show.

'What the Devil's up with you? Are you ailing or something?'

'No.'

'I'm your husband, Sarah.'

'In name only!' She paused, determined to stay in control. Then, lowering her voice, she continued, 'From now on – you sleep down here.'

'Like Hell!' He rose shakily to his feet. 'It's my house. It's my bed. And you'll do your duty!'

He reached for her but she stepped aside. The bandage unravelled like a May Day streamer. He made another grab. Sarah gripped his wrist.

'Touch me and I'll walk out now.' Her voice was as cold as the east wind in January. 'I swear you'll never see me again.' She let go and Dimer stood back, genuinely confused by her attitude.

'How long is this . . . banishment to go on for?'

He sounded pathetic and made her even angrier. But before she could answer, a dog barked out in the yard. Dimer's first though was that it was Jackson paying another visit. His stomach turned over.

'Well don't just stand there,' he whined. 'Go and see!'

Sarah went to the window. Her husband crossed his legs to prevent himself dribbling into his breeches.

Outside, all appeared quiet. It had been a bright day, and now the red eye of the setting sun cast an eerie light over the yard where, as the air cooled, a rising ground mist created the impression that the outbuildings were floating on some strange, colourless ocean. By the shippen, a mongrel sheepdog wrestled with the mangled remains of some unfortunate creature.

209

'It's only Drum,' said Sarah. 'He seems to have caught himself some supper.'

Dimer sat down again and waited for his heart to stop thumping. Sarah went back to him and started rewinding his bandage.

'Sarah?'

She avoided his eyes.

'Just tell me what it is I've done.'

Had she answered, they would not have heard the soft scuffling outside the door. Too late, Dimer sprang to his feet as two dragoons shouldered the door off its hinges. Suddenly, the tiny room was full of armed soldiers. A candle lantern crashed to the floor. Michael Shearer entered and, in the half-light, pointed at Dimer.

'Take him!' ordered the Collector.

'No!'

The troopers crowded their man into a corner.

'Sarah!' he shrieked. 'Stop them!'

And she tried her best, but she was no match for Kemp who held her so tight she could hardly breathe.

'Let go of him,' she gasped. 'Get your hands off me!' She stamped on the exciseman's instep and he grunted.

Shearer, meanwhile, stepped aside so that his men could drag Dimer out. A despairing hand clutched at his sleeve.

'Please, sir,' pleaded Dimer, 'I'm sick. An' I've not done nothing. On my life – I ain't!'

Shearer looked at the snivelling creature grovelling before him and felt nothing but contempt.

'Get the wretch out of here!' he snapped.

The pain shot up Kemp's arm as far as the elbow. Sarah's teeth drew blood as he ripped his hand from her mouth. Taking her chance, she was out of the door before he could stop her.

'Leave him alone!' she yelled at the top of her voice, running as fast as her legs would carry her. John, though, was already in the saddle with his legs tied beneath the gelding's belly.

'You've got no right!' she roared, then stopped in her tracks as George Sturt materialized from the mêlée. He had waited outside, hoping to avoid her. Now he wished he'd taken Shearer's advice and stayed in Poole.

A moan of deep misery died in the mist. Sarah's body seemed to sag and she shook her head. She knew that John was responsible for what was happening, but she felt betrayed by Sturt. Reason and the positive intentions of recent days fell away like flakes of dead skin. The familiar blanket of confusion descended as the dragoons rode away with John still pitifully protesting his innocence. Sarah felt more like a mother being robbed of her child than a wife losing a husband. Standing there, it occurred to her that God could not possibly be the compassionate entity the church said he was, not when He could continue to subject her to the remorseless spiritual battering that had been her lot for most of her adult life. The thought was un-Christian, blasphemous even. It should have shocked her but it didn't. The pain of the moment was too great. She needed someone to blame, so she lashed out at Sturt.

'Damn you!' she cried. 'Damn you! Damn you, George Sturt!'

Her nails gouged his cheek. A fist split his top lip, but he did not attempt to defend himself. He had no words to help her. All he could do was absorb the blows until her rage dissolved into great heaving sobs of anguish. Then he drew her gently to him. She did not resist and he held her tight, burying his face in her hair while she cried herself out.

Across the yard, Drum dragged the choice joint of beef that had bought his silence into the barn and gorged himself to the limit.

Harry Sheerman jerked his mount to a standstill. His ears were not playing tricks after all. He could hear horses, a dozen or more, heading west at the canter, closing fast. The snared roebuck slung across his saddle was still warm, and though he had nothing to fear from any keeper so close to Hawkhurst, something didn't feel right. Whether it was because the unseen riders were moving dangerously fast along a narrow rutted lane, or just a free trader's instinct didin't matter. He was not a man to take unnecessary risks. Melting into the trees some twenty yards from the road, he dismounted and clamped a hand over his horse's muzzle.

The horsemen came into view. He was right – they were travelling at reckless speed. A flash of scarlet, picked out by the waning moonlight, identified the dragoons. Sheerman muttered a curse to himself. His eye registered the armed civilians bringing up the rear but locked onto their shirt sleeved prisoner. The squat, toad-like figure hunched over the saddle was unmistakable. A shiver ran down Sheerman's spine. Anxious to make all speed, he dumped the stag's carcass in the undergrowth. He mounted up and was about to go when another, solitary, rider appeared on the road. It was Sturt but he did not recognize him. Preoccupied with the thought of John Dimer saving his own neck by landing them all in the hangman's cart, he saw just another exciseman lagging behind the rest. In a moment, Sturt too was gone and Sheerman was riding flat out for Hawkhurst.

Meanwhile, a quarter of a mile away, Dimer looked over his shoulder and gave one last cry of despair. His voice floated over the rolling downland, and Sturt rode on with Sarah's name ringing in his ears.

'George?'

There was no reply so, red-eyed and cried out, Sarah stood up and turned towards the open door. The cold light of dawn was creeping in, revealing the damage caused by Shearer's troopers. The sound of a horse breaking wind carried across the yard, followed by the rattle of riding boots on icy setts.

Sarah stepped over a broken chair and said again, 'George? Is that you?'

The visitor paused in the doorway. She blinked twice, not believing her eyes the first time.

'Mistress Dimer . . .' said Kingsmill softly.

Instinctively, Sarah stepped back. He entered the house.

'Where have they taken him?'

Instead of answering, she reached for her horse pistol, but Kingsmill was quicker and swept it from the mantel-

212

shelf. The firing piece clattered across the floor. He grabbed hold of her wrist.

'I said, where have they taken John?'

Again no answer, so he twisted her arm up her back and she gasped.

'I need to know.'

Sarah lifted onto her toes as her shoulder joint was threatened with dislocation.

'Chichester Gaol!'

'You're lying!'

Tendons were tearing and she was in danger of passing out.

'No!' she screamed 'It's the truth!'

He let go and she dropped into a chair, clutching her arm, waiting for the waves of pain to subside. Kingsmill crouched down before her.

'Who was it?' he asked. 'Who took him?'

Sarah looked into his eyes and saw the clinical coldness of an executioner. He placed a hand lightly on her shoulder.

'Soldiers,' she said, wincing, 'dragoons from Poole!'

'There were others. Civilians – not soldiers.'

'I don't know . . .'

Again, those probing fingers.

'Excisemen!' She'd said it before she could stop herself. 'I think they were excisemen!'

'One of them was called Sturt.' Kingsmill's tone changed as if he was willing her to confirm his suspicion. 'George Sturt.'

Sarah paused and this time he waited, giving her a moment to collect her thoughts. Sensing that an outright rebuttal would only cause her further suffering, she elected to do neither, saying boldly, 'Believe it or not, they neglected to introduce themselves.'

Her heartbeat faltered as Kingsmill got up. But, instead of striking her, he went to the fire.

Raking the embers with a spurred heel, he said, 'John will be safe so long as he keeps his mouth shut. They can do nothing without a witness. You see, it must be done legal. Someone has to name him in court.'

213

He moved behind her chair and leaned forward. His mouth touched her hair, making her skin crawl.

'John has a distant cousin or uncle,' he said, 'a shoemaker – name of Daniel . . .'

Terrified as she was of what he might do to her, Sarah shook her head. She could not – would not – be the instrument of Chater's death.

Suddenly, she was lifted bodily by the hair. Kingsmill turned her towards him and rammed the same arm back up between her shoulder blades.

'Who is he, Sarah? Where do I find him?'

'I don't know!'

Another inch had her shoulder sliding from its socket. The noise she made belonged on the killing fields of war. Kingsmill eased off a fraction. He was well versed in the refinements of inflicting pain and knew precisely when to stop. For what seemed like a lifetime to Sarah, he held her there on tiptoe. Then, panting into her face, he said, 'Make it easy for yourself . . .'

She bit into her lip, refusing to give him the pleasure of hearing her scream again. But her defiance only served to excite him. So he slammed her against the wall and clamped his mouth to hers. It was a bruising, joyless kiss. Sarah fought to break free – succeeding only when she sank her teeth into his tongue. Now it was his turn to cry out as he tore himself away.

Sarah flinched, but the expected blow never fell. Instead, she felt his swelling member pressing up against her belly.

'You'll tell me,' he breathed, flecking her face with blood. 'Sooner or later – you'll tell me.'

It was after midday when the house dogs woke Sheerman. Stretching stiffened limbs, he was vaguely aware of the bolts being thrown at the front door where Becky Leggatt admitted her master, exchanged a few words, then started up the wide mahogany staircase. Still half-asleep, Sheerman was wrestling with an obstinate boot as Kingsmill entered the back parlour. He looked like Hell. His face had sustained the kind of damage usually inflicted in a street brawl, and the flickering firelight somehow seemed to exaggerate it.

'Jesus, Thomas . . .'

Taking off his muddied greatcoat, Kingsmill poured himself a large measure of fine cognac. He dropped into the upholstered chair that Sheerman had vacated and dabbed at his wounds with his stock.

'His name is Daniel Chater.' He could not speak properly because his mangled tongue had swollen to double its size. Each word ran into the next as he continued. 'You'll find him living in Fairfield.' His face contorted as the grape spirit seared his mouth.

'What about the cargo?'

'Richard will be in France by now. We run it as planned.'

'And' – Sheerman made sure he was out of reach before saying it – 'George Sturt?'

Kingsmill nodded. 'As soon as it's safe stored.'

He closed his eyes and Sheerman took the hint. Picking up his boots, he turned to go as Robert Lamb entered. A vision of debauchery, the Magistrate had spent the night in one of Kingsmill's many spare rooms, sleeping off the effects of too much brandy. Sheerman closed the door behind him and, clutching a splitting head, Lamb stumbled over to the fire. 'Becky said you wanted a word with . . .' His voice tailed away as he caught sight of the bloody lacerations stretching from nose to throat, the torn ear, bite marks on the cheek. Kingsmill's eyes remained closed.

'Get your clothes on, Robert,' he said. 'You're going visiting.'

'I'm sorry, Chater, but the Law is quite specific. You must identify Dimer personally.'

Across the desk, the old shoemaker shifted his weight from one foot to the other and said, 'It just ain't a decent way of doing things, sir. Not decent at all . . .'

'The Hawkhurst Gang retain the most capable counsel,' explained Shearer. 'Every avenue of escape must be closed if he is to be persuaded to inform.'

'Name him and forget it ever happened – that's what Master Sturt said . . .'

He appealed to Kemp with his eyes, but the riding officer just shrugged his shoulders and looked out of the window.

'You're working yourself into a lather over nothing.' The tone was reassuring, almost friendly. 'Chief Officer Kemp himself will escort you.'

By pure chance, Shearer had struck the right note. The idea appealed to Chater's inflated estimation of his own importance. Nevertheless, he had no intention of making things too easy for them.

'I don't know. . .' he said, gravely. 'Happen I'll have to weigh the matter with my Dorcas.'

'I didn't offer a choice.'

The shoemaker sighed and sagged like wet washing on a windless day.

'Of course, there will be a reward . . .'

'How much?'

'Five hundred pounds for every man convicted and turned off.'

Chater had never had fifty, let alone five hundred pounds. In his imagination, he saw himself lording it over the poor folk of Fordingbridge – bestowing favours as the mood took him.

'For the rest of your life,' continued Shearer, 'you would want for nothing.'

The old man took a deep breath, then said with great sincerity, 'Oh the reward is of no consequence, your honour. It's more a question of duty, wouldn't you say?'

'Indeed.'

Chater exposed the stumpy remains of his teeth. 'When needs must, an honest citizen has to declare himself. Show the world where he stands!'

'Quite.' Shearer stood up and shook Chater's hand. 'Your public-spirited attitude does you credit, sir. I shall write you a letter of introduction to Justice Battine. You will, of course, be provided with lodgings in Chichester, and a good mount.'

The old man's face fell. 'I can't ride a rented animal!'

216

Such was the vehemence of the protest that Kemp turned away from the fishwives brawling on the jetty.

'With respect, sir, hired horses and myself is not built to get on. It's a well-known fact.' Chater puffed himself up like a mating woodcock. 'You'll have to send a carriage.'

Resisting the urge to box the old villain's ears, the Collector said, though not without difficulty, 'I shall loan you a horse from my own stable, Chater.'

'Now that's different.'

'I think you will find the beast more than adequate.'

Taking him by the elbow, Shearer marched him to the door. Henry Kemp opened it and Chater said to him, 'I'll expect you at nine sharp, sir. And mind you don't forget my letter.'

After he had gone, Kemp took advantage of his superior's offer of a glass. Tomorrow was going to be a long and tedious day.

The process had started with a glimmer of light pulsing in the blackest recess of his mind. Gradually it had spread, pushing the darkness back. Countless arbitrary collisions among the cloud of tiny fragments that had been, John Fairbrother had re-created the building blocks of the original whole. And the completion of one such block had rekindled the thought processes. From that point on, he knew that he was still alive. But with increased awareness came pain. At first, a dull throb at the outer limit of his consciousness, then, as the light grew brighter, like a spreading cancer – a terrible reminder of the true nature of the human condition.

A part of him craved a return to the comfort of non-existence. However, that intangible something which can only be described as the human spirit, proved stronger. For a time, time did not exist. Moments that could have been seconds or millennia propelled him towards the world in which, for a while longer at least, he belonged. Then a needle point of concentrated agony tore through the curtain of consciousness, ripped open gummed-up eyelids, leaving him blinded by the daylight. He was too weak to cry out, but the pain activated muscles causing his body to twist and jerk.

Something touched his forehead: a powerful, unseen presence that gradually calmed him. The pain ebbed. He tried to focus on the dark, featureless entity looming over him. Something glinted and he recognized a plate button touched by the morning sun. He shifted his gaze. A nose materialized, followed by the familiar slate-grey eyes with their stark intensity. Though he was a wasted wreck, the worst seemed to be over. He knew who he was and what had happened to him. Tension eased and a ghost of a smile lifted the corners of his cracked mouth.

At the bedside, George Sturt said nothing. He just edged his stool closer and sat with a hand resting on his shoulder.

'Bootie!'

The shout interrupted a private argument between cripple and monkey.

'Master Sturt?'

'He's come round.'

If it was possible for a blind man's eyes to express his feelings, Bootie's surely did so then. Grinning from ear to ear, he picked up his pipe and started to play with such vigour that the monkey, not to be outdone, turned back somersaults on the spot.

Bouncing down the street, Sturt was brought up sharp when he saw Sarah weaving between the street vendor's stalls.

'Sarah?' he called, taking in her ashen complexion and strange shuffling gait.

She stopped, seemingly on the point of collapse. Kingsmill had hurt her, humiliated her, done things to her that words could not describe, but he had not marked her face. Therefore, it was reasonable for Sturt, or anyone else who took an interest, to assume that she was ill rather than injured. He hurried towards her. She raised an arm, as if to deflect a blow.

'No!'

He stopped.

'Don't, George . . .' Bottled-up emotion caused her voice to crack. She paused, as if to gather strength, then asked, 'Did Daniel Chater inform against John?'

Sturt hesitated. Natural suspicion triggered what, deep down, he knew were unworthy thoughts concerning her motive for asking.

'Tell me!'

Heads turned. Passers-by slowed down, eager to eavesdrop on what appeared to be an entertaining domestic drama.

'Yes,' said Sturt.

Sarah leaned against the nearest wall. 'Kingsmill is looking for him.'

Again, those mean-spirited suspicions urged him to take her to task.

'How?'

'I told him.'

She gave him a moment in which to react but, for reasons he did not understand, he kept quiet, allowing her to explain.

'I had to. I gave him Chater's name – but I lied about where he might find him.' Her legs finally gave out and he caught her as she fell. 'They told me at the Custom House that I'd find you at the sick-bay . . .'

'Bootie!'

Down the street, the music stopped. A small crowd gathered as Sturt sat her down on the stone steps leading to the quay.

'What did he do to you?' he demanded, failing to hide his outrage.

'Help him, George.'

He sat down beside her and waited what seemed like an age before replying. 'He has to help himself.'

'By turning King's Evidence?'

'Yes.'

Bootie appeared behind them. 'Master Sturt?'

'Fetch the army surgeon.'

'No!' protested Sarah. 'I'm all right – '

'Do as I say!'

219

'Sir!'

Forcing a way through the forest of legs, the cripple knuckled down the steps with startling agility. Sturt turned to the ghoulish onlookers. 'Get back!' he ordered. 'Give her some air.'

The cutlass easing from its scabbard added weight to the authoritative tone of voice and sent bunter and fish porter, merchant and ostler's lad scurrying about their business. Sturt took off his coat and draped it around Sarah's shoulders.

'They hanged my father, George. I was six years old and my mother made us all go and watch, as a warning. I still have nightmares . . .' She looked him in the eye.

'I can't go through it again.'

'He has to name Kingsmill – in court.'

'I could have given him Chater! They'd have killed him and you'd have nothing against John!'

'There's nothing I can do.'

He hated himself for saying it – but he was so close to Kingsmill now. One word from Dimer and it would all be over. Mary could rest easy and he could – Could what? He didn't know. But at least the score would be settled.

Sarah shivered. She was suddenly cold and felt completely drained. His intransigence had claimed the last of her resources. She had deliberately appealed to him on a personal level because she needed him to do it for her. Now, having failed, she was left with no alternative but to present him with a strictly business proposition.

Holding his gaze, she said bitterly, 'They're running a cargo, George.'

He shook his head. 'Sarah – don't . . .'

'It's the truth. John told me before you took him away. I know where and when.'

He searched her eyes and detected no trace of deceit.

'Take them at the coast,' she said. 'And let my John go.'

Snorts of stifled laughter greeted the leathery little man's arrival in Fordingbridge soon after ten the next morning. Dressed in threadbare wrap rascal, worn-out bucket tops

220

and an over-sized Kevenhuler that obscured the upper part of his face, he was indeed a curious sight. To the casual observer, he was probably an old soldier fallen on hard times. However, a glance at his mode of transport would have contradicted such a hypothesis. Instead of a broken-down nag, the ideal complement to his personal appearance, he was riding a fine chestnut mare and leading a saddled grey gelding of similar quality.

Attracting children like a flame does moths, he crossed the Green and approached the church, where a young priest sent his tormentors packing with a flea in their collective ear. The stranger lifted his hat revealing a warty face and a cut wig made from goat's hair. He asked the whereabouts of Daniel Chater's house, and a moment later was dismounting outside the lime-washed cottage.

At ground level, he looked even smaller and moved with a peculiar ape-like gait thanks to arthritis in both knees. Straightening his hat, he knocked at the door and assumed what he considered to be a military posture.

Chater opened up and the welcoming smile on his face disappeared the instant he set eyes on the stranger.

'Who are you?' he demanded.

'Master Chater?'

'Who wants to know?'

The little man bowed as low as his bad back would allow, and said, 'King's Officer William Galley, sir. Your escort for Chichester!'

'The Devil you are!'

Chater tried to slam the door, but Galley managed to get a foot in.

'Get out of it!' snarled the shoemaker. 'Else I'll loose the dogs!'

'Give me but a moment and I'll explain – '

'Chief Riding Officer Kemp is to be my protector. Collector Shearer gave his word!'

'Summat come up,' said Galley. 'Ridin' Officer Kemp's bin assigned to other duties.'

'Then I'm going nowhere!'

Chater ground Galley's corns with his heel and the door slammed shut.

Perched on the water butt, nursing damaged toes, Galley bleated, 'Master Chater, I got my orders, sir.'

'Shove off! I've given fair warning!'

'Open up now – there's a good gentleman . . .'

'When I'm provided with an escort worthy of the title. And not before!'

Galley got up. He'd been warned to expect a hostile reception and had come prepared. Limping over to the gelding, he slapped its rump.

'I picked out Collector Shearer's best 'orse.'

'No!'

'And . . . I warrant you'll find my company passing agreeable.'

Chater pressed an ear to the door while Galley rummaged around inside his saddlebag. A brief silence was followed by the distinctive clunk of full bottles. Dorcas Chater watched in silence as her husband threw the bolts and eased the door open. Two bottles of cognac appeared before his eyes.

Galley grinned. 'We can take us time,' he said. 'And make a day of it.'

Chater picked up his riding coat and stepped outside. 'And just where is my letter of introduction?' he demanded.

The prison surgeon picked up the tools of his trade and nodded to the gaoler standing inside the door.

'I'm grateful to you, sir, for all your trouble and kindness,' said Dimer, fingering the fresh dressing that had replaced Sarah's handiwork.

'The Law will go to extraordinary lengths to ensure that a man is fit to hang,' replied the cadaverous sawbones. 'The next time I examine you will be on the gallows.' The gaoler opened up and he paused in the doorway. 'It always strikes me as a criminal waste of effort.'

The door banged shut and Dimer pressed his nose to the observation grille.

'You'd best scrub him down with vinegar before Justice

Battine sends for him,' said the surgeon as he followed his escort down the narrow passageway. 'I doubt his own mother could identify him in that state.'

Alone in the rat-infested cell, Dimer collapsed onto his cot. It was so unfair! Why had they chosen him when there were so many others to pick on? He closed his eyes and saw the Mare. Suddenly it was an effort to keep his breakfast down. He'd seen men dance the jig: eyes bursting, tongues turning black as they slow strangled at the end of a short halter. In desperation, he turned his gaze to the heavens, promising God that he'd never again break the Law – if only he might be spared such a hideous end. As an after-thought, he reminded Him of the hardship that would inevitably befall Sarah as a gallows widow. Surely, that was unfair too?

When God failed to respond, he curled up like a frightened child and railed against the injustice of it all. Things could have – should have – been so different! If only he'd kept his mouth shut when Jackson had wanted to kill Chater. If only he could go back in time. If only he'd listened to Sarah.

If only . . .

Fairbrother had had a good night and he lay quietly now, absorbing the sounds of the day as they floated up from the street below. Occasionally, an image of the raid flashed at the back of his mind, but he quickly suppressed it and concentrated on regaining contact with the everyday business of just being alive. Outside, the cripple started to play, having broken his fast at Swallow's Coffee House. Inside, he was vaguely aware of someone, probably the surgeon major, on the stairs at the far end of the corridor beyond the sick-bay.

He sucked the dank air deep into his lungs and sighed contentedly. At last he felt strong enough to sit up. A quick smile died with the realization that no one had yet told him the nature of his injuries. Admittedly, he hadn't asked. But that was because, until now, blanket pain had impaired his ability to identify specific detail. Imagination conjured the worst.

He tried to lever himself upright. His body refused to lift itself from the palliasse. He cursed. Perhaps something vital had been severed and he'd lost the use of both arms and legs ... Wriggling and shuffling, he tried again but succeeded only in exhausting himself. He fell back, breathing hard. A terrible foreboding twisted his innards. The shrill notes of Bootie's tune were exploding inside his skull like pistol shots. Closing his eyes, John Fairbrother summoned his courage. The fingers of his left hand gripped the top sheet. Then, eyes wide open, he threw it back – revealing the loss of his right arm.

Sturt's fingers curled around the doorknob as Fairbrother screamed.

It was a long, agonized moan of despair, and Sturt had never heard anything like it on the field of battle. But it reached deep inside him, causing physical pain as it penetrated the dark vault of intolerable memories he'd thought were safely out of reach of further experience. It ripped the scab off the wound of Mary's death and, inside his head, he heard himself making the same inhuman noise that John was making now, behind that door.

He did not turn the knob.

The moment was private, to be endured alone. His support would be required later, as John's was in Goudhurst. A momentary silence was followed by another rending cry. Sturt turned on his heel and walked quickly back down the corridor. Fifteen minutes later, he was riding past the sick-bay with Michael Shearer. Behind them cantered a crocodile of armed excisemen and dragoons that stretched all the way back to the Custom House.

Chapter 19

By late morning, the sky had cleared bringing an unexpected warmth to the day. Deep in the Sussex countryside, the sun glinted on an empty brandy flask bobbing in a flooded wheel rut. Close by, Shearer's horses were lazily cropping grass at the side of the highway. The mood was relaxed; the silence broken only by the soft sound of running water as Galley and Chater stood side by side, swaying like reeds in a summer breeze, pissing into a ditch.

'Strictly speakin', Daniel,' said Galley, concentrating hard on the job in hand, 'I ain't what you'd call a reg'lar ridin' officer. More like an auxiliary – if you takes my meanin'.'

He splashed Chater's Sunday boots and the shoemaker edged out of range.

'What sort of auxiliary?' he enquired, shaking off the last drip. 'Precisely.'

'That's 'ard to say. My official duties tends to vary from day to day.'

Chater buttoned his fall, and said, 'What do you do – most days?'

The answer was given with some reluctance.

'I rummage ships at anchor.'

Dismayed, Chater stared at him. 'A tide waiter?'

'Senior Tide Waiter!' Galley stressed the word senior. Then, boosting the inebriated shoemaker into the saddle, added, 'And sometimes I runs errands for the Collector.'

'What kind of errands?'

'King's business,' said Galley with a conspiratorial intimacy. 'I'm a sort of Special King's Courier, fetchin' an' carryin' all along the coast. I've even bin to Brighton – twice!'

Chater shook his head as Special King's Courier Galley hopped around trying to remount the chestnut.

'I'm promised an armed escort,' he said gloomily, 'and they send me – '

'An armed escort!'

Galley's rump dropped into the saddle and he pulled an ancient horse pistol out of his saddle bag. 'I borrowed it from Tom Hogg . . .' His mount continued to turn on its axis, and the business end of the gun passed dangerously close to Chater's head. 'A fine lookin' piece, eh?'

The shoemaker remained unimpressed until, the next time around, the 'fine lookin' piece' exploded whilst wafting under his nose. Luckily, the ball missed him by a whisker, but etched a neat groove in the gelding's rump before burying itself in the mud. A split second later, Chater sailed through the air and landed head first in the ditch. Mortified, Galley looked on as the wounded grey disappeared down the road. Then, with Chater in imminent danger of drowning, he leapt into action.

'Beg pardon, Master Chater . . .'

The shoemaker surfaced, and Galley dragged him onto the grass like a gaffed fish.

'You'll not say nowt now, will you? To Collector Shearer, I mean . . .'

Chater sat up and Galley flicked a piece of weed from his ear with the finesse of a barber surgeon.

'Get your hands off me!'

The smell was awful as the shoemaker rose unsteadily to his feet.

'I'd be safer with the Hawkhurst Gang riding escort . . .'

Something brown and nasty was dangling from the end of his nose. He drew breath and it vanished down his throat, triggering a violent coughing fit.

'Sweet Jesus,' cried Galley, thumping him firmly between the shoulder blades. 'Don't swallow it. Francis Felkin's 'orse died of sommat terrible 'avin' drunk from a ditch!'

A final, hernia-inducing effort expelled the glutinous foreign body, and left Chater gasping.

'My letter!' he croaked, frantically searching his water-logged pockets. 'Where's my letter of introduction?'

Before Galley could answer, he was back in the ditch, scrabbling around like a seven-year-old after tadpoles.

Galley, meanwhile, had retrieved the undamaged letter from the verge.

'Daniel . . .'

'What?' snapped Chater.

The tide waiter beamed as he showed the letter. Then his face fell as a singularly unpleasant thought occurred.

'God save me,' he groaned. 'What's Master Shearer goin' to say – when 'e finds out I shot 'is 'orse in the arse?'

'An excellent glass, Battine. I regret not having called on you before.'

Chichester's Senior Justice picked up the decanter. 'Always a pleasure to entertain a colleague with a discerning palate,' he said, refilling Lamb's glass. 'Your health, sir.'

'And fortune,' toasted the Magistrate.

Battine's eyes never left him while he drank. Even so, quite why Lamb felt so ill at ease with the man wasn't clear. Perhaps it was because he'd retained the air of the naval officer he'd been for so long. Or perhaps it was something to do with the reason for his own reluctant visit. The Magistrate drained his glass and accepted another. He was standing in the bay window of Battine's third-floor chambers and, in order to escape his host's gaze, allowed his attention to drift towards the massive gates of Chichester Gaol. As he sipped his claret, Dimer's brutish gaoler crossed the street before entering the building in which they stood.

'If I say so myself,' said Battine with considerable pride, 'you'd be hard pressed to encounter more secure accommodation outside the Tower of London.'

'A veritable fortress, sir – by anyone's standards,' said Lamb. 'And I believe presently holding a prisoner of distinction?'

Battine did not answer, and returned the decanter to its proper place on the inlaid table opposite the bureau.

Lamb, meanwhile, remained undeterred. 'Come, sir,' he coaxed, 'the tongues of the gossip-mongers are seldom still where the Hawkhurst Gang is concerned.'

227

'So it would seem.'

'Then it isn't true?'

A tight mouth, in Battine's opinion, was an essential factor in running a tight ship. He insisted on both from his subordinates and expected no less of himself. Unfortunately, he was prone to the occasional lapse when encouraged to flaunt his own successes.

'I didn't say that,' he said.

Lamb forced a convincing smile. 'Allow me to offer my whole-hearted congratulations – '

'You are a trifle premature, sir. The stubborn wretch is not yet persuaded that turning King's Evidence is the only way to postpone his descent to Hell.'

The knock at the door masked Lamb's sigh of relief.

'Yes?'

' 'Scuse me, your honour,' said the gaoler, bobbing like a fishing float.

'What is it?'

'The prisoner Dimer, sir. Bin yellin' the place down, 'e 'as.' He shuffled respectfully into the room. 'Seems 'e can already feel the 'alter round 'is pipe. Says 'e's got names – dozens of 'em. But for your ears only like.'

The invitation to witness Dimer's interrogation was impossible to refuse. However, entering those grim gates, Lamb felt more like a condemned man than an honoured guest. The pass-door slammed to and, for a moment, the Magistrate wondered if he would be allowed to walk out again.

In his cell, Dimer now sat quietly on his cot. The scrubbing had brought him up as pink as a boiled lobster, while the vinegar had made his eyes smart and run. Footsteps echoed down the passageway. He stuffed his shirt-tails into his breeches and stood up.

'Wait here until I call you,' said a voice he didn't recognize.

'Yes, sir,' came the gaoler's reply.

A key turned in the lock.

Dimer wiped bloodshot eyes, in case the Chief Justice should think he'd been snivelling. After all, to show weak-

228

ness in the face of the enemy was to surrender advantage. Kingsmill had said it often enough, though the use to which Dimer was about to put his advice was hardly what he'd had in mind. Loyalty and courage had never been his strengths, but his instinct for survival was stronger than most. Thanks to Chater, he knew he had to inform. He also knew that even if Kingsmill, Jackson and all the rest were turned off before he was released, he would not live to see another spring – unless he was guaranteed a government pension and a new start, a long way from Kent, for himself and Sarah. Therefore, instead of begging for his life, he had to strike a hard bargain with Battine. And in order to do that, he would have to present a confident appearance. He was still composing himself when the door swung open and the Chief Justice entered.

'Well, John Dimer,' he said, 'not before time.'

Dimer was about to open negotiations when he noticed the other gentleman hovering in the doorway. Even with a nosegay clamped to his face, he recognized Robert Lamb at once. A barely perceptible shake of the head and all Dimer's positive intentions turned to dust. The panic came flooding back. He turned away, knowing that if he kept quiet Battine would hang him. And if he was to inform, Kingsmill would have him murdered in his cell as sure as night followed day. If only he had someone to advise him. If only he'd not been so stupid.

If only . . .

A handful of kitchen scraps lulled the hens into a false sense of security. Squabbling over the tastiest morsels, they failed to notice the kitchen girl inching nearer. She timed her strike to perfection and snatched the plumpest bird out of the mêlée. A quick twist and pull and she crossed the yard, pinching the stable lad's backside as she passed. A handful of oats showered her hair and she disappeared with a laugh. Blushing like a bride, the pimpled youth slapped the grey's neck and suggested a painful, probably impossible, remedy for the girl's high spirits. Nearby, young Sam Payne finished grooming the mare and, pondering the anatomical

229

complexities of the lad's suggestion, entered his mother's inn.

In the tap-room, he tossed a fresh log onto the fire, in front of which Daniel Chater's boots and greatcoat were drying. Bloated on gin and self-importance, Chater was up on his stockinged feet, confidentially announcing to the White Hart's regulars that he and his companion were not really what they seemed, but men of importance going about the King's business. To his surprise, no one believed him. Fisting the tabletop, he insisted that Galley, who was stretched out on the hearth, sleeping off a skinful with the Widow's hounds, was in fact a senior excise officer – and his personal escort. The resulting gales of laughter roused him to a fury. A glimpse of Shearer's letter with its official seal silenced the disbelievers at a stroke – at which point young Samuel slipped out and fetched his mother.

Transfixed by the letter, Hannah Payne issued instructions to her son and approached the shoemaker who was, by now, well into his stride. Admiring the letter, fingering the seal, she glanced at Galley and remarked on the high quality of the current crop of King's officers. Then, laughing with Chater, she filled his tankard to the brim.

Outside, Samuel told the lad to get the grey gelding under cover at once. Then, walking Galley's mare out onto the highway, he mounted up and spurred her in the direction of Southampton Water.

There was only one way down to the secluded cove, a steep track winding tortuously amongst the crumbling buttresses of shale, and Edmund Luker was guarding the top end of it. He had been sitting there for the best part of two hours during which time the tide had started to fall, forcing the overdue lugger to anchor off instead of running onto the beach as planned. Now, with the tub warp in place and the skiff running the last of the dry goods ashore, he estimated that another hour would see them off the beach and safely on their way home. All in all, things had gone smoothly, so the Hawkhurst Gang's look-out relaxed a little and packed a favourite dudeen with duty-free weed.

230

Flint sparked on steel, and he was working out his share of the profits when a soft rustling set the hairs on the back of his neck on end. Pistol and musket lay close by. He chose the latter and scanned the headland. He could see nothing to cause alarm. A second look and he dismissed it as just a gust of wind moving the dead bracken. He sat down again – only to spring back up as a harness clinked somewhere beyond the headland. Man and beast appeared simultaneously, silhouetted against a clear night sky by a bright half-moon. Try as he might, Luker could not identify the figure so, to be safe, took aim at his head.

'It's all right, Edmund.'

The soft voice was familiar.

'It's me – Harry Sheerman.'

Luker lowered his musket. Travel-stained and weary, Sheerman approached. 'Where's Thomas?' he asked.

'Helping haul tubs. The ship were late, but they're almost done.'

Leading his horse down the track, Sheerman noticed the smouldering pipe where Luker had dropped it. He crushed it beneath his heel.

'He'd have your balls if he knew.'

Luker nodded and breathed a sigh of relief. Little Harry was a mate and could be relied upon. Nevertheless, he waited until he had disappeared from view before taking a second pipe from a pocket. Searching for his baccy, he didn't see what hit him. A blinding flash behind the eyes preceded total darkness, and that was the last he knew.

As he hit the ground, Sturt shoved the belaying pin back into his sword belt and rolled the look-out's body into the undergrowth. Then, waving the all-clear, he watched as Shearer and sixty armed men slid noiselessly over the skyline.

For Fairbrother, it had been the recurring fear of the army years: not death but maiming. Being crippled was the ultimate horror and now it had happened. A day to brood had left him totally drained. Uncontrolled panic was not sustainable, and the ifs, buts and maybes of how it might

231

have been avoided had soon crowded in, plaguing him until the onset of bitterness. That was a new experience. To date it had not been in his nature, and intellectually it fascinated him.

For a moment, he managed to stand outside himself, watching as the pus of human frailty boiled over, shaping the desire for revenge. A desire so strong that it transcended the defined limits of existence – searing the soul, as if another living entity was consuming him from within. For the first time, Fairbrother fully understood the beast that was driving Sturt. The difference between them, however, was that George no longer heard the tiny voice that was still advocating reason to him.

Confused, Fairbrother had tried to analyse thoughts and emotions that were tearing great gaping holes in the fabric of his mind. Caught in a vortex of despair, he was only saved by a surge of simple physical pain. Starting as a phantom in the region of his missing right hand, it ripped through his nervous system until it blotted everything else out. Whether real or imagined, it caused him to black out. And when he came to, that manic free fall towards the pit of insanity had stopped. Somewhere in the distance, he heard the faint echo of that tiny voice. He focused what was left of his energy on himself. The voice was saying that the survival of the essential John Fairbrother was all that mattered.

For the rest of the day, he did not eat or sleep, remaining locked in that inner world. He tried to see the future – caught what he thought was a glimpse and reached out. It dissolved as he touched it. But somehow, whatever it was gave hope.

Night fell, and the next thing that he was aware of was a church clock striking midnight. His candle lantern flickered and flashed in the fragment of mirror glass nailed to the wall. He got slowly out of bed. He was naked except for the bulky surgical dressing that encased the stump of his arm. Rag legs carried him to the glass. A spider's web of cracks exaggerated the disjointed image that stared back at him. He turned his eyes away – then forced them back.

Crude stitching had successfully closed the cutlass slashes across chest and shoulders. The rest appeared undamaged. His reflection suddenly changed. Bootie's sightless eyes gleamed in the candlelight. Fairbrother touched the glass and the cripple disappeared. Perhaps it was possible to survive the ultimate horror?

On a cot close by lay the possessions of a recently deceased trooper. With his left hand, Fairbrother slowly drew the hanger from its scabbard. Trembling fingers gauged the weight and balance. Back in front of the glass, a clumsy attempt to cut saw the blade sink deep into the woodwork. He jerked it out and swung again. Slash, parry; stab, parry . . . the classic strokes of swordplay repeated time and time again. The pain meant nothing. All that mattered was . . . Was what? Grotesque shadows leapt up the walls, danced on the ceiling, as he shut out the thoughts and just kept swinging.

'The slut lied to you.'

White surf rolled in, wetting Kingsmill's boots.

'Tell me,' he said.

'He don't live in Fairfield. Never has done – not a soul there has heard of him.'

Jackson tossed a pair of roped casks to the next man in line, and said, 'Faced with a witness, Dimer will talk. Even Lamb's silky tongue won't stop him.'

'Then we'll muzzle him! And Chater too!'

'How?'

'Kill them!' Kingsmill stormed off. 'Kill them both!'

He stopped at the rocks, his face contorted with rage. For fully ninety seconds he stood rigid, using every ounce of his will to regain control of his feelings. Finally, his features softened, though his eyes continued to glitter like live coals.

'Oh, Thomas . . .' Jackson said it to himself, not daring to intrude. He'd been with Kingsmill for a long time now, and his great strength had always been his ability to remain ruthlessly clear-headed when disaster threatened. That was what set him apart. But this was different. Yes, Dimer was a problem – but he could be silenced. Therefore, such an extreme reaction was unwarranted. There had to be something else. He watched as Kingsmill paced like a caged animal, and it occurred to him that he was fighting a war with himself. As if, inside, two Thomas Kingsmills were bludgeoning the life out of one another.

'Sturt . . .' said Kingsmill with chilling control. 'It must be Sturt.'

'Thomas?'

The voice was familiar. He turned as the skiff ploughed into the sand, and the twisted figure of Richard Perrin limped up the beach.

A hand closed around her mouth, gagging any attempt to scream. The arm that lifted her squeezed the breath out of her. But still she fought every inch of the way across the headland.

'Where on earth did you find her?' asked Shearer, an expression of disbelief on his face.

'Topside of the headland, sir,' replied the trooper, as an elbow jabbed him in the bread-basket.

His commanding officer, Major Ben Austin, ran an appreciative eye over her body. 'What in God's name was she doing?'

'Sitting, sir. Just sitting and staring at the beach.'

Born and brought up in London, Austin shook his head. 'Probably something to do with the in-breeding down here.' His eyes undressed her. 'Such a terrible waste,' he said, with genuine regret.

'Take her to the horses,' Shearer ordered. 'And see she stays there.'

A kick on the kneecap made him shout and brought Sturt sprinting up the track.

'Sarah!' he exclaimed, as she took another swing at the trooper.

Shearer nursed his throbbing knee. 'You know her?'

'Yes. Let her go.'

The dragoon didn't need telling twice. He dropped her like a hot cinder, making her even angrier.

'I'll go as I please, sir!' she yelled at the Collector. 'And I'll thank you to keep your orders for those in your employ!'

Sturt grabbed her and closed his own hand around her mouth. In an instant, her rage was re-directed, and in a thrashing tangle of arms and legs, he hauled her up the steep hillside. Out of earshot of those on the beach, he forced her down onto the ground and held her still.

'Sarah!' he said sharply.

She bit him.

He shifted position and held her from behind.

'Sarah – stop fighting me and I'll let you go.'

He buried his face in her hair and the resistance ceased. Cautiously, he removed his hand. Her lips were bruised and she licked a trace of blood from her teeth.

For a moment, Sturt said nothing. Her presence had thrown him, diverted his attention from the job in hand.

'You shouldn't be here,' he said eventually.

'I want to see him finished.'

'You could get hurt – '

'I gave him to you!'

'And that's enough. Go home.'

'No!'

'Please.'

'I can't!' Fighting for control she paused, then said very slowly, 'I've got better reason than you, George – for wanting him dead.'

Instinctively, he raised his hand and touched her face. His innermost feelings had slipped the leash and, though he could say no more, the gentleness, the caring concern of that simple action was too much for Sarah. At that moment, she just wanted to be with him. She wanted to show her feelings. She wanted to tell him what Kingsmill had done to her – because carrying the burden of that dreadful night, alone, was destroying her: turning her into a blinded, primitive creature thirsting for vengeance.

Her eyes filled up. The floodgates were close to bursting when her fingers curled around his. He drew her to him. She could smell his body, taste his breath as his mouth closed on hers. Their arms entwined and they were locked

235

together – the two halves of a whole. Each knew what was happening. Each was terrified. But neither had the will to resist. He was reaching into her, exploring her mind, her body, her heart – the very core of her existence. Like never before, she felt at one with the world in which she lived.

The taste of salt air intoxicated her. She could feel the heat of the day rising through the damp earth, enveloping them where they lay. It was as if she was being reborn, shown a crystal-clear vision of the future she deserved. His tongue danced in her mouth. The muscles inside her tightened, causing her juices to run. Causing a shadow as black as infinity to pass over her consciousness.

All at once, the nightmare returned and her blood ran cold. She pulled away from him. Kingsmill was no longer confined to the beach. His presence was all around her. Taunting. Humiliating. Hurting. Not once but twice – then again, and again . . .

'Sarah?'

She shrank from his touch. He knew why and tried to find the right words.

'It's all right,' he said lamely. 'I know – '

'George?'

Henry Kemp appeared on the track. 'They're horsed and ready to go,' he said. 'It's time.'

Twenty yards away, a pitch torch roared in the wind. Sturt stood up. He looked into Sarah's eyes and two tortured souls met on a different, altogether bleaker, plane.

'I'll take you to where you can see the beach,' he said.

'Who are they?'

Chilled to the bone, Shepherd Fairall pulled off his riding gloves and beat the life back into wooden fingers.

'I don't know,' replied the Widow, as Smoaker Mills helped himself to a quart of hot. 'That one says he has business at Chichester Gaol, while the one in the hearth boasts of being a King's officer.'

The leader of the Chichester Gang was in a murderous frame of mind. It was two in the morning. The Widow's boy had dragged him away from the card table. He'd ridden half-way across the county on a freezing night. And for what? He crossed to the fire and took a closer look at Galley and Chater.

'Damn it, Hannah, they're just two old tosspots!'

Chater turned in his sleep, and Mills said, 'No. Look again, Shepherd. The mudlark was in Poole – outside the Custom House.'

Hannah Payne produced Shearer's letter from the folds of her skirt. She gave it to Fairall. He stared uncomprehendingly at the copperplate handwriting.

'It's addressed to Justice Battine.' She turned it over. 'And that is the Poole Collector's official mark.'

Fairall fingered the wax seal, then glanced around the tap-room where a couple of journeymen weavers were still drinking in a corner.

'The back parlour?'

She nodded. 'I kept it empty.'

'Wake the bastards!'

Mills finished his drink in one swallow.

'Do it gently, Smoaker,' the Widow cautioned.

So, exuding goodwill and juniper cordiality, Mills shook Chater by the shoulder. 'Rouse yourselves gentlemen,' he said with a smile, then spitefully twisted Galley's ear. 'Can't have you hogging the grate all night, now can we?'

Fairall, meanwhile, picked up his riding whip and started towards the back parlour.

'Shepherd?'

The Widow took it from him and ran a finger down his chest.

'Just keep them company,' she said. 'There'll be others keen to talk to these two.'

Across the yard, young Samuel stabled Galley's mare with Chater's gelding, then, absolutely out on his feet, fell asleep in the hay.

Chapter 20

Shearer's voice broke the silence and every man on the beach froze where he stood. 'Thomas Kingsmill!' he bellowed. 'In the name of His Majesty, King George, I order you to surrender.'

Austin's troops were pouring down the track like an army of crimson ants.

'You have precisely thirty seconds to stack your weapons!'

'They're already on the path, Thomas,' said Perrin, tugging at his sleeve.

Jackson pointed to the skyline. 'And all over the headland,' he added.

'Thomas!'

The sound of Sturt's voice sent the adrenalin surging through Kingsmill's veins.

'Give yourself up! There's no way out!'

In Perrin's opinion, that was a fair assessment of their predicament. But, to his astonishment, Kingsmill merely smiled and searched the hillside for the man behind the voice. 'Perhaps so!' he called. 'But it will cost you dear to prove it, George!'

Again the smile – not a smile of joy or even pleasure, but a manifestation of something much more fundamental. For a second or so it puzzled Perrin, distracting him from the immediate danger. The word resignation occurred, and he dismissed it – that was not in Kingsmill's nature. Then it came to him. It was the smile of a man at peace. Almost priestlike, it expressed the inner calm of a man who had finally encountered his destiny. A fire on the headland sent a column of smoke into the night sky and broke his train of thought.

'What are they up to?' queried Jackson.

High above them, a second blaze burst into life, followed by a third, then a fourth . . .

Henry Kemp waited until each of the improvised, man-high, fireballs was alight then gave the order that sent them tumbling down the hillside, scorching fiery paths through the bracken until they crashed onto the shingle and lit the horseshoe bay from end to end. Perrin hobbled out of the way as one passed by en route for the surf where it died with a hiss.

Kingsmill laughed outright as his men waited for orders. There was no panic, but, with the dragoons closing fast, there were fifty pairs of eyes on him.

'William–twenty men to form a rearguard. Richard' – he turned to Perrin as the soldiers fanned out across the beach – 'take the horses around the point.'

Perrin stared at the sea crashing onto the rocks. 'But the tide has turned – it's not possible!'

A ragged volley echoed and a packhorse thrashed in the sand.

'Do it!' snapped Kingsmill, shooting dead the leading trooper.

A concentrated volley from the rearguard killed two more, then it was down to bayonet and cutlass. No quarter was asked or given. Casualties mounted on both sides as sheer weight of numbers pushed the free traders back towards the sea.

With Kemp at his heels, Sturt cut a way to the very heart of the battle. All around, men were screaming and dying. He took a shot at Harry Sheerman and missed. The ball struck a horse laden with tea and it fell on its handler, drowning him in two feet of water. Sheerman charged. Sturt threw his empty pistol. It took him on the forehead and he went down like a slaughtered ox.

'Thomas!' cried Sturt.

But there was neither sight nor sound of him. Then Jos Place tried where Sheerman had failed. Kemp parried, and Sturt despatched him at a stroke. Again, he cried out. And this time, Kingsmill did hear him.

He was making for the skiff with Jackson. Half his men were dead or taken, but the cargo was now safely out of reach. Common sense told him to break off the action and

239

take to the boat. Instead, he waded ashore – eager to confront the ghost that had haunted him for so many years.

At first, Sturt could not be sure. He saw no more than a vague grey shape floating in and out of the shadows. Then, with a hanger in one hand and a short dagger in the other, Kingsmill appeared through the smoke and flames like a warrior from another age.

Neither man spoke. Wise by experience, they circled one another, each looking to strike the first vital blow. Oblivious to the carnage all around, they abandoned the present and planted their feet firmly in the past. Not the recent past of Goudhurst and the river-bank, but the past of pre-history: of a time before man had acquired the fragile veneer of civilization. With the surf boiling around their ankles, each had but one thought – to rend and destroy the other.

It was Kingsmill who struck first. Sturt parried and countered. A flurry of blows and they both backed off, breathing hard, assessing relative strengths and weaknesses. Close by, a fireball broke up and sent a column of sparks spiralling towards the heavens. Held in the eerie glow, they fell upon each other again. Driven by hate, they collided and recoiled, struggled blindly, instinctively, for supremacy. Steel flashed in the firelight. Knuckles and boots smashed home as both men stood their ground, refusing to give an inch. They fought to the point of exhaustion: until, summoning the dregs of his strength, Kingsmill made one final effort. Sturt deflected the blow with his handguard, and opened Kingsmill's chest from collarbone to sternum. He staggered back, and Sturt was on him. But the scent of victory made him careless. Kingsmill side-stepped his mis-timed lunge and kicked the legs from under him. Falling face down onto the saw-toothed rocks, Sturt was momentarily stunned – spread-eagled like some sacrificial victim on a Viking altar. Bleeding heavily, barely able to stand, it was Kingsmill's turn to strike the death-blow. He dropped the dagger and raised his hanger with both hands, unaware that Henry Kemp was charging in behind him.

'Thomas!'

Sheerman's warning saved his master's life. Kingsmill

ducked and spun in one movement. The upswing caught
Kemp under the left ear. The blade broke on impact but
still took off the side of his head. Stone dead, he sailed
past, and, carried by momentum, ran on until he cannoned
into Sturt and flopped onto the rocks. Then a shot rang
out, taking Kingsmill in the arm. He went down and rolled
away from the light. Sheerman dragged him to his feet.

'Thomas . . .' he implored, his own bloodied face a mask
of pain and terror. 'For Christ's sake – come on! The
boat . . .'

A quick glance confirmed that to delay would be suicidal.
Dragoons were everywhere. And the few surviving smugglers were splashing into the sea in a desperate attempt to
reach the skiff or, as a last resort, swim directly for the
lugger lying hove-to beyond the point.

Kingsmill's knees buckled, he was close to passing out.
Sturt, though groggy, was back on his feet and Shearer was
almost upon them. Suddenly it was over. And with Harry
Sheerman's help, Kingsmill turned tail and ran for his life.

'No! Thomas . . .'

Sturt's words echoed like pistol shots as he plunged into
the heaving sea.

'Damn you to Hell! Come back!'

Head spinning, he blundered down to the water's edge
and watched helplessly as Jackson hauled first Kingsmill
then Sheerman into the skiff.

'Thomas . . .!'

The sound he made was barely human and skimmed the
waves, hounding Kingsmill as the darkness closed around
him. For a moment, Sturt stared into the night, willing the
skiff to return. Then, all hope gone, he walked slowly up
the beach towards the track, past Shearer as he drew a coat
over the remains of Henry Kemp's face. A movement on
the headland caught his eye and he paused.

Somewhere, a seal moaned and Sarah drew her cloak
tight around her shoulders as she disappeared over the
skyline. Her instinct had impelled her to go to him but,
emotionally, she was too exhausted and had nothing left to

241

offer. She needed time before facing him again. Time to gather her resources. Time to lick her wounds in private.

They came in the back way. Soon after dawn. In dribs and drabs. By the drover's road that cut through the ancient oak wood. A peculiarly sombre atmosphere descended upon the White Hart. Perhaps because a cloud bank blew in with them, bringing with it a steady drizzle that leached the colour from an already stark winter landscape. Or perhaps it was more to do with the aura of human misery that always clung to the Hawkhurst Gang like a second skin.

Richard Perrin waited at the skilling beyond the outbuildings and supervised the transfer of a cargo that had cost them dear. Jackson, meanwhile, took his ailing master straight to the inn where an anxious Widow Payne waited at the door. They were long overdue and she had not slept. One look at Kingsmill as he slid from the saddle and the opened letter in her apron pocket was forgotten. She helped him inside where, dead to the world, Fairall and Mills were stretched out in drunken slumber.

The rain turned to sleet and slapped at the windows. Jackson shivered. He too was close to the end of his tether as he walked the horses towards the stable. Glancing through the back parlour window, he glimpsed Galley and Chater sleeping like babes in front of a pulsating fire.

He started to cough. A wetting, followed by two hours in the saddle, was not good for his bad chest. The wind picked up, driving clinging flakes into his face. It was, he thought, one of those days when old men, tired of the pain of existence, decide that it is not worth going on. In short, a perfect day for dying.

Chapter 21

News of the mauling inflicted upon the Gang spread like wildfire. It had happened on a Tuesday night, and by Thursday noon it was the sole topic of conversation in every coffee house and drinking den in the southern counties. Within the week, Kingsmill had been named in the *London Gazette* as a common smuggler and murderer, which meant that, armed or not, he could be arrested on sight.

The pressure was mounting. For the first time, the Hawkhurst Gang had been seen to be fallible. Even so, such was Kingsmill's reputation that, despite a reward of a thousand guineas for information, his whereabouts and those of Galley and Chater, remained a mystery. It was as if forty free traders, sixty horses and the Crown's vital witness had never existed.

Then, ten days after Galley and Chater set out for Chichester, Shearer's chestnut mare turned up at Will Thurston's place outside the Hampshire village of Sway. At first, the less-than-honest farmer could scarcely believe his luck. To own a saddle-horse of quality had long been a dream and as, to the best of his knowledge, no one local was missing such an animal, he had no qualms about keeping it. What changed his mind was no stab of conscience, but the patches of dried blood staining saddle and flanks. The beast was uninjured except for a foreleg chafed by a broken horselock. Therefore, it stood to reason that it was the rider who had sustained some serious, probably fatal, damage. It occurred to him that if he was found out, he might well be accused of complicity in a crime that would see him turned-off and gibbeted on Sway Green. Three hours later, he surrendered the mare to the dragoons.

Nagged by what might have been, Thurston went back to ploughing his potato strip. Turning an arrow-straight furrow in the rich earth, he wondered if it all had something to do with those two old men the Excise had been trying so hard to find. The dragoon officer had given nothing away. But if he was right, surely his public spiritedness deserved some small consideration?

To the farmer, the mare meant a few extra guineas to tide him over the winter. To John Dimer, it meant life. Despite objections from Sturt and Shearer, Chief Justice Battine had had no choice but to release him. He had not confessed and there were no witnesses against him. So, at 8.00 a.m. sharp, the pass-door opened and he was unceremoniously thrown into the street. Twisting an ankle, he fell heavily, scattering a flock of sheep on their way to slaughter.

Sarah helped her husband to his feet. Eyes brimming, he threw his arms around her and kissed her on the mouth. She did not resist; neither did she respond. But helping him into the donkey cart, she wished the ground would open up and swallow her. She had not seen him, but she knew that Sturt was somewhere close to hand, watching her every move. She had sensed his presence in Battine's chambers when she had collected John's release order, and again as she had presented it to the Prison Ordinary. Now, steering the General through the market day crush, she could feel his eyes boring into the back of her head.

For a moment, she recalled their meeting in Goudhurst; remembered the exhilaration, the sense of purpose that came from having glimpsed the future. The future that had previously existed only in dreams. But she was no longer the same person. And suddenly it struck her that Sturt had been unable to face her because Kingsmill had violated her. Life, she knew, was not fair. However, until now, she had not realized quite how cruel and complex it could be.

She looked at John and he smiled. The thought occurred that had Chater identified him and the Law taken its course, there would have been one less complication to clutter her life. Such a thought was uncharitable, but so great was her misery that she felt neither guilt or shame. The ordeal of existence would go on and she, as always, would get on with it as best she could, because the only alternative was

244

to stop existing. And that was unacceptable. For Sarah Dimer, the game quite simply had to be played to the bitter end.

The cart crawled up the long hill that led to the Broyle, and Sturt turned away from the window. At that moment, the gulf between them appeared unbridgeable. And the irony was that it was all due to a misunderstanding. He had not rejected her because Kingsmill had raped her. On the contrary, the courage she had demonstrated had, if anything, increased his feelings for her. But he had failed her: abused her trust by allowing him to escape from the bay. And that was as unacceptable to him as giving up on life was to her. His own thirst for vengeance had not diminished, but now it was equalled by his desire to settle for Sarah.

He would not – could not – face her again until Kingsmill was dead.

After years of neglect, the house was again beginning to ressemble a home. The roof had been re-thatched, rotted window frames replaced and, by keeping the fires burning twenty-four hours round, the walls were finally showing signs of drying out. The barn though was still in a sorry state and for the past week Alan had been working all hours replacing the worst of the weather-boards.

Now, perched on top of a rickety ladder with a mouthful of nails, he was putting the finishing touches to the south side.

'He's got to be told, Alan.'

Jan's idea of footing a ladder was to sit on the third rung planning the vegetable garden that was currently no more than a mud patch between yard and corn strip.

'Not yet, he hasn't,' came the mumbled reply. 'There's no point in aggravating his humour before we has to – no point at all.'

'You're still scared of him.'

'I am not!'

A shower of iron raindrops rang on the flagstones. Jan smiled and looked up. Alan's shirt was open and, as he spiked the last board into place, she caught a tantalizing glimpse of straining muscle and sinew.

'Then tell him,' she said.

'When I'm good and ready.'

Satisfied with his handiwork, he came down.

'I just don't like family rows, that's all,' he explained.

'There won't be a row. He'll be as proud as a dog with two tails.'

'Till he does the arithmeticals.'

He moved the ladder round to the west, and worst, wall. Jan followed with his jerkin.

'Alan . . .'

'No!'

Her scheming voice was what old Edward called it; an inheritance from her mother that usually meant that he was about to agree to something he didn't want to.

'You wouldn't have things different, would you?'

He angled his ladder and eyed her suspiciously. 'Depends on what you mean by different.'

She smiled. 'You know.'

Again that tone.

He paused. Then, choosing his words carefully, said, 'All things considered, I reckon I should have done a George Sturt' – he picked up a crowbar and hooked it onto his belt – 'and joined the Army while I was still winning!'

Smiling to himself, he'd reached the fourth rung before her fingers ran up the inside of his thigh.

'Now Jan, that's not playing fair!'

'George disappeared before he knew what he was missing,' she said. 'The same could hardly apply to you.'

Interest stirred in his breeches. It always did when she started her tricks. However, this time he was determined to resist.

'It's the middle of the day,' he protested, though with scant conviction. 'An' I've got more to do than I can manage.'

'Never stopped you before.'

Crossing the yard, she flashed him that look which never failed.

'I'm still not telling him!' His voice bounced back and forth across the valley. 'Leastways, not until nearer the time, I'm not.'

Jan laughed and, entering the house, left the front door swinging on its new strap hinges.

It was dusk when Sarah stopped the cart and watched the plume of peat smoke spiral lazily skywards. The wind had dropped, and she wondered who had moved into the old place. For too long now, it had been hardly more than a ruin, but, when she was little, it had all been so different.

After her father's death, she and her brothers had worked in those fields at harvest time under the kindly eye of Enoch Trickett. At the end of a long day, his wife Ann fed them and always sent them home with something extra, usually bread and cheese or cold meat. It was, she said, to see them through to breakfast, even though their bellies were full to bursting. Years later, Sarah had realized that the ritual filling of the muslin bag was Ann's way of seeing that their mother got an all too rare decent meal without having to go cap in hand.

In retrospect, they had been hard but happy times, and she recalled them with affection. However, she was also aware that the ensuing years of decay reflected the course that her own life had taken – which was why she was so pleased to see that shambling collection of friendly flint buildings being restored to something akin to their former glory.

She smiled. It struck her that life, boiled down to its basic level, was nothing more than a series of blind corners. Turning them was compulsory, and most harboured a nasty surprise. But, in order to maintain the fragile sanity of the majority, every now and again a moment of pure delight, enlightenment or fulfilment sprang from the darkness, providing the impetus to carry on. And who knows? she mused. Perhaps such a moment still lay in store for her?

'Best get on, Sarah.' John's hand squeezed her knee. 'Else we'll still be on the road come bedtime.'

His lips peeled back, releasing a smile that was supposed to entice but only made her skin creep.

Meanwhile, up the hill, in front of a blazing fire, Jan Winchcombe slept in her husband's arms and dreamt of babies.

Having children. Making them with the man you loved. Pushing them out, screaming, into the daylight. Loving them. Guiding them through the battlefield of childhood. Preparing them, to the best of your limited ability, for the rigours of the adult world. Sarah too had wanted them desperately at Jan's age. After all, were they not the mortar of marriage? Woman's great achievement? An ideal to be pursued like some latter-day Grail?

If so, when did it all go wrong? She had traced it back to the morning she woke up knowing that the ideal had simply died in the night, taking with it the last vestige of her love for John.

She looked at him across the table, shovelling down cold mutton and potatoes, his eyes darting around the room like hungry rodents as he absorbed the comforting atmosphere of home. Behind him, a long case clock driven by wooden gears tocked with the metronomic regularity of a relaxed heartbeat. To his left, her ginger cat stretched in the hearth where an iron kettle sang on the hob. The brittle illusion of domestic harmony was complete until his gaze lighted onto his sick-bed, still made up in the warmest corner. He glanced at her and Sarah rose, leaving her own supper untouched.

'Sarah?'

She picked up a candle and, turning to him, said, 'Good night, John.'

He got up as she climbed the stairs.

'Wait!' he called. Then, as an afterthought, 'Please . . .'

The bedroom door closed and a wet log spat in the grate. He was hurt. Humiliated. Anger flared, then subsided when he saw her shawl draped across the arm of her favourite carver. He picked it up and buried his face in the soft woollen folds. For a long moment, he stood there, inhaling the sweet smells of her body. Then he spoke her name, just once, and so softly that the sound died almost before it had left his lips.

Chapter 22

They found them high on the Downs, at the bottom of a dry well near Lady Holt Park. Dying had been no easy transition for the two old men. Systematically beaten, whipped and half-strangled, they lay forty feet down, each with a short halter pulled tight around his unbroken neck. Galley's skull was levelled to the eyebrows as a result of being dropped head first. Chater lay on top of him, beneath a pile of large, jagged flints. Unfortunately, the tide waiter's body had broken his fall, and their murderers, perhaps hearing a whimper or a groan, had been forced to finish him off by stoning.

Retrieving the bodies was a grim business. They had been there for over a week when a dragoon patrol had chanced upon the grey gelding. It had been slaughtered and buried in a shallow grave a stone's throw from the well, indicating that those responsible were either stupid or so sure of themselves that they cared nothing for the forces of law and order.

Now, laid out on the sapless grass, those poor bloated corpses bore silent witness to the appalling end of William Galley and Daniel Chater. The atrocities that had been perpetrated upon them were all-too obvious. What would never be known was precisely how long they had suffered before finding merciful release in death.

Fairbrother's stomach heaved as he watched them being carried to the cart on tarpaulins. Sturt boosted him into the saddle. And, with the pale winter sun warm on their backs, that sorry procession made its way slowly back to Poole.

The harsh clatter of running feet. The rise and fall of excited voices. Bootie's perception of the commotion was no more than that. However, in his mind's eye, he saw it all. A rainbow stream of flashing bodies, a mass of animated faces, bright-eyed children jostling for position as they tumbled down to the jetty. Something was up – but what? He cocked his head to one side, like a fox on the hunt listening for the tell-tale rustle in the undergrowth.

Choosing his moment, Bootie reached out from the alley and seized a passing shirt-tail.

'Gerroff! Leggo a' me!' yelled the squirming soot boy.

'What is it, lad? What goes on?'

The cripple adjusted his grip, paralysing the urchin's stick-thin arm.

'The soldiers, they've gone an' found them two old fellers . . .' he whined.

'Where?'

'I dunno! But if they're as dead as wot they say they are – don't much matter, do it?'

Bootie let go. The monkey returned the boy's parting curse with interest, then held on tight as its master was swept away by the mob.

Ten minutes later, Michael Shearer met the patrol outside the Custom House.

'Both of them?' he asked.

Sturt nodded. 'And your gelding,' he said, dismounting.

On the quay, Austin's troops cleared a space around the cart, while Fairbrother shouldered his way through the gathering mass of humanity. Incensed by their ghoulish curiosity, he jumped onto the tailboard before anyone could stop him and drew back the canvas sheet.

'Feast your eyes!' he roared. 'All of you – take a good long look!'

Suddenly, there was dead silence. The sight of the bodies sent shock waves of revulsion reverberating through the crowd. Women covered their children's eyes. Even those who believed that informers deserved the rope were sickened. Only one brash youth, an apprentice sailcloth weaver called Hoop, made the mistake of accepting the invitation. Fairbrother's hand snaked out and grabbed him by the hair.

'Smell it!' he snapped. 'Witness Thomas Kingsmill's interpretation of Justice for yourself!'

With his nose an inch away from the putrefying mess

251

that had been Daniel Chater, Hoop sicked up dinner and breakfast.

'Think who's next!' said Fairbrother. 'Whose daughter, father or grandchild!' He paused. 'Each and every one of you! Ask yourselves – what are you going to do about it?'

He got off the cart and Shearer pulled him aside.

'Damn your blood, John,' he murmured. 'You should have known better!'

Somewhere, someone defended Kingsmill's right to protect himself and got a bloody nose for his trouble. That started it. Within the space of a few seconds, the mood of the mob was transformed. Shock and disgust gave way to shame and anger. The citizens of Poole were baying for blood – but those they wanted were beyond reach. However, with frustration at fever pitch and human nature being what it is, they simply diverted their anger towards the nearest available scapegoat.

A stone shattered Shearer's office window, sending Archibald Peckover running for cover. Then a trooper was kicked to the ground, and Austin gave the order to fix bayonets.

'Get those corpses out of here, Major' – Shearer glanced at Fairbrother – 'before we have a full-scale riot on our hands!'

'No,' said Sturt, stepping forward. 'Wait awhile.'

He turned to the mob as Bootie scuttled up the Custom House steps to avoid being trampled.

'After all,' continued Sturt, 'the people have a right to know.'

Another soldier went down. Outnumbered by at least twenty to one, Shearer saw the wisdom of, if not the reason for, Sturt's advice. He withdrew his men, thereby allowing the storm to rage without further provocation. And rage it did. The clamour was deafening as men and women who, in the past, had benefited greatly from the free trade called for Kingsmill and the Hawkhurst Gang to be brought to heel. It was an extraordinary sight. And, from the comparative safety of the Custom House, Fairbrother realized that, despite the violence, they were witnessing a sort of moral

252

reawakening. Sturt was aware of it too, though he cared little for the morals or motives of the masses. All that mattered was that public opinion had turned against Kingsmill. And that was the one mistake even the leader of the Hawkhurst Gang could not afford to make.

Unfortunately, Sturt had made a mistake himself. He had underestimated not only the power of Kingsmill's reputation for violence, but the populace's natural abhorrence of the excise laws. Yes, consciences had been stirred. And admittedly, breasts continued to be beaten in public, but that was, in essence, no more than a feeble attempt by the masses to salve a collective guilty conscience. The truth of it was that no one was prepared to inform. Therefore, Fairbrother's much-vaunted moral reawakening would be a thing of the past within two weeks.

Nevertheless, changes were occurring – albeit less dramatically. For instance, farmers who had previously been eager to hold run goods no longer had room in their barns. And innkeepers who had been regular customers suddenly stopped replenishing their stocks with Hawkhurst tubs. A subtle process of social ostracism had begun – though in John Dimer's case, the process was hardly subtle.

His part in the affair was, by now, well known. And, as a result, he faced constant open hostility. Recently, dogs had been loosed on him in Rye; children had hurled horse dung at him; and only that morning, he had been set upon by a gang of youths outside the Dog And Partridge in Flimwell. Quite why everyone continued to pick on him defeated him. But having suffered enough physical abuse of late to last a lifetime, he headed for home where, if not exactly welcome, he was at least safe from harm.

One final tug did it. The brush gave way. Sarah flew backwards and ten pounds of soot dropped straight into the grate. Black from head to toe, she picked herself up and rescued the cat from the debris where, totally bemused, it sat doing a passable impersonation of a witch's familiar. She cursed John. He'd been promising to sweep the chimney for months, then muttering to herself, she rolled up her sleeves and started to clear up.

The money bag was in the log basket, and she assumed, rightly, that it had been dislodged from its hiding place up the chimney. Whether John was responsible, or it was a forgotten legacy belonging to a long-dead tenant she did not know. But the temptation to open it was irresistible. Gold and silver coins spilled onto the tabletop. Her jaw dropped in amazement. She had never seen so much money. There must have been two hundred guineas – probably more.

'Blood money is what you called it.'

Sarah almost jumped out of her skin.

'God punish you, John Dimer,' she snapped, 'for creeping up on me like that!'

Standing in the doorway, he said smugly, 'Swore you'd never touch a penny – remember?'

'It fell out of the chimney that you should have swept!'

He took off hat and coat, then crossed to the table. Turning his face to the light, Sarah examined the eye that had been blackened in Flimwell.

'What happened this time?'

'I walked into a door.'

Pulling away, he started to pick up the coins.

'I've never seen so much money,' said Sarah.

He drew the drawstring tight, then, wiping the soot from the carver, sat down.

'How much is there?'

He did not answer.

'John?'

Pulling off a boot, he poked a finger through a new hole in the sole.

Sarah sat down opposite. And after a pause, she said, 'Is there enough to buy passage to America?'

Now it was his turn to look astonished. 'America!' he exclaimed. 'And why the Devil would I want to go to America?'

'To stay alive.'

He shook his head patronizingly. 'You don't know what you're talking about, woman.'

'Someone informed, John.'

She was looking him straight in the eye, all the time hating herself for what she was doing.

'The soldiers were waiting at the beach. Kingsmill lost half his men.'

'Well, it wasn't me!'

It never occurred to him to ask how she knew so much. His eyes slid away and he chewed the inside of his mouth like he always did when worried.

'You are the obvious choice.'

'I didn't! I wouldn't.'

'I know.' The tone was sympathetic, and she moved a little closer. 'But you know that he never takes unnecessary risks. You've said so yourself – often. Sooner or later, he'll kill you just to be sure.'

Sarah paused and he felt a familiar tightening in his innards.

'That money could buy a new life,' she said.

He reached out, but she withdrew her hand.

'What about you?'

She remembered Sturt as he'd been on the headland – saw those hard angles soften as they kissed. Then the image dissolved and it was Kingsmill breathing into her face. Expressionless. Driving into her.

'I've nothing to stay here for,' she said, her voice as brittle as ice.

'Then we'll go as man and wife.'

Again that dead-eyed projection of inhumanity. Hurting her. Bearing down on her . . .

A dog barked in the yard, and she looked out of the window.

'Who is it?' Dimer asked nervously.

She peered into the gathering gloom of evening.

'Sarah?' His mouth was as dry as dust, causing his voice to crack.

'It's Jackson.'

Though momentarily paralysed, he just managed to beat her to the horse pistol.

'Give it to me!' she screamed.

'No!'

They were pushing and shoving, like children squabbling over a favourite toy.

'If he catches you with this – he'll kill us both!'

Breathing hard, Sarah backed off. Stupidity and terror, in equal measure, reflected in his expression.

'What do we do?' he asked helplessly.

'What does he want?'

'I don't know! Hawkhurst business, like as not.'

Forcing herself to calm down, she thought for a moment then said, 'Bed.'

'What?'

'Get into bed.'

'Why?'

'Just do it!'

Wiping soot from her face, Sarah bundled him into his sick bed and opened the door.

Jackson made it plain that he knew what Kingsmill had done. Ignoring her grubby appearance, his eyes roamed all over her body.

'Where is he?'

'Taken sick,' she replied, refusing to give ground. 'Something he picked up in Chichester Gaol.'

He gripped her arm and moved her out of the way. Crossing the room, he studied the patient languishing in bed with the blankets pulled up under his chin.

'Not too uppish, Master William,' Dimer said in a whisper, trying hard to give the impression that he was at death's door. 'Feelin' a bit done-in, like.'

'Fresh air.'

'Beg pardon?'

'Have you on your feet in no time,' explained Jackson as he pinched the swelling around Dimer's eye.

'If only it would,' he winced.

'The Widow is holding a few tubs,' said Jackson. 'They're to be shifted come Friday night.'

256

Half-way out of the door, he paused.

'And you are expected,' he said.

Closing the door, Sarah waited for her pulse rate to slow down then pulled back the blankets. To her surprise, John was still clutching the pistol.

'You should have shot him!' she snapped, snatching it.

'What if I'd missed?'

In her opinion, even he could have hit a target as big as Jackson at two feet. She put the gun on the table and sat down. Tired in mind and body, she could have slept for a week.

'America,' she said, without looking at him.

'Yes,' he answered. 'But, like I said, as man and wife.'

'September?'

'Late September.'

Edward Winchcombe tapped the last spoke into place and leaned the half-completed wheel against a trestle.

'A bit quick off the mark, wasn't you?'

Jan glanced at the door that she'd left ajar. Outside, a shadow bobbed nervously back and forth.

'Very late September,' she said, weakly.

Edward shot a beady look in her direction and picked up his spokeshave.

'These things happen, father,' she offered by way of an explanation. 'Sometimes. A quirk of nature.'

'With its source in Coppett's Wood, I should fancy.'

Jan felt the blood rush to her cheeks. Edward threw his arms around her.

'I'm right pleased for the both of you,' he beamed. 'And for myself too!'

'I knew you would be really,' said Jan, kissing his bristled chin.

'In which case . . .' said the wheelwright, 'you can tell him it's safe to come in now.'

She laughed and did as he said.

'Father . . .' said Alan sheepishly, standing back just in case, 'or should it be grandfather now?'

Edward was having trouble keeping his face straight, so

257

limited his response to a strangled grunt. Taking that as a sign of approval, Alan moved closer and produced a flask of brandy from behind his back.

'Bearin' in mind the nature of the occasion,' he said, 'I reckoned a glass of summat special was in order.'

The old man roared with laughter and, with an arm around each of them, said, 'And for once in your life, boy, I reckon you're right!'

The flask was almost empty and potential boys' names had been reduced to a short list of six when they heard the horses on the hill.

'Soldiers,' said Alan, peering out of the grimy window. 'With – God save us! – Jonathan Place and Luke Wilderspin in chains!'

Jan pretended not to hear the expletive as her father tripped over a wheel iron in his haste to get to the door.

'Come on!' said Alan, grabbing her hand.

Jan hesitated.

'Place and Wilderspin?' she queried. 'Aren't they – '

'Yes,' came the reply. 'And this I've got to see.'

The reason for the excitement was that the two men in question, both from the nearby village of Cranbrook, were known members of the Hawkhurst Gang. And to see them in irons, flanked by a dozen dragoons caused a sensation. In fact, so great was the outpouring of feeling that they were lucky to get through the village intact.

Adding his own two pennyworth as they passed, Edward recognized a third civilian riding at the rear of the column. Francis Rooksbee, a regular customer and tenant of Wadswell Farm, stopped outside the workshop and bobbed from the waist.

'Edward . . .'

'Good day, Francis. What's happening, then?'

'They came to the farm last night,' said Rooksbee, as the soldiers took the road to the west. 'Said they'd be back today for my pack animals.'

'And got more than they bargained for, by the looks of it.'

258

'Yes.'

'So you . . .'

The farmer turned and said, 'Aye, young Alan, I informed against them.'

'And you'll name them,' asked Edward, 'in open court?'

Rooksbee took a moment to answer.

'Someone has to,' he said, not without trepidation, 'so it might as well be me.'

Edward lifted his cap to him. 'God keep you safe, Francis.'

Back in the workshop, the atmosphere was quieter – more thoughtful.

'I'd never have believed it,' said Alan, perching on the bench. 'He wouldn't lend so much as a musket when we took 'em on in the village.'

It was true. And they were all thinking the same thing when Jan said it.

'It's Galley and Chater, isn't it? Because of what they did to them.'

Her father nodded and drained the contents of Alan's flask. The vagaries of human nature never failed to surprise him – which was perhaps why, unlike Sturt, he still had a modicum of faith in it.

The dragoon sergeant floated across the yard with a quarter of a pint of gin warming his ears and struggled into the saddle. Taking the reins from young Sam Payne, he turned to the Widow, who had escorted him as far as the door, threw up an extravagant salute and led his men out onto the highway. The artificial smile was switched off the instant his back was turned, but Hannah Payne did not budge until the last trooper had disappeared from view. Then, sure they were not coming back, she went inside and hurried upstairs. In her room, a fire blazed in the grate and Kingsmill was sitting up in the four-poster. Naked except for the dressings wound around his chest and shoulder, he put down his pistol as she closed the door behind her.

'Well?'

259

She sat on the bed. 'He was asking after Galley and Chater.'

'So what did you say?'

'That anyone who could do such a thing to two poor old men deserved hanging, drawing and quartering.'

The corners of his mouth lifted a fraction. He drew her to him and kissed her. She rolled on top of him, taking care not to lean on his wounds, and sucked the tip of his tongue. A hand slipped inside her bodice searching for a breast. She pulled away.

'Later,' she said, rising, and this time her smile was genuine. She kissed him where Sturt's blade had cut deepest. He made a grab, but she was a split-second too quick for him.

'Hannah?'

She paused at the door.

'Who else knows they were here?'

'No one,' she said. 'Leastways, no one who'd dare say so.'

The letter came on the evening mail coach from Rye and was addressed to 'George Sturt, the Custom House, Poole.' It was short, to the point, and bore no signature. Shearer thought it a hoax or, as is so often the case, a clumsy attempt to settle an old grudge. He dismissed it out of hand. Fairbrother remained noncommital. Sturt read it a second time, then called the Collector's clerk into the room.

'Tell me, what do you know of Hannah Payne?' he said.

Peckover had developed a raging dislike of Sturt, and shot a glance at his master before speaking. Given the nod, he shrugged his shoulders and said, 'Not much. She keeps the White Hart at Cadnam.'

The briefest of looks passed between Sturt and Fairbrother.

'They say she deals in run goods,' continued the clerk when pressed. 'But then again, what innkeeper don't these days? Everyone hereabouts knows her as the Widow.'

The name brought a wry smile to Fairbrother's lips. 'Henry Kemp's informant,' he said.

Sturt nodded. And before Shearer could butt in, ordered Peckover to find Major Austin. Then, while the miserable clerk trudged around the eating houses and taverns favoured by the military, Fairbrother gave his master a brief account of how, courtesy of the Widow Payne, the Poole dragoon squadron had been chasing wild geese in Chichester at the time Kingsmill was running contraband at Chamber Cove.

Sturt half-listened but took no part. His mind was elsewhere. In Rye, to be precise, pondering the identity of the anonymous scribe who had done them such a service.

Chapter 23

Dimer helped himself to another drink. He had been working himself up into a state since eight o'clock, and it was now approaching midnight. The round trip should have taken three hours, three and a half at most. Something must have gone wrong. And if it had – what? Had she lost her nerve at the crucial moment? Were they coming for him? His instinct told him to run. But where? He knew that left to his own devices, he'd go under in next to no time. Right now, he needed Sarah. She made the decisions – that was what she did best. But where was she? Why was she so late? Was her plan, so convincing in the comforting light of day, merely a clever device to make it easy for herself? Had she finally lost patience and abandoned him? On the evidence available, the answer had to be – yes.

The prospect frightened the life out of him. He paced the floor, cursing her, calling her every vile name he could think of, going so far as to wish upon her a lingering, painful death. His knotted guts turned over and he tasted the bile at the back of his throat. He shuddered and washed it down with warm gin. Then, losing control, he slung his holed boot at the cat and was about to start on the crockery when he heard her in the lane. Breathing an enormous sigh of relief, he apologized to God for doubting her integrity, lit a candle lantern and dashed out to meet her.

In the yard, the General dropped his head as the cart drew to a halt. Dimer offered a hand. She ignored it and got down unaided.

'Did you find him?' he said, tugging at the folds of her cloak.

Her face was grey with tiredness. She looked at him dispassionately, studying him with the clinical eye of a surgeon. 'Yes,' she said. Then, removing his hand, she entered the house.

'And?' he said, following her in.

'He called me a liar.'

'Damn you, Sarah!' He smashed both fists onto the tabletop. 'I told you it wouldn't – '

'But,' she said, with grim satisfaction, 'he did decline the invitation to come and see for himself.' She paused, then added wearily, 'you can rest easy. They'll not bother you now.'

The load was suddenly lifted from his shoulders. He wanted to jump for joy; throw his arms around her; shout to the world that everything was going to be all right. But he didn't, saying instead, 'I'll get off at first light – '

'You'll go nowhere before nightfall. And then you'll stay off the highways and speak to no one!'

'All right, whatever you say,' he conceded, taken aback by the controlled anger in her voice.

'You will arrange passage at Greenwich and wait for me there.'

'Why can't we go together?'

'Because the stock will starve, and that's not fair.' Taking off cloak and hood, she was conscious of the slight tremor affecting both hands. 'When I find a buyer, I'll join you.'

Moving to the fire, she removed the heavy pattens from her only decent shoes and put them in the hearth to dry. The adrenalin that had kept her going was draining away. She sat down feeling old and worn out. Her eyelids drooped. She needed sleep – the release of oblivion.

'Sarah?'

Dimer crossed the room and squatted at her feet. Soft-lit by the fire, he looked about twenty – the age he'd been when they married.

'I'll work hard.' He said it with deep sincerity. 'On my life – I'll do my best to put things right between us. I promise.'

Again that quizzical look from her. He could feel her eyes lifting the top of his skull, exposing the essential John Dimer. He did not like it and wriggled like a worm on the hook.

263

'I'll see to the General,' he said, rising. 'You get yourself into bed – and I'll be up before you know it.'

Left alone, Sarah fell into a half-doze, and the events of the past few hours recurred in a series of jolting images. At first, they were all out of sequence, but her tidy mind soon marshalled them into the correct order.

From the safety of her own fireside, she saw again the lights of Hawkhurst blinking against the velvet night sky. Felt the stunned silence as she entered the Black Dog. Remembered, so clearly, the fear she felt but would not show as she faced William Jackson. Remembered, with pleasure, the fear she saw in his eyes at the mention of gaol fever. Later, back on the road, the cold night air had shocked her to her senses, and she had taken the whip to the General in her haste to put as many miles as possible between her and that godless cradle of evil. The journey home remained a blur. And only now did the enormity of the risk she had taken really sink in.

She awoke with a start, aware of something moving on her lap. Her instinct said lash out. But a tiny rough tongue dragged across the back of her hand and she smiled. Outside, the stable door banged shut. The smile faded and she felt her innards shrink. It was, as John had said with such relish, time for bed.

The wind funnelled down the chimney and blew out a candle as the two men circled one another in the centre of the room. What furniture there was, they'd pushed back against the walls and their shadows danced a grotesque reel on the ceiling. The light of battle was in Fairbrother's eyes. He feinted and backed off, revelling in the physical effort of combat. He changed direction. Adjusted his guard. Then, choosing his moment, bored in. Sturt parried a clumsy slash. It was one in the morning and the bell-clear ring of steel on steel echoed around the labyrinthine passageways of the lodging house. Fairbrother came again and, anticipating the sidestep, barged Sturt with his shoulder and pinned him against the wall. The success was short-lived. Sturt punched him sharply in the stomach and he collapsed, breathless.

'That's enough,' said Sturt, sheathing his hanger.

Fairbrother took his hand and pulled himself upright. 'I'm all right,' he grunted.

'You might be,' said Sturt, 'but I've had enough.'

He picked up his friend's blade and helped him to a chair. 'Sit awhile,' he advised. 'Catch your breath.'

Poking around in the grate, Fairbrother tried to tease some heat out of the dimly glowing embers. A fragment of unburnt wood flared, causing the hoarfrost on the cracked window pane to glint and gleam. Such was the trick of the light, that the crystals took on a life of their own. He watched, fascinated, as a pair of ice warriors stood toe to toe, locked in mortal combat. The firelight shimmered. One cut. The other slashed. Fairbrother mirrored their actions with his stump. Then the flame died and they were gone. Off into the night. Off in search of another bottleglass battlefield.

Fairbrother flexed cramp-locked fingers. A blister burst and he licked the warm trickle. The skin had not yet hardened, but he knew that was only a matter of time.

Sturt joined him, bearing generous measures of brandy.

'It's come on apace, wouldn't you say?' said Fairbrother. 'A week ago, I could scarce lift a cutlass. Now, it's simply a question of practice.'

Sturt put down his glass and looked at him. 'You're right,' he said, 'the arm has come on.'

Fairbrother read the thought and completed the sentence, 'But not enough.'

'No matter how good it was, I'd have stuck a knife in your belly.'

'I'm going with you, George.'

Sturt took a dudeen from his pocket and filled it, slowly, taking time to consider his words before speaking. The problem was that, on the one hand, he did not want to be unnecessarily brutal; whilst on the other, he knew the danger of delusion. Eventually, he said, 'You'd be putting yourself – and everyone else – at risk.'

The point was skilfully made. But Fairbrother dismissed

it, arguing, 'I'm not asking to be wet-nursed, George. I'll take care of myself.'

'How?' Sturt asked. 'With a pistol perhaps?'

He took his own from the table and threw it.

'Show me.'

The catch was fumbled and Fairbrother yelped as the hammer caught him across the knuckles. Sturt picked it up and sat down again.

'John.'

Fairbrother looked at him.

'You've faced your Maker once already – and walked away. No one is that lucky twice.'

Flint sparked on steel, and Sturt sucked the flame into his pipe bowl.

Fairbrother said nothing. Sometimes, George had a way of presenting an argument that, in itself, made perfect sense; yet also served to conceal a secondary or deeper meaning. He sat, lost in thought, for some time. But it was late. He was tired. His mind was running in circles. And he had neither wit or imagination to divine what Sturt was trying to say. Irritated, he drained his glass and got up.

'You may well be right,' he said with grim determination, 'but I'm going – and there's an end to it.'

Ironically, Sturt had no ulterior motives this time. His concern was, quite simply, John's safety. Nevertheless, Fairbrother passed the night fitfully, plagued by ignoble thoughts that reflected his own, rather than Sturt's, state of mind.

Dawn broke cold and grey. The town clock struck seven, calling the working population of Poole from their beds. Fairbrother, however, rolled over and buried himself beneath the blankets. He felt like death. Another ten minutes was all he wanted, but the squeal of greaseless hinges penetrated the fog inside his head and he was instantly awake.

'George?' he murmured, blinking the world into focus.

A key turned in the lock, and by the time he reached the door Sturt was half-way down the stairs.

In the hallway, Bootie was vaguely aware of someone

266

stepping over him. He turned onto his side as Sturt closed the door behind him. Then, with Fairbrother's curses ringing in his ears, Sturt pulled on his riding gloves and hurried down the street.

Later, riding hard through the New Forest, he suffered a twinge of conscience. He knew better than anyone the anguish John was experiencing. But he also knew the risk involved in what he was about to do. And, old soldier or not, it was too great for a one-armed cripple.

The stable door slammed shut and she leaned her weight against it. Outside, Kingsmill hammered at the woodwork.

'Hannah,' he called, menacingly, 'I give you fair warning! Hand it over, or else I'll . . .'

'Go to the Devil!' she retorted with a grin.

The banging stopped. Anticipating what was about to happen, she moved away from the door and looked for somewhere to hide. One hefty kick and Kingsmill was inside. 'Damn you,' he yelled, 'give it back!'

He lunged and missed. So, snatching a bridle from the tack rail, she threw it at him and backed away. Breathing hard, they circled one another in silence – just as Sturt and Fairbrother had done at the lodging house. Bedding straw crackled beneath their feet. A horse stamped nervously in its stall, sending a roosting pigeon clattering from the hay loft.

The Widow glanced at the door. Moving swiftly, Kingsmill cut off her avenue of escape. She reversed direction, taking care to stay out of reach.

'Just tell me why you want him here,' she said, 'and you can have it.'

'Hannah . . .' he threatened, making another grab.

'No!'

She slapped his hand away, and a feed bucket cracked his shin. Hitching her skirt, she made a run for it but got no further than the loose box before an outstretched foot hooked her legs from under her. She fell, cursing, into a pile of hay. Rolling onto her back, she got in one good kick then he had her by the ankle.

'Give!' he demanded, straddling her, pinning her arms.

'Not until you tell me why!'

Using all her strength, she arched her back and twisted in an attempt to topple him. It almost succeeded. But, about to go over, he managed to brace an arm against the wall. However, in saving himself, he pulled the stitches in his chest. Suddenly, the game was over. A clenched fist hung above her head, threatening to batter the life out of her. Memories of Galley and Chater came flooding back and she flinched.

'All right!' she conceded.

For a moment, her looks hung in the balance; then he lowered his fist and sat up.

'I told you . . .' he breathed. 'It's business.'

His shoulders slumped as the pain surged. He waited until it eased then continued. 'I mean to set the Hawkhurst/ Chichester alliance on a more permanent footing.'

The intent behind the word permanent was obvious, and the Widow shook her head.

'Shepherd Fairall is nobody's fool, Thomas. And he has a suspicious nature. He'll never agree to meet with you.'

'Not me,' explained Kingsmill. 'You. Send for him. Promise whatever it takes – but get him here. The rest you can leave up to me.'

The Widow propped herself up on her elbows.

'When?' she asked.

'Tonight.'

'But you're alone. He'll . . .'

Kingsmill smiled, then held out his hand, saying quietly, 'The timepiece, Hannah.'

Timepiece was a slight misnomer. The case had been mangled almost beyond recognition, and all that remained of the innards was the face and mainspring.

In her mind's eye, the Widow saw again the way it had shattered against the brew-house wall. Saw in detail the expression on his face as he'd lashed out, scattering shards of glass, fragments of brass and steel about the yard.

'It belongs to George Sturt, doesn't it?' she said.

268

He nodded. Then he took it from her and felt the silver case warm in his hand.

'I gave it to him a long time ago – as a token of friendship,' he said.

'Then you must have thieved it.'

He half-smiled. 'No. Just the money to pay for it.' The smile faded and his voice hardened. 'We were fifteen years old at the time – and George swore that this would be buried with him.'

For a long moment, the Widow said nothing. Then, as he started to rise, she traced a line down his shirt-front.

'You're leaking,' she said, showing the blood on her fingers.

He licked it off, and lowered himself on top of her as she fell back. She offered her mouth and tasted the blood on his lips. Feeling him grow, she opened her legs and guided his hand to the spot. Her conduct was blatant – whorish even. And though her own desire was real enough, it belied the true nature of her feelings. A part of her genuinely cared for Kingsmill, but she knew better than to let it show. Lust – his not hers – was the key to their relationship. And while she continued to manipulate it with such consummate skill, he would remain in the palm of her hand.

His mouth worked down her neck and he murmured her name. Warm fingers touched and teased, and she gave herself over to the moment, unaware of the silent watcher high above their heads.

An eye blinked at a crack in the hay loft floor. A fine thread of dust spiralled earthwards as Sam Payne made himself comfortable. He had seen the act performed before, in the wood behind the inn. But he was eight years old at the time and, though curious, had soon lost interest, preferring the thrill of ferreting for rabbits. Now, he was aware of the changes in his maturing body, and childish curiosity had given way to something more powerful. Down below, clothes were discarded as the tempo quickened. Surprisingly, he felt no animosity, no revulsion towards Kingsmill

269

or his mother. Their coupling was wild and passionate, yet the lad saw it as a thing of beauty.

Then the Widow cried out. Her face contorted. Her voice soared to a pinnacle of uninhibited, shuddering release. And all the while, Sam lay with his face pressed to the pitch pine, absorbing the most intimate details of adult pleasure. Details that would be recalled, exaggerated and embellished, time and again, until the day dawned when he too would know them for himself.

From the top of the hill, the figure walking away from the house was unrecognizable. Jackson stopped and the rest followed suit.

'Dimer?' suggested Richard Perrin.

If Jackson heard him, he didn't show it. For a moment, he remained silent, concentration focused on that diminishing silhouette merging into the lifeless landscape. Lamenting his failing eyesight, he touched his mount's flanks with his spurs.

'If I've not caught up by Uckfield,' he said, 'wait for me at The Golden Lion.'

The track that led to the house was pitted and icy. Jackson rode slowly: the smell of woodsmoke in his nostrils, a glint of pure malice in his eye.

Behind him, cart and riders slid over the western skyline one by one, until Perrin was left alone. He had never trusted or taken to Dimer, but his wife had shown great courage in pleading his case at the Black Dog. Her face sprang to mind. True, she was no raging beauty, but she was not unattractive. And she certainly deserved better than Dimer.

Watching Jackson cross the river, it occurred to Perrin that, come the day, it would not be the weak who inherited the earth but the likes of John Dimer. They were the opportunists. And when the Sturts and Kingsmills had finally destroyed one another, Dimer's sort would rise to the top of the dung heap because of their ability to anticipate the wind of change and bend with it. Pride, self-respect, principle – such trivia would never hinder their struggle for survival. Even now, with Jackson descending like the Angel of Death, Perrin felt sure that Dimer would emerge unscathed – though probably at some other poor wretch's expense.

He turned his horse and hurried after Sheerman and the rest. It was a long ride to Cadnam, and Kingsmill had sent explicit instruction to be there by nightfall.

Sarah had banked up the fire before leaving and the heat was making him drowsy. He took the last nail from his mouth and hammered it home. He grunted with satisfaction. Life was looking up. One more tack and he would again have a pair of waterproof riding jacks. He was back in Sarah's bed. And come spring, they would be starting a new life in the Colonies. He helped himself to another mug of ale and searched the table for nails. Finding none he cursed, more out of habit than in anger, and crossed to the fire where he tossed the cat off the mantelpiece. He cursed again. His tack box was not in its usual place. Muttering darkly, he wished a pox on Sarah's tidy mind and set about turning the room upside down. Shelves and drawers surrendered everything but boot nails. So, in a fit of pique, he kicked over the small oak chest that contained Sarah's few clothes. Unfortunately, he did so with his stockinged foot, not the booted one. Howling with pain, he hopped over to the settle where he promptly sat on – his tack box. He'd left it there while he'd looked for his hammer, but a selective memory laid the blame squarely on Sarah's shoulders.

For a moment, he sat nursing bruised toes. Then, as he righted the chest, a sheet of cheap writing paper fell out. Curiosity aroused, he looked inside. Discovering quills and ink hidden beneath the petticoats and coarse cotton stockings, he returned to the table and sat down.

The paper bore the faint impression of a letter written on the sheet above. He lit a candle and studied it closely. He could not decipher the letters, the fragments of words, so dusted them with fine flour. Outside, a dog barked, but so engrossed was he that it went unnoticed. Blowing gently, he cleared the excess flour and gradually revealed the gist

271

of Sarah's letter to Sturt. He sat bolt upright as if he'd been shot.

'Oh no, Sarah,' he moaned. 'No! You couldn't!'

'Gaol fever surely ain't what it used to be.'

The sound of Jackson's voice put the fear of God into Dimer. Yelling with fright, he shot to his feet and turned to face him.

'Nevertheless . . .' said Jackson from the doorway. 'You must have the strength of an ox, John Dimer.'

Gabbling frantically, Dimer backed away as Jackson sauntered towards him.

'I was lucky, praise God,' he said. 'It were just a touch. I'm feelin' much improved now.'

He stopped, panic-stricken. Jackson was idly casting an eye over the paper on the table. Desperation forced Dimer's hand. He made a grab for it. Jackson caught him by the wrist and his fingers hovered inches above what amounted to a death warrant.

'I knew nothin' of it, Master William!' he whined. 'On my life! I chanced on it in Sarah's chest – '

A fist struck him on the temple and sent him sprawling across the floor. Instinct sent the cat running for cover as Jackson scanned the page.

'It's nowt to do with me, I swear,' Dimer sobbed, cringing in the hearth.

Jackson turned on his heel, eyes blazing.

'No!' squealed Dimer as he leapt to his feet. 'No! Don't . . .'

Wailing like a lost child, he crabbed around the room with Jackson in pursuit. Tears streamed down his face. He brandished a chair in a futile attempt to keep Jackson at bay. A vicious kick sent him crashing into the dresser. He slid to the floor. Crawled under the table. Screamed hysterically as Jackson dragged him out and slammed him against the wall. The blade broke the thin skin covering his pulsing jugular and he filled his pants.

'Pl – please . . .' he stammered, voice reduced to a strangled whisper. 'It wasn't me.'

272

The knife remained at his throat, but Dimer sensed an infinitesimal hesitation.

'Sarah!' he croaked. 'It was Sarah what wrote it. She's had it in for you an' Master Thomas from the beginnin'.'

He knew that if Jackson believed him, he was sentencing her to death. But he did not care. What mattered was immediate survival. Life. His life – regardless of the cost. He felt Jackson's breath clinging to his face like a shroud. Shooting stars were exploding inside his brain, emphasizing the difference between light and dark. Existence and eternity.

'As God is my witness,' he breathed, 'it's the truth.'

Sarah saw Jackson leave from the edge of the wood. Such was the shock that she reeled as if struck, and had to brace herself against a towering elm. Then, fighting the panic rising in her gullet, she dropped the mushrooms she had picked and flew down the slope as fast as her legs could carry her.

The door was half-open. She stopped and listened. There was no sound or movement. For a moment, she was at a complete loss, paralysed by a feeling of utter despair. A torrent of memories suddenly filled her mind, drowning objectivity and judgement. Even though John no longer occupied a place in her heart, he was her husband – another human being, no matter how weak or stupid.

A pair of carrion crows circled the farmyard on noiseless wings. It started to rain. Dredging depleted reserves, Sarah steeled herself and pushed the door open. The house was in semi-darkness. The stench was overpowering. And as she waited for her eyes to adjust to the gloom, she heard herself murmur his name. The weight of silence crushed whatever faint hope she had retained. Crossing the threshold, she stepped inside, out of the drizzle.

The room was a shambles. Every piece of furniture except the table had been overturned. She stared at it: an image of domestic normality where John's boot last and leather knife lay next to her writing materials.

Her heartbeat faltered.

In an instant, she knew what must have happened. Touching the tabletop, she left her fingerprints in the flour dust. She wanted to run, but stood mesmerized by that blank sheet of paper. It seemed to be taunting her: accusing her of the worst kind of treachery. Every word she had written to Sturt came flooding back. She closed her eyes and, at the forefront of her consciousness, saw a face. John's face. Twisted into a mask of hatred. Mouth working. Shaping one word. Judas. Over and over again.

She felt as if she had been stripped naked, exposed for what she truly was. But before she could find words to describe such feelings of self-disgust, the softest of sounds emanated from the upturned settle. The hairs on the back of her neck stood on end. She turned and, without wanting to, crossed the room.

The toes of a stockinged foot were all that betrayed a human presence. And with shaking hands, she took hold of the high-backed bench and tipped it over.

Inhuman best described the howl that split the silence. Sarah cried out too – as a terrified bundle of ginger fur brushed her leg and disappeared through the door.

For a long moment she stood panting, unable to move. Then, turning slowly, she looked down at her husband's outstretched body. He lay face down, a spreading crimson stain beneath his head. Sarah knelt down and touched his cheek. Still warm, he might have been sleeping. Great racking sobs welled inside her, but no sound escaped her lips. With tender care, she turned him over and looked into clouded eyes that still bore an imprint of the last frenzied moments of a life brutally cut short. Her tears dropped onto the cooling clay of being. Salt tears ran down his cheeks creating the impression that he was crying. And between chin and collar, his slashed throat gaped like a second mouth, giving the impression that he was screaming.

At about the same time as Sarah was drawing a sheet over her husband's corpse, Sturt was entering the White Hart. It was dinner time and the country inn was bursting at the seams. So, taking care to avoid the Widow as she ferried countless plates of beef and potatoes from the kitchen, he found himself a seat in the shadows and settled down to wait. Young Samuel brought food and drink. Sturt sipped warmed ale, and his volucrine features took on the intensity of a hunting hawk as he followed the Widow's every move with his eyes. He did not eat. He spoke to no one. And all the while, his right hand remained in his coat pocket where it rested on the polished butt of a horse pistol.

One hour later, Sarah was feeling no sense of loss and wondered if she was in a state of shock. She thought for a moment, and decided she wasn't. And that shocked her. Her behaviour appeared callous, even to her. But the truth of the matter was that she had used up every last scrap of guilt and anguish whilst living with John. Therefore, his death – horrible as it was – had somehow failed to reach her. Of course she had cried, but that had been a conditioned response. What she was really experiencing, though she was loathe to admit it, was an intoxicating sense of freedom – as if a journey that she had always assumed to be endless had suddenly ended. However, having arrived she now needed to discover precisely where she was.

Sturt came to mind. The thought of what might have been made her eyes fill up. But, gritting her teeth until her jaw ached, she told herself that she no longer harboured any illusions. The future lay elsewhere. And despite all that had happened, it was still her duty to make the best of it. So, driven by that positive intention, Sarah Dimer lifted herself out of her chair and took John's money-bag from its hiding place up the chimney. Then picking up her pistol and shawl, she strode purposefully out of the house and closed the door behind her without so much as a backward glance.

A sharp north-easter stung her eyes as she harnessed the General to the cart. The wind tasted of the sea. And crossing the little bridge over the river for the last time, she willed it – more in hope than expectation – to carry the past away with it.

Chapter 24

By four o'clock the tap-room was empty, except for Sturt who had moved to the fire and fallen asleep. Clearing plates, the Widow leaned across him and felt the firing piece in his coat pocket hard against her leg. She paused. His face rang a bell but she could not place it. Then the trap-door that led to the cellars opened with a bang, making her jump. She glowered at Samuel as he stepped off the ladder with a tankard of her best ale in his hand. She fingered her lip; gestured to him to sit down. Intrigued, the lad made himself comfortable and watched his mother slip a hand into Sturt's pocket. He did not stir. So, taking hold of the butt, she slowly extracted the gun. Her touch would have made a professional thief envious. Nevertheless, Sturt's fingers closed around her wrist and she froze.

'A hemp halter is the regular penalty for picking a gentleman's pocket,' he said quietly.

The Widow looked into cold, piercing eyes that revealed nothing.

'In my experience, sir,' she retorted, 'no proper gentleman carries a loaded horse pistol in his coat.'

'That depends on the nature of his business.'

He took the weapon from her and put it on the table. Then drawing out a chair, added, 'And mine is with you, Hannah Payne.'

She sat down, took a moment to regain her composure and said, 'I make it a rule never to do business with strangers.'

'I'm an old friend of Thomas Kingsmill's.'

It was the tone more than his actual words that told her who he was. And the realization struck with the force of a thunderbolt.

'Then you can trant your business elsewhere!' she snapped, rising.

'Sit down!'

Again she paused, and this time scanned the room. To her horror, Samuel had vanished, leaving her alone with him. An unfamiliar restriction in her airway was making it difficult to breathe, and it dawned on her that she was genuinely frightened for her life.

She sat down, and Sturt pushed Sarah's letter across the table.

'Read it,' he said, then studied her face as she did so. A tiny muscle flickered beneath her left eye.

'Who else has seen this?' she asked, voice as tight as a drumskin.

'No one. As yet.'

Moving with a speed born of desperation, she threw it into the fire, only to see Sturt snatch it out before the flames could take hold.

'Damn you!' she snarled. 'What is it you want?'

'Tell me where to find him.'

'And if I don't?'

'I'll take you and the letter to the nearest magistrate.' He leaned across the table. 'I'll see you dressed in tar and chains – hanging outside your own front door.'

'You'll scorch in Hell first!'

Springing to her feet, she shoved the table with all her strength. Caught off guard, Sturt went over the back of his chair and fell heavily across the fender. Reaching for the pistol, she cried out as he kicked the legs from under her. Rolling across the floor, he caught hold of her dress and, despite furious resistance, pinned her down. His hand closed around her throat.

'Where is he?'

By way of an answer, she drove her knee into his groin.

Hurt, Sturt gave her a shake that almost dislocated her neck. He tightened his grip.

Flat on her back, the Widow clawed desperately at his face, but the world was growing dim and she was forced to concede.

'All right . . .' she rasped. 'All right!'

The pressure eased – just enough.

'Where?'

Her eyes felt as if they were about to burst as she glanced over his shoulder.

'Here,' she breathed, an agonized note of triumph in what was left of her voice. 'He's here.'

Now it was his turn to be thunderstruck. He did not know whether to believe her or not. So ... His fingers were again squeezing the life out of her when a shadow fell across her face.

'Let her go, George.'

Sturt's body went rigid, as if he'd been turned to stone. The voice was all-too familiar. It was also calm – completely under control. A pistol barrel touched the back of his neck.

'I said – let her go.'

Furious with himself for being so careless, he did as he was ordered. He looked down at the Widow. There was something grotesquely sexual in the way she was spread-eagled between his legs. Tattered lips parted in a spiteful grin. She spat into his face.

'Get up.'

Cold metal ground against the base of his skull. And from the top of the stairs, Sam Payne watched as Kingsmill stepped back, thereby allowing Sturt to release his mother.

'Slowly,' came the caution.

All at once, the two men were standing close enough to smell one another's sweat. Even so, each remained hidden behind a mask of impassivity. Both pairs of eyes glittered like those of wild animals. Nevertheless, they failed to reflect the all-consuming depth of feeling, the pain and turmoil, the gross injustice that each had suffered at the hands of the other. For fully thirty seconds, neither man moved. The Widow watched, fascinated, as an aura of impending violence gathered like a gigantic storm. Suddenly, it broke. And Sturt, disregarding his instinct for self-preservation, leapt forward in a desperate, flailing attempt to lay hands on Kingsmill. It was a brave, though ultimately useless, gesture. As he reached out, Kingsmill struck him with the barrel of his pistol.

'Bastard!' croaked the Widow, kicking his inert form beneath the ribs.

'No!'

An arm swept her aside. She bounced off the wall, and Samuel ran to her as Kingsmill dropped to his knees.

'He's not to be touched, Hannah,' he murmured, gently fingering the wound he had inflicted on Sturt's head, 'by you, or anyone else.'

Soon after eleven, a shadowy figure moved noiselessly between the skilling and the brew-house. Taking care not to disturb the geese in the yard, John Fairbrother slipped into the stable.

The smell of tobacco smoke hung on the dank air. And, hanger raised, he spun on his heel as something rustled in the hay behind him. Reeking of stale ale, young Samuel sighed contentedly and turned in his sleep. A smouldering dudeen, packed with weed stolen from the Hawkhurst cargo in the cellar, fell from his mouth. Fairbrother caught it and dropped it into a water bucket. Then, satisfied that the drunken boy constituted no danger, he quickly searched the stalls. He found what he was looking for at the very back of the rickety building: Sturt's horse – hobbled and blanketed. Doubtless, thought Fairbrother, awaiting a similar fate to Shearer's grey gelding.

Leaving the yard, he heard riders approaching from the west and dropped out of sight behind a stunted hawthorn. At first, the two horsemen were just silhouettes against the night sky. As they got closer, a shaft of pale moonlight touched their faces. Fairbrother's pulse quickened. Then, as the Widow's geese sounded the alarm, he cut through the undulating rough pasture that bordered the beech wood and disappeared among the trees, where Shearer and the dragoons waited.

'Did you see them?' he asked softly.

Michael Shearer lowered his spyglass as the Chichester smugglers entered the White Hart. 'Yes, but I took them for honest patrons,' he said.

There was no humour in Fairbrother's smile.

'Shepherd Fairall and his man,' he said. 'They were both at the Custom House.'

'And Sturt?' queried Major Austin, stepping out of the shadows.

Fairbrother nodded. 'His horse is in the stable.'

They both looked at Shearer.

'Would it not be to our advantage to know who else is in there before we move?' he asked.

'Yes,' said Fairbrother, 'but the longer we wait, the less chance we'll have of finding George alive.'

The Collector's fingers drummed on his sword pommel. He looked down at the inn where, with smoke curling from the chimney pots and a soft glow in the windows, all appeared deceptively normal. He shook his head. Sturt had over-stepped the mark and he was furious with him for jeopardizing the entire operation with his ridiculous heroics. Nevertheless, he knew that Fairbrother was right. So, against his better judgement, he ordered Austin to move his men down the hill.

'And mind you tread softly,' advised Fairbrother. 'The Widow Payne keeps geese.'

The dragoons' Commanding Officer drew his sword, but, before he could speak, more riders appeared on the highway. They came from the east, and this time there were six of them and a cart. From the wood, it was impossible to identify anyone. And though it was always possible that they were ordinary working people going about their legitimate business, the consensus – as the dragoons ghosted through the trees – was that it was so unlikely as to be not worth considering.

Fairall had barely had time to swallow a glass of geneva before he heard the horses in the yard. Mills peered out of the window and a look of astonishment swept his face.

'Jackson!' he said. 'William Jackson!'

Fairall turned on the Widow who was moving towards the stairs. His cutlass was clearing its scabbard when Kingsmill spoke from the top landing.

'Put it down, Shepherd.'

Looking down the barrels of two pistols, the leader of the Chichester Gang saw no advantage in arguing.

'You too, Smoaker,' said the Widow.

Mills's sword belt clattered to the floor, and he shot a glance at his master.

'Business – and pleasure,' he said contemptuously. 'I told you the whore wasn't to be trusted!'

Jackson rattled the locked door as the Widow flew across the room, intent on shoving her knife into Mills's belly.

'Save it, Hannah!' snapped Kingsmill, descending the stairs. 'And let them in.'

Fairall caught her arm as she passed.

'Why?' he asked. 'I thought we – '

'It's nothing personal, Shepherd,' she explained with a degree of genuine regret. 'But business is business.'

Outside, Jackson was working himself into a frenzy. Riding west, his limited imagination had been racing. And haunted by visions of arriving too late, of Kingsmill already languishing in Chichester Gaol, he hammered at the heavy oak door.

'Damn your blood!' he roared. 'Open up! Thomas . . .'

The name ricocheted around the darkened outbuildings and stopped Fairbrother in his tracks.

'Kingsmill . . .' he murmured.

Shearer stole a glance across the yard as the Widow threw the bolts.

'This time,' said the exciseman, 'the Fates are with us.'

Fairbrother cocked his pistol.

'Just pray they've not neglected George,' he said.

Such was his state of mind, that the presence of Fairall and Mills hardly registered with Jackson. Ignoring them, he blurted out his story, describing in detail what he'd done to Dimer. Kingsmill listened without interruption. Then, when Jackson had finished, he got up and entered the small snug where Sturt sat bound and gagged with his own stock. Jackson's jaw sagged, creating the impression that he was even more stupid than he was. Sarah's letter breezed under his nose.

281

'You had it half-right, William,' said Kingsmill. 'There was a letter. But it was Dimer's wife who wrote it – not Dimer.' He moved closer to Sturt, adding, 'And it seems that George here kept it all to himself.'

Jackson's brain was labouring away, but the information was coming too fast for him to take in. He stared at Kingsmill with blank eyes.

'Dimer's wife?' he mumbled. 'You're telling me it was Dimer's wife?'

'Yes.'

There was a long pause, broken only by the scuffle in the tap-room where Harry Sheerman was tying Fairall's hands behind his back. Then a huge malevolent grin cracked Jackson's face as the irony of what he'd done finally sank in.

'Thomas?'

Richard Perrin spoke from the doorway.

'About the Shepherd . . .'

'What about him?'

'There's no need to . . .'

'To what?'

Perrin hesitated. Choosing his words carefully, he said, 'There's no need to do anything – rash.'

For a second or two, Kingsmill considered what Perrin had said, then he turned to Jackson.

'Get rid of them,' he ordered.

'Where?'

'Anywhere you like. There must be more than one dry well in Hampshire.'

Jackson squeezed past Perrin, who made one last attempt to save Fairall's life.

'At the very beginning,' he said tentatively, still nervous of Kingsmill's mood, 'I gave my word there'd be no treachery. He trusted me, Thomas.'

'Then he deserves all he gets! Now get out.' He turned. 'You too, Hannah.'

The Widow moved from the fire where she'd been absorbing every word.

'Not here,' she said. 'Not after Galley and Chater. Take him somewhere else.'

Kingsmill picked up a long coachman's whip.

'Out,' he said.

The Widow closed the door behind her and he turned to Sturt.

'Seventeen years is a long time to wait, George.'

Sturt's bloodshot eyes followed him as he crossed the room.

'And there hasn't been a day when you were out of my thoughts.'

A charred log split, sending a fountain of sparks spiralling up the chimney. Kingsmill sat down and placed the whip on the table between them.

'When word got back as how you'd enlisted,' he said, 'I'd wake up in a sweat. Night after night. In that stink-hole of a gaol – imagining that some Highland renegade had got to you before me. The same dream. Every night for five years.'

He poured himself a brandy from the flask that the Widow had left behind.

'The only thing that ever changed was who finished you off. If it wasn't the Scot, it was a French sniper. Or one of your own mates in a pot-house brawl. Always someone else. Never me. Time and again, I was the one standing to the side – watching them cheat me.'

He drained the glass in one and refilled it.

For what seemed like an age to Sturt, Kingsmill remained locked in his own thoughts. Then, turning slowly, he looked Sturt in the eye.

'When I got out,' he said, 'I asked Mary to marry me.'

Sturt strained against his bonds, but succeeded only in tightening the knots.

Kingsmill half-smiled, and continued. 'I told her what happened at the river. All of it. As a way of getting back at you.'

He leaned across the table – as Sturt had done with the Widow – and the firelight danced in his eyes.

'She didn't believe me.'

283

He shook his head. The passing of time had not made it any easier for him to accept.

'And nothing I could say would shift her. She had no idea why you'd gone – but she was convinced you were alive. Certain you'd be coming home.'

He paused.

'So was I.'

The tone was harder now. And his eyes were blazing – boring into Sturt's.

'But not for her,' he said. 'For me. You see, I knew that owing me would eat you out. Rot your soul – bit by bit – until the account was squared.'

Suddenly, Sturt was losing control. Kingsmill's words were blasting holes in his defences. Killing was the only thought in mind. But he was helpless. Trussed like a chicken waiting on the butcher's knife. A long moan of despair erupted from the depths of his being as he railed against the injustice of existence. And even that was wasted. Stifled by the gag, a pathetic whimper was all that eventually dribbled from his lips.

Kingsmill got up, delved inside his coat, and produced the broken timepiece. He put it in Sturt's vest pocket then loosened the gag.

'It's time to settle the account, George.'

Sturt stared at him. Saw his own reflection in Kingsmill's eyes. Saw the pain and hatred that were the mirror image of Kingsmill's feelings towards him.

'Cut me loose, Thomas.'

Kingsmill shook his head.

'We used to be an even match,' he said, touching the cutlass slash across his chest, 'but I reckon you've come on apace.'

'This isn't the way! I owe you for the river. You owe me for Mary!'

'Mary was an accident!'

He had him by the throat, but Sturt's gaze did not waver. Kingsmill let go and turned away.

'When she died,' he said, quieter, more controlled, 'we both lost.'

For a moment, Sturt's mind was a cauldron of confusion. Had he heard right? Was Kingsmill trying to say that he too had loved Mary? His Mary! The surge of emotion rising in his gullet scrambled his thoughts even further. In another time, that hunched figure bracing himself against the fireplace had meant more to him than anyone else in the world. Sturt groaned. The past was threatening to destroy his sense of purpose. He jerked against the hemp that was shredding his wrists. Blood flowed. And the pain rekindled his rage – shocked him back to the present.

'Thomas . . .'

He turned – the very essence of darkest human nature.

'Any way you like,' said Sturt.

Kingsmill picked up the whip.

'I never did understand your sense of fair play,' he said.

In the tap-room, the Chichester men were being herded towards the front door when the crack of Kingsmill's whip split the silence.

Terrified, Fairall turned to Perrin.

'Richard?' he pleaded. 'Please . . .'

'I tried!' said the buyer, despairingly. 'He won't listen to me!'

A vicious dig in the back sent Fairall cannoning into Mills.

'Out!' snapped Jackson, opening the door.

Sheerman led the way. But the instant he set foot outside, a musket butt crashed against the side of his head and sent him sprawling back across the floor.

In the blink of an eye, a wave of scarlet and steel had funnelled through the doorway and sent Hawkhurst and Chichester smugglers alike reeling in all directions.

In the next room, Sturt cried out as plaited leather bit deep into his neck. Kingsmill prepared to strike again but, before the blow could fall, the back door was burst off its hinges. Shearer entered first and took the lash full across the eyes. Screaming with pain, he blundered into Fairbrother and knocked him across the table.

Kingsmill swept the lamp to the floor. The snug went

285

dark and he slipped into the tap-room – where a desperate battle for survival was in progress. From the other side of the room, Hannah Payne called his name. He cut his way towards her as she made her way to the trap-door that led to the cellars. Lifting it, she paused, waiting for him. However, the delay was just enough for an eager young trooper, anxious to make a name for himself, to catch hold of her. A short kitchen blade ripped the life out of him. His legs buckled and, dying, he fell across the trap, effectively blocking her escape route.

She was trying to shift him when, like some nocturnal creature afraid of the daylight, Richard Perrin scuttled out of the shadows. Between them, they rolled the twitching body clear. The Widow opened up. But, before she could step onto the ladder, Perrin shoved her aside and dropped into the darkness. Cracking her head on the hearthstone, she lay stunned as Kingsmill followed Perrin.

'Hannah!' he called. 'Get up!'

Senses scattered, she staggered to her feet.

'Thomas, help me!' she cried.

'Damn you, woman! Come on!'

He stretched out a hand.

Too late, she started towards him. Shearer seized her and, though half-blinded, saw the knife and twisted it from her grasp.

'Never mind her!' yelled Sturt from the snug doorway. 'Kingsmill, take Kingsmill!'

A brace of troopers bore down. Bayonets glinted in the candlelight. A last glance at the Widow and Kingsmill dropped the trap.

'Thomas!'

With her voice ringing in his ears, Kingsmill rammed the bolts home and hurried after Perrin.

'You're wasting your time!' snapped Sturt, as the troopers battered at the trap. 'Outside!'

Weak from loss of blood, he stumbled. Fairbrother caught him.

'George,' he said, 'no more. You've done enough.'

Sturt levered himself upright.

286

'The cellars . . .' he breathed. 'Help me find the cellars and we have him.'

'Private Pym?'

The soldier guarding the stables stepped outside and shook his head. 'Quiet as the grave, sir.'

'Major!'

Austin turned. Lit by torchlight, the yard and outbuildings were swarming with troops.

Fairbrother called again. He and Sturt had found the door to the cellars behind the brew-house – but needed help to break it down.

From the stable entrance, Private Pym watched two of his biggest mates put their shoulders to the task, unaware that something was moving in the hay bay behind him.

Very slowly, a well-oiled trap swung open. Kingsmill appeared and lifted himself out of the tunnel. Pausing for a moment, he gestured for Perrin to stay where he was. Then, knife in hand, he stalked his unsuspecting victim.

The first – and last – that Pym knew of it was a hand closing around his mouth and the pleasing sensation of his throat being stroked – as if by an attentive lover. Strong arms jerked him out of the light. Held him until the death throes subsided. Then let him flop to the floor.

Choosing the nearest horse – Sturt's – it took Kingsmill less than a minute to saddle up. Perrin, however, was still fumbling with his girth buckle.

'For Christ's sake hurry it up, Richard!' hissed Kingsmill.

'I can't! My hands . . .'

Kingsmill threw him a bridle. 'Never mind the saddle!'

Across the yard, the cellar door finally gave way. Voices echoed down the tunnel, and Perrin stared at the open trap.

'It's no use, Thomas, we're finished!'

Kingsmill dropped the trap and hoisted Perrin bodily onto his horse.

'Not yet, we're not! We'll lie up awhile – then take a boat for France.'

'Boats cost money!'

'Keep your voice down,' Kingsmill whispered. 'And don't you fret – I can get all the money we need.'

As he mounted, Sam Payne pressed an ear to the hay loft floor. He'd managed to slip out via the kitchens when Austin's men had piled in through the front. Now, still trembling and hardly daring to breathe, he strained to catch the muffled conversation below.

In the cellars, meanwhile, the escape tunnel had been discovered.

'The stables!' said Fairbrother, quickly working out the subterranean geography. 'It's got to be the stables.'

Sturt was already out of the door as the soldiers disappeared into the blackness. Staggering across the yard, he heard the crash of splintering timber inside the stables. A split-second later, Kingsmill and Perrin were bearing down on him. Raising his blade, Sturt stepped in front of his own horse. Sparks flew as both men struck simultaneously. Then Sturt flew backwards through the air in a shower of shattered steel.

In an instant, the fugitives were out of the gate. And though Austin got off a hurried shot, they melted into the night unscathed.

'Damn it, man,' yelled Fairbrother, hoarsely, 'don't just stand there – get after them!'

Austin sheathed his sword.

'There's no point,' he said quietly. 'The Hounds of Hell couldn't catch them now.'

'It doesn't matter . . .'

Sturt dragged himself to his feet. Battered and bleeding, he looked more dead than alive. However, turning to Fairbrother, he smiled.

'This time,' he said, 'he's got no one left to run to.'

Chapter 25

For once, the Law acted quickly and decisively. Chichester, not London, was chosen as the venue for the trial. Within the week, King George had granted seals to hold a special Assize of Oyer and Terminer, on the grounds that Justice should be seen to be done by those who had suffered most at the hands of the free traders. The effect on the population of Kent and Sussex was electrifying. It was as if peace had been declared after a long and bloody war. They descended upon the city in droves. In anticipation of the verdict, a new high gallows was erected on the Broyle. And even the Dean was swept along by the mood, delivering a sermon before the judges that left not a shadow of a doubt as to the outcome demanded by the people. The fact that Kingsmill was still at large was of no consequence. Turning off the five in custody would prove to the world that his power was finally broken – and provide an entertaining day out into the bargain.

Sturt, however, cared little about what happened to Jackson and the rest. He was as single-minded as ever. So, while the legal circus gathered momentum, he and Fairbrother rode with the dragoons as they scoured the countryside for Kingsmill. For days, they investigated every alleged sighting, every rumour or whisper. But it was as if the earth had opened up and swallowed him.

Few words were exchanged on the long ride back to Chichester, and Sturt sank deeper inside himself with each passing hour. At first, he thought of nothing but Kingsmill and how he might have already slipped across the Channel. That depressed him further, so he made a conscious effort to think about something else. Unfortunately, what sprang to mind threw him completely off balance. A stream of faces flashed before his eyes, like a spout lantern on a moonless night. But instead of smuggler's blue, they were red. Blood red. Slashed or shot away, staring, grinning in death. Peter Glover, Galley, Steven Diprose, Chater, Henry Kemp, Cobby, a dozen others ... But why? The significance of those dead faces eluded him: not because he was being particularly stupid, but because his mind had been closed to everything except killing Kingsmill for so long that he had lost his sense of perspective.

The rain turned to sleet as the coast came into view. He stared at the leaden sea and suddenly it was Mary's face haunting him. Alive and smiling, he saw her in her father's house the day he suggested it would make good sense for them to marry. He murmured her name. He saw her turning in the firelight at Jan and Alan's wedding party. Again he spoke – only this time the name that carried on the wind was Sarah's. He repeated it. Then, angry without knowing why, he spurred his mount and left Fairbrother wondering what new form of mental torture he had just devised to inflict upon himself.

The sound of sawing drifted in through the open window. Jan finished straightening the bed and caught her reflection in the looking glass behind the door. Turning side on, she inspected her profile. She pulled her dress tight across her belly, then pushed it out, imagining the changes to come in the months ahead. A shiver of excitement ran through her as she bent her knees, felt the living weight cradled in her pelvis.

'I was counting on your company.'

Her father's voice intruded, and she looked out of the window as he dismounted.

'Chichester's a long way for an old man on his own.'

'I'm sorry,' replied Alan, still sawing. 'We talked it over last night. Jan says no. She don't want nothing more to do with it.'

'I might peg out on the road. Think of the embarrassment!'

Alan sat on his saw-horse.

'I seen a hanging when I was a lad,' he said. 'It made me sick.'

Edward cast a quick eye over the house and Jan stepped back.

'She's a bossy madam, Alan. Once she gets her hooks into you – '

'She's right, Edward.'

That brought a smile from Jan, and left her father at a rare loss.

'The Hawkhurst Gang is finished – and as far as I'm concerned, it's all over and done with. History. A piece of the past.'

'George wouldn't see it that way.'

'That's up to George.'

In the distance, the storm that was gathering over Chichester darkened the horizon. Lightning flashed and, shaking his head, the old wheelwright made a real performance of climbing back into the saddle. Jan's pig-headedness was obviously rubbing off.

'I don't know what the world is coming to,' he sighed. 'In my day, women held their opinions close. And they done how they was told – if'n they knew what was good for 'em!'

'If you want to take it up with Jan – I'll give her a shout.'

'No!' came the quick reply. 'No need to bother her now. Happen she's fixin' your dinner . . .'

Edward pulled his muffler up to his chin. 'I'll call in on my way home,' he said, 'if I survives the journey, that is.'

'You'll do all right,' said Alan, rising. 'Just see that you stay out of the alehouses.'

A slap on the rump sent his father-in-law's fat mare on her way. Then, selecting another weather-board from the pile, he measured it off in handspans.

'Alan . . .'

Two arms slid around his waist. He turned and Jan kissed him, gently, with a great deal of affection. His mouth watered.

'What's that for?' he asked suspiciously.

Jan stroked his face. 'Just a token of respect,' she said, 'for my lord and master.'

A smile, all sweetness and light, lingered in the memory

after she'd gone. Sawing away, Alan wondered if he would ever understand the workings of the female mind.

The smell of new wood hung on the air. Thunderclouds crowded the setting sun. And sky-washed by an extraordinary, shimmering light, the Broyle took on the atmosphere of an eighteenth-century Calvary.

A brooding figure stood dwarfed by the oaken mare. Lattice-work shadows caged him as Sturt struggled to put his thoughts in order. Glover, Kemp, Galley, Chater – they would not let him be. Diprose, Cobby, Collier . . . Kingsmill's victims, yes. But all sacrificed on the altar of his blind quest for vengeance. For a fleeting moment, Sturt understood. The consequences of his actions were snapping at his coat-tails. His conscience was whispering in his ear. And it frightened him. He could not afford such a luxury. Not now. Not when he was so close. He shook his head, as if trying to exorcize a personal devil.

Lightning flashed.

He stared up at the gallows where a bonfire burned in the night. Through the heat haze, he saw himself dancing with Mary. She laughed. They turned in the firelight and it was Sarah in his arms.

Somewhere – in another time – thunder rumbled and the rain started to fall.

The bonfire flared and it was Kingsmill now. Dancing with Sarah. Touching. Holding. Sarah.

Turning.

Mary. Kissing. Mary. Holding. A pistol. Locked together. Beneath her breast.

Turning.

Firing. Falling. Mary – wrapped in crimson shroud.

Sturt dropped to his knees.

Beneath the mare – Kingsmill in the cart. Laughing. Halter tight around his neck. Faceless hangman. Horses whipped. Kingsmill – dangling in mid-air. Eyes burning. Laughing. All the time – laughing . . .

A shot rang out.

292

Sturt's ball punched a bloodless hole in his forehead. Spun him like a dervish.

Yet still be laughed – louder. And spun – faster.

Casting aside his pistol, Sturt knelt blank-eyed in the mud.

Behind the empty gallows, day gave way to night. And with the darkness came the spectre of impending madness.

Meanwhile, less than ten miles away, Fargus Cope was being relieved of purse and jewellery on Slindon Common. In itself, that was nothing unusual. After all, the desolate heath had long been a favourite haunt of highwaymen and footpads. However, routine robbery it was not. And had the corpulent corn dealer known that it was Thomas Kingsmill who faced him, it is unlikely that he would have protested quite so vigorously. As it was, objection gained him nothing but a cracked skull. Indeed, he would not have survived the encounter at all if Richard Perrin had not spotted the dragoon patrol approaching at the gallop.

Kingsmill sheathed his knife and quickly remounted. Then, inwardly ranting against the indignity of reduced circumstance, he turned tail and ran – like the common criminal he now was.

Later, outside Justice Battine's chambers, Bootie and the bonnet monkey were counting their takings to the genteel accompaniment of a string quartet. Inside, a lavish reception for the three trial judges was in full flow. All of Chichester society had been invited, and many a gentleman had been persuaded to reach into his pocket by the monkey's bizarre impersonation of the state executioner – complete with mask and string noose.

Someone approached. The cripple stopped counting and listened to the rhythm of the footsteps.

'Sergeants Sturt and Fairbrother!' he said with a grin.

'Bootie!' exclaimed Fairbrother.

'At your service, gentlemen. But you're late,' he chided, 'an' you've got 'is honour's flunkeys in a right ol' sweat. Bin bobbin' in an' out all night, they 'as, lookin' for you two.'

Fairbrother glanced as Sturt, who was tugging at the over-tight new breeches that had been forced upon him after he'd been dragged out of the tap-room at the Royal George.

'A slight hiccough at the tailor's,' said Fairbrother, none too convincingly. 'But what on earth are you doing here?'

'Come for my pound of flesh, ain't I?'

Bootie felt the frown on Fairbrother's face.

'Believe it or not, Master John, there was a time when the Hawkhurst Gang didn't have it all their own way.'

The monkey jumped onto his lap.

'Nine year ago, the Third Foot caught 'em bang to rights runnin' tubs across the Marsh. Half the damned night, we chased 'em. Killed some; took some – though not wi'out cost . . .' Purely by chance, his sightless eyes settled on Sturt.

'Me an' Jack Flack, God rest him, took on Kingsmill himself.'

Sturt removed the crude hood and gently scratched the monkey's ears.

'You know he's not taken?'

Bootie nodded.

'I can wait, Master George. An' stretchin' 'is crew will whet my appetite nicely. Now you'd best get on,' he said, jerking his head towards the door, 'before them over-puffed turkey cocks drinks the place dry.'

They climbed the great double staircase in silence. Sturt, though back in control of himself, was hardly in the mood to be put on display like some exotic wild animal. And Fairbrother's thoughts remained in the street with Bootie. Announced at the door, he winced as the sharpest of pains ripped through where his arm used to be.

A solitary handclap broke the curious silence. A sea of powdered, painted faces beamed, nodded approval. Then, one by one, judge and justice, landowner and churchman, followed Robert Lamb's lead. The applause reached its peak. Fairbrother gave a sigh of resignation and disappeared amongst the crowd of fawning admirers. But Sturt remained in the doorway. His guts turned over – he was feeling distinctly queasy.

Major Mills closed the door on the dragoon sergeant and put the candle lantern back on the grime-encrusted mantel-shelf. The old house had seen better days, but it suited the retired colt breaker. Squalor, as he saw it, was in the eye of the beholder. And since his tidy-minded wife had passed on, he and Smoaker had lived mostly as they pleased, which was, in a nutshell, like pigs.

The hoofbeats faded and he opened the back door.

'All right – they've gone.'

Chilled to the marrow, Kingsmill and Perrin entered.

'Seems I seen two scabs answering to your likenesses riding hard for Walberton,' said Mills, extending a gnarled hand.

Kingsmill threw Cope's purse.

Catching it, the Major counted out twenty guineas won at the card table of Ma Cappe's Chichester establishment. He frowned.

'Considering the circumstances, Thomas,' he said, 'you'd be hard pressed to find cheaper lodgings.'

Kingsmill eyed the shrewd old scroat. They went back a long way – to the days of his predecessor, Arthur Gray, in fact, who, with Mills's help, had had the misfortune to fall down a dry well twelve years ago.

'Better give them to him,' advised Perrin.

The rings and pocket watch were worth at least as much again, and brought a thin smile to Mills's crusty lips.

'Just look on it as being a fair price for my boy, Smoaker,' he said, sinking worn-out teeth into a ring.

'The boat?' said Kingsmill.

He nodded.

'When?'

'Night tide. Day after tomorrow.'

'Where?'

A dry laugh echoed.

'I'll take you myself,' said the Major. 'A man of your standing should at least be seen off in style.'

Before Kingsmill could respond, he took a large kettle from the hob and filled three mugs.

'How much?' asked Perrin.

'Five hundred. Each.'

The old man's feet lifted off the floor as Kingsmill grabbed him.

'The Excise is offering two thousand just for you, Thomas, so you can take it or leave it,' he rasped, hot ale dripping from his greasy beard.

The idea of beating the whereabouts of the boat out of him really appealed to Kingsmill. But the possibility of him dying of a seizure and leaving them stranded persuaded him to let go.

Nursing his windpipe, Mills sat down. Then, speaking with difficulty, he said, 'You can hand it over to me – now, if you like – '

'To the captain!' said Kingsmill. 'And not before we're under way!'

Perrin glanced at him with anguished eyes. Mills might just as well have asked for a hundred thousand. The slightest shake of the head warned him to keep his thoughts to himself.

However, the unspoken conversation did not escape the Major.

'In which case, gentlemen,' he said, pocketing Cope's money-bag, 'you'd best put your minds to retrieving your nest-egg. 'Less you mean to earn it all on Slindon Common, that is.'

'You've got a visitor.'

Hannah Payne turned from the tiny barred window that was now her only contact with the outside world. Over-tight leg irons chafed her ankles, and the rats vanished as if by magic when the heavy oak door swung open.

Back-lit by the gaoler's smoking torch, a half-sized figure stood in the narrow passageway.

'Samuel?' queried the Widow, as her pupils adjusted to the light.

'Mam!'

Before she could speak, the lad flew into her arms and, sobbing his heart out, buried his head between her breasts. Perplexed, even embarrassed, by such an uncharacteristic outburst, she appealed to the gaoler who, hardened as he was, nevertheless had six children of his own.

'Five minutes,' he said. 'No more.'

The door banged shut. The rats re-appeared. And the Widow attempted to extricate herself from her son's not altogether childlike embrace.

'All right, he's gone.'

Fingernails gouged her flesh, and the wailing got louder.

'Samuel!'

Instant silence. Then tearless, cunning eyes blinked up at her.

'What the Devil are you up to, boy?'

Across the street, the lively strains of a jig danced on the air. Letting go of his mother's shapely behind, Samuel swayed in time to the music and grinned.

'Come to get you out of here, ain't I?'

Moods change, often for no apparent reason. And Fairbrother, far from finding the reception a chore, was experiencing a heady sense of freedom as he whirled Judge Foster's daughter around the floor. Fine food and drink, music, pretty women, intelligent conversation; in fact, all the trappings of civilized society combined to make him feel as if he had just stepped back into the real world. The half-life of recent months was suddenly no more than a bad dream. He could not remember when he had last enjoyed himself so much. He glanced at Sturt, brooding, trapped in a corner by the judges' over-scaffolded wives and a gaggle of sycophantic hangers-on. He smiled to himself. With a large proportion of the British Army combing the southern counties for Kingsmill, he refused to feel guilty about having a good time. After all, they had earned it. There was nothing they could usefully do. So, come Hell or high water, he intended to re-acquaint himself with the trivial pleasures of everyday existence.

Robert Lamb was also determined to enjoy himself – but

for an altogether different reason. His position was, to say the least, tenuous, in that, if any of those in custody decided to turn King's Evidence, he could easily end up in the cart himself. Therefore, he determined to establish the highest possible profile with those who mattered. So, flitting from pillar to post, he entertained the ladies with amusing stories, exchanged the crudest of jokes with the gentlemen, and created an effective diversion when the Dean, drunk as a gin widow, keeled over and had to be carried out on a board.

Then, growing bolder, the Magistrate forced himself upon the judges, and was airing his views on the appalling social consequences of the free trade when Major Austin entered with the Chief Gaoler.

Austin sought out Collector Shearer. Shearer spoke with Justice Battine. Battine whispered with Judge Foster. He summoned Sturt and, without so much as a by-your-leave, left Lamb to imagine the worst.

Fairbrother ignored the mass exodus, and drew his partner indecently close. The softest of lips brushed his ear. The most wanton suggestion brought a smile to his face. And deep within, a spark that he had thought to be extinct was rekindled.

'Curse the woman!' muttered Harry Sheerman, his ear pressed to the observation grille.

Mills grunted as his chain brought him up sharp, four feet short of the door.

'For Christ's sake, man,' he grumbled, 'what's going on?'

Sheerman ignored him, and strained to catch the gist of the angry conversation taking place in the cell next door.

Fairall, seemingly unconcerned, relieved himself in the slop pail. And caught in the grip of some mysterious fever, Jackson merely moaned in his cot.

Suddenly, Sheerman turned from the door, a look of incredulity stamped on his face. Fairall buttoned his fall, and smiled wryly.

'She's turned King's Evidence?' he said.

A nod confirmed it.

298

'Thomas . . .' said Sheerman. 'She's spillin' all she knows.'

'Then pray they take the bastard soon,' replied Fairall, packing a pipe. 'It would be an abomination if we were to dance the jig with him still free.'

Footsteps chattered in the stone-flagged passageway. Snarling with rage, Sheerman spat at Judge Foster as he passed. The response was immediate. A club handle jabbed him in the face and sent him reeling.

'Master Sturt?' called the gaoler.

Last to leave, Sturt was still staring at the Widow. The image in his mind was of her and Thomas. He could see the attraction. And under different circumstances, he could easily have taken an interest himself. However . . .

The turnkey, anxious to lock up, shuffled in the doorway, so he turned to go.

'Sturt?'

He paused.

'It's something you and me have in common,' she said. 'In years to come, we can both boast about how we betrayed him.'

The smile was a mistake. But Samuel recognized the danger and stepped between them.

Sturt squatted on his heels, and looked the lad in the eye.

'You'd better not be lying, boy,' he said, quietly, 'or I promise – I'll sit you up in the cart when they hang her.'

The funereal strains of a pavanne drifted in through the glassless window. Left alone, Hannah Payne drew her son to her. And next door Jackson ranted and raved as goblins and ghosts sprang from the subconscious to pick the flesh from his bones.

299

Chapter 26

With time passing, Austin set about the daunting task of mustering his troops. Finding them was not difficult. Taverns and brothels spewed them out in droves. It was the condition they were in that was the problem. The possibility of having them ready to ride before dawn receded by the minute as, progressing up Broad Street, he supervised the twentieth horse trough baptism like some crusading priest eager to swell the ranks of the converted.

Still dancing, Fairbrother heard about it from the Prison Ordinary. So, willingly supported by his equally intoxicated partner, he set off in search of Sturt.

The stables were off an alleyway behind the gaol. Across the way, a bonfire burned on the corner, warming whores and clients alike. From the shadows, Sarah Dimer saw Fairbrother and companion sail majestically through the maze of verminous sewers. She had taken lodgings that morning for the singular purpose of attending the trial. However, against her better judgement, she had been drawn to Battine's chambers on the off-chance that Sturt would be present. Failing to gain entry, she had waited outside. And seeing him had destroyed all her good intentions at a stroke. The thought of making a new life alone was suddenly ludicrous. The old contradictions returned with a vengeance – bringing with them a few new ones to add to her dilemma. Fate had made it perfectly clear that they were not meant for one another. But, as she fended off the attentions of a drunken cooper, Sarah knew that, without him, the future would be nothing more than a matter of marking time before death.

'Just give me five minutes,' said Fairbrother, swaying in the stable entrance.

One quick look told Sturt all he needed to know. Shaking

his head, he lengthened a stirrup leather and led his rented horse out of its stall. Fairbrother, meanwhile, was blundering around searching for his saddle.

'No, John.'

'What?'

'I said no. You're no use to me in that state.'

'I'm going!' affirmed Fairbrother. 'So you might as well save your breath for riding.'

Heaving his saddle from the tack rail, he overbalanced and crashed into a low beam. Stunned, he sank to the floor, clutching his head.

Sturt picked up a brimming pail.

'When he's fit,' he said, 'tell him it's Goudhurst. Trickett's Farm.'

Henrietta Foster had never held a bucket before. Nevertheless, Sturt's instructions were clear — even to one with her limited practical ability. So, as Fairbrother rolled around, moaning and groaning, she raised it, giggled – and did precisely what she'd been told.

Fairbrother's outraged yell echoed around the yard as Sturt prepared to mount.

'Don't go, George.'

He spun on his heel.

'Sarah?'

Initial shock gave way to relief as she stepped into the light. He reached out, but she kept her distance.

'Please,' she said. 'Wait for John and the soldiers.'

He paused.

'I can't. There isn't time.'

'Then he will destroy you.'

'No.'

'He will!' She said it quietly, with total conviction. 'I know it in my bones.'

The politics of human relationships were discarded there and then. In a run-down Chichester stable yard, George Sturt and Sarah Dimer abandoned their defences. Yet, like spinning magnets, they were attracted and repelled with such bewildering speed that neither could see the nature of their relationship clearly. It was fundamental. Spiritual.

Their feelings went beyond anything either had ever experienced. With him, she had turned dreams into reality – and not been disappointed. With her, Sturt felt whole for the first time since childhood. Quite simply, they loved one another with a passion so rare, so powerful, that it constantly threatened their very existence. Together, they had the potential to harness that power – to conquer the world. However, the tragedy was that their present dealings with that same world continued to block their every attempt to do so.

For a long moment, neither spoke. And the chemistry bubbled.

Then Sarah went to him, saying, 'I'll not tend your grave for the rest of my days, George Sturt. Sunday visits. Fading flowers. Year after year. You and Mary . . .'

Her head dropped onto his chest.

'I couldn't bear it.'

'Sarah . . .'

He lifted her face.

'It isn't only for Mary.'

She held him tight.

'That's my shame, George. And it isn't worth dying for.'

'He is what he is because of me. Every murder. Every maiming and rape – tied to my cowardice.'

He buried his face in her hair.

'I owe it to myself, Sarah. Thomas is my shame.'

'Oh, George . . .'

Words were no longer adequate. So, for a timeless span, they clung together, mouths and minds joined. Then drawing away, he mounted up.

'Your horse pistol?'

Puzzled, she frowned. 'At my lodgings. Why?'

'Just see that you leave Jackson to the hangman,' he said. 'I'd find it difficult to fix flowers to a gibbet cage.'

'It's expected.'

'Over my dead body,' he said, stacking new weather-boards two at a time.

'Alan . . .' coaxed Jan, nuzzling his neck. 'You're being mean-spirited. He'd be so pleased – '

'I don't care! Not Edward.'

'What then?'

'George. George Alan Wynter.' The early morning light poured in as he opened the barn doors.

'And that's my last word.'

'Even if it's a girl?'

Such an appalling prospect had never occurred. So, oozing a smug smile, Jan picked up the duck eggs that she had gathered and left him to consider it.

'If it is,' he yelled, 'it's your fault!'

Across the yard, the farmhouse door slammed shut.

'The Wynters ain't sired a girl in two hundred years . . .'

His ladder was inside, propped against the hay loft. He took hold of it, still muttering to himself.

'Not as can be proved anyhow!'

The door swung to, shutting out the daylight, wiping the smirk from his face.

'I didn't mean it. I swear – '

Spinning round, he saw not Jan, but two shadowy figures swathed in travel-stained greatcoats.

'Alan Wynter . . .' said Kingsmill, as he removed his muffler.

Sorting eggs, Jan heard the barn door again. Anticipating a change of heart, she smiled and glanced out of the window. To her surprise, Alan was not alone. An oddly twisted individual was limping along at his shoulder – with a pistol clutched in his misshapen fist. An egg slipped from her fingers. She stared blankly at it. Then, with Alan almost at the door, she dashed out the back way.

'Where is she?'

Alan was asking himself the same question when he noticed that the back door was off the latch.

Perrin poked him in the ribs. 'I heard you in the yard!'

'Goudhurst,' blurted Alan, 'she's gone off to Goudhurst. To her father's . . .'

Eggshell crunched underfoot. Both men stared at the mess on the floor.

'Not strong on housework,' said Alan, lamely. 'Never was.'

Perrin scraped his boot on the fender.

'Goudhurst?'

'Yes.'

'Without so much as a goodbye?' he asked, shuffling towards the door.

'She's got a terrible temper . . . Acts on the spur of the moment, she do.'

Perrin paused.

'What you heard at the barn – you and Master Kingsmill – was our very first family set-to.'

The word family stung. And throwing the bolts, Perrin wondered if he would ever see his own again.

Outside, Jan stood pressed against the wall. Hands shaking, guts churning, she took a moment to gather her wits. Then, with a plan born of desperation in mind, she turned and slipped away.

Two feet down, the spade struck gold – literally. Scrabbling with bare hands, Kingsmill unearthed the leather satchel that he had had the foresight to bury in the days when Enoch Trickett was holding contraband. He wiped away the mildew with his sleeve. He shook it. Coins jingled. Laughing out loud, he did not hear the soft footfall behind him. A pitchfork pricked his spine, and he froze.

'If you so much as breaks wind – I'll send you to the Devil.'

His head half-turned.

Jan prodded him. 'I mean it!'

'All right.'

Kneeling motionless, he looked ridiculous – almost as if he was praying.

'You know who I am?'

'I know you!'

There was no trace of fear in her voice, and he shivered – someone had walked on his grave.

304

'Your man and my husband,' she said purposefully, 'you'll call them from the house.'

When he hesitated, she stabbed him, drawing blood.

'You'll call them!'

'Yes!'

Jan ordered him to get up. As he did so, she stepped back and trod on her best layer. Squawking in agony, the injured bird flapped at her ankles. And in one movement, Kingsmill turned, jerked the pitchfork from her hand and swung the heavy money-bag at her head.

Hurt, dazed, Jan rolled onto her back and watched helplessly as he struck.

'She damn-near did for me, Richard!'

He threw her across the room and she smacked into Alan.

'Jan!' he cried. 'You should have run . . .'

'I didn't want to leave you!'

Her knees buckled. Helping her to a chair, he examined the bruise across her throat, where the pitchfork had pinned her.

'Was it still there?' Perrin asked, anxiously.

A small fortune spilled onto the table.

'Passage,' grinned Kingsmill. 'And more than enough to finance the first run.'

'What do you mean?' asked Perrin. 'The first run?'

'Within the month, there won't be a smuggled tub between Bristol and London. We'll be able to name our price.'

A brittle laugh reverberated.

'There's no one left, Thomas! How in God's name do we run contraband?'

'With a French crew – and Robert Lamb organizing distribution.' Kingsmill smiled. 'Nothing changes,' he said. 'We just move our base across the Channel.'

He was mad. Perrin was now absolutely convinced of it. The strain of past weeks had taken its toll and he had finally lost his grip on reality. He glanced at the money. One shot when his back was turned would do it. He dismissed the

305

thought at once. Even if he had the nerve and the hands to hold a gun steady, he couldn't. Whatever else Richard Perrin was, he wasn't a murderer. And anyway, they had known one another for too long . . .

His shoulders sagged, and his head felt like a ton weight. He was very tired – so tired that the panic just drained away. And though the thought of death – particularly on the gallows – continued to terrify him, he suddenly felt easier with himself.

'I'll fetch the horses,' he said, quietly and without fuss.

Kingsmill took off his coat.

'No,' he said, 'stable them. We'll wait until nightfall.'

He was counting the second thousand guineas when Alan plucked up the courage to speak.

'When you go,' he said, 'what happens to us?'

It had been a grand theatrical occasion. Defence and Crown performed with panache. Witnesses pointed the finger. Informers sang like birds. The packed gallery bayed and stamped as each successive nail was driven into the collective coffin. And even the accused – excluding the Widow who was to be tried separately, and Jackson, so ill that he languished in the dock oblivious to the proceedings – gave good value by displaying an arrogance that was as entertaining as it was unexpected.

By mid-afternoon, the verdict was in and Judge Foster prepared to pass sentence. Silence fell. Black silk was taken. And, across the gallery, old Edward caught a glimpse of Sarah easing her way to the front. Failing to catch her eye, he squeezed past Robert Lamb and watched as the prisoners were ordered to stand. Two gaolers lifted Jackson. The court was completely still as the awful words were spoken. Then a fleeting movement caught the wheelwright's eye. Again, he looked at Sarah. Something glinted in the candle-light. Wriggling like a demented eel, he tried to get to her before she did anything stupid. But so tight was the crush that he could scarcely move.

As he called her name, the shot rang out.

The ball took Jackson in the chest and propelled him

clean out of the dock. His legs thrashed in the air. Suddenly, there was pandemonium. Lamb called to the guards, pointed to the culprit. Fairall, Mills and Sheerman were bundled off, protesting, to the cells. On the Judge's orders, a surgeon was sent for. And not thirty feet away, Sarah was knocked to the ground by a soldier eager to lay hand on Dorcas Chater. The shoemaker's widow surrendered her pistol. Then, offering no resistance, she was dragged away as the court was cleared.

Outside, Edward and Sarah sat on the steps, unable to speak. At that moment, the old wheelwright felt worn out by the weight of experience. He shook his head. The Law of the land – even the law of natural justice could not bring Mary, or any of the others, back. He put his arm around Sarah's shoulder and gave her a squeeze. There was nothing to keep him in Chichester. Tomorrow he would go home – to await the arrival of a new generation.

The sickly stench of burning flesh assaulted Michael Shearer's nostrils, and he closed his eyes as the prison surgeon cauterized the crater in Jackson's chest. Jerked screaming back to consciousness, he sat bolt upright despite being held by two burly officers. Then, as the iron went in again, he fell back in a merciful dead faint.

Picking up the flattened ball that had wreaked such havoc, the exciseman hammered on the cell door. The turnkey let him out, and he hurried away before he disgraced himself.

Next door, the Widow peered through the bars.

'Well?' she said.

A quick look at Jackson and the gaoler shook his head.

'And the others?'

'What do you think?'

The man was on his way when she called him back. A gold coin wafted under his nose.

'My release . . .' she said. 'If it were hurried on apace, there'd be two more.'

The bribe was taken, examined and pocketed.

'You ain't goin' no place,' said the gaoler. 'Leastways, not before the prison hulk sails.'

At first, she thought it was just a joke at her expense. She even smiled. The gaoler did not.

'What do you mean?' she said, uncertainly. 'Judge Foster promised . . .'

'That you wouldn't hang. He didn't say nowt about lettin' you loose.'

The Widow seemed to shrink, and he pressed his deeply pitted face against the bars.

'Transportation.'

'You're lying!'

He grinned and walked away.

'Damn you! You're lying!'

She beat her fists against the door, skinning knuckles, drawing blood.

'That wasn't the agreement . . .'

Strapping creature that she was, Dorcas Chater appeared bird-frail as she stood before Judge Foster. Ignoring her, he toyed with the pistol ball while Shearer informed him that Jackson would live long enough to be turned-off – just so long as there was no delay.

'Battine?' said the Judge.

The Chief Justice nodded. 'The hangman is already ensconced at the Spread Eagle.'

'Tomorrow then.'

'And the blacksmith?'

'Have him fetched this evening.'

Bows all round saw Chichester's Senior Magistrate taking his leave. For a moment, the only sound in the exquisitely panelled room was that of three people breathing. Then rising to his feet, Judge Foster expounded, 'Vengeance, my good woman, is the prerogative of God and the Law!'

A kerchief trimmed with smuggled lace dabbed at a powdered nostril, and Dorcas dropped her eyes.

'Even the loss of a husband cannot condone murder. If the man had died, you would have left me with no alternative. As it is, the Law demands a penalty of seven years in the Indies plantations.'

308

Like an actor or priest, he paused for effect. Then, in danger of losing his audience, he continued in softer vein.

'But considering the somewhat unusual circumstance, I see no purpose in detaining you further.'

He pocketed his kerchief and beamed.

'You are free to go, ma'am.'

The expected expression of gratitude was not forthcoming. However, increasingly aware of the enfeeblement of advancing years himself, the Judge ascribed Dorcas's lapse to her age rather than lack of manners.

Shearer opened the door and took her by the arm.

'Mistress Chater,' said Foster, speaking slowly, exuding paternalistic goodwill, 'Seek comfort and guidance in the Lord. Show true penitence and He will pour balm upon remorse.'

Feeling her stiffen, Shearer tightened his grip. But Dorcas shook loose, saying in a strong, clear voice, 'I regret but one thing only, sir. And that is that William Jackson still lives.'

And with no more to say, she strode out of the room; leaving Sir Michael Foster, Kt., Judge of The King's Bench, to contemplate the intrinsic boorishness of the lower classes.

The air temperature was dropping like a stone as a pair of adenoidal rooks beat their way across the face of the setting sun. Richard Perrin stood at the window, watching the day fade. Something moved on the western skyline. He scanned the hillside but, deer or whatever, it had already melted into the twilight.

Alan lit a lantern. Jan stood by the fire, watching Kingsmill eat at table.

'Richard,' he said, without looking up, 'it's time.' Putting on hat and coat, Perrin limped towards the door.

'Your pistol.'

'No, Thomas. We've got what we came for . . .'

'Leave it.'

Alan squeezed Jan's hand while Perrin pleaded their case.

'The Winchcombe girl – Mary – '

'Was her sister. I know.'

'And did you also know that she's carrying the boy's child?'

Perrin placed his gun on the table.

'He let it slip – while you were digging in the barn.'

The door closed and Kingsmill picked at the remains of his supper. Caught in the firelight, Jan bore an uncanny ressemblance to Mary.

'The same eyes . . .' said Kingsmill, rising.

He touched a cheek and her teeth snapped at his fingers.

'And spirit.'

She caught her cloak as he threw it.

'Put it on.'

'What for?' Alan demanded, drawing her close.

'They're looking for two men. She'll see us safe to the coast.'

'And Alan?' said Jan.

'Will sit tight and say nothing – until he's sure you're safe.'

The clasp caught him across the nose as she threw her cloak back at him.

'I'm going nowhere without him!'

Side by side, the Wynters presented a united, if petrified, front. So, without further argument, Kingsmill took aim and fired.

Jan screamed and fell to her knees as Alan writhed in agony.

'Oh, Jesus!' he cried, clutching his foot. 'Sweet Jesus – it hurts!'

Tearing at his boot, Jan froze when she heard that awful, metallic click. She turned. Primed, Perrin's pistol was pointing at her husband's head.

'No – don't!'

She placed herself in Kingsmill's line of fire.

'Please don't,' she said. 'I'll do anything. Anything you want.'

Justice Battine, his clerk, six armed foot soldiers, and two gaolers led Jonathan Felkin into the labyrinth. Passing the

Widow's cell, they stopped next door and the duty officer opened up.

'On your feet!' ordered Battine.

At supper, the condemned men were dragged from their seats.

'Have a care!' Fairall complained. 'You'll ruin an excellent dinner.'

'Master Felkin?'

Battine stepped aside, giving the fire-singed blacksmith room to work.

'All four of them.'

'Gibbet irons,' wailed Mills. 'The bastard is to measure us for chains!'

'Shut it!'

The gaoler's fist silenced him.

'Get on with it.'

Jackson, conscious now but barely breathing, came to life at the sight of the smith's measuring rod.

'Bugger off . . .' he wheezed, trying to rise from the cot.

'A damnable injustice, sir!' Fairall said to Battine. 'The sentence was hanging – no mention of the gibbet . . .'

'Get away from me!' moaned Jackson.

A feeble kick caught Felkin on the knee.

'You'll not black my face with tar . . .'

Two soldiers held him but, from somewhere, Jackson found the strength to break free. A third man sat on his chest, undoing the surgeon's work.

'In the name of God,' murmured Harry Sheerman, 'show mercy.'

One last great heaving effort proved too much for Jackson. His heart gave out. And haemorrhaging from nose and mouth, he uttered a dreadful, shuddering scream, rolled his eyes and rattled into oblivion.

Covered in dead man's mess, Felkin blundered, retching, into the passageway. Shepherd Fairall picked up his measure as a soldier tried to close Jackson's lids.

'At least we'll be hanging in the sweet air, while he lies rotting in the ground,' he said, with bleak satisfaction.

311

Chapter 27

The stable door swung open, throwing a hard-edged wedge of light across the yard. Well wrapped against the cold, Perrin led the horses out and tethered them to the hitching ring.

'Thomas!' he yelled.

A figure moved at the window and Perrin braced himself, expecting a second shot. When it didn't come, he relaxed and went back for the lantern.

Entering the stable, he suddenly sensed that he was not alone. He reached for his pistol – cursed Kingsmill for taking it – and slowly drew his sword from its scabbard.

'Who is it?' he said calmly, trying not to let the panic show. 'Who's there?'

Somewhere, something moved. He raised his hanger. But just then, the light went out plunging the building into darkness.

A split second later, his blade clattered to the floor. And soon after that, the lamp flickered back to life.

'Trickett's Farm?'

Henry Newdigate picked himself up, and blinked at what looked like a dozen fiery horsemen.

'Eh?'

'Trickett's Farm!' repeated Fairbrother.

'Dead,' said Goudhurst's resident drunkard.

'What?'

'Enoch Trickett. Dead. Kicked by his old mare . . .'

'His farm!'

'Not now.' Henry said, sadly. 'Bought by George Sturt – an' he give it to Joe Wynter's lad.'

'I know that,' said Fairbrother, losing patience. 'What I don't know is where it is!'

'Well, why didn't you say?'

312

A work-worn finger waved in a vaguely northerly
direction.

'That way. Three mile – but – '

A horse struck him a glancing blow, and put him back
on the seat of his breeches.

'It weren't my fault,' he called from the gutter. 'I warned
him, time an' again, not to trust that mare!'

Down the hill, beyond the Gore, Becky Glover's dog
yapped at the window as Fairbrother and the dragoons
passed at the gallop.

Skilful fingers had stopped Alan's bleeding and were putting
the finishing touches to a makeshift dressing when Kingsmill pulled on his coat.

'That's good enough,' he said, picking up the money-
bag.

Jan helped Alan to stand.

'Jan . . .'

'I'll be all right – be back before you know it.'

A hefty shove in the back took her breath away.

'Kingsmill!'

Alan's voice carried unexpected authority. Kingsmill
stopped.

'Even if you get to France, there's still George Sturt.'

'Alan – don't . . .' pleaded Jan.

But braced against a chair, he leaned over the lantern on
the table, determined to finish what he had started. The
light sharpened the angles of his face. He looked older as
he spoke.

'So you'd better keep running.'

The pistol barrel split his ear, scrambled his senses. Jan
screamed, lashed out, but Kingsmill bundled her out of the
door. Then quite deliberately, he knocked the lantern onto
the floor.

Dragging Jan towards the horses, he glanced at the figure
limping from the stable.

'Richard,' he snapped, 'fetch another horse!'

The silhouetted figure kept coming.

313

'Richard . . .'

It was almost within touching distance when the flames inside the house licked at the windows and lit Sturt's face.

'Thomas . . .'

Both Jan and Kingsmill stood rooted to the spot. Neither believed eyes or ears as Sturt, dressed in Perrin's greatcoat and hat, levelled his pistol.

'Step away from her,' he said, 'and throw the gun.'

The pause was a long one as Kingsmill instinctively played for time – probed for the slightest sign of weakness.

'And if I don't?'

'I'll shoot you where you stand.'

An extraordinary exhilaration seized Kingsmill. Fair play! he thought to himself. His absurd sense of fair play! Had it been the other way round, he would have shot Sturt without a second thought.

For an instant, Jan masked him as she ran. So he kicked the nearest horse, hard, and it wheeled around, crushing Sturt against the wall.

Disarmed and winded, he went down. Iron shoes struck sparks from the flags, numbed his shoulder as they trampled him. Rolling clear, he cried out when Kingsmill's boot cracked a rib. A second kick burst a cheek, broke teeth. A third missed. However, such was the onslaught that he could not get up. Then a knife glinted in the firelight. Kingsmill lunged. But Jan took his legs from under him with a rake and the blow never landed.

Hurt and bleeding, both men scrambled to their feet. Behind them, the windows of the house blew out.

'Alan!' cried Jan, already running as they tore into each other.

The heat drove her back. So she wrapped her cloak around her head and was half-way through the door when Fairbrother pulled her out. A heavy beam crashed to the floor.

'Alan!' she sobbed. 'He's in there!'

Dismounting, Major Austin went in, followed by his sergeant.

'Jan, where's George?' asked Fairbrother.

A thick, choking cloud billowed out of the doorway.

'The stable . . .' she answered, hoarsely. 'He's at the stable with Kingsmill.'

A dragoon swept her aside as three blackened figures materialized. They collaped at her feet and a dozen willing hands beat at their smouldering clothes.

'No, John!'

Spread-eagled, Sturt was clinging to Kingsmill's knife arm.

'Stay out of it!'

A scything blow sent Kingsmill sprawling, the knife spinning.

Fairbrother took aim, and again Sturt yelled at him. Conscience, common sense, decency – all demanded that he should shoot. He tried, but something was stopping him. Something other than Sturt. He felt again Kingsmill's blade biting into his body. Looked at the empty sleeve flapping in the night breeze. Yet still he could not pull the trigger. The answer came to him as the two men circled one another. They were in a world of their own. And despite his own suffering, he was an outsider. An intruder who had no right to come between them.

And so they fought.

And this time there was no thought of Mary, no memory of events at the river. The weapons were bare hands. The conflict was cold and clinical. Awesome to watch. With each attack and counter, the movements became more refined – the senses more attuned to achieving the ultimate goal. Each man was filled with a tremendous sense of power and well-being as he strove to destroy the other. They passed through pain. Ignored exhaustion. Shifted onto another plane where George Sturt and Thomas Kingsmill were one again. The same light shone in both pairs of eyes. Pure. Unadulterated. Carrying them towards a pinnacle of human experience. A pinnacle where each – in his way – would find peace. Where both would be released from the agony of existence as they knew it.

It was a perfectly timed, paralysing blow that ended it.

All at once, the vision faded and reality reclaimed them. In a Kent farmyard, two broken, hideously beaten men lay entwined like lovers in some dark fantasy of a crippled mind. Sturt's left arm was locked around Kingsmill's neck, while his right hand clawed at his face. One quick jerk and it would be over.

'George.'

Fairbrother's shadow fell across them.

'It's for the law to say.'

'That's not enough!'

'Then finish it! Finish it now!'

Kingsmill's words were bursting inside his head like star shells. One quick jerk . . .

'Leave it to the hangman.'

'No!'

For the briefest interval, there was terror in Kingsmill's voice. Sturt's grip relaxed – no more than a fraction – but enough to allow him to swivel his head.

'For pity's sake, George, spare me the gibbet,' he said.

The mist had not yet lifted from the valley. Around the farm, there were deep pockets where, two by two, horses' heads and half-soldiers sailed westwards on a granite sea.

'What will you do?'

'Go home,' answered Fairbrother. 'Take to the cloth trade, if my father will have me.'

'He'd be a very foolish man if he didn't,' said Jan, her voice thick with emotion.

Fairbrother smiled and kissed her. Sturt joined them.

'You'll keep to your agreement about the farm?' said Alan, not without difficulty as his burns were giving him gyp.

'It's yours,' replied Sturt. 'And dead or alive, there's a considerable reward. Use it to put the place in order.'

'You've given us more than enough already.'

He patted her belly and glanced at the house.

'No godson of mine is going to inherit that awful shambles, Jan Wynter!'

'Who says it'll be your godson?'

A blister burst as Alan slid an arm around a thickening waist.

'It just might be a girl,' he said.

'Boy or girl,' replied Sturt, smiling, 'see you take good care of them both.'

Jan took his hand.

'What about you and Sarah?'

The smile faded and he shook his head.

'I don't know . . .'

Tears flowed freely and unashamedly as she clung to him.

'Our Mary really wouldn't begrudge you, George!'

Sturt's eyes filled up too. But the words turned to dust in his mouth. There were times when silence and a heartfelt embrace could say more than all the words in the language.

After they'd gone, Jan and Alan stood amongst their scattered possessions. For a moment, it felt as if the end of the world had come. Then the sun broke through and swept the yard like a new broom. They had survived the worst that could happen. Grown older and stronger in the process. Learnt that such was the nature of existence that nothing could be taken for granted. That it could all happen again tomorrow.

However, today they were alive. The sun was warming their bones. They were together. The future was wriggling in Jan's belly. And for the Wynters, that was more than enough to be going on with.

Chapter 28

Why hadn't he killed him? The question had kept Sturt awake all night. He had tried to be honest: freely admitting that he wanted to prolong the agony, subject him to the humiliation of a public turning-off. But in the cold hours before dawn, that had not rung true. So now, as he and Fairbrother rode hard on the heels of the dragoons, he was forced to consider another possibility.

Sarah.

He'd done his utmost to shut her out of his life but she had refused to go. Perhaps he too had glimpsed the future? The thought terrified him. To have abandoned all hope and then accept a lifeline demanded courage of a high order. And, in truth, he did not know if he possessed that sort of strength. But inside, something had changed. It was nothing so definite as the return of reason – more a faint glimmer of light in the void. A glimmer so insubstantial that just to admit its existence threatened it with extinction. Nevertheless, the weight of its presence had been felt.

Approaching the crossroads, Sturt relived the moment when Kingsmill's life had hung in the balance. Recalled Sarah's words outside the stable. 'Destroy' she had said. 'He will destroy you' – not 'He will kill you'. Understanding had dawned as Kingsmill's neck was slipping out of joint. And Sturt knew then that by killing Thomas, he would be killing a piece of himself. A piece without which he could not function.

The gibbet cage rattled in the wind, and the thought occurred that by leaving it to others, he was rejecting a responsibility that was indisputably his own. Doubt and guilt stirred in the darkness. And so the wheel keeps turning . . .

'If you should get restless or bored . . .' he said.

'I won't,' said Fairbrother.

They sat in silence. And for the first time, Sturt was

318

aware that the light – the childlike spark that had so often sustained them both – had gone from John's eyes. In its place was caution – as if he was now keeping a vital part of himself tucked out of harm's way.

They shook hands, awkwardly. This time, there was no embrace – just names, murmured. Then John Fairbrother was riding for Tonbridge and Sturt for Chichester.

He caught sight of the dragoons in the distance and drove his horse on. There was a pain rising in his chest, pounding in his head. Pounding with the precision of a military drum beat . . .

And the beat got louder as Sturt rode up the hill towards the Broyle. Approaching the gallows, his mind was in turmoil. He had won everything, yet felt defeated. It was his hour of triumph, but life had never tasted so bitter.

The Mare stood stark against the skyline. Behind him, Austin's troops closed ranks as the mob, eager to lay hands on Kingsmill and Perrin, threatened to unhorse them. A sea of angry faces flashed by. Sturt did not see them. The drum was reverberating inside his head. Driving him on. But towards what? Deliverance? Or Oblivion? The deeper he plunged into that seething mass of humanity, the greater became his sense of isolation.

A nod from Battine silenced the drummer. Robert Lamb craned for a better view. The hangman raised his whip. A hum of expectation. Then silence – except for the horses.

Shepherd Fairall looked out from the cart. He saw Kingsmill not thirty yards distant. A smile of satisfaction creased his face.

'I'll see you in Hell, Thomas.'

And then the cart was gone.

Legs thrashing, Smoaker Mills, Fairall and Little Harry Sheerman twisted in the air, beating time to the hempen jig.

It was Kingsmill's tearing cry that cracked the silence. It came from the bowels of despair – chilled the blood of all who heard it.

Sturt turned and they looked deep into each other's eyes.

319

Neither could speak. The moment seemed frozen in time – on a plane between life and whatever lay beyond.

Then Sarah stepped out of the crowd. In her mind's eye, the mob disappeared. She stood alone beneath the Mare. She called Sturt's name, but it was Kingsmill who came out of the darkness. The life that he had implanted crawled in her belly. Again, she called to Sturt. He appeared at Kingsmill's shoulder. She ran towards them and both figures converged. Falling into Sturt's arms, she heard someone sobbing. Peering into the void, she detected a glimmer of light, pulsing like a tiny star at the outer limit of existence.